Y0-DDO-160

Taylor and Seale Publishing, LLC

Daytona Beach Shores, Florida 32118

Copyright 2013

Second Edition

ISBN   978-0-940224-12-1

Cover Design and Page Layout by WhiteRabbitGraphix.com

All rights reserved. Except for use in any review, the reproduction or utilization of this work in whole or in part, in any form by any electronic, mechanical or other means, now known or hereinafter invented including xerography, photocopying and recording, or in any information, storage or retrieval system, is forbidden without the written permission of the editorial office of Taylor and Seale Publishing, LLC., Daytona Beach Shores, Florida 32118.

Rec'd
Tues
4-7-14

i

This novel is dedicated to

my family and friends

and to strong women everywhere,

past, present, and future.

Marie Bartlett

Pearl, MD

by

Marie Bartlett

While all characters and events in this book are fictional, a debt of gratitude is owed to the family of Herschel Springfield Harkins for allowing me to use his real name.

Chapter One

Taney County, in southern Missouri

Autumn, 1882

The office door burst open. An unshaven man, his arms weighted with an unconscious woman, pushed past the young physician and placed his sister on the hard wooden table. Russet-red stains ran like ribbons down the folds of her long skirt. Her feet, covered in thick stockings, were shoeless. As he positioned her on the table, the startled doctor thought the woman might already be dying or dead.

"She was brought to bed with child, been bleedin' like this for nigh on three days," the man said. "Family's outside on the stoop, too scared to come in. They be watchin' for her husband, too!"

Dr. Pearl Stern dropped the mortar bowl and its club-shaped pestle used to mix medicinal spreads. She rushed to help the man position the pregnant woman on the table. Grabbing the nearest heavy woolen blanket, she placed it under the patient's head, noting her chalky white skin; the twitch and tremor of her eyelids.

"What happened?" Pearl asked. Her mind raced to place the familiar face and the woman's possible condition. "Tell me her name."

Breathing hard, the man leaned in. "Lori Singleton ... Keith Singleton's wife. This is her fifth young'un. My aunt, our mama, and my own self, we came by to check on her today. Hadn't seen her in weeks. Found her like this. Her young'uns say she's been gettin' weaker and weaker till she wouldn't even take vittles anymore."

Stepping back, he wiped his beard with a paw-like hand. "Can you save her, Doc? I ain't never seen her like this. It's frightful."

Pearl looked up with a frown. "And her husband, Mr. Singleton? Where is he?"

"He don't put much stock in doctors. Says birthin' is a natural thing. Flat out refused to let her come here after that last time. But we was worried about her, Doc. My brother-in-law, he went out to hunt up some rabbit and we decided in secret to bring her here. He won't like it none."

Pearl remembered now. Mrs. Singleton was a para-prima, a woman with multiple births and a history of complications. She had come in to see Dr. Stone only once, weeks earlier, and was among the first patients to whom Stone had introduced Pearl. Pearl recalled the almost frightened demeanor of the woman during that meeting.

Mrs. Singleton, her head bowed, had raised her eyes and stared intently at Pearl. "Ain't never seen no woman doctor." Her voice was little more than a whisper.

Walter Stone had grunted. "I disapprove myself. But she was all I could find."

He had turned to Pearl, who was staring at Stone, shocked

2

over his blunt remark. How dare he put her in an embarrassing position in front of a patient? She must say something to him later. But he was already directing his next words at her.

"Now that you're fresh out of medical school, maybe you'll learn something with a real flesh and blood case away from the useless institution of a hospital." He had pushed at his round spectacles as though to emphasize the insult before turning back to their patient.

Pearl had seen plenty, having worked a full, mandatory year at the teaching hospital near the Women's Medical College in Pennsylvania. There, she had treated everything from smallpox to scurvy, performing autopsies, changing dressings, cleaning instruments and even emptying chamber pots when the nurses needed an extra hand.

For birthing, it was true that only the poorest of the poor turned to Lying-In facilities . The population still had a superstitious dread about hospitals, especially when most doctors were willing to travel to the patients' homes. But Pearl believed hospitals had their place, too, particularly for complex cases like this one.

She knew better than to argue with the aging physician, however. He had made it clear he had hired her only because of his long-standing friendship with her father. One of the longest practicing physicians in Taney County, Walter Stone was now considered by his younger colleagues as "out of touch" – still refusing to sterilize his hands and follow the new Lister technique, or to use anesthesia for complicated childbirths.

Pearl had observed, however, he was generally kind to his patients. And, she admitted to herself the only doctor in Missouri who had offered her a position.

She had patted Lori's calloused hand when she asked,

3

"Is your husband with you?"

Lori had looked startled and grabbed Pearl's slender wrist. She squeezed it tight. "Oh no! He don't know I'm here. And I don't want him to know. You won't tell him, will you?"

Then she said in a sing-song voice like that of a child repeating verses, "In the Bible it says, 'in pain thou shalt bear children,' and my man, well, he says the more pain, the healthier the child." Her head drooped as she let go of Pearl's hand and mumbled softly, "But I gotta tell you, Miss…Dr. Stern. This one is different. Somethin's wrong. I can just feel it."

Pearl had exchanged looks with Stone, who instructed the patient in a confident voice, "Lie back now and let me and this lady doctor see if we can feel the baby move. I'm sure everything is fine. You look a healthy enough specimen to me."

Now the young mother appeared near death. It was the climax to a series of events that seemed increasingly dreamlike. Only two weeks earlier, Dr. Stone had died suddenly from what appeared to be a massive heart attack, leaving Pearl in shock and in charge of a very long list of patients. Working fourteen-hour days, six days a week, she was just now beginning to gain control of Stone's large, solo practice. She saw that some patients had left, unwilling to have a female doctor in charge, but others were determined to compete for her time and attention by coming in at unexpected hours. With no one to oversee the front door or set appointments, Pearl did the best she could, performing every routine duty.

But Lori Singleton was her first true emergency.

"You need to leave the room," she told Lori's brother. "If one of your female relatives would like to assist, have her come in. But I'm sure your sister wouldn't want you here."

He nodded, noticeably relieved. As he disappeared

behind the door, Pearl lifted Lori's skirt, pulling back layers of billowing fabric and bloodied pantaloons.

"Lori, can you hear me? It's Dr. Stern. I'm here to examine you and see what's going on."

There was no response. Pearl placed her hand atop Lori's abdomen, recalling from her medical classes that the uterus was the strongest muscle in the body. She pushed down. It contracted in her hands like a vise. She felt for the infant's form, its head, feet, coiled arms and legs. The baby moved against the pressure of Pearl's firm hands and she sighed with relief. At least the infant was alive, for now.

Just as Pearl was about to turn from her patient to the large glassed cabinet, looking for carbolic acid to douse her hands and instruments, Lori moaned and then gasped. Blood gushed from between her legs, spilling onto the table, her stockinged feet, over Pearl's white physician apron and onto the wooden floor where it formed a small red river that ran across the room.

"Oh no!" Pearl said. The door opened and an older woman appeared.

"I'm Lori's aunt." she said. "What's going on? How can I help?"

"She's bleeding! We must get this infant out now, or neither will survive. Come here and hold her undergarments. I need to see if the baby is coming."

Lori had stopped pushing and lay motionless, her skin an alabaster white. Pearl snatched a pair of forceps ("hands of iron," her instructor called them) and began applying the cold metal to the baby's skull, a melon-like purple mass still inside its mother. She pulled gently in an effort to force the fetus out. A small round head appeared, followed by a miniature set of

5

shoulders and a tiny pair of arms, bent legs and curled feet. With her bare hands, Pearl pulled the newborn upward and out. It slid forward and caught between Lori's bloodied garments.

Pearl ignored the rank, putrid mix of blood and mucus that suddenly filled the room, but she could hear Lori's aunt gasp and take two sharp breaths. If the woman fainted away, Pearl determined, she would have to leave her lying in a heap.

There was no time to spare. Pearl spoke to her quickly, with authority. "Quick. Hand me that stack of cloths behind you and grab a pair of scissors!" She wiped at the infant's eyes, ears and mouth. The slimy, umbilical cord hung, eel-like, between mother and child. Pearl cut the cord, allowing it to remain in the mother's womb for now.

"It's a girl," Pearl said. "She's weak, but she's alive." Pearl cleared the bloody mucus from its mouth and nose, hoping for a robust cry. Soft and fragile as a kitten, the baby only mewed.

After wrapping the child in a thick cloth, she handed it to Lori's aunt. "Here, tend to her. Can you put her to your breast?"

The woman raised her crescent brows. "No, I cannot. I'm a spinster...and mournfully old!"

Not that old, Pearl thought, guessing her age at late thirties. "Then take her to your family. I must tend to Lori. The child will need to suckle soon."

Lori was breathing but still remained inert on the wooden table. For now, the bleeding had slowed to a steady trickle. "My baby," she mouthed.

As Lori tried to tend to her, she heard a commotion coming from outside – men's voices – yelling – a woman's high, shrill cry. Keith Singleton pushed at the exam room door and stepped inside. He looked from Pearl, to his wife, to Lori's aunt, then back at Pearl.

"What in thunder is going on here? What have you done to her and…is that..?" He stopped in mid-stride.

Without turning toward him, Pearl continued to care for Lori. "It's your newborn daughter, Mr. Singleton. Would you like to hold her? I need to see about your wife. She's not doing as well."

He shook his head and nodded toward Lori's aunt, who was already half-way out the door with the baby, as though to shield it from its father.

Rooted to the floor, Singleton was speechless.

Pearl's attention was fully focused on Lori's womb. There was no time to waste. The bleeding had resumed, coming in strong red rivulets. She needed to pull on the umbilical cord in order to force the placenta out and hopefully, stem the flow.

She heard Singleton spat, "Well, is she dyin'?"

Pearl ignored the rude question, but she could hear a slight panic in his labored breathing. As she thrust a bare hand into the uterus to bring the afterbirth forward, from the corner of her eye she could see Singleton clench and unclench his hands. The best Pearl could hope for was that he wouldn't interfere. But his next words dispelled any notion she was dealing with a reasonable man.

"I hold you and those worthless relations outside responsible for this," he said, pointing at Pearl. "And you – you lady doctor – which is an abomination in the Lord's eyes all by itself. Whatever you done here, whatever happens, it's your fault! Now I aim to take my family home."

Struggling to stay calm, Pearl continued working, her head bent over her patient. She had grabbed the stack of

7

cloths and was packing the uterus now that the afterbirth was out. It seemed the sensible thing to do. Had she learned that in medical school or was she responding to instinct? She couldn't remember. Her head felt as though it was stuffed with cotton. These past few weeks had been so far outside her normal experience, she felt as if she had stepped outside her life and was peering into a surrealistic dream. Reaching up, she wiped her forehead with the back of her red-stained hand.

Shooting a glance at Singleton, who was now looming over his wife, she said softly, "I don't recommend she be moved right now. I've got the bleeding under control, but I need to watch her closely for the next forty-eight hours. I can also give her something for pain...opium or laudanum...so that she heals quicker."

Pearl recalled Lori's Bible quote, and Singleton's attitude about pain and healthy babies. That was easy enough for him to say. Maybe if he thought giving her pain medication would make her well sooner, he would settle down.

Singleton took a step closer to Pearl, close enough for her to smell his coarse body odor mixed with that of stale tobacco and a hint of rye whiskey. She wondered if he was normally this difficult or if his bad behavior was coming from the bottle.

"I don't give a damn what you recommend." His lips formed a thin, angry line. "She and this here baby belong to me and I aim to take 'em home."

Pearl met his steely look with one of calm resolve, her voice steady.

"Then she will die, probably from loss of blood. It's as simple as that. And the baby might die too. She's already weak and with no mother to nurse her...do you want that on your conscience?"

He pushed her aside. "You don't worry none about my conscience, young lady. Now step aside."

When Singleton left, holding his barely conscious wife, Pearl knew the woman and the newborn's fate were uncertain at best. All she could do now was wash up, scrub the blood-soaked exam table and mop the floor with a soapy mix that would help remove the dark red stains.

At her back, sunlight crept in from the bare, streaked windows, while shadows danced along the thick, papered exam room walls. It was nearing dusk; another long day was nearly over. Moving to the supply drawer, she pulled out a box of stick matches and lit the kerosene lamps, carefully placing the dust-encrusted globes atop each flickering light. As her hands began to tremble, she steadied herself against the cabinet. Too much, she thought, it's all been too much.

A sudden burning itch at her left arm drew her attention. Tugging at the lace edge of her dark-colored sleeve, she unclasped the buttons and pulled back the fabric. A silver-white plaque circled the tender skin around her elbow. From the medicinal cabinet, she extracted a bottle of mercurial ointment and rubbed some of the compound into the inflammation.

Psoriasis – a scourge she had lived with since the age of fifteen. Now that she was twenty-nine, it still showed no signs of relief. Through the years, it had appeared at her knees, on her lower back, even in the most womanly part of her body. From what she had read of the disorder, it could also appear suddenly on the palms of her hands. How would she explain to her patients that she suffered from a chronic condition some might view as a type of leprosy? Even learned physicians were unsure of the correlation between the two. Nor did they know the prognosis.

9

She began to scold herself. This fretting isn't getting any work done. Untouched instruments lay scattered across the tall oak cabinet, their silvery gleam catching the fading light. They needed sorting and putting away. A heap of soiled, stained rags were piled in a dark corner. Once the mopping and the wiping were done, there were still handwritten patient notes from the day's events to record, papers to file, lamps to extinguish, and doors to lock.

But she was so tired, as bone weary as her father's oldest mule when it finally collapsed at the end of a long, hard season. She reached up to touch the dark braid on top of her head. Even her hair hurt.

Stone's books, medical tomes, a dictionary, and his most recent acquisition, *Ben Hur: A Tale of the Christ*, lay in reckless abandon on his dusty bookshelves. She could picture him, his white head bent in concentration, flipping dog-eared pages. Maybe he was not nearly as bad a sort as she had first thought. Perhaps in time, they would have gained, if not affection, at least a measure of respect for each other.

Opening the storage closet, she reached for the heavy, cumbersome mop, its weight nearly equaling hers. The water pump and the pungent liquid lye soap mix Stone kept in a barrel was in the adjoining room. She would have to form a one-person relay: fill the bucket, mop the blood-soaked planks, empty the bucket, refill the mop and empty it again until the floor was finally clean. Wipe down the exam table. Swipe the used instruments with carbolic acid and set them out to dry. At this rate, it would be midnight before she could head back to the farm where she lived with her parents.

As Pearl pulled and pushed the weighty mop across the oak plank floor, her thoughts turned again to Dr. Stone, who had inhabited this space, for more than twenty-five years.

What would he have done today for Lori Singleton? Would his techniques have been vastly different from hers? She knew he had still practiced bloodletting for certain cases, though more progressive physicians had stopped this practice. She recalled debating with him about the merits of using opiates instead.

"An opiate combined with sedatives and antispasmodics may afford some relief," he argued, "but bleeding will leave the patient much better during the interval." He went on to recommend up to sixty ounces of blood be removed in a single treatment. Pearl had shaken her head and walked away, uncertain she would ever change his mind.

Now, after her own efforts, she replayed her most recent episode with Lori. What would now become of the mother and child? Would they even live? What about the other children in that troubled household? Pushing the mop in deep concentration she worried. What else could she have done? What else? Something began to gnaw at her.

She stopped mopping and stared at the patterns on the walls, beginning to visualize forceps, blankets, cloths to push against the bleeding, laudanum, carbolic acid. The litany ran like a series of picture cards across her weary mind. Suddenly she lifted her head. Carbolic acid. I didn't use the carbolic acid. I didn't clean my hands, or the instruments – the forceps. I forgot, I forgot, I forgot!

Her rational mind told her that if Lori died, it would probably be from blood loss that had begun even before she had been carried in. But Pearl also knew that puerperal sepsis – childbirth fever – was one of the most common reasons women and infants died after birth. This condition was also preventable – as long as one believed and followed the Lister technique taught in every progressive medical teaching fa-

11

cility: Douse instruments and hands in carbolic acid. Easy – simple. She had made this argument repeatedly, touting the technique wherever she went, including throughout her short stint with Dr. Stone. That he hadn't believed in the procedure – calling it "unnecessary poppycock" – hardly mattered now. He was no longer here and the decision, or lack of, had been hers alone. She was as guilty as he was. No – she was guiltier – because she had examined Lori, inserted her exposed un-washed hands into the womb, handled the infant, and packed the womb, all without applying the technique every first and second-year medical student should know.

Keith Singleton would be right: if anything happened to his wife and child, it was probably, at least in part, her doing. Pearl set the dripping mop against a corner wall. She would come early in the morning to complete the cleaning, hours before the day's regular patients arrived.

She ran to the sink, scrubbed at her hands, and patted them dry on a coarse white cloth hanging near the door. Re-moving her soiled, bloody apron, she placed it near the rags on the floor. She could wash them all tomorrow or take them down the street to the Chinese laundry.

A quick look in the hall mirror caused her to pause and pat her loose hair into place. Vanity is a sin, her mother had lectured - therefore implying this was yet another failing on Pearl's part. It was true Pearl had always cared about her ap-pearance, especially as a professional woman. But it should matter little now. Grabbing her cape and black leather satchel, she locked the front door and hurried to the stables two doors down.

"Where you headed, miss?" the lanky young stable-man asked. Thank god he was still here when she had burst through the door, out of breath, explaining she needed the

12

doctor's buggy and a steady horse right away.

"The Singleton home," she said. "I must go check on the family and I must go now."

Chapter Two

The Singleton family lived twelve miles from the farm Pearl shared with her parents but in the opposite direction, according to directions the stableman had provided. He informed her he knew the entire clan and that Keith and his brood had been given the land by her parents and now lived in a half-decent two-story clapboard they had built. "Even has a fenced yard for the young 'uns, a good thing too since Singleton never lets them go much of anywhere." It was more information than Pearl needed in a hurry, but at least she could now find her way there in the dark.

Leaving town, she could see the outline of the Ozarks looming in the distance. A biting wind nipped at her face. The smell of wood smoke and cooked beef grazed her nostrils as she passed homes where families were probably now sitting down to dinner. Soft, inviting lights flickered at their windows. As she pulled on the reins, it occurred to her this would be her due, making house calls at all hours. Since Dr. Stone had made frequent calls during the evenings, she would be expected to do the same. She would miss dinners, family, a warm hearth. Her mother would not approve.

With a free hand, she tugged at her cape to keep warm. Her back began to itch from another scaly patch but she couldn't reach behind her to relieve the irritation, not with the horse to manage. There was no time to stop.

Pulling up in front of the white, clapboard home, she noticed the lights were still burning. At least they were not yet in bed. She dug at her back to relieve the ongoing itch and hitched the leather horse straps to a post. As she reached into the wagon to retrieve her leather bag, the horse gave a loud snort. Pearl heard the front door open.

"Who goes there?" Singleton's voice boomed in the still air.

Pearl, bag in hand, approached the gate in slow measure. "It's me, Dr. Stern. I'm here to see about your wife and baby, Mr. Singleton. After you left today, I grew worried about them."

Singleton stepped from the porch and as the moonlight hit his shadow, Pearl realized he had a rifle in his hand. She froze in place.

"Now look here, Miss," he growled. "I ain't never shot no woman and I don't aim to start now. But I told you today that this is my family and my business. You got no right to be here uninvited and unannounced."

"But…"

"Don't give me no buts," Singleton said, raising the gun's barrel. The gun's long arm was poised just over Pearl's head. She realized he meant to scare her rather than shoot her. Still…

She clasped her bag in both hands and stood her ground, though her heart felt it was beating at a gallop. "Then can you tell me if Mrs. Singleton is all right? Has the bleeding stopped?

15

Is she awake and taking food? How's the baby? Is she nursing?"

"You ask a hell of a lot of questions for somebody with a gun pointed toward her head. You must be one stubborn cuss of a woman." He spat what appeared to be tobacco juice on the ground between them.

Pearl cleared her throat, unsure what to say next. Her back began to itch horribly but she dared not reach behind her. Singleton might think she had a weapon and draw down on her. "I've been accused of that," she said in the darkness. "But I come here solely for your wife's welfare, Mr. Singleton. May I at least come in and speak to her? Then I will leave you and your family in peace, I promise."

He lowered the rifle and pointed it at her chest. She heard a click; he had pulled back the hammer.

"Get off my property now. Don't come back. What happens here is none of yer business."

Pearl's hopes fell. She lowered her head, then slowly turned and retreated from Singleton's obstinate form. Until she was fully off his land, he could easily shoot her in the back for trespassing. Her fright that he would do so was matched only by a growing sense of despair that once again, she had failed to protect her patient.

The next day, Pearl returned to Walter Stone's office, firmly determined to clean the place thoroughly, organize Stone's outdated patient files, and decide how best to conduct a practice that might soon belong to her. As his assistant, it seemed a logical assumption that she would succeed him in business. The town needed a family doctor; she needed a job.

For days on end, she worked morning till dusk, stopping only when a patient came by to ask if Dr. Stone's office would remain open. She had the funds in the Taney County Bank to purchase his entire enterprise, including his equipment. Each time she was asked if the office was closing, she answered "Certainly not. In fact, I hope to become your official physician in residence once the sale is final."

Yet her plans could not be fulfilled. A week after her visit to Keith Singleton's home, the county Sheriff, Fred Billings, appeared at Stone's office door.

"Sheriff Billings, come in," Pearl said. She had recognized him from the flyers plastered all over Taney County prior to his recent election. "What can I do for you?"

Billings removed his hat and sat down in front of Pearl's neatly rearranged desk. "The place looks good, shiny as a new copper penny," he said, nodding his approval. He reached inside his pocket. "I came here for this." He slid a paper toward Pearl. "I'm sorry ma'am...Dr. Stern." He reached up to smooth his long drooping mustache.

Looking at him quizzically, Pearl unfolded the paper; then she began to read. The first word that caught her eye was "Eviction."

"I don't understand," she said. "I put in a bid to purchase Dr. Stone's practice. It was in the paper. I responded to an advertisement by his widow. She seemed anxious to sell. I thought I handled it properly. As Dr. Stone's assistant, I also thought I had a right to remain here until the sale was final."

Glancing toward the ceiling, the Sheriff shifted in his seat. "Well, technically, that's true ma'am. But, here's the thing. The widow Stone...she does want to sell. She just don't want to sell to you. So she took out this eviction notice through a civil court and now I'm here to serve it. She wants you out by end of the day."

"End of the day?" Pearl sputtered. "You mean today?"

"Yes ma'am."

Pearl drew back in her chair. "Oh, my," was all she could muster. She rose, paced the room, and then returned to her chair. She scratched at the raw patch on her elbow. The flare-ups had gotten worse since the incident involving Lori Single-ton. Efforts to find out how she and the baby were doing had proven futile and it had frustrated her no end – not good, she suspected, for a chronic affliction.

Wrinkling her brow, Pearl looked at the sheriff. "Did Mrs. Stone say why? Why she won't sell to me?"

"Might have something to do with the Singleton case since the lady was one of Doc Stone's patients. Or might be just 'cause you're a woman and she don't want to sell to no woman doctor. I ain't real sure." He rose to leave. "All I know is that I came here to serve papers, I done it and there you are." He looked at her with concern in his eyes. "Do you have some help gettin' your belongings out of here?"

Pearl clasped her arms with both hands. "I actually don't have much here yet. But Papa will bring the wagon and help me clear out my things." She felt as though Billings had walked in and thrown a physical punch at her. Her cheeks burned. She dreaded telling her parents the news.

Billings turned at the doorway. "I'm sorry again, Dr. Stern. I heard you was actually a pretty good doctor…except for that Singleton case. Damn shame about that whole family."

Pearl's eyes widened. "What do you mean? Has some-thing happened?"

18

Billings put his hat on. "Yesterday, we got word that both mother and baby went to Jesus. I don't think even Singleton saw it coming. They just up and died, both of 'em, the young'un cradled in her arms. Well, bye ma'am. Take care of yourself."

And he was gone. Pearl clapped her hand over her mouth and burst into tears.

Chapter Three

Spring, 1883

A figure moved in the wingback chair near the fireplace where, just a month earlier a toasty fire had sizzled and a bowl of deep red apples had perched on the hearth waiting for a good roasting.

"Yes?" came a voice from the chair.

"Mrs. Stone?" Keith Singleton said. "You sent for me?" Clutching his hat, he moved quietly into the room and stood before the elderly woman.

Three sparkling blue stones set atop a massive ring adorned her hand as she shifted from the shadows to meet his gaze. Her voice was faint, like that of an old frail woman. As light from the window crossed her face, a crown of frosty white hair gave her an almost angelic appearance.

"I did," she said, waving him toward a chair. "Have a seat. We haven't spoken since you completed renovations on my veranda after my husband died. You're a hard worker, Singleton, and a good carpenter."

"Thank you, ma'am," he said, shifting from one foot to the

other.

"I'm well aware you have obligations that are far above your means," she said. "And so I asked you here for a very special reason," Reaching for a small wooden box the house-keeper had set near her chair, she placed it on her lap, and opened the lid.

"Oh?" said Singleton. "What would that be, ma'am?"

"It's about that woman," she said, "the one that worked with my husband last fall. I think he fancied her with that slim waist and pretty face." She gave a loud sigh. "Walter was a ladies' man, God rest his darkened soul. But I'm convinced she threw herself at him. Why else would a proper girl with good breeding choose to spend her days in such dreadful cir-cumstances, working among the poor and the sick? She was after him, and, with her immoral ambition, his practice too."

"I don't know nothin' about that," Singleton said. "All I know is that she helped send my woman and baby to the Lord way before their time. No one's seen her for months, not since you ran her out of your husband's office. Last I hear'ed, she was lookin' to move elsewhere."

"Where she will find and lure another man, no doubt." She reached inside the box and pulled a thick wad of fifty dol-lar bills from the stack, slamming the lid shut tight. "Here, take this and do exactly as I say."

Singleton hesitated. "She found out quick not to come around me and mine," he said, "and she ain't been around since. I don't see her as a problem no more."

"You are a widower left alone with young children, isn't that right?"

"Yes ma'am, that's a correct statement."

"And this lady doctor, this Pearl Stern, is she not the one

that caused the tragic loss of your wife and infant?"

"Well, now, it's true she had a part in it, but since then…"

"Since then what?"

I've had others tell me that my wife and young'un probably would have died anyway."

"No!" Mrs. Stone said. "That's not so! Now listen to me. Your future and the future of your motherless children depend upon you following my instructions."

Singleton shook his head. "I don't understand, ma'am. What is it that you're asking me to do?"

"It's what we'll do together," Mrs. Stone said. She settled back in her chair. "We're going to destroy that woman and her reputation. Not only will she never work again in Taney County in her chosen field of endeavor, we'll make sure she never works anywhere, ever again."

Chapter Four

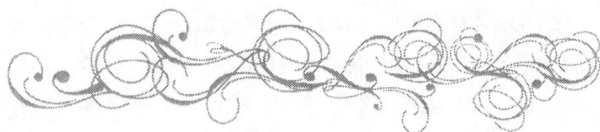

At the family farm where Pearl had grown up an only child, Pearl was relieved that her father had asked few questions about what had happened at Dr. Stone's practice before she returned home. There had always been a silent trust between them, and this time was no exception.

He had brought the wagon into town at her request and helped her remove her few belongings from Stone's office – mostly leather-bound books, a decorative leech jar Pearl had bought as a keepsake, the brass microscope her father had given her as a graduation gift, and a small live plant she had placed on Stone's desk to soften the room's atmosphere.

Papa had treated her as an adult guest, respecting her private business. Within a day, he had returned to his normal routine: working the fields till mid-afternoon and then sitting in his overstuffed chair near the fire fall through spring, reading with his spectacles askew atop his sun-burnt nose. Pearl knew she could go to him at any time and seek his counsel.

Her mother, however, was a different story. "I don't understand about any of this business," she said one morning at breakfast. "Of course I never knew why you had to go off to medical college anyway; such a waste of a lovely young woman. Any man worth his salt would have been fortunate to have you as a wife, and now that you're freed from all that doctor nonsense…"

Pearl interrupted, "Mother, we've had this discussion many times." Taking a bite of thick, buttered toast, she continued calmly. "I don't expect you to understand. But thank you for allowing me to stay while I decide what to do next." She knew her mother meant well, and she loved her for it. Yet, even as a child, she and her mother had never shared much common ground. It was as though she never saw Pearl as anyone other than an extension of herself.

"Humph. Allow you to stay? You're our daughter! Of course you can stay here as long as you like. In fact, I was thinking I might invite that attractive Mr. Witherson over for dinner next Sunday. I'll show you how to make a nice roast. What do you think?"

But Pearl had already cleared her place at the table and was leaving the room. "I have a few letters to write, Mother. I'll be in my room."

Pearl heard a muttering at her back and what sounded like a crystal glass slam against the counter: "Just like her father; all head and no heart."

Pearl closed the door to her childhood room, leaned against the frame and sighed. She would consider herself lucky if she were even half like her father. His quiet strength and steady hand had seen them through times good and bad. When he had supported her decision to become a doctor over her mother's objections, it was to him that she wrote letters home, describing the head nurse who, on principle alone, appeared to detest all women students; the steady throng of patients, many destitute and unable to read or write; the tricks

Pearl and her classmates played on their male professors.

Papa would answer that he had laughed out loud when Pearl wrote to say they had filled the stage at graduation with skeletons decked in caps and gowns. Victoria – Pearl's best friend at school – had helped her keep her resolve, and her sanity, throughout their seemingly endless classes.

She now clawed at her arms, itching like the devil, as usual.

Victoria: she must write to her and tell her what had happened. Now living in Richmond, Virginia with her physician husband, Walter, Victoria seemed to have landed in the best of all worlds, at least according to societal standards . She had a medical degree, a doting well-respected husband, a large richly decorated home, servants and fine leather carriages. She and Pearl still corresponded but only infrequently. Although Victoria often invited Pearl to come visit them, the time had never seemed right.

Now a plan began to form. Sitting at the weathered desk in her room, Pearl pulled at the creaky drawer holding her best box of stationary, dipped her pen in the thick black inkwell and began to write:

My dearest Victoria…

The response came more quickly than Pearl had imagined, and by May, she had purchased her train tickets and set a date to stop in Richmond, Virginia to visit with Walter and Victoria. Then it would be on to a place she had selected at random by closing her eyes and sticking a jewel-tipped hat pin onto a map that had been hanging for years on the back of her closet door.

This is where she would start a new position and a new life if the fates allowed. She had written to her college professor, asked for a reference, and then, following some research, sent a letter to the town's city council signing it "P. Stern, M.D." in a flourishing hand she hoped would not appear too feminine.

Breaking the news to Papa and her mother had been much more difficult. Sitting in the parlor, hands on her lap when she told them she was leaving, her mother had grabbed a tassel-rimmed pillow from the settee to stem her outburst. "You're an ungrateful child!" she had cried. "Now I'll never have a normal life...or grandchildren. God is punishing me!" She fled the room.

Pearl's father sat with head bowed, tapping his thick fingers together.

"Papa," say something," Pearl implored.

He raised his head and Pearl thought his eyes looked sadder than she had ever seen them. For a moment she thought of reaching out to grab his hand and tell him she had changed her mind; she'd stay right here and do his bidding for as long as he wanted. She might even consider marriage if anyone would have her after all this time.

"You've always been a spirited one," her father said, "and are braver than anyone I know, including myself. But why go so far away, Pearl? Where is this place, this Appalachian town in North Carolina?"

"It's a mountain town called Asheville. Not too big or too small. They're looking for a new town physician. I've applied, Papa, and they sent a letter requesting that I come. It sounds promising. First, I'll take the train from Springfield and stop to see Walter and Victoria for a while. You remember my letters about Victoria, don't you?"

Her father gave her a faint smile. "Of course, a lively

young woman, as I recall. But Pearl, are you sure this is the right thing to do? Your mother will swear it's not part of God's plan for you."

What he failed to add, but Pearl knew he was thinking, was that he would have to live with her mother's disapproval long after Pearl departed. Raised a Calvinist through her mother's influence and insistence, Pearl was aware of what her mother believed: all people are at the mercy of God and are depraved or inadequate in making their own decisions. "Fallen people" – people like Pearl who didn't follow the religious doctrines she'd been taught as a child – were incapable of redeeming themselves.

"I know Mother thinks I'm a lost soul," Pearl said. "But what do you think?" She reached out and placed a hand over his.

"I think you should use the brain God gave you and let it lead you wherever it, and your heart, says to go."

"Oh Papa!" Pearl said, clasping his neck. "Thank you. I'll miss you so!"

~

Finally, her stop was just ahead. Nearly forty hours had passed since Pearl left Taney County, Missouri by train, a thousand miles to the west. It seemed they had slowed to a crawl at every small turn. At least Pearl had a chance to see parts of the country she had never seen before, images that stayed with her each time the train pulled away: stout oaks forming a canopy over an abandoned campsite; a tattered Confederate flag hanging from an arched window; a Negro woman standing beneath a bent tree with a basket on her arm; soot-crusted factories belching thick black smoke; horse-drawn wagons at a public square standing patient while their drivers conversed, tipped their hats and spit tobacco; a large sign proclaiming "Lard Oil Factory"; textile mills and warehouses; a family, dressed in Sunday best and poised for a group photograph along the steps of their veranda.

The engine hissed, lurched and came to a faltering halt at the Richmond station. Pearl recalled that Richmond, capital of the Confederacy during the war, had been torched by its own troops to prevent looting from the enemy. She wondered if any remnants still existed of the city's vibrant youth. There were certainly signs of progress, including the new telephone lines everyone was predicting would soon appear in all large cities. They drooped like fat, lazy ropes along the street parallel to the depot.

As Pearl stepped onto the platform, she saw Victoria ahead, virtually bouncing on her heels from the excitement. Immediately, her spirits rose. Victoria's exuberance was one of the things Pearl remembered and loved most about her.

Dropping her bag, Pearl threw herself into her friend's arms. Dear Victoria, the perfect antidote to a long, hard trip. The pair released each other and Pearl stood back to study her college roommate. Heavier than Pearl by about thirty pounds and at least two inches shorter, Victoria wore a dark blue skirt with a ruffle that made her waist appear even thicker.

"Do you like my new dress?" Victoria said, twirling away from Pearl. "It's the latest in Paris fashion! Look, it's so short you can see my boots!"

She lifted the hem of her flounced skirt and pointed. "And the bustle is back this year!" She turned so that Pearl could see the high puff of fabric that made Victoria's hips appear even broader.

28

"I see that," said Pearl, laughing. Victoria hadn't changed a bit; still a breath of fresh air. Stopping here first had been the right decision.

"You're a sight for these silly eyes!" Victoria said, cocking her head to one side. "Look at you – slender as a reed and that skin – as dewy as a rose petal. You were always the envy of the other girls for your looks alone. But I thought your brain was much more attractive!" She giggled at her own joke. "The train was over an hour late…again. But I told Walter I'd wait here all day if I had to. Now where are your bags?"

Pearl reached for her satchel. "I'm traveling light and will buy whatever else I need. Mother is shipping my trunks to a hotel in Asheville." She searched the platform for Victoria's husband. "Where's Walter?"

A doctor of family medicine, Walter had convinced Victoria to drop out of the Women's College of Medicine in Pennsylvania and marry him before he brought her to Richmond. Unlike Pearl, who would have weighed the pros and cons before giving up her hard-earned career, Victoria had impulsively said yes. It crushed Pearl at first, for the two were more like sisters than friends and had even talked of going into practice together.

"Walter had a patient," Victoria explained as they walked along the platform, "an old man with signs of stroke. I left the good doctor with the befuddled poor thing. But he said to bring you straight home and we'd have a nice dinner and a glass of sherry. We have an excellent cook, Mrs. Mammoth. If she stays with us much longer, I'll be her namesake, that's for certain." She patted a bulging hip and smiled at Pearl.

Pearl laughed again. "I've missed you. Seems like forever since we parted."

29

The two women moved toward a waiting carriage, its black leather gleaming in the noonday sun. "Well, it's been a year," Victoria said. "Between our graduation and the wedding, you know how frantic things get during such celebrations." She stopped and looked at Pearl. A hand went to her mouth. "I'm so sorry. That didn't come out right. I just meant..."

Pearl reached up and clasped Victoria's hand. "It's fine. Once I got over the shock, I was thrilled for you and if you're happy, I'm thrilled for you now."

"I know that," said Victoria. "I was referring to that other matter of the heart."

Pearl reached down to smooth her skirt. "I have no idea what you're talking about." But she did. A Chinese-American with a razor sharp mind and exotic good looks, Caine Lee had captured Pearl's attention the first time she'd seen him and, she realized after he'd left town, had almost captured her heart. She could still see the curve of his mouth, the gentle almond-shaped eyes that seemed to penetrate right through her, smell the soapy scent of his aftershave, and hear the low smooth tones of his voice. What would he make of her now with doubts and fears haunting her every move? For that reason alone, she was glad he was nowhere in sight.

"You don't think of him at all?" Victoria teased, as though reading Pearl's mind.

"Think of whom?"

"You know perfectly well whom," said Victoria, climbing into the carriage and offering Pearl a hand. "You do recall that Caine and Walter were friends, don't you? Caine writes to us often about his business ventures. Don't you want to know if he asks about you?" She tilted her head toward Pearl.

"No I don't," said Pearl. The open carriage had thick cush-

30

ioned seats heated by the blazing sun, and, though she was already beginning to perspire, Pearl was relieved to be out in the summer air.

The two women entwined their arms as the driver flicked the reins. Pearl saw he was dressed in a gray flannel coat and top hat and wondered how he could endure such clothing in this hot weather. She felt sorry for him. When the horses pulled forward at a steady clip, Victoria turned to face Pearl.

"I know you. You appear as tough as the bark on an oak tree. At least you give that impression. But inside, you're like clear jelly. I can see right through you. Caine hurt you, I'm sure of it. He had his reasons for leaving, but you'll never believe where he is now."

Unwilling to look at Victoria and admit that she was right, Pearl continued to admire the stately, columned homes on the tree-lined street. Not asking about Caine's whereabouts wasn't just bravado. Her belief was that deep down, people basically do what they want to do. If Caine had wanted her with him, he would have asked. If he had wanted to stay, he would have. They had kissed, but only once. Had he wanted more, he would have made that known as well. Yes, she thought of him, more often than not. But it was over and done with.

"He's in Tombstone, in the Arizona Territory," Victoria said, "and doing quite well for himself from his letters. He speaks highly of the place."

Pearl sighed. Victoria had all the subtlety of a run-away coal train. "All right, I give up," she said. "What's he doing in Tombstone? That's Apache territory, isn't it? And didn't they have some big shootout in the center of town? It was in all the Eastern papers."

Victoria smiled. "It was at some Corral. Yes, it's rough

31

country but according to Caine, it's now a huge boom town. Silver mines, a lot of money and a good bit of finery. He says they have a theater with plays and performances, wine shops and an ice cream parlor, for goodness sakes. Caine writes that he even found one of his relatives in the Chinese district. He had no idea the person was there!"

"You sound like an advocate for the place," Pearl said. She couldn't help but smile at her friend. "So what took him there? What, pray tell, were his reasons for leaving?" She glanced at Victoria and noted the pleased look on her face. Truth be told, Pearl did want to know why he left in the first place.

"A business venture he couldn't refuse. If you recall, he was always ambitious. And guess what? He wants Walter and me to come out there. He says Walter can set up a lucrative practice in Tombstone." Victoria sat back, and her eyes lit with what looked to Pearl as sheer excitement.

"You're not serious!" Pearl said. She was genuinely shocked. Victoria, with her latest fashions and private carriage moving to an isolated town in the Arizona desert?

"I'll let Walter explain. We haven't decided yet."

The carriage stopped before a large, lemon-yellow two-story frame house, its eaves trimmed in a gingerbread design. Purple asters and spotted geraniums splashed vibrant colors across the low veranda. A late-blooming dogwood had shed its creamy, off-white petals but was still bursting with small, glossy red fruits. To Pearl, the soothing scene looked like something from an oil painting. This must be what domestic bliss was like. Once more, she could hear her mother's voice. "You could have had all of this but you chose another life, one that will no doubt lead to loneliness and has already led to harm."

"It's charming," Pearl said, wondering how on earth Victoria could even consider leaving this. For the first time in her life, Pearl was envious of her friend and the path Victoria had followed.

Once inside, Pearl heard someone bustling about in the kitchen. Voices murmured and a black house maid appeared. Victoria introduced Pearl to the woman, who curtsied and took Pearl's overnight satchel.

"Beth, this is Miss Pearl, who'll be staying with us a few days. Please take her bag upstairs and turn down the bed in case she needs a nap before dinner. And make sure you open all the windows. Fresh clean air is good for the body."

"Yes um," Beth said. She took Pearl's bag and hurried off.

Pearl turned to Victoria. "Thank you, dear, but I'll wait and call it an early evening." Though weary from the long trip, she was anxious to see more of Victoria's home and learn about the couple's future plans.

Pearl glanced about the foyer. The furnishings, expensive and elegant at first glance, were worn; the walnut staircase was chipped in places, its carpet runner threadbare. In the adjoining parlor a rose-colored velvet settee with matching chairs and tassel-fringed globe lamps had a weary look, as though they could use a good cleaning or replacement.

Victoria peeled off her gloves, removed her hat and set them on the foyer table. "Walter's out back in his office with a patient, though the gentleman has probably left by now. Let's go through the kitchen. I'll introduce you to our cook. She's the best one I've ever had."

Despite her name, Mrs. Mammoth was a wiry woman who looked about fifty and appeared fit to Pearl's trained eye. Pearl had expected another Negro, but Mrs. Mammoth was white. As she bent over a large ceramic bowl of dough, her arms were covered to her elbows in the powdery flour.

"Never you mind us," Victoria called as they entered the kitchen. "This is my friend, Pearl, that I've been going on about. I told her what a wonderful cook you turned out to be."

The woman looked up, gave Pearl a gap-tooth smile and nodded a greeting. "Ma'am," she said, "it's a pleasure. I got a big ole pan of biscuits in the oven and this one near ready to go. Hope you're hungry." Pots of green and yellow vegetables simmered on the stove, emitting wispy fingers of steam. A large pink ham rested on a sideboard.

"I'm famished," Pearl said. "Dry crackers and an apple on the train is all I've had since this morning. It smells like heaven in here." Though it seemed as if Victoria's possessions had seen better days, Pearl felt as though she had stepped into a classic Southern plantation, complete with luxurious surroundings, well-mannered servants, and rich foods. Another stab of envy took hold, and she pushed it away, scolding herself. Victoria deserved all this, and more.

From a lace-curtained window at the door, Pearl could see a small building at the far corner of the yard, painted the same cheery color as the house. A sign hung from a white post with Walter's name and credentials in full view.

Victoria waved a hand toward Mrs. Mammoth. "Come get us when it's time," she instructed. "We'll be with Walter." Pearl thought it unusual that Victoria had both a Negro house maid and a white cook, especially here in the South. She was about to ask Victoria about this, but her friend was already off on another subject.

"Wait till you see Walter's apothecary collection!" said Victoria as they crossed the yard. "The cabinet takes up the

34

entire front room. That's where he does his mixing too. I keep telling him not to let his patients witness too much. It's not good business practice."

Though Victoria could be flighty, she was no dullard when it came to medicine. Pearl recalled how competitive the two of them had been during exams and thought wistfully that Victoria would have made an excellent physician in her own right. Yet she seemed happy and content as Walter's wife and helpmate. If only women could learn how to combine both a career and marriage. Pearl wondered if she would ever have even one of the two.

Walter greeted them at the door, wiping his palms on a tattered cloth. He tossed it aside as Pearl extended her hands. Trying not to look surprised, she realized he had physically changed in only a year. A decade older than she, he had gained a considerable amount of weight and was beginning to lose his hair. He now resembled any portly, well-dressed gentleman she might have passed on the street.

"Pearl, it's good to see you again. Victoria was so excited when she knew you were coming." His voice boomed in the small room. "And of course, anything that makes my wife happy makes me happy." He winked at Victoria and Pearl realized the spark between these two was genuine. Victoria deserved this too.

"Would you like a quick tour?" Walter motioned toward the back rooms.

A former lecturer, he was in his natural element when going on about his favorite subjects, Pearl recalled. Pearl followed him with Victoria trailing. "A tour would be grand. I love that your office is separate from your home. I hope to do the same when I'm in Asheville."

He turned and gave Pearl an inquisitive look. "Yes, Victoria mentioned that. She said you're headed to some place in the Carolinas, a little Appalachian town. How many physicians do they have? It's a competitive business, you know, and not one that's likely to bring you a big wage."

"They have eight doctors." said Pearl. "But it's growing. I hope to be the first one to work for the city as a municipal employee and I'm quite sure I'll be the first woman."

Victoria took hold of Walter's arm, looking up at him. "Pearl was always the forward one in school. It was she who spoke up when the professors talked to us as though we were children. And do you remember, Walter, when I told you about the trick we played on the staff? The one where we dressed skeletons in caps and gowns and lined them up on stage behind the graduation presenters? We got in trouble for that one, but it was Pearl who talked our way out of it."

Pearl smiled at Victoria. "I seem to remember it was your idea."

Walter grinned. "Well, it sounds like you two have much catching up to do." He motioned for the women to follow him. "Here's the latest in examination tables. But this…" He gestured to a tall narrow cabinet with two sets of artificial legs propped alongside each other in the glass case, "this is my real treasure." The contraption appeared to Pearl as all leather and straps.

"It's among the first artificial limbs," Walter said. "It was designed by a noble Virginian, a war veteran who wanted to help our Confederate wounded. That one on the right, the wooden peg, is made from whittled barrel staves. See the hinge at the knee? Most likely the first one was designed for the wealthy, and this second, simpler one for the working man. I bought them at a Richmond Medical Society fund-raising event."

"They're both quite dreadful," Pearl said, shaking her head. Among the few patients she had treated, she had yet to meet an amputee.

A tapping sounded at the office door followed by the musical tinkling of a bell as someone entered. "Dinner's on!" Mrs. Mammoth called from the front room. "We got the table all set if you folks are ready to come eat."

"Starved," said Pearl. After the long, torturous ride in which she had to transfer trains numerous times, she couldn't wait to sit down to a real, home-cooked meal.

In the dining room, Walter took his place at the head of the table and said a hurried grace while the two women bowed their heads on either side of him. A crystal chandelier cast soft shadows about the room. Pearl looked up and squinted at the sparkling jewels.

"All the rage now," Walter remarked, "new-fangled electric lights. We just had them installed. Don't ask me how they work. Anyway, I believe they are likely a passing fad."

"I hope not, for what they cost," said Victoria.

Pearl wondered again why the couple would want to leave this place. They had everything on these beautiful premises anyone could desire.

She scanned the feast of colorful vegetables, summer fruits and meats set before her. Cooking was not one of her strong suits so she had great regard for the expertise that went into planning and preparing a hearty meal.

"Deer steak," said Walter, catching Pearl's roaming eyes. "A delicacy in summer but we stored it in the icebox for a special occasion. Nourishment is not complete without meats and vegetables. At the age of twenty most of us can digest cast iron. The gastric powers diminish after that."

A lecture, Pearl thought. She hoped, as she gained more experience, she wouldn't come across like that. She could certainly tell others what not to do.

He stabbed the meat with an oversized fork and placed a large chunk of deer and a slice of roast beef on his own plate, then motioned for Pearl to pass hers along. "Excess at the table, especially at my age, causes derangement of the stomach so I'll willingly share our good fortune," he said.

Pearl raised her eyebrows as he overloaded her plate. She seldom ate more than small portions at a time, but as a guest, it was bad manners to complain of anything.

"Save room for dessert," Victoria said. "Mrs. Mammoth has plum tart, rhubarb tart and your favorite, Pearl, rice pudding with cream. I told her how much you loved it."

"You'll both be the death of me," Pearl said, smiling first at Victoria, then at Walter. "But thank you for your generous hospitality." Once settled in Asheville, she would be lucky on her planned budget to afford entertainment for the field mice.

Victoria raised her glass of sherry. "A toast to our friend," she said, sipping from the crystal rim. "And now, in return, you must reward us by telling us about your decision to leave Taney County. What did your parents say when they found out you were coming south? You being the only child, I can't imagine they were happy about it."

"They weren't," said Pearl. She took a bite of speared roast and savored its juicy flavor. "Now that they're both in their sixties, I think they expected to have me nearby as they get older. But they supported my decision." Well, that was half true. At least Papa had supported her. Her mother had helped her pack but had barely spoken to her as both parents escorted her to the station.

"Are they still on the farm in Taney County?" Victoria asked.

Pearl nodded.

"So about this destination," Walter said, "this mountain town where you're headed. "Why there?"

"Well," said Pearl. "I wanted to stay in the East because of my parents and I'd read something about the health benefits of the pure mountain air in North Carolina. Of course, Papa said you don't have to go clear across the country when the natural air in Missouri would do just fine."

Victoria was grinning at her. "That sounds like something I would say!"

She explained to her hosts that Asheville was considering a municipal physician, the first of its kind in the country, and had advertised as far west as Missouri. "So I sent an application and a letter of reference. I'm to meet with the Board of Aldermen after I arrive."

"That's quite progressive for a small town," Walter said. He took another bite from his steak. "But why leave Taney County at all?"

Pearl froze. She knew he was only making casual dinner conversation. The problem was how much half-truth she could muster. She had shared none of the details in her letters to Victoria about the Lori Singleton incident. It was too complex to explain through personal correspondence, especially with someone like Victoria who would want to know everything.

She had started to respond when Mrs. Mammoth entered the room and placed a tray of silver dishes with three cinnamon-topped puddings and a pitcher of fresh cream near Pearl. Walter rubbed his hands together like a child with a new toy.

"Oh my," Pearl said. "That looks sinful."

"I'll bring coffee in a minute," Mrs. Mammoth said. She hurried out.

"You're so lucky to have such a fine cook," Pearl said. She caught Walter and Victoria exchanging glances and wondered briefly what that was about. It did seem odd that for such a large home, there was only one cook and one maid. But then she had grown up on a farm. What did she know of servants, cooks and housemaids?

"Enough about me," she said, relieved to change the subject. "Walter, I want to hear about this new venture in Tombstone. Victoria mentioned you might be moving across the country."

Walter frowned at his wife. "You're already talking about this when we haven't made a final decision?" Victoria's face fell and his tone softened. "I'm sorry, dear. I didn't mean to snap at you."

He turned his attention toward Pearl. "It's premature. It's true that I've heard from Caine. I know you remember him. After last year's Chinese Exclusion Act – a short-sighted move from our government in my opinion – Caine was concerned about his relations on the West coast. That, and a prime business opportunity in Tombstone, is what compelled him to go. He says there is much to recommend the place."

Pearl set her fork down and folded her hands in her lap. She was surprised that hearing Caine's name for the second time that day would sting. She had worked hard to push him from every waking thought. She glanced across the table at an empty chair and envisioned him there, dressed in his spotless linen suit, his brown hair brushing his brows. Chin down, he would raise his eyes toward her and smile ever so slightly,

40

as though they shared a special, mysterious secret.

"Walter!" Victoria said. "All I told Pearl is that Caine has written to us about the many possibilities in Tombstone and that he thinks you could set up a rewarding practice there."

"I didn't mean to pry," Pearl said in a low voice. She felt as though she had intruded on a married couple's private business.

"Of course you didn't," said Walter. He ladled a generous portion of cream over his rhubarb pudding. "It's no different than us asking you about your own move. But I have an established practice here and I don't want it getting out that we may uproot and leave when that's not final."

He shot a glance toward the closed kitchen door and it occurred to Pearl that he was checking to see if Mrs. Mammoth was within hearing distance. It seemed odd, but then Pearl rarely trusted her instincts these days.

"I understand," Pearl said. She reached over and placed her hand atop Victoria's. "But you'll certainly write and let me know what you decide?" More than anything, she wanted to maintain her ties with Victoria regardless of where either of them was living.

"You'll be the first," Victoria said, squeezing Pearl's hand in return. "And you, of course, must let us know how everything works out in the Carolina hills."

Walter rose and took a short, thick cigar from his shirt pocket. "If you ladies will excuse me, I'm going to the veranda to enjoy a smoke. Then it's off to bed for me. Pearl, if I'm gone when you awake in the morning, I hope you sleep well. How long are you staying?"

Pearl tipped her coffee cup toward him. "Not long enough. My stage to Old Fort leaves in a few days. I take the train from there up the mountain into Asheville."

"It's disgraceful how little time we have to catch up!" Victoria said, rising. "Let's go into the parlor, Pearl, and have another glass of sherry. We have so much talking to do."

Pearl smiled. She suspected that Victoria, as usual, would be doing most of the talking.

As daylight seeped into dusk, the two women sat side-by-side on the settee and reminisced about their mutual dislike of the hateful head nurse at the teaching hospital where they had trained; the flirtatious professors who were proper in class and lecherous in a darkened hallway; their rare but shared love of reading poetry between required texts; the strain of constant studying. Victoria poured one, two and then three glasses of sherry while they chatted and laughed in the darkness like two mischievous schoolgirls.

Finally, Pearl's head began to swim. "Stop!" she said, stifling a giggle. "If I drink anything else you'll have to drag me up the stairs and throw me across the bed with my boots on!" Seldom one to imbibe more than a single drink, Pearl knew that being with Victoria always made her feel more open and adventurous. Maybe this diversion, this visit, was exactly what she needed.

But Victoria had grown unusually quiet. Pearl set her glass down and reached over to clasp her friend's hands.

"What is it, dear?" she asked. "Is there something wrong? Did I say something?" She thought she heard Victoria sniffle. "Are you crying?" Pearl asked. She sat upright, her light-headedness dissipating. "Tell me what's wrong."

"It's Walter," Victoria whispered. "No, really it's us. We're in trouble, Pearl."

"What? Everything here is so... perfect."

"It isn't," Victoria said. "We're in such financial straits that we're in danger of losing everything. Neither one of us has a good head on our shoulders for finances, and as you can see," she waved a hand about the room, "we both like the finer things, Walter as much as I."

"Is that why you have so few household staff?" Pearl said. On the one hand, she was stunned at Victoria's disclosure, but on the other she was relieved it was about money troubles and not the couple's relationship. Finances could be fixed; often marriages could not.

"I might as well tell you all of it," Victoria sighed. "Mrs. Mammoth is Walter's poor cousin. She was in dire need of a home and we took her in with the agreement that she would serve as our cook. Our Negro maid, Beth... we owe her a month's wages and I wonder every day if she's coming back."

Victoria choked back a sob. "Walter has creditors all over town. Some come by here. Others send threatening letters. I can barely hold up my head in Richmond. In fact, I'm no longer comfortable in the social circles that once welcomed us. It's because I feel like such a fraud."

Pearl rubbed her friend's hand. "I'm so sorry." It seemed pointless to ask how two well-bred and well-educated people had arrived at such a state. "What do you and Walter plan to do?"

Victoria's voice was tinged with sadness. "Leave. Walter says we'll go to Tombstone, start over and see if we can rebuild our finances and our future."

"But his patients, his office, your home," Pearl asked. "What will you do with it?"

"It will soon be for sale, including his list of patients," said Victoria. "Then everyone in town will know about us. Our creditors will get most of it. We'll take what's left for the move." She bent forward and put her face in her hands. "I'm so ashamed," she moaned, "especially when you wrote to tell us of your new adventure and your brave plans. You're so strong, Pearl, and you have so many traits I admire. I wish…"

"Hush," Pearl said, reaching out to grab Victoria's hand again. "Now sit up and look at me. I have something to share with you too."

Moonlight filtered through the open window. As Victoria raised her head and turned to face her friend, her shadowy figure seemed surreal to Pearl. Perhaps it was the wine altering her judgment, perhaps the weight of all that she had endured these past few months. Maybe it was just time to unload the burden she carried onto her best and most loyal friend.

"I left Taney County for my own escape," she told Victoria. "Asheville was selected at random, just a dot on a map. But I had to leave. I had no choice."

Victoria placed a hand to her breast. "What do you mean, Pearl? What happened?"

Pearl cleared her throat. "You mustn't tell anyone, not even Walter. Promise me, Victoria, that you will take this secret to your grave. Can you do that?"

Victoria nodded, her hand still pressed against her bosom, as though she was holding her body in place. Pearl immediately regretted her decision. Silence filled the room.

"Go on," Victoria whispered. "You know you can tell me anything."

Every muscle in Pearl tensed. She took a deep breath and continued. "I believe I was responsible for the death of a mother and child back in Taney County. I failed them both.

44

It was as dreadful a thing as if I had shot them through the heart."

Chapter Five

Like two sisters irretrievably bound by their respective secrets, Pearl and Victoria were inseparable right up to the day of Pearl's departure.

They had taken the carriage into Richmond and spent their days exploring the city's rich past – once they looked past the few remnants of war that remained. Despite a few crumbling walls, a still-burnt building here and there, much was left to admire: clean swept sidewalks and sturdy brick museums filled with art and historical artifacts; charming cafes with white, wrought iron chairs and colorful flower carts; a stunning catwalk perched in mid-air over a half-built wire-strung bridge.

Pearl loved the elegant lamp-posts along the wide streets, the tall buildings with arched trim and the small window-front shops filled with all manner of ladies fashions, house wares, foods and other goods. She bought a small, framed painting that would always remind her of Richmond and this special visit.

Ever since she had confided in Victoria, it seemed as though a heavy weight was lifted from Pearl's shoulders. It wasn't as though she could forget about what happened, but she did gain some perspective after Victoria told her it sounded as though Pearl had done all she could do in a terrible situation.

"You were suffering from exhaustion, shock and threats from a demented husband," Victoria had said. "Besides, do you really know what ended the poor woman's life? No, you don't. I'll tell you one thing. If I'd been married to that vile creature, that Mr. Singleton, I might have ended it myself!"

"Victoria! That's dreadful. She was a mother. She wouldn't have done such a thing and leave her children alone with him. Now that you know about it…let's not talk about it anymore." And so they didn't.

They passed a young woman on a busy boulevard with her hair cut so short, Pearl gave her a startled look, trying hard not to turn around and look twice.

"Did you see that?" she asked Victoria. "That's quite a spunky look."

"I heard it was a home remedy for contagious ringworm and nits," said Victoria, linking her arm in Pearl's. "At least that's what Walter says."

Pearl jerked away, grabbed her elbow and began to scratch.

"I'm sorry!" Victoria said. "Did I hurt you?"

"No, it's this confounded skin disease. Remember, I suffered with it in school?"

"Well, let's go visit the druggist and see what we can find. There's something called Wizard's Ointment that may work. It's a mix of petroleum, camphor, wintergreen and a dab of mercury. It may just be the miracle cure."

~

As Pearl mingled with the other passengers at the stage depot in Richmond, ready to depart for Old Fort, she realized how fortunate she was to have friends like Victoria and Walter. Victoria had brought her a modicum of peace of mind while Walter had talked to her at length about her skin condition, explaining new treatments he had studied and remedies she might attempt.

"I'm suspecting it's a lifelong ailment," Pearl had said. "Is that so?"

Walter had nodded. "From all indications, it appears such. But it's a condition you can manage, Pearl. We also believe that extreme distress and exhaustion can worsen it, so be cautious and don't over-exert yourself."

In other words, had Walter known what Victoria knew, no more killing of your patients.

The two women had parted with warm hugs and promises to write long and frequent letters.

"You mustn't worry," Pearl had said. "Your finances will straighten out in time, the move to Tombstone will prove exciting, and I'll be starting a whole new practice and a whole new life."

Someone was coming through the station handing out printed pamphlets for the stage passengers and calling out, "Study this before you depart! Important safety rules that all must obey! Any questions? Come to me or the stage driver over there by the platform."

Pearl opened the folded paper and read:

• *All passengers must abstain from the bottle while en route, unless they're willing to share. That's only neighborly.*

48

- *All gentlemen must refrain from the use of foul language in the presence of the gentler sex. That's only Christian.*

- *If you must smoke cigars or pipes, keep in mind the odor may be repugnant to those around you. That's common sense.*

- *Topics off-limits include politics, religion and the Civil War. More passengers are injured through unfriendly discussions than in all the coaches out West with hostile Indians and other bad elements combined.*

- *Chewing tobacco is permitted but you must spit with the wind, not against it.*

- *Pistols may be kept about your person but don't fire them for pleasure or friction may result, as in you and your neighbors being thrown from the carriage. That makes a bad travel experience for you and bad business for us.*

- *Follow these rules and we will welcome you as a repeat customer.*

Pearl chuckled, wondering how many passengers actually followed the instructions. Caine would have, but then again, he was unlike most men. She imagined him taking a stage somewhere between Pennsylvania and the Arizona Territory. Unlike most men she knew, he didn't drink, smoke or use tobacco products. She had never seen him carry a gun. He intrigued her with his quiet strength, seldom speaking unless he had something relevant to say. In that sense, he reminded her of her father. With a start, she realized that she missed that rare quality. She missed Caine.

Knowing her bags were stowed safely overhead, she climbed aboard the stage and squeezed into a seat next to a man whose substantial girth forced her against the hard wooden interior. Though dressed in current fashion, in a tailored sack suit and wingtip collar, he smelled of sour sweat and stale cigars. Across from her sat an older woman and a young boy who appeared about twelve. Since no one seemed inclined to talk, Pearl tried nodding off as the coach rattled forward, rocking side to side on its way south and west over rock-strewn paths and rutted roads lined with leafy oaks and maples. The steady rocking only gave her a slight headache.

Along the way, they stopped to water the horses and allow the passengers to relieve themselves in the primitive outhouses at the way stations. Pearl wandered off alone to watch a flock of Bobwhites calling to each other. Someone had told her Great Horned Owls and Whip-poor-wills were common in this part of the country too. She hoped to see even a hawk or a Downy woodpecker.

Nearly eight hours later, as they approached the small village at the foot of the Blue Ridge Mountains, Pearl spoke up for the first time since entering the stagecoach. "Does anyone know how Old Fort got its name?" Her father once told her that natural curiosity was a curse and a blessing and since Pearl had the two in abundance, they would both help and hinder her. What harm could come from asking a simple question?

"Called Old Fort after the Cherokee Injuns tried to kill off all the settlers," said the rotund man beside her. "Whites had to build a fort and then man it to stop the slaughterin'. You can still see dark blood marks on some of the buildings." He leaned back, pleased with his discourse.

Pearl's heart skipped a beat. Was she entering Indian Territory? The thought had never crossed her mind when she decided living in the East was preferable to the still-untamed West.

An older woman sitting across from them, her knees

50

nearly touching Pearl's legs waved a gloved hand. "Oh, posh! That's just a lively old story. I'm from around here. It's true the town was built to help protect the early settlers. But there was no slaughter. The place wasn't even named Old Fort till about ten years ago." She gave the man a withering look.

Pearl was grateful when she saw the sign above Henry Station where they pulled up. So far, she hadn't seen much to recommend this part of the country other than the thick, beautiful forests that surrounded the hamlet. But the station was nothing more than a small, wooden structure in the center of a field with a railroad line running westward. A hand-painted sign across the street announced a circus would be passing through on its way to Asheville.

"There's a pretty little spot called Round Knob Lodge about two miles northwest of here," the heavy-set gentleman said to Pearl as they entered the depot together. "'Till the railroad was done, that's where you had to go wait on the overland stage that took you up the mountain. Only one trip a day though, and a rough ride it was up that steep incline."

"Well, thank goodness for the railroad," Pearl murmured. It seemed her fellow passengers were doing little to make her introduction to the mountain region a happy one.

Grabbing her bags, she made her way to the platform along with a group of twenty or more other adults, some dressed in business attire, others in their Sunday best. All were attempting to board at once and she heard the occasional "'cuse me, Madam," "Beg pardon," common to civilized folks everywhere. At least these fellow travelers appeared to have manners. She felt somewhat relieved.

As the engine belched and pulled forward, Pearl finally relaxed, staring out the windows blackened with dust. Someone two rows up was talking about the tall mountains ahead, how at the top was the Eastern Continental Divide, blanketed in towering oaks and thick white pines. Rain on the west side ended up in the Gulf of Mexico while rain on the east side fell right into the Atlantic Ocean.

"That's a mighty good reason to live in these parts," another passenger commented. "We got it all."

Across from Pearl sat a white-haired, well-groomed gentleman. As she noticed his almost continuous, hacking cough, she estimated his age at seventy-plus. When he spoke, his voice grew raspy, as though a smoldering fire burned within his lungs.

"They call this the railroad that couldn't be built," he remarked to no one in particular. "Took convicts, even women prisoners to get it done. It's one of the steepest grades in the country; been plundered ever since."

"Beg your pardon?" Pearl said.

"Ever since the war, this rail line has been in the hands of rogues and swindlers," he said. "They've stolen everything but the roadbed and would have taken that had it not been so inconvenient. It cost a fortune in money and lives: three years and two million dollars to build and more than a hundred lives lost after six of the tunnels collapsed."

Pearl was unsure how to react to his remarks. Though she felt sympathy for the victims, what did she care about corrupt railroad officials? Deciding he was simply making conversation, she said, "I'm sorry."

"I take it you're not one of the defrauded contractors traveling to Asheville for monetary recourse?" he asked, with a mischievous grin.

"Hardly," Pearl said, returning his smile, "I'm headed to Asheville on business. It's my first time here. May I ask, sir, what's the region like?"

He leaned forward, a pleased look on his face. "I was hoping you would ask. I seldom get a chance to extol the virtues of my fair town." Pausing, he turned his head toward the window and coughed into a dingy grey cloth. "Well, much like me, these hills are old and tired," he said. "As for Asheville, it's still a pup with growing pains; a population of a little more than two thousand. We do have a Thespian Club and a public library with a free reading room, however. One writer calls it "an awkward mountain town" while another says it's "a land that reaches to the sky." So take your pick."

"What do you mean by growing pains?" Pearl asked. He reminded her of the kind but outspoken elder pastor in the country church she attended with her parents: the same weathered face, the neatly trimmed white beard, the smell of cigar smoke that wafted from his tailored suit, the wingtip collar stained. Like most men, including her pastor, he wore a white shirt and a simple tie; a fedora hat resting in his lap.

"It's like a willful youth that can't make up its mind what it wants to be when it's all grown up," he said, "a rough-and-tumble cow town or a sophisticated city. It's something in-between right now. But it's no matter. Whatever happens in the next decade or two, I won't be around to see it."

It occurred to Pearl he might be returning home for the last time. She thought he looked and acted sick, perhaps even gravely ill. At least he had the courtesy to cough into a kerchief. So many people still had no knowledge of germs and how they spread. Even worse, some didn't care, including a few of her own peers. Her thoughts flashed to Dr. Stone and his antithesis to the new germ theory. He had been wrong, yet she knew she was in no position to judge him or others, not after what she had done.

"You'll find two kinds of people in the mountains," he continued, "those who are comforted by the tight embrace of these ancient hills and those who are smothered by them."

"And which are you?" she asked. How presumptuous of her. Her mother would not approve of her impertinence. But the gentleman seemed not to take offense.

"Oh, I'm deeply rooted here. My family owns one of the oldest haberdasheries in town. And I have several, shall I say, prominent relations." A coughing spasm erupted. He took a labored breath and leaned back. "Forgive me," he said. "Consumption; it's why I'm returning to the mountains. I've been away a few weeks on business and it seems that anytime I leave, ill health follows. I should refrain from leaving again."

Despite his obvious discomfort he didn't seem overly burdened by it and Pearl couldn't help but admire his cheerful spirit.

"And what about you?" he asked. "May I inquire what brings you to our lovely up-and-coming city? I'm Jeremiah Dickson."

"And I'm Dr. Pearl Stern," she said, nodding at him from across the aisle. "I hope the town fathers will hire me as their first city-employed physician. I've written to them about it." He gave her a surprised look. That was the normal reaction when anyone learned of her profession.

"Do tell! You know, I remember reading in the Asheville Weekly last month that we were receiving a visit from a new doctor, a Dr. P. Stern. But I had no idea *he* was a *she*."

"You have a good memory," she said, then almost added for a man your age. "How do you recall that detail?

"I've spent many years learning to pay attention," Jeremiah said. "Pays off when you're doing business. Customers appreciate it when you remember their names, dates, things like that. Besides, most everybody knows everyone else in Asheville."

Pearl's brow furrowed. So everyone knew everyone else's business? She forced a smile for this Mr. Dickson.

"I doubt the town fathers know I'm a woman," she said. "All they have are my credentials and the letters of reference I sent at their request. But they'll know soon enough."

He burst out laughing, followed by another, shorter coughing fit. "That they will and it serves them right if they're blindsided. All politicians are fools and knaves."

The snorting train lurched and came to a stop.

"Ah, the Swannanoa Gap," Jeremiah said. "We must see what stale refreshments are featured today at the way station." He rose slowly, placed the sweat-stained fedora on his head and reached for his cane.

Pearl stood and moved in behind him. If he stumbled, she knew that she would instinctively reach out. But he made his way deftly toward the opened door, his cane tapping on the train's metal floor.

Inside the way station, they shared a small table. Pearl ordered lemonade; her companion asked only for water. Following a short, gravelly cough Jeremiah tucked his soiled handkerchief into his pocket. Eyes animated, he sat more erect than he had on the train. Pearl could tell he was beginning to enjoy the attention from a younger lady and in public, no less.

He told her of the first woman doctor he had met, Elizabeth Blackwell, who had visited Asheville briefly nearly forty years past, "You know where she is now? She's a professor of gynecology at the London School of Medicine for Women.

Been there since 1875."

Pearl was entranced. Dr. Blackwell was one of her icons. She knew that in 1849, the physician had been the first woman to obtain a medical degree in the United States, and that she had earned it with the highest honors. Pearl was pleased to meet someone who knew of her.

"She was a woman with a mind of her own," Jeremiah continued. "You remind me of her a good bit."

Pearl smiled, "If only..."

At Best, the depot near Asheville, Pearl left the train and adjusted her long, olive green skirt with one gloved hand while she shooed a summer blowfly with the other. With a single satchel for luggage, she felt liberated. It was nice to travel such distance without the burden of leather-strapped trunks and crates. Now if her mother would follow through with shipping her other items. Otherwise, she would have to make multiple purchases, dipping into her already tight budget.

Jeremiah had tipped his hat and bade her farewell, explaining he lived near the train station. "The walk will do me good," he said. "Oh yes, Dr. Stern, when you're ready, I'll be happy to send patients your way." Another racking cough overtook him and he bent double, using his cane for support.

"Are you all right?" Pearl asked, unsure that anything would do him good. "I'll see that you get a ride home."

He waved her away. "No, dear, but we'll meet again soon," he said as he ambled off.

She stood in the harsh sunlight waiting with the other passengers for a horse and carriage driver who would transport them on the two-mile trip into town. Two of the women had removed their gloves and were fanning themselves. A nervous young man who looked barely out of his adolescence was mopping his brow with a kerchief.

One by one, they piled into the carriage, passing tree-lined streets with tall pastel-colored houses and open verandas, small shops with white hand-painted signs in the windows, a hardware dealer, a carriage shop, a feed and livery stable offering FINEST BUGGY AND SADDLE HORSES AT CHEAPER THAN THE CHEAPEST PRICES.

Nearby, a grocery and a finery shop competed for attention with their THIS-MONTH-ONLY advertisements. Incomplete sidewalks made of small, round stones alternated with rough-hewn planks for an unfinished look to the streets. Pearl's eyes caught references to hand-lettered street signs: Pulliam and Bailey Street, North and South Main. They rode South Main where a welcome breeze accompanied them up the hill toward Public Square.

It was a bigger place than she expected; more commerce than Taney County. That was a good sign for any new practice.

As they neared Public Square, Pearl raised a gloved hand to cover her nose and mouth, overwhelmed by the pungent smell of newly tanned leather and the earthy odor of fresh horse droppings.

On the east side of the Square was a tailor shop and the W.O. Wolfe Marble Yard with what appeared, at first glance, a gargoyle perched over its entrance. Pearl stared at the obscure sculpture and finally recognized it as an angel.

They passed X. Brand & Company, which, upon closer inspection, Pearl realized was an undertaker business. Next door was Misses Coffin's Boarding House. Pearl laughed softly. Someone here had a sense of humor. Her fellow passenger, the nervous youth, gave her a disgruntled look as

57

though to say 'what's so funny that you won't share?' Intent on seeing as much as possible on the short ride, she turned to her left and resumed her study of the city as the sound of horse's hooves beat a steady rhythm. They were almost at the Square.

Pearl could see an arched building, identified by a sign as the Asheville Police Department. It adjoined the volunteer fire department next door. Slightly further ahead was a three-story courthouse with a rounded entrance and a turreted tower running through its center. An observation deck sat perched, bird-like, on the roof.

The place had a raw energy and Pearl felt a renewed sense of excitement that she was here, at this juncture in her career and the town's growth, and that she might become an important part of it. Earlier doubts were disappearing as fast as the dust that swirled about the horse-drawn carriage. No one knew her here. No one could judge her past. In time, even she might forget.

Blue-gray mountains surrounded the town and loomed against a cloudless light blue sky. But it was hot, much warmer than she expected. Wasn't this where people came for the cool climate and the clean mountain air?

Tiny rivulets of perspiration stained her moss green blouse and trickled down her armpits. It didn't help that she was wearing gloves. Her mother's early teachings came to mind: "A lady must wear gloves in public if for no other reason than to protect fair skin from the sun and retain a sense of sanitation."

At the Square itself, the open grass-less expanse was packed with dirt. Tethered horses stomped and snorted while their owners left them to idle as they tended to business inside the shops. A few men sat atop their wagons conversing while others gathered around the water pump to cool off. Many were bearded, rough-hewn men in tattered clothes; some were clean-shaven but plainly dressed. These were working men probably taking a noon break.

As the buggy halted, Pearl stepped from the carriage and reached in her purse for a coin to tip the driver. Exhausted from her long trip, she was anxious to get settled for her first day in Asheville. She retrieved her bag, marveling at its dead weight, no doubt the result of her having stuffed a critical number of medical supplies and instruments among her clothing. Her remaining luggage would not arrive for days, possibly weeks.

Bent over, she didn't see the wagon until it was nearly too late. The driver, a slender colored man, was swigging from an earthen jug. As he attempted to drive the rig, the wagon veered perilously close to Pearl, so close she could smell the animals' bristled hair in the summer heat, so close that two of the wooden wheels caught the hem of her skirt and pulled her onto the ground. She lay there, momentarily stunned.

Then she heard yelling.

"You goddamned heathen!"

A shot rang out. Was someone firing at her? She managed to pull herself up, but her skirt was still hung under the wheel. Grasping the heavy fabric, she attempted to pull at it but neither the wheel nor the skirt would budge. She sat there on the ground, helpless.

A man holding a pistol, his hat askew, yelled at the driver. He was so angry his face appeared as nothing more than a red blob to Pearl. "What are you trying to do, kill this young woman? Get down! Now! You're under arrest!"

The colored man shook his head, climbed from the driver's perch and stumbled to the ground with the jug attached to his thumb, like a separate, ill-formed appendage. "No sir," he mumbled. "I ain't done anything like that. Wouldn't hurt no woman, white or otherwise."

"Shut up," said the man, who opened his jacket to reveal a police badge. "I'm arresting you for public drunkenness and attempting to run down a pedestrian." Then he turned his attention to Pearl. "Are you all right, ma'am?"

"I'm fine, she said. "If you'd be so kind as to help me get my skirt untangled." The officer kicked hard at the sunken wheel and splintered a spoke, whereupon the wagon immediately sagged toward Pearl. She drew back.

"There," he said, "that ought to do it." With a final jerk, Pearl pulled on the fabric, freeing herself. The officer helped her to her feet. She brushed the dust from her torn skirt.

"You done broke my wagon," the colored man moaned, shaking his head.

"I'll break your damn neck next time," said the officer. He pulled a pair of iron cuffs from his belt loop and grabbed the driver's hands, snapping the restraints in place.

"Excuse my language, ma'am," the officer said. "But this isn't the first time ole Jim here has created a bother on the streets."

"Officer, wait," Pearl said. "There was no real harm done. Is it really necessary to put him in jail? By the way, what's your name?"

"Callahan, Officer Callahan. And beg your pardon, ma'am, but this is official business. Our drunken Negro here is a well-known public menace."

Pearl noted the policeman's rising color and that she was likely making things worse. "I meant no disrespect," she said.

She turned to the man in handcuffs. He gave her a mournful look as the officer pushed and prodded him along. Several of the workers at the Square were hollering and one yelled "String him up now! Save us the time and trouble later!"

"Sir, what's your name?" Pearl called to the Negro, appalled at the uncouth jeering.

"He ain't no 'sir'," the officer growled. "He's just a plain ole coon, and there's plenty more where he came from. You'll figure that out, if you stick around long enough."

"Harrison, my name's Jim Harrison, ma'am, and I'm real sorry about what happened."

Pearl, shocked at the officer's coarse language and over-eagerness to use his weapon, gathered her belongings and looked around, uncertain of which way to go. Her fellow passengers had already scattered. No one else came to her assistance as she attempted to reassemble herself. Surely someone could see she was just as lost as she appeared.

A place no more civil than the Wild West, Pearl concluded. Her friendly, intelligent exchange with Mr. Dickson must have been a rare exception to people that – at least on first impression – seemed rife with poor breeding.

Good lord, she thought, what have I done?

Chapter Six

As she lugged her bag across Public Square in the hot July sun, Pearl regretted her decision not to have anyone, even a town official, meet her upon her arrival. It was one thing to be fiercely independent, another to find herself disoriented and alone in a strange town, especially one that was proving inconsistent in its welcome. But she was here now and must deal with it. Such pragmatism ran deep in her nature, a gift from her father's side of the family.

She headed toward the Swannanoa Hotel, an imposing four-story brick building on South Main that sat directly opposite its main competitor, the Eagle. She thought the Eagle stately but weary-looking. Its weathered gray entrance needed a fresh coat of paint.

Entering the Swannanoa, she saw a clerk behind the desk and in a far corner of the dim-lit room, several people dining. It gave her a hopeful sense that hospitality was nearby. A densely-worded sign propped on the counter declared

THE SWANNANOA: THE LARGEST AND BEST

ARRANGED HOTEL IN ASHEVILLE. OPEN YEAR

ROUND. Rooms and halls well-ventilated. Superior

views of surrounding mountains. Cistern and mountain
well water. Hot and cold baths. Telegraph office and

Electric Annunciator.

"Good afternoon," Pearl greeted the waiting clerk, "it's so hot outside. How nice to be indoors!" She glanced at the sign again. "Sir, what's an electric annunciator?"

"It means you can press a button and get somebody to come to your room post-haste," he said. "Now, how can I help you, miss?" He was short, stout and wore his hair parted in the center. Slicked back, its oily shine caught the lamplight. He had not once smiled, Pearl noticed, and came across as though the daily grind of greeting guests was well beneath him. Everything about him sent the message that he was behind the desk against his will.

"Yes," said Pearl, "I need a room for a few nights and perhaps a good meal."

He handed her a brass key. "It's three dollars for the night, includes all meals."

Pearl's frowned. "Three dollars? That seems high."

"It's three dollars. We're the newest in town and consider ourselves the finest. You can go to the Eagle across the street or walk a few blocks to the Grand Central. They're cheaper but not as nice and sure not as clean…or friendly."

"No, it's fine," said Pearl, rummaging in her cloth handbag. "I'll take it. And thank you." As she went up to her room, she noticed a large poster at the door of the hotel dining room proclaiming "world class entertainment – unlike our neighbors across the street." She could already hear the clang and high-pitched whine of what sounded like a band warming up to play.

When she descended and ordered the daily special – a bowl of chicken gumbo with a thick mixture of rice, vegetables, and chopped meat, soft biscuits slathered in fresh apple butter and a slice of the cinnamon-topped sweet-potato pie, she enjoyed every succulent bite – a delicious, a mix of sweet, spice and tart. At least the food in Asheville was pleasing.

Preparing to leave, she noticed someone approaching her table. In the shadowy light, she could not distinguish much, but he was certainly a big man – tall, broad shouldered, with a commanding presence. Several of the diners glanced up and made a point of acknowledging him as he brushed past to get to her table. As he came closer, she noticed that his thick auburn hair formed a smooth line at the nape of his neck, that he wore a dark blue coat with a shiny gold badge pinned to his vest and sported a handle-bar mustache. Unlike the majority of the men in the room, he was hatless. A rather fine-looking man, very different from Caine, whose Asian features give him an exotic appeal. Was he approaching her?

"Miss?" he said, reaching for a chair. "Forgive the intrusion but I heard you had a little mishap in town. One of my officers – Callahan—told me what happened." His voice was a deep, baritone tinged with a thick Southern accent.

"And you are?" Pearl asked, surprised by the fast-traveling news of her arrival.

"Hershel Springfield Harkins, Chief of Police. It's a pleasure to meet you, ma'am, and welcome to our fair city." She reached out and placed a small soft hand in his rather large one. To Pearl, it felt as though he could easily break a person's fingers with the sheer strength of his grip. "Watch for a man with a strong handshake," her father had always advised. "It means he has character."

Herschel released his hold. "I came to assure you of your

safety while you're in Asheville."

Looking up at him, Pearl wiped her lips with her napkin, pleased by his warm gesture. "That's very kind, Chief Harkins. But how did you know I was here?"

"They were still talking about you at the Square, and it wasn't hard to follow your trail. It's not every day we get attractive single ladies arriving by train cars, and not every day they almost get run over by a drunken black man. A highly unusual event, I assure you. Please accept my apology on behalf of our citizens."

"I was about to have coffee," said Pearl. "Would you like to join me?" There was something about him, maybe the piercing gray eyes. They seemed to bore right through her, so different from Caine's, whose eyes always held a hint of mystery.

He nodded, motioning for a waiter to attend them. Then he took a seat, ordering a cup of coffee, "strong and black."

"So," he began, "I take it no harm came to you from the incident?"

"I'm fine," Pearl answered, crinkling her brow, "but your officer Callahan was quite rough with his handling of the gentleman he arrested, and very rude to the man, I might add. Mr. Harrison was his name, I believe. What became of him?"

"He's in jail, of course. Don't worry yourself with him. May I ask why you're alone in town? Here to visit family? Are you staying long?"

Pearl thought it forward that he asked so many questions. That probably made him a good officer, but not much of a gentleman, at least in some social circles. She decided she might as well be direct, too. After all, he was an officer of the law and here for business purposes alone.

"My name is Pearl Stern. I'm the new physician invited by your town fathers to discuss the possibility of becoming their first municipal doctor. That's assuming all goes well. I came from Taney County, Missouri, south of Springfield. What else would you like to know?"

He grinned. "We're not much used to ladies coming to town for upstanding business in these parts. But I find it refreshing. So you're Dr. Stern. Saw the announcement in the paper that a new physician was arriving on the train from Old Fort. Our weekly rag reports every visitor. Not much else to attract newsworthy attention."

"Apparently, however, a lot of locals read the newspaper," Pearl said. "That's the second time I've heard about my arrival today." Sitting across from her, his physical presence loomed large. She felt small in comparison. Studying his blank expression, she guessed he was good at poker, since he didn't even register surprise that she was a female doctor. She chose her next words carefully.

"Well, I learned from my father that it's better to make myself clear from the start." It suddenly struck her that she had done just the opposite by sending her letter to the town council without clarifying her sex. She hoped the police chief wouldn't bring that up.

He reached for a spoon as the waiter returned with his coffee and set it before him. "I'm happy to make your acquaintance. You know, I once wanted to become a doctor myself."

Sipping from the thin china cup, she looked at him with smiling eyes. "Really? And why didn't you?"

"Family obligations, other opportunities, that kind of thing. Then the war came along. I have an uncle in Jackson County who's a general practitioner. Went to study with him for a while but I didn't stay long. It's still a real interesting business, though."

"Family obligations? Did your wife not approve of the profession?"

"She did," he replied. "She supported whatever I chose. I lost her a few years back."

Pearl placed her cup back into the saucer. "I'm so sorry. Forgive me."

Herschel shook his head and mumbled, "No need."

Pearl thought it best to steer the conversation in a new direction. "I see you became a police officer instead. That's an interesting business too."

"It can be. I spent some time first with the U.S. Marshal's office as a revenuer."

"You chased moon-shiners?" Pearl stared at him intently. "I've never met a Marshal."

He caught her eye and she looked away quickly, embarrassed by their sudden connection. Such intimacy with a virtual stranger was foreign to her. Caine was the only man, besides her father, she had ever felt pull at her heartstrings. She had never allowed males to take up her time, considering her focus should be on more serious and therefore more important things, than a boy's fleeting affections. She pushed at her empty dinner plate, rearranging it slightly in an effort to regain her composure.

"It's not all it's cracked up to be," he said. "There are some dangerous people out there just like here in town, some right under your nose."

Pearl gave him a shy smile. "Hopefully, I won't turn out to be one of them."

He laughed aloud, and a few of the diners turned to look their way. One woman shot Pearl a disapproving glance. They talked a while longer, Pearl describing her trip up the mountain and the comments made by her newfound friend, Mr. Dickson.

"Yes, I know that old coot," Herschel said. "The only thing he loves more than causing a stir is causing a big stir. Don't take everything he says too seriously."

Pearl frowned. "He's an intelligent, very pleasant man, who, I think, is very ill. He has a terrible cough that keeps him nearly breathless in between all that talking. Do you know about his health?"

Herschel shook his head. "I know he's stubborn as a Missouri mule — no offense ma'am — but I don't know anything about his constitution. Of course, we have a lot of people who come here for the clean air and the fresh water. I reckon there's something to it. I'm a pretty healthy specimen." He patted his midriff as he stood up.

Pearl couldn't help but smile at him. She was almost sorry to see him go.

"I better get back to the station," he said. "Lost track of what time it is! Sounds like your next order of business is letting your prospective employer know you're here. I'd like to help with that, if you'll allow me."

"You mean the Board of Aldermen?" Pearl said. "As police chief, I'm sure you know some of them."

"I know all of them. My cousin is also the mayor."

As she considered his offer, Pearl wondered if that was good or bad. Her first instinct was to say no. She had come this far alone and could certainly handle her own business affairs. But his assistance might help with an introduction, especially if there was a negative reaction when they learned of

68

her sex. "That's very kind of you, Chief. Give me a few minutes to freshen up and I'll come to the police station."

He reached into his pocket for change to cover his drink. "I'll be happy to return to the hotel and escort you," he offered, smiling.

"That's not necessary. I'd enjoy the walk to the station." Noticing him scrounging in his pocket, she leaned toward him and whispered, "Though you may think me forward, the least I can do, in exchange, is to buy you a cup of coffee." Noticing his frown, she continued, "I insist."

"Well, that's a first for me, a young lady covering my drink." Herschel gave a wry smile as he rubbed his right hand behind his neck. "And no, I don't think you're forward. Furthermore I'm glad you're here."

As he turned to leave, Pearl glanced about for a waiter to bring her ticket and heard murmurs from the other diners. They probably thought she was brazen. They could whisper all they wanted. She had more pressing things to worry about, like whether or not she'd even have a position once she met the aldermen.

Chapter Seven

She had put on a simple black dress with a hint of lace at the collar, smoothed her dark shiny hair, and searched her luggage for a toothbrush and a dollop of the newly patented baking soda mixture that, according to its advertising claim, was "tonic for the mouth."

The double bed, spread with a bright patchwork quilt, served as her makeshift desk due to its size. An hour-glass lamp squatted on a tiny oak table near an open window. Thick, wheat-colored tassels on the lamp shade danced in the afternoon breeze. White-washed walls offset the colorful hues of the furnishings, giving the room a homey cheerfulness. She felt a sense of warmth and safety within these walls.

She sifted through her stack of papers, arranging the documents she would need during her introduction to the aldermen: Certificate of graduation with honors from the Women's Medical College, her gold-embossed degree from the state of Missouri which allowed her to practice medicine east of the Rockies, academic letters of reference from her all-male college professors and a personal reference from the pastor in Taney County, Missouri. Also tucked away was a copy of the recently published manual *The Physician Himself*, a guide to setting up a successful private practice she might be using later. She had stopped taking offense that such directives were aimed only at men.

As she fingered the silver locket her mother had given her before Pearl's departure, she was reminded of her mother's words: "This will keep us close even as you travel long distances." Inside was a sepia-tone photo of her parents, appearing as hardy and formidable as ever. The gift of the locket had been an unusual display of affection from her mother. Sitting on the edge of the bed, Pearl wondered again if her mother really believed in her ability to make her own way in the world. She had never given her a vote of confidence, and Pearl felt that unspoken words sometimes signified the dissimilarity between love and indifference.

Their years together had been uneven at best, sometimes distant, sometimes as close as those Pearl and Victoria had shared. Though Pearl knew her mother probably loved her, she wasn't sure she approved of her own daughter, particularly as she grew into adulthood and began to show a fierce independence.

"You don't need me," her mother once accused her. "You don't need anyone." It had broken Pearl's heart to see the hardened look on her mother's face. Shocked, Pearl couldn't respond to this untrue accusation. Her mother had given her a speculative look, shouting "You just proved my point."

Pearl gave herself a final check in the full-length mahogany mirror that stood guard in the corner of the room and decided her appearance, simple but professional, would do. Taking a deep breath, she sighed. She would need all the courage and confidence she could muster to pull this off, to make the Board of Alderman see that she was well-qualified for the position they needed to fill. Gathering her things, she closed the door behind her.

The Asheville Police Department was only a few blocks away, up South Main and around the corner toward Public Square. Thick, gray clouds had rolled in during the afternoon and were hunched over the distant mountains like angry old men. Pearl had forgotten to bring her parasol, so she hoped the summer storm would hold off at least a short while.

Nearing the Square, she passed a cigar shop and breathed in the not unpleasant aroma of rich, dark tobacco, remembering that Jeremiah Dickson had informed her the region was a booming tobacco market, with most of the crops sent to Virginia in barrels. He boasted that the city had four brick tobacco sale warehouses with sales of several million pounds of the coveted "bright yellows".

Next door was a barber shop filled to capacity with male customers. Two men dressed in suits and vests, their chained pocket watches dangling, stood at the doorway talking. One was in the process of lighting a stubby cigar while the other studied the darkening sky. Both tipped their hat as she walked past. "Looks like a thunder boomer," she heard one say. "Maybe it will cool things down a notch. Were you here in '81 when we had that storm on the west end of town that brought us such destruction? I lost nearly half my lumber supply in that flood." Pearl knew mountain weather was unpredictable. At least they didn't have tornados here like they did in Missouri.

A street vendor hawked his wares from a wooden cart. "Ma'am!" he called out as she approached. "You look like a refined young lady. Silk scarves, customized hand-made genuine Indian jewelry from right here in the mountains; items never seen before."

Pearl brushed past him with a "No thank you" and crossed

the wide intersecting streets to the police department just ahead. As she walked, she noticed a large clearing among the burgeoning young oaks, a hand-carved park bench and a small, man-made pond.

Inside the stone-arched police station, she went directly to the dark brown wooden counter where a young officer, dressed in a baggy uniform, sat reading the paper.

He looked up at her with a bored look. "Yeah?"

"I'm here to see Mr. Harkins," she said.

"Who?"

Pearl realized she had not made herself clear. "Chief Harkins," she said. "You know, your Chief of Police?"

"Oh, you mean Big Hersch," he said. "Yep. Stay right here, miss. I'll go get him."

Dapper in his blue buttoned uniform, shiny black shoes, and badge, Herschel strode down the hallway toward her carrying his white helmet in one hand.

Pearl was impressed. Now that's how a policeman is supposed to appear!

Herschel gave her a teasing smile. "I see you're already looking real doctorial," Herschel said.

Pearl chuckled "I'm not even sure that's a word, but thank you. Have you had a chance to speak to any of the aldermen? Do they know we're coming?"

"I went by after lunch and talked to them. We barely got a majority for a vote to see you, but several of the aldermen have offices either in or near the courthouse so they aren't hard to round up. But here's one problem."

Pearl looked up with a frown. "What? Have they already changed their minds?"

"Not that I'm aware. But it'll be a few days before they can see you. You didn't expect this meeting to take place as soon as you stepped from the buggy, did you?" He was grinning even as he shook his head at Pearl.

"Of course not," she said, attempting to hide her embarrassment. But she had hoped it would. The sooner the better as far as she was concerned.

Herschel offered her his arm. "What I suggest we do instead is take a stroll around town."

"I'm fine," she said. To her, the gesture implied they were on intimate terms when in fact, they had just met. "Lead the way and I'll follow you."

"Yes ma'am," he said. They walked side-by-side, her height barely reaching the level of his shoulder. A slight breeze had lifted the oppressive heat from earlier and Pearl found the walk pleasant. Despite her initial encounter with the police officer at the Public Square, she was beginning to feel Asheville might be a friendly little town.

She glanced up at the Chief. "Did you happen to mention that I'm…not…did you mention my sex?"

"Did I tell them you're a woman? Oh no, that would spoil half the fun."

Pearl stopped in mid-stride and glared at him. "Is that what this is about?" she said, her face flushed. "It's some game you 'gentlemen' are using to toy with the little woman? Well, if that's the case, I don't need you for introduction or support and certainly not as your means of amusement."

"Now hold on a minute," he said as she moved ahead of him, "'Don't get your dander up." His voice had taken on a new seriousness, and Pearl realized this is how he must sound when confronting an adversary. Good. Maybe she got her point across.

"You're taking this all wrong," he said. "What I meant was no, I didn't tell them you're a woman because it's not my place. That's your business and as you made clear, you're right capable of handling it. Though, if I might be so bold, you really should have told them yourself, in your letter, that you're a woman doctor. Not disclosing that fact is risky business; maybe even downright foolish."

Pearl's face turned a deep crimson. "I know that. I took a big chance and it could backfire." But he had no idea how desperately she needed this position, a fresh start in a place where no one knew her, or her past.

"I'm not done," Herschel said. "Furthermore, I was wrong."

"What?" Pearl had no idea what was coming next. She wondered if his assistance would turn into a liability, and just when she was starting to like him.

"I was wrong to put it the way I did, about it being half the fun. You're new here. You don't know how set in their ways some of these old codgers can be. I swear to God I think most of them still believe women are of no real consequence other than as housekeepers and do-gooders."

"And your point?" she said, hope rising that he was still on her side.

Herschel looked down at her. "I want to see you put them in their place."

Pearl gave him a half-hearted smile. "Do you believe I can do so?"

"Yes, Doctor, I do. But what does it matter what I think? I'm just a simple country boy."

She burst out laughing. She could hardly imagine him as

a boy. He extended his arm once more. This time she took it, and they walked together.

He pointed out the Bank of Asheville that had recently moved to the western side of South Main Street, the two-story public library located in a former mercantile building and the broken remnants of a Yankee Negro garrison where riots had erupted after the Civil War.

"People were shot right after they were tried," said Herschel. "The execution was held at these two junctions." He motioned toward two intersecting streets. "Some of the Negroes killed here are probably buried below the street."

"That's horrid!" Pearl said. She thought of Jim, the drunken man who had nearly run over her upon her arrival.

"That man named Jim," she said. "The one your Officer Callahan arrested. I really don't think he meant any harm. Is it absolutely necessary he be in jail?"

"I don't know," said Herschel. "I'm not opposed to looking into it. But he does have a record for trouble-making."

"Thank you. Now, can you tell me something about your town that is of a more promising nature? What do you love about this place?" She remembered what Mr. Dickson had said about these mountains either drawing people in or making them feel smothered.

Herschel stopped at a small ridge overlooking the French Broad River in the distance. Pearl stood quiet, looking up at the imposing man beside her. When he finally spoke, his voice had an intimate timber, as though they had known each other for years.

"See that river yonder? That's a grand ole lady. She's been winding her way through here for hundreds of years. She's seen it all – the rise of the Cherokee nation, the hard-

76

scrabble life of the first settlers who came to these mountains. She's seen the wars we've fought; the men we've lost; those who have come before us and those who are here now; generations of people good and bad. She's rugged and strong, just like these mountain people. You'll find us peculiar in some ways, Dr. Stern. Hardheaded, stubborn, set in our ways. But you'll also find kindness, forgiveness and a real willingness to get along. I've been other places, lived elsewhere. But something draws me back here every time. Maybe it's the mountains like Jeremiah says. I like their steadfastness. They comfort me."

He glanced down at Pearl, smiling. "Good huntin' and fishin' too. Best in the land."

~

A few days later, with Pearl spending her idle time cooped up in her hotel room reading and writing letters to her parents and Victoria, she finally received word that the Board of Alderman was ready to meet. She hurried to the police station to find Herschel.

Together, they walked the block to the courthouse. Inside, the building smelled of old wood, smoke, and the collective sweat of dozens of people milling about, some attempting to find a courtroom where they could sit and wile away the hot afternoon. Others, awaiting verdicts, were nervously pacing, unsure they would be going home anytime soon. A few men dressed in denim coveralls and simple work clothes seemed to be exchanging gossip or discussing the latest news. Pearl caught snippets of their conversation as she walked past.

"Did you hear about that man in Candler? The one whose

wife ran off with the doctor? Brought a suit against the doc for five thousand in damages. Hell, I would have drawn blood instead. At least that might improve my standing in the community!"

"Stamps going up to three cents. Hells-bells."

"Ole President Arthur, I hear he's starting this civil service thing. Nothin' civil about it from what I can tell." Low snickers followed.

Herschel guided Pearl up the L-shaped stairwell and down the hall toward a door shut tight. Feeling her heart rate rise, she forced herself to stay calm by taking deep breaths, disappointed with her sudden lack of confidence. Mentally, she thanked Herschel for his presence. Alone, she would have found the stress unbearable.

Herschel opened the door and stood back while she entered. Six men seemed to crowd a stuffy room with a lone half-cracked window. Pearl saw a blur of gray and black suits, smelled the aroma of starch and stale cigars, and heard the wooden floor creak beneath her feet. She saw a row of framed photos displaying prominent judges, governors and city officials lining the walls. She wondered briefly if Herschel's Chief of Police photograph was among them but was too nervous to look.

The councilmen greeted Herschel in loud voices, one slapping him on the back as he moved past. At first hardly anyone noticed the petite young woman at his side. Then eyes began to flit nervously from Herschel, to her, to each other.

Pearl took a seat front and center, arranging copies of her paperwork on her lap. Herschel had already taken a chair in the far corner of the room, though she could sense his physical presence.

"Good day, gentlemen," she began. "My name is Dr. Pearl Stern. I'm delighted to meet you. I'm here to present my credentials but I must begin by asking your forgiveness for not disclosing my sex. I sincerely hoped it would not be a major deterrent, for as you see by my documents, I'm well qualified to serve as your prospective municipal physician."

She heard a clearing of throats and then a cough amidst a growing silence.

Pearl tried again. "I arrived a few days ago from Missouri." She motioned toward Herschel. "Chief Harkins was kind enough to escort me here to meet with you. While I understand you may be a little taken aback..."

"Miss," interrupted a heavyset man who identified himself as Will Owen, senior alderman. His voice boomed in the tight quarters. "Are we to believe you are a real doctor? We've studied the credentials sent to us by Dr. P. Stern and his... the...associates. But nowhere is there a hint of your true nature."

Pearl stiffened. "My true nature being that I'm a woman?"

"Correct," he said. "And we can only conclude that this discrepancy, this distortion, was of a purposeful nature." The others nodded in agreement.

"In my experience," said Pearl, "it's not unusual for physicians responding to letters of intent from prospective employers to use their first initials."

"Your experience?" Owen repeated. "Young lady, you have no experience. It says here that you – if indeed this is you – graduated from medical college only in the past eighteen months."

Pearl struggled to keep her voice steady. "Sir, Mr. Owen. If you'll look closely at my certificate, you'll see I'm a graduate of the Women's Medical College of Pennsylvania, which in turn should lead you to conclude the obvious." She could hear Herschel in the background stifle what sounded like a chuckle.

Papers shuffled around the table.

"Well, yes, I see that," said Owen. His only hint of embarrassment was a slightly reddened face. "But is it not true all of this school's professors are men of great talent? And is it not true that men graduate from there as well? So I don't think that we should be judged for assuming that our candidate is... was...a gentleman."

Pearl shifted in her seat. She should have expected a cross-examination. This predicament was by her own hand and now she must suffer the consequences. Perhaps another approach was in order.

"Your need for an additional physician is great," she said. "From others I have spoken with, I believe that Asheville is on the verge of major growth. At present, you have only eight doctors to treat the thousands of people within the city limits alone, none of them employed to do your bidding as a municipal physician. Isn't that true?"

She had a momentary flashback of closing her eyes and stabbing a pin into the map that led her here. She hoped they wouldn't question her on prior research about Asheville. In truth, she came for reasons unknown to anyone but herself, her parents and Victoria.

"Uh...yes," the alderman said. "We could certainly use a man of medicine in our employ or as an addition to the established healers we have in town."

"You could use a doctor," Herschel called out from the back of the room. "What does it matter man or woman? Get off your high horses. If truth be told, some of the quacks we have around here need a little healthy competition. You know who I'm talking about."

I'm handling this, Pearl thought. Don't make it worse. Quacks? What did he mean by that? Face flushed, she looked down and fumbled with her paperwork. Didn't they realize her credentials were legitimate?

"No need to get personal, Hersch," Owen said. "Let's not forget you are a Republican partisan from the ground up. And while you have ability enough to manage the police department, in retrospect it should have been entrusted to a Democrat. Don't interfere with our task at hand. You're not qualified."

Herschel audibly groaned.

"Yeah," another alderman added. "But politics aside, just because Doc Hanson had a few setbacks, let's not lose sight of the fact that if it hadn't been for him there are several of us here who wouldn't be in such fine health, myself included."

A loud round of agreement followed. A moment later, the men were gesturing toward each other. One told Herschel that he had no business bringing this young woman into their meeting, wasting their time, at which point Herschel rose and moved toward the table. Owen and two of the other aldermen scooted their chairs away from the table and stood up.

Both men faced the Chief of Police, all glaring at each other.

Heart racing, Pearl was stunned. Her proper job interview was turning into a near brawl. She placed her fingertips on both temples, then stood up, too, facing the row of aldermen as they gathered themselves, their faces an angry red. Her paperwork fell and scattered to the floor.

"Gentleman!" she called out. "If you'll excuse my interruption, can we get back to the business at hand? Your town needs a doctor. I need a job. Will you employ me? If not, I'll be on my way." She leaned over to gather her things from the floor. What she wouldn't give for a breath of fresh air. She headed toward the door. She should have known better than to come here. Trying to start over was a mistake.

"Wait!" said Herschel. He had moved away from the angry Owen and was now close to the chair she had vacated. He turned to the small group of men, all in various stages of rear-ranging their seats. "She's right. Let's get down to business. Does she stay or does she go?"

There was a low rumble; a putting of heads together, and another cursory glance at the paperwork.

"She can't be worse than what we've got already," Herschel added. He shrugged at Pearl.

Pearl rolled her eyes at him. Oh thank you, she mouthed. This man, this Chief of Police notwithstanding, was unbeliev-able.

"We'll discuss among ourselves and take a vote," Owen said, brushing his rumpled coat. "In the meantime, Miss…Dr. Stern, do you have any idea where you might set up a prac-tice if we choose to employ you? It's up to you to find and support your own office."

Pearl felt a resurgence of hope. This was a good sign. She should be diplomatic. "Actually, I could use your guidance on a suitable location," she said. "I noted some vacant store-fronts on my way here. Perhaps close to Public Square? That seems to be where the other physicians are housed."

More grumbling ensued. "We'll get back to you," was all she could make out.

"Very well," she said. "I'm staying at the Swannanoa

Hotel." A wave of the hand by one of the aldermen was her dismissal.

Once outside the courthouse in the cooling air, Pearl took a deep breath. She sat down on a plain wooden bench near the dirt path that circled back to the Square and retrieved a pink floral fan from her purse. Unfolding it, she flapped it about her face like a distressed bird.

Within moments, Herschel exited the building and walked toward her as though nothing untoward had happened. She studied his purposeful stride and took note as people entering the courthouse stepped aside to let him pass.

"So do your town meetings generally turn into a free-for-all?" she asked as he approached.

"No, not all of them," he replied. "If that blasted Owen hadn't started in." Taking a seat beside her, he wiped his brow on the sleeve of his uniform. "There's something about that weasel. He gets my goat every time. I told you they were a bunch of thick-headed old fools. At least now you know what you're up against."

Pearl knew better than to point out that had he kept his own head and not tried to rile the councilmen it could have turned out differently.

"I'm not worried so much about them," she said. "They will do whatever they choose with or without us. But what you said about these quacks. What were you talking about?"

"Doc Hanson, that's who," said Herschel. "He doesn't know his ass from the bottom of a rum glass. We tried petitions to get him fired, letters to the editor of the Asheville paper, subtle threats and not-so-subtle threats. Nothing worked."

"Is that because of his friendship with the councilmen?" Pearl said.

"That, and the fact that no one wants to confront him direct. I once saw him put a cast on a young kid all the way up to the top of the boy's thigh."

"What's wrong with that?" Pearl asked.

"The boy had a broken toe on the other leg," said Herschel. "I'm telling you Hanson is a carbuncle on the human race."

"He can't be that bad," Pearl said, suppressing a laugh at Herschel's florid description. "Are you not employed by these same councilmen you just insulted?"

"Technically, they appointed me but I answer to the Mayor. The Board sets my salary and tells me what I can and can't do as far as enforcing the laws. But I don't pay them much mind. I find common sense, of which they have little, works about as good as anything."

It mortified Pearl to think he might have put his own job in jeopardy on her behalf. "You don't worry they can influence others against you?"

"I make it a rule not to worry," he said. "I just do my job. The rest takes care of itself." He stood. Pearl rose too. "I need to get back to the station," he said. "I'll see that you get to the hotel."

They strolled toward the Square, saying little. Herschel seemed to be pondering something. He suddenly spoke up. "How much money do you have?" he asked.

Pearl's eyebrows shot up. "I beg your pardon! What business is that of yours?"

"How much money did you bring with you? If the town doesn't hire you, you can set up your own practice, pick and choose your own patients and make house calls in or outside the city limits. You won't be beholden to anyone."

84

Pearl considered his suggestion. "I have enough to live on for a few months but I need a steady income, Chief. I've known too many country doctors who set themselves up in private practice and are lucky if they are paid in chickens and eggs. It's a hard way to making a living, if you can even call it that."

"Well, at least chickens and eggs allow you to eat."

A pragmatic man, Pearl thought, much like her father, and herself. "True," she said. "But there are other considerations. I also need to pay rent, buy supplies, things of that nature. You heard what the council said, that even under their hire I'm responsible for my own office. I didn't see signs of many merchants on the Square bartering with poultry. Do they?"

"It happens," Herschel said. "People do what they can to pay in hard times."

When they reached the station, he offered to walk her to the hotel. "That's not necessary," she said. "But thank you for everything."

He tipped his officer cap. "My pleasure, Miss Stern... Pearl."

She turned and walked away sensing, at least for a moment, that his eyes were on her back. Under normal circumstances, she couldn't wait to sit down and write another letter to Victoria about her unexpected alliance with the intriguing Chief of Police, the bizarre job interview unlike any she had ever heard about, and her impressions of her newly adopted hometown. But she wasn't sure if Victoria, struggling with her own domestic problems, would even respond.

Instead, Pearl would write another perfunctory letter to her parents, telling them she had undergone her first job interview and that she would keep them informed of the outcome.

She knew her mother would write, if only to admonish Pearl for not selecting a city where she at least had friends or relatives.

A wave of loneliness washed over her as she covered the block and entered the lobby of the Swannanoa Hotel. This was her home for now. But where and what was her future?

Chapter Eight

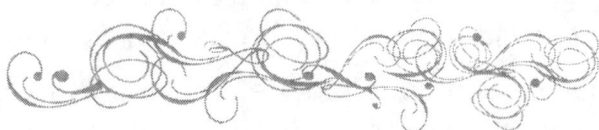

Pearl spent most of the next morning and early afternoon in her hotel room thumbing through her texts, particularly the section on proper forms of conduct for a town doctor. She read from the chapter on office practices in *The Model Physician*:

One must not be seen loitering around drug stores, hotel lobbies, saloons, clubrooms, cigar stores, billiard parlors, barber shops, corner groceries, or with 'splendid' fellows who love doing nothing. You are a public figure about town and must be held to a lofty standard.

In your office avoid the temptation to display untoward curiosities. Do not hang shark heads, stuffed alligators, tortoise shells, impaled butterflies, miniature ships, mummies, snakes, tape worms, devil-fish or anything else that will advertise you in any light other than an educated and cultivated physician.

She would be lucky to find an office and adequate equipment, much less a roomful of exotic exhibits. She read on:

Take care neither to ask any questions twice at the same time nor to do anything else that would indicate lack of memory, lack of interest or incompetence. Allow everyone a fair hearing even though their long statements are often tedious. Endure them so that you may bear the greatness of their trust and the glory of your divine mission.

In the classroom she had argued with the professor, to no avail, that such advice was sometimes contradictory. What is wrong with asking questions more than once to confirm a patient's age, condition or any other useful information?

"We have a service to provide and an oath to uphold," Pearl had said to the class. "In order to perform that service properly, why not just say that listening is imperative, clarify when needed and treat everyone with the same respect?" Heads nodded, but, as Pearl recalled, the male professor dismissed her muted outburst. She had exchanged knowing glances with Victoria, whose look said she approved of the effort to be heard.

She laid the book aside and went downstairs to the lobby to check for messages from the Board of Aldermen. There were none. Strangely, she felt both disappointment and relief. Did she really want to be employed by such a cadre of bigoted men? Not one of them seemed to take her seriously as a trained professional. The only exception was Chief Harkins. And he was…what was he? Intelligent and kind, at least on the surface, yet with a hair-trigger temper. She thought of Caine's mellow face and calm demeanor, the smooth, measured tones of his voice. She could not recall ever seeing him angry. His demeanor had both puzzled her and endeared.

Pearl was startled to hear the clerk. "Waiting to hear from a fine feller?" That was the last thing on her mind.

"No, nothing like that," Pearl said. At least the man was trying to be civil, unlike the cold employee she had first encountered at the desk. Returning to her room, she realized that regardless of whether or not she was chosen to work for the city, she should first start looking for decent real estate. She had passed two or three offices with signs advertising commercial property. Maybe Chief Harkins was right. Maybe she should consider opening a private practice and the town fathers be dismissed.

By early evening, with her stomach rumbling from hunger, she went downstairs and ordered a simple dinner of braised beef and potatoes. She decided the food was good, and the hotel was as clean as any establishment she had ever been in, but she had found pesky bedbugs. However, a handwritten notice on each door announced the wooden beds would soon be dismantled room by room, the mattresses aired and the slats and frames soaked in kerosene as part of the hotel's annual battle against infestation.

When she was ready to order after-dinner coffee, she noticed a thin elderly man entering the dining room. As he drew nearer, she raised her water glass to get his attention. "Mr. Dickson, is that you? Please, come join me." A gasp from two women diners made it clear she was violating social etiquette by calling out to a gentleman. But she had liked him from the start and appreciated the fact that he was one of the few people in Asheville who had been kind to her. At least she had two new friends – -him and Chief Harkins.

Jeremiah put a trembling hand to his hat and removed it. "Well, well, what a delightful surprise. I will join you."

As he settled across from her, Pearl handed him her leather-bound menu and asked, "What on earth are you doing at the Swannanoa, especially this time of evening?"

He chuckled and broke out coughing, grabbing a cloth napkin to stifle the sudden outburst. "Even at my advanced age and poor condition, I'm allowed out after dark. I'm actually meeting a business client here this evening for a drink and a bit of conversation. I can't seem to stay confined for too long. It affects my spirit."

"How is that dreadful cough?"

"It remains much the same," Jeremiah said. "But thank you for asking."

The waiter brought coffee for Pearl and stood by while Jeremiah studied the menu, then set it aside. "Just coffee and a warm biscuit. Oh yes, and some water," he said before turning to Pearl. "How are things rolling along for you since you are still so new to town?"

"I had an interesting encounter with the Board of Aldermen and the Chief of Police," Pearl said. "In fact, the Chief escorted me to the meeting."

"So you've met Big Hersch."

Pearl thought it amusing that even this formal older gentleman referred to the Chief by his nickname. She was anxious to tell Jeremiah about the prior day's events but even more anxious to ask one particular question. Taking a sip from her coffee, she looked at him intently. "What can you tell me about him?"

"Hmmm. Did you know he was once a Deputy U.S. Marshal?"

"He mentioned that."

"Did you also know he captured one of the most dangerous men in all of the western part of the state and brought him in single-handed after a skirmish in Dark Corner?"

"Dark Corner?"

"It's a well-known moonshine haven in South Carolina just across the border, the place for blockade whiskey. Herschel was sent there after a fellow officer failed to make the arrest.

It was a bad situation. Several kinfolk moved in to protect the man and threatened Herschel with guns and knives. Big fight broke out."

Pearl leaned forward. "What happened?"

Jeremiah, now in full story form, sat up and cleared his throat. "Well, Hersch talked them down, calmed everybody, and got the moonshiner to ride with him to Polk County and the Blue House."

"The what?" Pearl said.

"The Blue House, an old abandoned school used for federal court cases. But about the time they arrived, the kin showed up too, all riled again. Said there was no way their man could get a fair trial in Polk County."

"How did Chief Harkins take that?" Pearl was curious to know how he would handle a volatile situation.

"From what I heard, he was mostly aggravated. You may have already witnessed his hot-headed tendency. If not, you will soon enough. But he's a hard man to scare."

Pearl nodded. Jeremiah took a sip of coffee and carefully set the china cup on its saucer. "Should I keep on talking?" he said with a slight smile.

He's enjoying this, Pearl thought. And his hacking cough seems to have quieted. She tipped her cup toward him. "Go on."

"You must understand the spectators at the court, as well as the kin, were half drunk on home brew themselves," Jeremiah continued. "But Herschel got the offender inside and the court was called to order." He rapped on the table with his knuckles for effect. A few of the other diners looked over at their table. One shook his head in annoyance, but resumed eating.

Pearl smiled, recalling Chief Harkins' comment about not taking Mr. Dickson too seriously. "He likes to make a big stir," the Chief had said.

"What happened next is quite remarkable," Jeremiah said and paused. "A hail of bullets smashed through the window. Everyone scattered – some leaped for the door like a flock of panicked sheep. Herschel drew his gun and looked for a firing position. By now the room was filled with broken glass, overturned benches and quivering men everywhere."

"Was anyone hurt?"

"Not just then," said Jeremiah. He sat back.

Pearl spread her hands and held them up. "So then what happened? Was it the Chief against all those angry armed men?" She was now caught up in the story, visualizing the tall, strong-willed officer fending off a crowd of drunken men.

Jeremiah rushed to complete his story. "There was another officer in the courtroom but he ducked for cover. Someone pulled a knife and lunged toward Herschel, who had his revolver ready but only had three bullets. Herschel used them all to shoot at his attacker. Didn't kill him, but he sure could have. When it was over, only two men out of thirteen remained standing. One was Herschel. The other was the mean rascal who started the whole thing."

"Where was the judge in all this?" Pearl asked.

"Oh, he ran out the back door," Jeremiah said with a wave of his hand. "I don't think he's been seen or heard from since."

Pearl tried not to laugh.

"Well," Jeremiah said, "the varmint made a last desperate lunge at Herschel and stabbed him a few times, though the wounds ended up being minor. I think his heavy coat is what saved him from that torment. He also had bullet wounds from the fire fight but didn't yet realize he was hit."

Pearl could see the Chief staggering about like a wounded bear. "How did he get away?"

"He was out of bullets by then. So he picked up his empty pistol and threw it at the man, struck him square on the forehead. Down he went, where he lay dead-like while Herschel pulled himself together. About that time the Polk County sheriff and his men showed up. Then things got bad."

Pearl nearly choked on her coffee. "What do you mean things got bad?"

"They got worse," Jeremiah said. "The sheriff proceeded to arrest everyone, including Big Hersch for – of all things – disturbing the peace."

"What did the Chief say to that?" Pearl said. She could hear Jeremiah's labored breathing during his rushed monologue. He coughed, gagged, and then sputtered, "Told the sheriff to go to hell, of course. You will pardon my language as I am only repeating the truth."

Pearl got up and moved to his side of the table, reaching out to pat his shoulder. "Are you all right?" She ignored the diners looking their way. "Mr. Dickson, would you allow me to examine you? I can get my medical bag and we can go into one of the hotel's meeting rooms."

"Oh no, I'm perfectly fine. Just too much talking, as I tend to do. A little water is all I need."

Pearl reached for the crystal glass near his empty plate and handed him the drink. She returned to her seat, wondering if he was hesitant about an examination because he refused to acknowledge he was more ill than he let on, or because she was a woman. It was likely both.

She gave him an imploring look. "Thank you for sharing your tale with me. But you must seek medical help." She thought of the hospital patients with consumption she had helped treat during her training and knew that in most cases, their prognosis was poor.

"It's not a tale. It's all true," said Jeremiah, underlining Pearl's fears that he minimized his condition by refusing to fully acknowledge it. "You can read the account for yourself in the local paper. They printed the full story."

"Maybe I'll just ask Chief Harkins," Pearl said. She wondered what his reaction would be if she brought up the subject. He would probably make light of it, though how could she know that about a virtual stranger? Somehow, she concluded, she just knew.

Jeremiah shook his head. "He won't tell you a thing. Doesn't like to talk about it. Says it's old history now."

Pearl watched him closely. "Let's talk about you for a moment," she said. "I think you are ill, perhaps seriously, and I want you to either see your own physician or come and see me as soon as I have my practice established. Would you consider doing that?" She hoped they could maintain their paternal-like relationship regardless. To Pearl, whose instincts were usually on target, Mr. Dickson had the earmarks of a good, kind man. At the least, she felt safe and secure in his presence.

"I'll give it pause," he said, "though Doc Hanson has been treating me for years."

Pearl realized this was the same physician Chief Harkins was railing about at the Board of Alderman meeting. He had referred to Hanson as a quack.

"There's more to the Blue House story," Jeremiah went on.

94

"Well, I won't deprive you of a proper ending," she said. "Just don't over-extend yourself." She thought it better to indulge him than to tell him to stop talking. Besides, she wanted to know what happened.

"Herschel managed to walk away from the sheriff after arguing with him about the unruly offenders. He was on the trail back to Asheville when he spotted an old mountaineer on a mule. Herschel told the man he was hurt and needed the animal to get himself back to town. When the mountaineer refused, Herschel just up and took it. I think he had it returned to the man later."

"And did he get back to town and receive proper treatment for his wounds?" Pearl realized her medical training was so ingrained, getting treatment was her first thought.

"Yes indeed," said Jeremiah. "From then on, as the story spread Herschel became known as the officer afraid of neither man nor devil."

He must be afraid of something, Pearl thought, though she found the story believable simply because she found the Chief credible too.

Someone approached their table and patted Jeremiah on the shoulder.

"There you are!" the man said.

Jeremiah looked up. "Dr. Stern," he said, turning to Pearl, "let me introduce you to my acquaintance, Mr. Cecil Whitener."

Pearl extended her hand. The man was small and neat, his shirt a spotless white, his wiry hair combed and clipped. A pencil-thin mustache and round gold-rimmed spectacles, along with his nervous squint, gave him the look of an oversized owl.

"My pleasure," she said. She found him a little prim and

fussy compared to most of the Missouri men she knew. But his smile was genuine.

He removed his hat and bowed slightly. "The pleasure is mine. You are a doctor? My, I don't believe I've had the opportunity to meet a physician so young and…attractive." His face flushed.

Jeremiah laughed. "He's used to our stodgy old physicians about town. Mr. Whitener is a land agent and knows everyone in Asheville."

"And what does a land agent do?" Pearl asked, both out of courtesy and her natural curiosity.

"A wonderful question!" Whitener said. "As you may know, Asheville is growing rapidly. I help clients like Mr. Dickson find good tracts of land to purchase and develop. I also negotiate for the city when a land parcel is needed for street widening or other worthy projects." He reached up and adjusted his glasses.

"That's important work," Pearl said. She realized Mr. Dickson, despite his tendency to regale people with stories, was likely a man of worth and stature within the community.

Whitener beamed down at her. "Indeed," he said.

"Well," said Pearl, rising from the table, "I'll let you two gentlemen get down to business. Please excuse me Mr. Whitener. Do take my seat while I go settle my ticket. And Mr. Dickson, don't forget what we discussed. In the meantime, take care of yourself."

Jeremiah bid her good night then added, "I trust you have more important things to worry about than a sick old man."

Pearl smiled at him warmly. "Other things are never too important. Good evening to you and to you, Mr. Whitener."

As she prepared to leave, she overhead the land agent whisper to Jeremiah, "she's lovely," and the elder gentleman respond, "Clever too, but a little sad."

Pearl was so struck by the comment she stopped at the doorway and hesitated as though she might return to the table. How on earth...how could Mr. Dickson know that she carried any burden? Was her face that transparent?

Catching her reflection in the gold-framed lobby mirror, she saw a somber young woman whose expression appeared almost vacant, a practiced, expressionless look she had learned in medical school. Patients should never know what the doctor is thinking. She brushed a hand across her cheek, winced at her image in the mirror, and moved on.

Chapter Nine

During her second week at the Swannanoa Hotel, Pearl awoke early and wondered how much longer she would have to wait to hear from the Aldermen. Were they deliberately avoiding her, or simply could not make up their minds? Either way, she was losing valuable time and potential income to a group of indecisive men unwilling to provide her the courtesy of an answer.

She penned a quick letter to her parents and a short note to Victoria, thanking her for the hospitality in Richmond: *Please let me know how you are doing, she wrote, and remember that your friendship means more to me than anything. While I wait for your reply, you are always in my thoughts.*

Next on her list was how she would go about setting up her office. She knew exactly what she wanted for combined work and living space. Finding it was another matter. Forty-five minutes later, fully dressed, she had ordered a quick breakfast of porridge and fruit in the dining room downstairs, had her second cup of coffee and was heading out the hotel door.

Two blocks down the street, she glanced up to see a red-and-white real estate sign. Inside the small office, visible from the street, a middle-aged man sat bent over a desk. Maps and photos of land, buildings and houses snaked along the walls. A blackened kerosene lamp perched at the end of his desk along with a smattering of papers.

"Can I help you?" the man said, without even looking up, as if accustomed to people walking in unannounced.

"I'm seeking office and living quarters near Public Square," Pearl said.

He glanced up, gave Pearl an admiring look and then resumed working. "My hat is off to you, madam, if you find the ideal location. Anything around the Square is at a premium. You might have to consider something further south, towards the depot in Best. If it's for your husband, you'll need to tell me what type of commerce he engages in."

"I don't have a husband," she said. "The space is for me."

He looked startled. At last she had his full attention. "Intriguing," he said. "In what business are you involved?"

"I'm a doctor. I need a medical office and a place to live."

The realtor stopped his work and leaned back in his chair. "Very interesting. Now please, have a seat. Let me see how I can help you. Do you have specific requirements?"

"I do," said Pearl. "I want the office on the ground floor with a sitting room and one, maybe two exam rooms. I need a heating stove downstairs as well as a sink and plenty of shelving. Plus, I want a small apartment upstairs." Pearl had the layout already in her head, as though an architectural map had been implanted, waiting for the proper time to make itself known. She was a planner by nature, a trait that had helped her make good grades in medical school.

"And your living quarters?" he asked, jotting notes in his ledger. "What did you have in mind?"

"A simple kitchen, parlor with heat and one bedroom," she said. "I would also like to have windows that face the street." She not only loved the natural light, she needed it to feel at her physical and mental best.

"A woman who knows her own mind," he noted. "How large an apartment?"

"I don't require a lot of personal space," she said. "Most of my time will be spent in the office." She prayed she would have enough patients to make that a true statement.

He tapped his pencil on the note pad before him. "I don't have anything at the moment," he said, "but if you'll tell me how to reach you I'll get right on this. It's possible we could have a cancellation on a pending lease arrangement."

"Thank you," Pearl said. "I'm just up the street at the Swannanoa. You can leave your calling card and a message at the desk." She hoped he would be more diligent than the Board of Aldermen in getting back to her.

Next she stopped at the druggist. Her list of medical supplies and equipment was lengthy: laudanum, an anesthetic in four ounce bottles, twelve to a case; essence of peppermint for stomach upsets; spirits of camphor and turpentine; carbolic acid for antiseptic cleaning; nickel-plated hypodermic syringe sets complete with vials in a dark morocco case; funnels, mortars and a hand scale; worm syrup for children and dyspepsia powders for that most common ailment, "irritable and weak stomachs." She needed corn and bunion plasters, ague pills for chills and fever and eye water manufactured by an oculist for inflamed and sore eyes. Those she would get later.

She briefly considered the purchase of one or two of the newer products she had read about: Nerve and brain pills "for those who are miserable and suffer with indescribable bad

100

feelings," Dr. Barker's Blood Builder and Skin Remedy "which destroys poisons in the blood." On the apothecary shelves she spotted Female Pills for Weak Women alongside a complexion beauty nerve and blood maker called Dr. Rose's Obesity Powders, on which was clearly stated on the box "too much fat is a disease and a source of great annoyance to those afflicted." More to the point it warned that "obesity causes sudden death."

Most of these remedies were hogwash, but even she had to admit a few had some value. She understood how people could fall prey to their outrageous promises. At the least, their outlandish claims were entertaining.

"I like this," she murmured to herself as she toyed with a device, four to six inches in diameter. It was described on the empty carton as "a new scientific help to nature when nature has not favored you." Made of nickel and aluminum its shape resembled a sink plunger. The accompanying Princess Bust Developer and Bust Cream claimed that with daily use of the device along with the cream "it fills out shrunken and undeveloped tissues forming a rounded plump, perfectly developed bust." Pearl chuckled, finding it amusing that many people took such promises at face value.

"We just got that in," the male clerk said shyly, watching Pearl's reaction. "We'll sell you both for a bargain price."

Pearl's face registered shock. "It's five dollars! That's exorbitant." She caught the clerk eyeing her. "I'm a doctor," she added.

"Yes ma'am. Then I bet you know Doc Hanson. He just bought a set. Said he thinks his patients will like it, men and women alike."

"No doubt," Pearl said, turning away. She spied insect

powder which promised "sure death to all insects," sealed in a metal airtight container. At fifteen cents per can it was a bargain. She went to the counter and handed the clerk her list. "I don't need these right away, but I'll need them within the month. I expect some items must be ordered."

"You really are a doctor?" he remarked as he recorded her information.

"I am," she said. She shrugged off his look of disbelief. What did it matter if he was taken aback by her profession?

"Sorry. We never had no lady doctor in here."

Pearl began to pull her letters of introduction from her purse. "It's perfectly fine. Here are my credentials. May I set up an account? I'll need regular supplies."

"Oh yes, doc," he said, "I mean yes ma'am Doctor."

She gave him a pleasant smile and thanked him for his help.

Her final stop was across the street to look at furniture and household goods. Even a small apartment was unlikely to have furnishings or window treatments. Considering her budget, she moved to the back of the store for used and reduced items. Almost immediately she found a four-poster bed made of wormy chestnut, simple and sturdy in design and made a mental note to have the clerk tag it for purchase.

This is beautiful, she thought, moving toward a solid oak dry air refrigerator and sideboard combination. It would be perfect for a small kitchen. Attached to the carved top was a beveled French plate mirror. The entire piece, close in height to her own five-feet four, was decorated with raised wood carvings and a star-burst centerpiece.

"That's got a lift-out ice reservoir too," the bearded sales clerk said as he approached. "And the ice rack is made entirely of metal so you can store your supply of ice. It's one of the most modern styles we have."

"How much?" Pearl asked. She was already sold on it, but it never hurt to bargain, a trait she had learned early on from her father.

"Just marked it down to eleven forty-seven."

Pearl's tone grew annoyed. "Eleven dollars and forty-seven cents? But it's used. That sounds like the cost of a brand new piece."

He cocked his head, as though unaccustomed to having a woman argue with him. "Well, madam, this is retail."

Pearl moved toward the door. "There are other furnishing establishments just down the street. I'll look elsewhere," she said over her shoulder.

"Wait! Perhaps we can work something out."

Pearl stopped and turned to face him. "I'll give you eight dollars even."

"Nine," he said.

"Eight fifty."

He frowned and then reluctantly nodded. As she filled out the paperwork, she suddenly realized she had bought a dry air refrigerator minus a kitchen. In fact, she didn't even have a place to live. How foolhardy was that?

"Hold up!" she called.

The clerk halted in mid-stride and turned. "Don't tell me," he said. "You've changed your mind."

"No. I just wanted to say that my quarters are not quite ready yet. I'll pay for the purchases but I need you to hold onto them for…how long can you keep them?"

"Ten days," the man said. "We can hold your items for ten days as long as you pay cash up front."

She paid for her purchases, tucked the receipt in her purse and headed back toward the hotel. In ten days, she decided, she would have answers. One way or the other, she would know where she would work, where she would live and how she would likely fare in her newly-chosen city. And if not? Well, she would worry over it later.

She remembered her father saying to her, "You must learn to control your fears, or they will control you," the first time he had handed her reins to the wagon. She was eight and they were on their way into town for supplies. Hands trembling, she had grasped the leather straps and looked up at him.

"What if we crash, Papa?" she said. "What if the horses run away and the wagon tips over and we tumble out...what if we get hurt or killed?"

"The world is made up of what-ifs, Pearl," he had said. "It's your job to control what you can, just like you're doing now with the reins. As for the rest, don't let fear take over as the driver."

When she reached the hotel, she found two messages waiting at the desk. One was from the realtor she had spoken to that morning. The other was a sealed, cream-colored envelope with the City of Asheville as its return address.

It was her answer from the Board of Alderman. Clutching the papers against her bosom, she climbed the stairs to her room. After shutting her door, she sat on the edge of the bed and took a deep breath. Her future could well be inside the letter's thin envelope. Setting the note and her purse aside for now, she took off her gloves and peeled back the envelope flap.

104

Chapter Ten

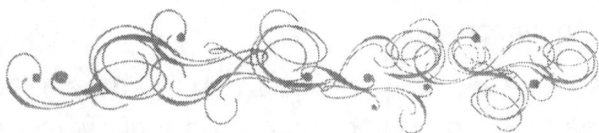

Her hands steady, Pearl began to read:

Dear Dr. Stern,

It is with great regret that we inform you we cannot offer you a salaried position as our municipal physician. After much aforethought and careful deliberation, the honorable City Board of Aldermen have reached a unanimous decision to forfeit this proposed position in favor of free enterprise so that our illustrious city may continue to flourish as the western economic centerpiece of our grand state.

She didn't even know what that meant. All she knew for certain was that the Board had voted unanimously not to hire her. She would probably never know their real reasons. Her first big disappointment in Asheville, coupled with her inauspicious entry, once again made her question her choice for relocation.

The setback stung, and she sat on the bed, allowing the inevitable self-pity to take hold. It lasted no more than a few minutes, long enough for her to realize that at least now she had an answer and could move forward. She opened the folded note from the realtor.

I think I've found the perfect location, it said. *Come by my office at your earliest convenience.*

Her spirits lifted. She would visit him this afternoon. But first, there was something she had to do. As a courtesy to the man who had assisted her in getting an audience before the Aldermen, she should inform Chief Harkins, in person, about the letter and its contents.

Descending the hotel stairs, she walked past the main desk. It was near noon, and people were crowding into the hotel dining room to order lunch. The smell of frying chicken, yeast rolls and fresh-baked pies tempted her to wait till after the noon-day meal, but she decided to catch the Chief first and hurried outside.

At the police station, the lobby, with its high ceiling and spacious windows, appeared nearly empty. A different officer from the former languid young man was on duty. The sign on the counter read Desk Sergeant.

"Where is everyone, Sergeant?" Pearl asked.

"Out on call. There's been an incident at the Titus farm."

"Chief Harkins as well?" Pearl said. "I'm looking for him."

"Yes ma'am, they're all out there. It's a pretty bad scene."

"May I ask what happened?"

He hesitated. Pearl thought he seemed unsure whether to provide details to someone he didn't recognize. "What's your business here, ma'am?" he asked.

She flushed at his impertinence, as though he assumed there was a personal connection between her and the Chief. "I'm a doctor and yes, I'm also a friend of...I'm a friend of the Chief."

"Well, in that case," he said with relief, rattling on. "It ap-

106

pears to be suspicious from first reports. We're not sure yet. Got no coroner to go out there and tell us anything. He's laid up with a broken leg because he fell off a ladder doing volunteer work for the fire department. Always saying he's too old for such as all that, but he does it anyway. If you ask me, he just likes to get away from his wife."

Pearl waited for him to finish. "If you can lend me a wagon," she said, "I'll go see what I can do. Just tell me how to get there." It occurred to her this was a good time to prove her usefulness and her competency not only to the Chief, but to the townspeople.

He stepped out from behind the desk and yelled down the hall. "Callahan! Come here! I got a job for you!" Within moments, Officer Callahan was lumbering down the hall toward Pearl.

She recognized him immediately. "Officer, it's nice to see you again."

He scowled. "Do I know you?"

Pearl gave him her best smile. "Why yes, just a couple of weeks ago, you helped rescue me from the wagon incident on the Square. I had just arrived in town. Remember?"

"Oh yeah," he said. "That was the day Jim got busted... again...for drunk and disorderly." He grinned. To Pearl, his smirk-like smile displayed too much enthusiasm for such a minor offense. She had met people like him, bullies who enjoyed lording it over anyone weaker than themselves. In any other circumstance, she would have given him a wide berth.

"Need for you to take this young lady out to the Titus farm," the desk sergeant said. "She says she's a doc and a friend of Chief Harkins. She might be able to tell for a fact if ole Titus croaked, had a little help or just went to meet Jesus on his own terms."

Callahan nodded but appeared less than enthusiastic for the task. "All right," he said, "I'll get the wagon. But don't expect me to get all my paperwork done by end of the day."

The farm lay at the outskirts of Asheville on a wide berth of land nestled between two high ridges. This was Pearl's first trip outside the city limits, and she was curious to see how the landscape differed from the Missouri Ozarks. Here the Blue Ridge Mountains rose and fell in steeper, higher grades but the hard-scrabble earth itself seemed similar to her parents' farmland. Pearl also noticed tall green stalks of silk-laden corn, plump cabbages, potatoes, tomatoes, squash and row after row of shiny, green-leaf tobacco.

She noticed the wooden privies made of plain, raw, cut timber. One stood out, painted in bright yellow with a hand-drawn sign over its door: *Enter at own risk*. Another was white-washed, two stories in height and with a connecting walkway attached to the main structure. Pearl had seen elaborate privies up north and wondered what it revealed of residents whose outhouse was more ornate than their home.

Just down the road was a crude log cabin whose irregular logs protruded stick-like in all directions, as though constructed by the wind. A woman wearing an over-sized bonnet sat in the open doorway stripping husks from a wooden barrel of corn. Her hands worked fast and furiously. A string of dried beans hung like a necklace near the door. Two dogs panting in the noonday heat rested on either side. The woman looked up, waved at the strangers passing and resumed her work.

Arriving at the Titus' farm, Pearl spotted Herschel standing among a small group of men. She was relieved to be there as Callahan had proved a poor travel companion and tour guide. Each time she attempted to speak to him or ask a question, he responded with a grunt, followed by a large spit of tobacco juice.

Almost immediately Herschel looked up and saw Pearl. Leaving the group, he walked toward the wagon. "Pearl! What in blazes are you doing here?" He reached out to lift her from the sideboard, settling her onto the ground in one swift, light motion, his eyes grazing hers as their faces nearly touched. Pearl felt a sudden shiver as she cast her look downward. Good manners, she thought, ignoring the electric feel of his hands on her waist.

"I was told a doctor might be needed to determine cause of death," she said. "Your officer here," she looked at Callahan, "agreed to bring me." Pearl realized she was giving Callahan an overabundance of credit. She turned to Herschel. "What's going on?"

"Well, appears we got us a dead body," he said. "Ole man Titus. We think it's a self-murder, that he hung himself in his barn. One of the neighbors found him when he came by to get hay."

Pearl placed a gloved hand over her eyes and scanned the property, looking for other officials. "I understand your coroner is laid up. Would you like me to take a look?" She hoped, almost in desperation, he would not turn her away.

Herschel folded his arms and stared at her for a split second. "You sure you want to do that? We can wait for the coroner from the next county over. I mean, it's not like Titus is going anywhere."

Officer Callahan spoke up. "Why are we even here boss? This ain't our jurisdiction. I see the Sheriff and his boys over yonder. Can't they handle it?"

"The Sheriff wants us here," Herschel said, his voice gruff.

"Considering the family history, there might be more than a suicide involved. Told me the scene didn't look right to him. Right now, I wouldn't rule out any of the Titus clan as suspects in a murder."

"So you don't think it's a suicide?" Pearl asked. She wondered if the Chief had handled many of these types of cases.

"I don't know," answered Herschel. "What I do know – this is one crazy family and that they all bear a strong hatred for each other. They're also chronic lawbreakers. Every one of them except Mary has served time for something. About a month back, we were called out here. The eldest boy brought a sawed-off shotgun to a funeral and scared everybody so bad they fled the church. It was something about the dead man owing him money."

Callahan snickered. "The last time that many people ran from a church was when Mabel Sawyer sang "Why Did They Dig Ma's Grave So Deep?""

Herschel scowled at the officer. "You're not helping, Callahan."

"So where's the Titus mother in all this?" Pearl asked. It was hard to believe that an entire family could be so disturbed.

"Died," said Herschel. "Some say from knowing all her children went bad."

He turned to see the body of Arthur Titus being carried from the barn by two of his officers and two deputies.

"Whoa boys!" Herschel called to the officers. "Where are you going with him? I thought we were here to investigate a suspicious case. How are we supposed to do that when you've cut him down?"

A deputy approached. "Sheriff's orders. Said it didn't appear to be a crime after all."

110

"Well, he could have talked to me first, dammit," Herschel said. "Where is he?"

He turned to Pearl. "Stay here. I'll be right back." Herschel marched toward the barn as the Sheriff and two of his deputies came around the back of the wooden building.

Pearl stepped away from the wagon so she wouldn't have to listen to Callahan and any more of his crude remarks. She remembered her medical bag was back at the hotel. How could she have been so foolish as to forget to bring it? Then she remembered: she had only gone to the police station to thank the Chief in person, not get involved in a suspicious death. A superficial, visual exam was all that she could offer.

"I'll be with the body," she said to Callahan.

"Better you than me." He released another wad of blackened tobacco juice.

The Sheriff greeted his regional rival.

"Howdy Chief," he said.

Pearl, propped against the wagon that held Titus' body, could clearly hear their loud voices from where she was standing and thought it was possible they were friends as well as colleagues. But the next words out of Chief Harkins' mouth proved her wrong.

"Don't howdy me," Herschel said. "I was already in a foul mood when I got word you wanted us out here. Now I find out you've got Titus cut down and the case solved."

"Boys," the Sheriff instructed his men, "go on back to the others. I need a word here with the Chief." The men ambled off, leaving Herschel and the Sheriff alone.

Watching them from a small area full of weeds and small, hardscrabble rocks, Pearl noted that compared to Herschel, the Sheriff was short and muscular and about a decade older. She guessed he had an ego that never shrank when up against another person in authority. She wondered if the two men had any regard for each other at all.

"Don't be talking to me like that in front of my men," the Sheriff warned Herschel. "It don't look good. Now just settle down, Hersch. I have my reasons for asking you out here."

Herschel towered over him, his arms folded.

"Well, what are they?"

"We found a will," the Sheriff said. "It was dated yesterday and signed, I believe, by the hand of Arthur Titus himself."

"So?" Herschel said.

"It's a danged peculiar document. You and I both know any one of these kin could have come out here and done Titus in on their own, especially if they thought there was anything of value to be gained. I think the ole man knew it too."

"I still don't know why you need me," Herschel said.

"I want you to see it, be a witness to the fact that it was found and that we read it right here. Then you can make up your own mind if you think it's for real."

"Wait a minute," Herschel said. "Let me get Pearl. She might be able to tell us something from looking at the body."

"Who the hell is Pearl?" the Sheriff growled. "Never known you to have a woman tag along with you. What business is this of hers?"

"She's the new doctor that just came to town, that's who," said Herschel. "She's out here to help in whatever way she can. And she's clever. So if you got any more snide remarks about the young lady or me, I suggest you keep them to yourself or you and I will go behind the barn again. Only this time

112

we won't be having a friendly discussion."

Pearl watched the unfolding scene, thankful that Herschel had come to her defense, yet offended by the Sheriff's remarks. The Sheriff should be grateful she had volunteered her time to assist in the case at no cost to the county.

"You're a lot of talk, Harkins," the Sheriff said, hitching his belt. He turned his back on the Chief and walked toward Pearl and the wagon that held the cold, dead Titus. Herschel was close behind.

The scrawny, angular body was draped with a muslin cloth and lay in the Sheriff's official county wagon as they approached. Pearl, at the Sheriff's nod, climbed inside and bent over the dead man, examining his head, neck and upper extremities. He looked undernourished and sunken in, as though he had been withering away even before this latest insult. She tried to recall details from her anatomy class and the few dissections she had attended as a student. The work had to be done expeditiously and usually in winter since the bodies deteriorated quickly.

"Officers, come close and look at this," Pearl said to the two lawmen. She pointed to Titus' neck. "He does appear to have ligature marks here and here. But he also has marks that could be hand prints. He's too discolored to tell."

"You mean like somebody had their hands around his neck?" Herschel said.

"Precisely," said Pearl. "I just can't tell for sure without instruments and a closer look."

"How long do you think he's been dead?" the Sheriff asked.

Pearl, relieved that the Sheriff was taking her seriously, could only guess. "I'd say at least eight hours. That's an estimate based on the extent of the rigor mortis. It usually takes about twelve for full rigor. He's cold to the touch."

"Well, leave him be for now," said the Sheriff. "I need you both to come with me. I want to show you something in the house." They left the two small bands of men behind: police officers on one side of the wagon guarding the body, deputies on the other.

"Any fist-fights break out and I'll have all your badges," Herschel called to his men as he headed toward the Titus home.

Inside the dilapidated four-room home, the first thing that hit them was the smell, a mix of rotting food, trapped body odors and soiled clothing. Cobwebs hung like white moss from the rafters. Musty newspapers, pots and pans were stacked waist-high in the corner. A used chamber pot squatted in the corner, emitting a strong aroma. Encrusted food, too old to identify, had spilled onto the sparse wooden furniture where Titus must have sat and eaten his meals. On the cook-stove was a pan of boiled beans encircled with a dark green mold. When something skittered across the floor, the Sheriff instinctively drew his weapon.

"You could have warned us about the conditions, Sheriff," Herschel said from behind him and then turned to Pearl. "Are you all right?"

Nodding, she wrinkled her nose. This was bad, but in medicine she was accustomed to foul odors. She should certainly be able to tolerate poor sanitation.

The Sheriff reached for the handwritten letter he had left on an empty chair. "Come over here by the window so you can read this," he said to Herschel.

Taking the letter, Herschel held it up to the natural light, standing aside so Pearl could join him. It was dated the prior day and written in print block letters with numerous misspelled words:

All my worldly goods aren't worth a shit. So here's what my offspring get.

I give to my son John, my bony frame and my consumption. To my daughter Mary, I bestow my sallow skin and my torpid liver which was the result of my bad living. To my son Arthur junior, I give my love for liquors and my outlook on the dark side. And lastly to my coarse daughter Jane, the one that spent half her time with evil men even when they don't pay her, well I don't give her anything except my tendency to commit self-murder.

Arthur C. Titus

Herschel handed the paper back to the Sheriff, who had removed his hat and was scratching his head.

"I'd have to agree this is the most unusual last will and testament I ever laid eyes on," Herschel said. " If it is legit, one of them might have figured he or she had good cause to kill Titus, considering all the property connected to the farm. If it's a cover for what really happened here, well I guess we got to figure that one out."

"Know any estate lawyers in town?" the Sheriff asked. "I think we ought to run it past one of 'em to see if this will stand up in court if it does prove self-murder."

"May I offer a suggestion?" Pearl asked. She agreed with Herschel's assessment that the letter could be fake. "If I can better pinpoint a time of death and you can compare the signature against the handwriting of each adult family member, including Mr. Titus, maybe we can determine when it was written and by whom. I'm sure we can find something around here with his signature on it."

"I told you she was clever," Herschel said.

The Sheriff nodded. "All right, I guess that's as good a start as any. Herschel, you handle your people, including this young lady here and I'll handle mine. Technically, this is still my case. I'll send my boys after the two Titus brothers and that daughter Mary listed in the will."

"Pearl," Herschel said, "we'll get you and the body back into town so you can better examine Titus. Our coroner, Stokes, might be willing to come in. He's a good man. I'll get one of my boys to make a visit to Jane in the city jail for a handwriting sample. Maybe we can sort this thing out."

"Let's see first if we can find something with Arthur Titus' handwriting," Pearl said. All three began searching the disheveled room looking for documents, correspondence, old mail, anything that might prove useful. But nothing turned up they could use or take with them.

En route to Asheville with Callahan driving the police wagon and the Sheriff's wagon carting the body behind them, Herschel turned his attention to Pearl on the seat beside him.

"Now, why were you here other than to help? Callahan let it be known you came looking for me."

"Oh, I almost forgot!" Pearl said, reaching into her purse. She retrieved the letter from the Board of Aldermen. It felt to Pearl as though months had passed since she was sitting on the bed in her hotel room feeling sorry for herself. Then, the letter was a huge disappointment. Now it was a mere distraction. A sudden death could put such things in perspective.

"Here, read it," she said, handing it to the Chief. He scanned the words.

"I'm not surprised," he said, handing it back to her. "Their

116

sound decisions could be captured in a half-full thimble. What now?"

"I've been thinking about your idea that I go into private practice," she said. "It seems the reasonable thing to do in view of the Board's decision. Besides, I already bought a dry ice refrigerator."

Herschel snickered. "You bought a what? Did I hear you say you bought a refrigerator?"

"Yes," said Pearl, watching the back of Callahan's head. She didn't want to see the amused look on the Chief's face.

"And would you mind sharing why, almost immediately upon your arrival in Asheville, the first thing you buy is a dry ice refrigerator?" Herschel asked. He leaned back to wait for her response.

"No, I don't mind," said Pearl. "And it wasn't the first thing I bought. Actually, a bed was my first purchase. As for the refrigerator, it so happened that I liked it. Now all I need is an office and living quarters to go with it."

Herschel shook his head. "I may live to be much older and wiser than ole man Titus. But may the good Lord help me if I ever understand the female mind."

"It was a practical decision," she said, "nothing more and nothing less."

"Practical," he repeated.

"Yes, Chief Harkins."

"I'd like it if you would refer to me as Herschel. I've taken the bold step of calling you Pearl, despite our brief acquaintance. Is such a fair exchange practical enough for you?"

Pearl cut her eyes at him. "I suppose I could do that."

"Thank you, Dr. Stern...Pearl."

117

"You're welcome...Herschel." Pearl rolled the name around in her head in an attempt to make it sound natural. It came surprisingly easy. She glanced at the imposing man sitting beside her and found herself comparing him to Caine. Where Caine was soft-spoken with polished manners and – she admitted – a hint of cool mystery, Herschel was bold, brash and transparent as a streak of sun in a darkened room. Caine would never have questioned her motives or her personal decisions. Nor would he have assumed anything.

Callahan pulled on the horses' reins and the police wagon came to a halt in front of what looked to Pearl like an abandoned two-story warehouse. In the distance, she could see the police department building and knew they were back in Asheville. Herschel exited the wagon and turned to reach for her hand.

"Where are we?" she asked. The Sheriff's open-bed wagon had pulled up behind them, the corpse covered head to toe in a tattered woolen blanket. Someone had failed to wrap the body carefully and a shoe, half its sole missing, protruded from Titus' stick-like leg.

"Coroner's office," Herschel said. "You're about to meet one of our more colorful citizens, Bailey Stokes, the county coroner. You'll either like him or hate him. There's not much in-between."

The small contingent of officers, including Herschel and the Sheriff, positioned themselves near Titus, hoisting him by the feet and shoulders from the wagon while Pearl stood back and watched. Poor old thing, she thought. What an indignant way to end a life, even if it turned out to be by his own hand. In medical school, during autopsy class, while she and some of the students had, at first, made macabre jokes to hide their discomfort, she soon learned to approach each corpse with a subdued respect. What stories had brought them here, she wondered. Who had loved them, or not, and why? What were their greatest strengths and weaknesses? What made up the fabric of a human life? And having left an empty shell behind, where did their souls now reside?

Even ole man Titus had a story to tell, she was sure of it. She pulled at her summer shawl, glanced up the empty street and followed the men inside.

Chapter Eleven

Inside, Titus was laid out on a thin concrete slab in the center of the vacant autopsy room. Above him hung a metal hook and a thick rope strung from the overhead rafters. An adjacent doorway led to the morgue where Pearl could see that other bodies awaited a similar fate, all placed on double-layer wooden tables, each ventilated with a large block of ice beneath them to cool and preserve the human remains.

Pearl was apprehensive. Would her presence be tolerated by the men – officers who had carried Titus in and the yet-to-be-introduced official coroner who had to get up from his sick bed to come here? She heard one of the officers remark, "He sure isn't going to be in the best frame of mind." From a few feet away she heard another call out "No different from any other day."

As though on cue, the coroner appeared from the morgue side door, hobbling across the floor on crutches for his broken leg. With his gruff demeanor, his white beard and hint of a pot belly, Bailey Stokes seemed to be much older than she had expected. Pointing a crutch at her, he gruffly demanded, "What's this girl doing here?"

"She's a…" Herschel started to say.

Pearl stepped forward. "I can speak for myself. Dr. Stokes, I'm Pearl Stern, also a physician and newly arrived in Asheville."

"Hmmph," Stokes grunted. "What kind of physician? Are you a coroner?"

"No. I'm in general practice. But I've performed autopsies."

"Where?" said Stokes. "What's your experience?"

She suspected he would not find her credentials impressive. Nevertheless, she would present herself with a self-confident demeanor. In her best professional voice, she responded, "I'm familiar with the text *System of Human Anatomy*. At the Women's Medical College in Pennsylvania, we used it frequently in our dissection classes." She wanted to add, "And I turned out to be quite competent in human anatomy. At least I made high marks in class." But she kept quiet. It would not pay to antagonize him.

"You mean in school?" he said. "Then you're a recent graduate."

"That's right," she answered. All the men, including Herschel, watched as though intrigued by the exchange between the crusty old coroner and the young lady physician. At this point, Pearl concluded her sex probably had less to do with their differences than did her lack of expertise.

"Very well," said Stokes. "Then perhaps we'll learn from each other. I could use some fresh blood in this room." He looked around him to see if anyone caught his clever line. No one acknowledged it. He sighed and stepped forward, leaning on his crutches and then raised his voice to the officers behind him.

"You gentlemen can leave now. Dr. Stern and I have work to do. I'll be her eyes and ears. She'll be my hands." No one moved. "GO!" he shouted. "Get out of here! We'll send for an officer when we're done, or in your case, Herschel, just show up when you can."

Pearl kept her eyes on Titus to hide her shocked expression. She had expected him to order her out of the room. Instead, he was offering her a chance to work with him as a peer. Just as the officers hurried out, she looked up and could swear Herschel winked at her before he turned to leave with his men. But then, she thought, maybe I'm hallucinating.

She didn't know whether to be flattered or offended by his actions and was annoyed at his tendency to stir conflicting emotions. She had come to Asheville for a new beginning and a chance to redeem herself, not get involved in a complex relationship that did not fit her goals, not after Caine, the man who had more potential to break her heart than anyone she had met thus far.

Alone with the cadaver, the two physicians began to prepare. Pearl found a large cotton apron hanging from a rack near the door and wrapped it twice about her middle, covering her dress but leaving the sleeves exposed. Stokes retrieved an amber bottle of ammonia from an overhead bin. "Here," he said. "Expose your hands to this. It'll produce an irritation on any break in your skin. That way, you'll know the possible sites for infection from handling the corpse. It's not pleasant, but believe me, you'll thank me later."

Pearl took the bottle, held it arm's length and splashed its contents onto her bare hands. She wondered if it might also work on her upper arms, where the psoriasis lay hidden for now. In time, she might consult with Dr. Stokes about her condition.

122

Moving to the side of the table, she pointed to the marks on Titus she had noted at the farm. "I suspected hands were here, applying pressure around the neck," Pearl said, showing Stokes the purplish hues on the old man's throat. "What do you make of it?"

Stokes leaned in, his rounded stomach squeezed against the table. "There's a marvelous beauty in the tissues of the human frame," he said absently. "The neck, oh yes. Well, I find it totally inconclusive, Dr. Stern, due to the indented ligature marks. So we'll need to do a complete autopsy, one that we can only pray will determine the true cause of death."

Pearl nodded. "All right, I'll follow your lead."

"We'll start with the peritoneum here at the abdominal cavity after we fix our subject in the correct position. Capture that rope above your head, Dr. Stern." Next, he instructed Pearl to grab Titus' feet and using the cord, wrap the rope noose-like around them. It was a stretch for her diminutive height, but she managed to grasp the thick twine and loop it around the man's ankles. She didn't recall learning this in dissection class.

"Now pull on the end that is looped through the ceiling hook," he said. Pearl did exactly as she was told. Titus' lower body swung forward and then up, giving the dead man the appearance of a shriveled-up ham ready for curing.

"Now," said Stokes, "we have full exposure of the membrane that encloses the viscera. Dissections demand a degree of delicacy and manipulation, as I'm sure you learned in school. We'll make an incision that completely surrounds the exposed area."

Pearl realized she would not be seeing the realtor today. It was already well past three, and they still had several hours of work ahead. She had not eaten since breakfast and should have been starving. Yet here, in this cold barren room with this grumpy old physician, she had never felt more energetic or alive. They were embarked on a journey to find the answer to a real-life mystery: who or what had killed Arthur Titus?

At the police station, Herschel had dispatched an officer to the city jail to interview Jane, Titus' wayward daughter who had been jailed for prostitution. Herschel had surmised she was likely in need of funds and would be willing to talk if she thought a windfall was headed her way. He directed his junior officer to make her put whatever she said in writing, and include a signature.

At seven p.m. Pearl looked up to see Herschel entering the coroner's office while she and Dr. Stokes were washing up. An assortment of metal bowls squatted on the tables situated about the room; some were filled with strange opaque liquids. Both doctors were blood-splattered and Pearl's hair, normally coiffed with every strand in place, had come loose and was hanging, thread-like, on both sides of her head.

"I know, I'm a sight," she said to Herschel as he crossed the room. "But we're finally done here. I was just helping Dr. Stokes clean up." Stokes was sitting in a high-backed chair against the wall with his injured leg propped on a stool while Pearl, sleeves rolled up, washed and rinsed the utensils.

Herschel looked from one doctor to another and asked, "Is there any word on cause of death?"

"That old man had more ailments than my wife has complaints about me," said Stokes. "Married nigh thirty-two years, that's a lot of belly-aching. We found everything from an enlarged heart to cancer in his gut. Even worse, his testicles resembled two little bird eggs."

Herschel raised his palm. "That's enough. No need to use indelicate words like that in front of the lady."

"She's a doctor, for god's sake," growled Stokes. "In fact, she's the one that said it."

Pearl's face turned a bright red as she busied herself at the sink to avoid looking at Herschel. She might be willing to call the Chief by his first name, but when it came to describing male body parts, she was nowhere ready for that kind of familiarity with the handsome officer.

Herschel now looked directly at Pearl and repeated, "Cause of death." Getting no answer, he turned toward Stokes and asked, "What do you think Stokes?"

The coroner shook his head. "Can't say for sure, but I think he was poisoned and strung up to make it look like a suicide."

"Poisoned?" Herschel said. "With what?"

"Likely arsenic," said Stokes. "That's the most common means with this type of wicked behavior. I recall one murderess who attempted to kill her husband three times with arsenic to obtain his life insurance. Guess that's why they call it 'the inheritance powder.' Claimed she bought it to keep her eyes bright. It's a downright fashionable way to send someone you love to the great beyond."

Listening to both men, Pearl felt the need to explain something. "It's often untraceable in the liver as it metabolizes into natural occurring chemicals,but we found some that lingered in his hair, nails and urine. We also determined the time of death as approximately midnight last evening. How about on your end, Herschel? Did you gather anything from the daughter?"

"Learned old man Titus couldn't read nor write," said Herschel, "not even poorly. That is, if Jane is telling the truth. We may have us a good ole-fashioned murder-for-profit. She had a pretty solid alibi though. She's been in jail for two months."

"So is the Sheriff going after Titus' other three children?" Pearl asked.

"They're still on the lookout for them," said Herschel. "My money's on the favored daughter, Mary."

Stokes grabbed his crutches and was now on his feet. "Why do you say that?"

"Because, of the four adult children she's the most intelligent," said Herschel. "She could have written this so-called will from spite. Or, another motive would be an attempt to get sympathy from a jury if she ever got caught and the case came to trial. She could convince a jury her father wrote it, therefore look what a bastard he was. And it's true. He was that. Everybody around here knew it."

Stokes moved toward the covered corpse on the flat concrete table. He had stuffed its chest with straw to prevent complete collapse and reattached the scalp at the base of the skull.

"Herschel, help me transport our friend Titus into the morgue. I'll get Elkins Funeral Home to come by first thing in the morning and pick him up. They can put him on ice and deal with that queer family. I don't envy them that."

"I'll be through here shortly," said Pearl. There was no means of hot water so she pumped cold water into a basin to rinse off the surgical instruments they had used to carve up Mr. Titus. She scrubbed at her nails with lye soap and glanced in the mirror above the sink. She felt she looked like a mess.

"I've had enough excitement for one day," Stokes said upon his return to the autopsy room. "I'm headed home.

126

Chief, do you plan to escort this lovely young lady back to her quarters?"

"If she'll consent," Herschel said, watching Pearl unwrap the bloody apron and return it to its hook.

"Food," said Pearl. "I need food first. I haven't eaten all day." The thought of Herschel escorting her to dinner was pleasant enough, but getting something to eat was even more important right now.

"I know just the right place," Herschel said, "an easy walk from here." He offered to take Stokes to his house first.

Stokes hobbled toward the door, waving them away. "My wife is on her way to pick me up. I'll wait for her in the fresh night air. It'll give me strength before I have to listen to her all the way home."

As Herschel waited for Pearl to tidy her hair in the small mirror hanging on a nail over the sink, he spotted a damp linen cloth and folded it into his hand. "Come here," he said. "Now turn around and face the wall. You missed a spot."

"A spot of what?"

"Blood," he said, dabbing at the back of her neck with the rag. "We can't have you terrorizing the public looking like some axe-murderer."

With her back to him, his bare hand brushed the nape of her neck. She involuntarily shivered at his touch just as she had done when he wrapped his hands around her waist and lifted her from the buggy at the Titus farm. What was wrong with her?

"Are you cold?" he whispered, inches behind her.

"No," she said firmly. "Hungry." Was it possible, she thought, that he was gently swiping at nothing more than the tender skin on her neck? If so, what would she do? Would she dare turn to face him and whatever might happen next? Instead, she forced herself into the present moment. From the corner of her eye she saw him toss the cloth aside. Her moment of uncertainty passed.

"Thank you, Herschel," she said. "You're very thoughtful. But we should go. We should go now."

Chapter Twelve

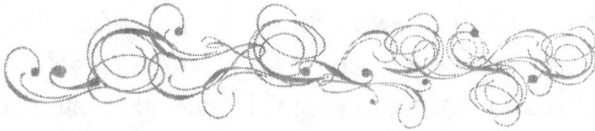

Pearl woke early the next morning with sunlight rippling through her hotel room. Still groggy from the long hours at the Titus farm and then with Stokes, followed by a late dinner with Herschel, she tried to recall what important tasks she had today.

It might be weeks before she received a letter from Victoria or her folks, so there was no reason to write to them again. Better to hoard her most exciting news and share it all in her next letter. Better to take care of the pressing matters she needed to attend to now.

The realtor, I must respond to his message.

As she dressed in her plain brown taffeta, checked her boots for residual blood, combed her hair and grabbed her handbag, her thoughts went to Victoria and Walter, wondering if they were in Tombstone already. Had they seen Caine? What would Victoria think of Herschel and the scandal at the Titus farm? Would Victoria point out the stark differences between Herschel and Caine? She missed her friend when she felt the need to confide her thoughts.

"Any messages?" she asked the unfriendly clerk at the

receiving desk. He was the same one who had greeted her upon her first arrival.

He gave her a curt nod.

"Just this."

Pearl unfolded the small note and read: *My second message to you. If you do not respond by end of next business day, I have another client expressing great interest.* That was today. Maybe she wasn't too late. Unwilling to stop even for coffee, she hurried down the street to find the realtor outside his office unlocking the door.

"Dr. Stern!" he said. "Good morning. I wondered if I would see you today. That's a prime piece of real estate I'm holding for you."

Pearl tried to explain her delay in getting back to him but realized he wasn't listening; his attention set on getting inside his office to work. Time was money to him. "Where's it located?" she asked. She recalled her initial arrival at Public Square, a place that was busier and more crowded than she had expected. Good commerce could translate to good, paying patients – a rule of thumb she learned in school.

"It's right on the corner near the druggist and just up from the undertaker with a cigar business next door. The new lessee skipped town, no doubt owing money. I got word a few days after you left my office; a ner-do-well fella."

"Then I'd love to take a look."

A former haberdashery, the two-story brick-front shop and apartment was as close to an ideal location as she would find. The minute she walked in, she sensed this was it. The entrance opened into a small foyer and a space large enough for a waiting room to accommodate five patients. Behind a slick oak counter were rows of shelving, the perfect spot for her many books. A fresh coat of off-white paint and a plant or two would give it a polished, professional look.

Beyond the counter she spied a short hallway with two large rooms on either side. With more shelving, she could use a corner for her laboratory equipment and her prized possession, the brass microscope her parents had given her when she graduated. A wooden bench would serve for storing her black leather bag made from alligator skin and guaranteed to last a physician at least a decade.

Seeing no visible stairwell to the living quarters, she asked, "How do I get upstairs?"

The realtor smiled triumphantly. "That's the beauty of this place. Mrs. Bagwell, one of our prior tenants, was quite taken with privacy. She installed the stairwell here at the back through this clever doorway." Opening what appeared at first glance to be a large closet, he motioned her to follow him.

Although solid, the stairwell creaked with each footstep and ended in a commonplace L-shaped landing. Fingering the smooth polished banister, Pearl admired its chiseled details. When the realtor reached for a white ceramic knob and opened the door at the top of the stairs, Pearl gasped. Before her stood an open, expansive room complete with a kitchen, a living area with an inlaid tile fireplace, two tall windows on either side, and a sturdy door leading to what must be a private bedroom.

Pearl was entranced. "It's lovely. Oh, and look...windows!" Reaching inside her purse for a kerchief, she cleared a spot on the soiled glass so she could see better. Natural light was a must for her, the more the better.

"I can see the Square! And the police station and the courthouse and trees. This is just what I need. How much is it?"

"Thirty dollars a month, a year's lease and a deposit of sixty dollars for first and last month's rent."

"What about utilities?" She knew she would have to monitor every penny until she could tally her income minus her expenses.

"Water is included since we got a well on the Square. The city is working on more lines. You'll have to buy your own kerosene lamps. Gas gives brighter lights, but we caution all our clients it can produce headaches and nausea. I know bigger towns have the new-fangled electric lights, though if you ask me, I think that's just a passing fad. Lots of wood out back for heating the fireplace and kitchen stove. Let's see what else… we got no ice factory here in town but you can buy blocks from suppliers. They haul it straight from the French Broad River. It's usually gone by August so you might want to place an order soon. I consider ice a miracle product…prevents rotten or infected meat."

He paused, tapping his finger to his chin.

"Oh, I almost forgot. You must abide by the city ordinances. Mayor Lusk is real strict about enforcing that kind of thing."

Pearl was nearly skipping through the rooms, opening doors, peeking into corners. "Like what?" Having never opened her own business, nor ever lived alone, this was all new and exciting to her.

"Well, you being a doctor and all, I don't know if this applies to you but you can't throw a dead body, an animal, a fowl, even a fruit or a decayed melon rind into the street. In fact, nothing that has obnoxious odors. If you're caught, it's a twenty-dollar fine and another twenty every full day thereafter."

132

"I'll keep that in mind," said Pearl. "Nothing of foul or ob-noxious odors." She thought that was well within reason. She opened the wood-burning stove in the kitchen and examined the oven interior, which appeared ample for the small amount of baking she expected to do. A white-enameled warmer with louvered doors provided storage over the stove's cast iron surface with enough room for a kettle and one or two cooking pots.

"There's a place out behind the building for slops, gar-bage and contents of your chamber pot," he said. "Residents were throwing the refuse and waste out their kitchen doors and windows. Can't do that anymore. Your privy must be in a water-tight vessel and securely covered or that's another twenty-dollar fine. And you can't transport the pot across town except between ten p.m. and four a.m. or it's another..."

"Twenty-dollar fine?" Pearl said. She smiled at the realtor, who suddenly dropped his stiff formality.

"That's right," he said, grinning. "Now that our grand state legislators have officially declared us a city, I guess we should start behaving like one."

"You'll get no argument from me," said Pearl. "I agree with such rules on cleanliness and hygiene."

"Anything else I should know?" she asked.

"We got a couple of bad neighborhoods around town. You being a single lady, don't go out after dark near Hell's Acre. That's down at the corner of Sycamore and Valley. Greasy Corner, over near South Main and Eagle is rife with loafers and bums. I don't even go there myself." He drew a deep breath and watched Pearl's face to see if her enthusiasm had waned.

But she was clapping her hands and looking at him with

something akin to glee.

"It's perfect. I'll take it!"

Chapter Thirteen

By week's end, Pearl had made considerable progress in moving out of the Swannanoa Hotel and into her new quarters on the Square. Hanging summer curtains, a blend of white muslin with lace overlays, she thought about all the things that had happened in these few short weeks: new town, new friends, her very own office, and the open mystery of Arthur Titus finally resolved.

The two brothers had been located by the Sheriff's Department operating an illegal still across the line into Madison County. Within an hour of their arrest, they had given up their sister, Mary, as the instigator in a scheme to poison their father, gain sympathy and split the proceeds from the farm three ways. Her sister, Jailhouse Jane as Herschel called her, had not been involved in the nefarious plot. To add an extra layer of punishment to Mary while she awaited trial, he arranged to have her share a cell with her irate sister who, thanks to a loose-lipped guard, knew all about the siblings' evil intent.

"Seemed like the just thing to do, having the two dear sisters share a cell," Herschel told Pearl. "Arthur Titus' body was never claimed from the funeral home. Don't know anybody that's willing to pay the twenty-five dollars for a casket, or pay the fifty-dollar fee to give him a decent burial. No choice but to send him to a potter's grave. Even for a man like that, it's a terrible end."

Pearl agreed, glad that she and Dr. Stokes had at least helped bring Titus' killers to justice. That they were his own children only added to her empathy for him. Grateful for the unconditional love and support from her own father, she resolved to work harder at patching up the rifts between her and her mother and to write this very night , telling her she was sorry for any distress she had caused within the family.

With her first few days now behind her, Pearl thought hopefully about what might lie ahead. Meeting Bailey Stokes was an important connection. He seemed to like her work and expressed an interest in calling her as needed in the morgue. Herschel vowed to sing her praises to Mayor Lusk, which could result in occasional work for the city. Despite the trauma that had brought her here, her prospects seemed good. Perhaps in a year, she would have a solid contingent of patients and a reputation as a knowledgeable, respected doctor. That was all she wanted, all she felt she would ever want.

With renewed confidence, she placed an ad to hire an assistant. As her practice grew, she would need someone to help set up her quarters, stock supplies and serve as another hand whenever patients began to stream through the door. Patients would come.

When a knock interrupted her quiet reflections, Pearl crossed the room and opened the door. "Please come in," Pearl said to the Negro woman who stood before her. Her first thought was that the girl appeared frightened. To her immense shame, it was followed by the fear that hiring colored might hurt my business prospects in this southern town. Determined to counter her own internal bias, Pearl stepped back and motioned for the slender young woman to enter. It was hard to tell her exact age.

Pearl noted that her clean cotton dress still smelled of lye soap and that her skin had a series of sharp angles softened by eyes as large and round as brown buttons. When she spoke, which Pearl quickly learned was not often, her voice was soft and low-pitched.

"You're early but we can get started," Pearl said, as she motioned her toward a plain wooden chair. "I'm sorry the place is so barren. I have yet to furnish the upstairs quarters. My name is Dr. Stern, but you may call me Pearl. We would, after all, be working close together. What's your name?" Pearl's tone was calm and conversational.

"Loomey."

Pearl smiled. "That's very unusual. How did you get such a name?"

The young woman placed both arms across her chest, crossed and then uncrossed them, finally tucking them beneath her lap to prevent their escape.

"It's all right," Pearl said. "There's no need to be anxious."

"Back before Mama went to school and got herself educated, she ran out of good names." Loomey's voice was low. "I'm one of six. Poppa could read and saw LOOMEY PRODUCTS, Chicago, Illinois on a flour sack, came home and said 'There you go. Now she has a proper name.'" She stared at Pearl, her hands still tucked beneath her.

"All right," said Pearl, shifting in her chair, wondering if she had already offended the young woman. "What's your last name?"

"Harrison."

"Harrison," Pearl repeated. "I've heard that name. Are you by chance related to a young man named Jim?"

"He's my husband, the one that done run over you in town. Want me to leave now?" Loomey rose from her chair.

"No! Sit down. He didn't run over me. It was an accident, plain and simple. I was perfectly fine. It's my understanding that Jim is still in jail. Is that right?"

Loomey hung her head. "Yes ma'am."

"Well," Pearl continued, "tell me why you're looking for work."

Loomey's head remained down. Pearl strained to hear her muffled words. "Ain't got no young'uns havin' lost my baby last year but I help my mama 'cause I live with her now that Jim's in jail again. Mama's the one that told me some new lady doctor was in town and might need a hand. My Mama, she's real smart. She's a teacher."

Pearl tried to hide her surprise. A Negro teacher and a woman at that; how interesting.

What Loomey didn't say, but Pearl knew, was that it could be months before Jim had a court appearance. Herschel had confided they had to wait for a riding judge to come through the county. However, the Chief did say he would look into it.

Pearl pressed on. "Let me ask you another question, Loomey. Can you keep supplies arranged on the shelves, fold bandages, fetch hot water and hold an instrument if I instruct you?"

"Yes ma'am. I can sew, clean and cook, too."

To Pearl, she sounded confident for the first time during the interview, an admirable trait.

138

"I also know all about laundry – how alum and vinegar preserve the green colors, baking soda for purples and oil of vitriol for reds. And I sing. I know 'I'll Be Ready When the Great Day Comes,' and 'When the Mists Have Cleared Away.' I've been told I have a strong voice."

Pearl smiled. "That's wonderful! You're also obviously bright. Your references will tell me if you are also hard-working and reliable. If all of these things are true, this is a job that is best learned by doing. What do you think?"

"But…" Loomey went quiet.

"What?" said Pearl. Something was gnawing at this young woman and rather than be impatient, Pearl wanted to learn what it was.

"I'm colored," Loomey said.

Pearl waited a moment before she answered. "I can see that." Seconds ticked by. "What about it?"

"What white folks are gonna come see you when they may get touched by my darkey hands or breathe my same air? That won't help your doctor business not one little bit."

Pearl reached out and patted her hand. "You let me worry about that. I think we can help each other out if you're my choice. I do have two other people who answered my advertisement."

"Whatever do you mean by 'help each other out?'" Loomey said.

"You need a job and I need an assistant. You showed spunk in coming here and I thank you for that."

"Mama taught us we have to look after ourselves," Loomey said. "She says hard work and thrift pay off."

"Your mother sounds wise."

Pearl heard heavy footsteps on the landing outside, soon followed by a man bursting through the door. "Doc!" he yelled. "Can you come downstairs? We got an officer shot!"

Recognizing him as one of the merchants from next door, she quickly rose from her chair. "Where is he?"

"We put him in your exam room. But he's real bad, Doc, and you was the nearest one around."

Pearl grabbed a clean cloth from the table and motioned Loomey to follow her down the stairs. "Stay close and listen for my instructions," she said. Her feet had no sooner hit the exam room than she recognized the young officer lying on her table. "Is that who I think it is?" she asked.

"Yep, it's Callahan," one of the men said, standing back so Pearl could move in. The bleeding officer lay on a wooden exam table surrounded by open shelves of medical supplies and equipment. The room smelled of alcohol, carbolic acid and a metallic odor. Both men were still trying to catch their breath from the officer's dead weight. One stood back and wiped his brow with the sleeve of his arm, his face a deep crimson.

Pearl grabbed a tinted bottle of carbolic solution and doused her hands. It was the best she could do when every second counted. "What happened?" She wrung her hands for a quick air dry.

The merchant who had run upstairs spoke up. "Shot twice. Took a bullet in the mid-back and upper arm trying to stop a dispute near the Square. I saw it from my window. Zach here" – he motioned to the man leaning over the officer – "was in my store when he heard the shots. We ran out together. Callahan is his brother-in-law. It was awful, Doc."

Zach was leaning over the patient, telling him "Shhhh, it's

all right Donnie. It's gonna be all right."

"Step back," Pearl ordered Zach. "Let me take a look at him." From the corner of her eye she could see Loomey's thin form frozen in the doorway. "Don't just stand there Loomey! Run and fix some hot water. You'll find a kettle on the stove and a basin in the sink. And there's an earthenware hot water bottle on the counter. Bring that too!"

Nodding, Loomey ran toward the kitchen.

"Hand me some bandages from the shelf," Pearl said to the merchant. "Zach, I know you're upset but I need you to help me remove some of his clothing so I can examine his wounds."

Callahan, eyes closed, skin pale and moist, appeared lifeless, though his chest rose and fell in an unsteady rhythm. Fumbling with the blood-soaked uniform buttons, Pearl knew she was running out of time. The man could well be mortally wounded.

On the opposite side of the table, Zach attempted to help, but his hands were shaking so hard he was nearly useless. "Donnie, oh Donnie," he repeated.

"Someone hand me a pair of scissors from the shelf, a knife if you have it," Pearl said. The merchant slapped both hands onto his pockets, found his knife, opened it, and thrust its bone handle toward Pearl. "Help me turn him onto his side," she told the two men. "Now take off your coat Zach and tuck it under him for support."

With the knife, she ripped at the officer's clothing, peeling back the blood-sodden layers one by one. A jagged bullet hole, the size of a small coin, was visible on his upper left back. "Can't tell where it stopped," Pearl said.

"Do you see the bullet?" Zach asked. "Do you see it?"

"Not yet," said Pearl. "We need to stem the bleeding first."

Loomey had returned with a water-filled basin, sloshing its contents as she struggled to carry it into the room. Under her arm was tucked the hot water bottle, precariously sliding forward. She placed the basin on a small wooden table near the patient and grabbed the bottle, all in one swift motion.

"Good," said Pearl. "That's good Loomey. Quick, wet a clean bandage and hand it to me." She was well aware of the new aseptic routine touted by Dr. Joseph Lister, who advised cleaning all instruments with carbolic acid and twenty parts water before touching a body. Hand washing and clean clothes were also strongly advised. Even the air should be sprayed with an atomizer, especially before operating.

Pearl knew that it was mostly the younger or more progressive doctors who believed in Lister's Antiseptic System, as she did. But there was no time for any of that now. She stifled a sense of rising panic, similar to what she had encountered with the mother and baby in Missouri. This can't happen again, she thought. I won't let it. At least the carbolic rinse on her hands would help. Think straight, push on, her father would advise. His words calmed her and she re-focused her attention. Nothing would go horribly wrong, not this time.

But human bodies had a way of following their own physiological path.

Callahan's breathing grew more labored as she hurriedly packed wet bandages against the gaping wound in his back. His upper arm oozed bright red blood though the amount was small, an indication no artery had been hit. On closer inspection, it appeared as only a flesh wound. There was no sign of a second bullet entry or exit.

When Zach kept asking "How is he, Doc?" It occurred to

Pearl that despite Callahan's rough exterior and coarse demeanor, he had managed to win the affection of this young man and somewhere must have a wife who loved him too.

"He's alive," said Pearl. "That's all I can say for now. Loomey, we'll need blankets. They're behind me on the shelves. Grab two or three and run the hot kettle over their length. Despite the heat, our patient is chilling."

Loomey took off running again. Pearl could hear men's voices in the background. It sounded as though they were coming through the walls. Within moments three additional men had crowded into the small room.

"Zach!" a voice boomed, "I just heard what happened to Callahan. Is he alive?" Pearl sensed Herschel's presence at her back. Zach had gone mute in the corner of the room and was slumped against the wall, his head bowed. "My poor baby sister," he said, moaning into his hands.

"Is he alive?" Herschel repeated to Pearl.

She didn't look up. "Barely, but I'm working as hard as I can."

"I've got Doc Stevens here with me," Herschel said, "and Hanson too. They came to see if they could help."

Pearl took an instant to glance up and catch a look at the infamous Doc Hanson, who appeared normal enough with his salt-and-pepper hair, a trim beard, and medium height. The two physicians quickly removed their coats and began rolling up their shirt sleeves.

"I think I've got his bleeding under control," Pearl said. She stepped back, dipping her bright red hands in the basin. The water turned from clear to a milky rose.

"We need to get that bullet out of there fast," Hanson said. "If you'll step aside, young lady, I'll poke around and see what

143

I can do." His breath released a whiff of alcohol.

Aghast, Pearl turned on him. "You'll do no such thing to my patient! The bleeding is staunched for now. We'll keep him warm, give him something for pain that will induce sleep and watch his signs."

Hanson's eyes widened and he motioned to Herschel. "Talk to her, Chief. This is preposterous!"

When Herschel ignored him, Dr. Stevens spoke up. Like Herschel, he was a handsome man, but of shorter height with a shock of thick black hair and a trim mustache that gave him a dapper appearance.

"Dr. Stern is correct in her assessment," he said. "I believe she has the situation under control, Hanson." He turned to Pearl. "With your consent, madam, may I take at look at your patient?"

Pearl nodded. Loomey stood like a small shadow in the background, her arms now stuffed with dark woolen blankets. She's a quick thinker, Pearl concluded.

"Bring them here, Loomey," Pearl said. "Help me spread them around him. We must keep him warm." Loomey followed Pearl's direction and returned to the doorway, as though to wait for more instruction.

While Pearl and Dr. Stevens discussed which medications were best to administer – laudanum, opium, or morphine for pain or perhaps homeopathic powdered herbs as poultices and clotting agents – Herschel grabbed Hanson by the sleeve and pushed him past a startled Loomey into the other room.

Pearl excused herself and stood near the doorway. This was her patient; her office. She had a right to know what was going on.

"Listen to me you son-of-a-bitch," she overheard Herschel say. "Wasn't my idea for you to show up. In fact, if I could make it stick and you didn't have so many fancy-foot friends in high places, you'd be at my station on any halfway plausible charge I could muster."

"Now Hersch," Hanson said, "you know that's highly improper."

Herschel kept at him. "You're a disgrace to decent doctors everywhere and a menace to society. And if I ever hear of you harassing that good lady," he motioned toward the door, "you'll be the one lying in a treatment room. I'll see to it."

"Wait just a minute," Pearl said, stepping forward. "I won't have either one of you making a scene while Callahan is fighting for his life. If you can't be civil to each other, why, you can both leave."

Hanson straightened his clothing and glared at the Chief. "You can't talk to me that way, Herschel. I'm an important public figure in this town and I can have your job for threatening me. I also know things about you."

Herschel stabbed a finger at Hanson's face. "Try it. Now get the hell out of here and go back to your quackery. I've got a real crime to solve."

Hanson shook his head at Herschel but backed down. Unsteady on his feet, he bumped against the door frame. Herschel could hear him cursing as he left. "How's Callahan?" he asked Pearl.

She frowned. "Too soon to know, but this isn't helping. Now you may stay, but I insist you be quiet and do not start a fracas."

Herschel gave her a sheepish look.

Loomey was standing silent against the wall, her arms wrapped around her waist, eyes darting from Pearl to Herschel.

"Fine," said Herschel. "But before I go, I need to speak with the merchant."

Pearl glanced at her sleeping patient, nodded and then pointed to the merchant.

"John," Herschel said, "what can you tell me about the shooting? What exactly did you see?"

"Well, I was at the window looking at the new display across South Street when I saw Callahan. Guess he was on foot duty because he approached a young couple. They were arguing right there in front of my store! What is it with these young people today? Have they no sense of decorum?"

"Just tell me what you saw," Herschel said.

"Well, I guess it was the husband, he seemed riled about something. As Officer Callahan came up it was like things just got worse. Callahan is not exactly salve on a wound, you know. Couldn't hear what he said but all of a sudden I saw something flash."

"Like a gunshot?" Herschel asked.

"No, not a shot; it was shiny and metal, like a gun."

"So you saw the gun?"

"Well, looked like a derringer to me, one of those little single-shot models. I couldn't see it up close of course. But it sure surprised me."

"What do you mean?" Herschel asked.

"Well, right before it went off I thought, my oh my, that's quite a piece for a young lady to have, though I dare say the pair were probably nothing more than riff-raff come to town."

Herschel's raised an eyebrow. "You mean the woman

146

had the gun?"

"Why yes," said John, bobbing his head. "As Callahan approached, she reached down in the fold of her skirt and drew it out. I don't think he ever saw it coming. I was just about to run out and warn him when Zach came up behind me and asked me what was going on."

"Did you see her shoot Officer Callahan?"

"Zach and I both saw Callahan turn and start to walk away when all of a sudden...." John's voice broke and he stumbled over his words.

"Go on," Herschel said with a touch of kindness.

"We saw him fall face forward. It happened so fast, Hersch, I didn't see the shooter. But it was cold-blooded, right in the back. And whichever one shot, they did it twice. They meant to either knock him silly or kill him dead."

"What happened next?"

"Well, they took off running together," said John. "It was all we could do to get to him and carry him inside to Pearl's office. She was the nearest doc."

Herschel nodded. "You did the right thing. I'll want you and Zach to come to the station. We'll need a full description of the couple, everything you can recall."

"Of course," said John, "whatever I can do to help. But I can't speak for Zach, poor fella. He's mighty close to his sister. She'll be done in by this."

"Herschel?" Pearl called out. "Can you come here for a moment?"

As the Chief and the flustered merchant entered the exam room, the officer's eyes fluttered and then closed. He groaned and moved his head as if trying to speak.

"Don't overtax him," Pearl cautioned. "But he wants to say something."

Herschel bent his large frame over the prostrate officer. "How you doing, son?" he said.

Callahan grimaced. "I didn't do my job right, Chief," he said. "I never should have turned my back. You always told us..."

"Hush. Don't worry about that now. We can talk about it later."

"But Chief..." he said. Herschel leaned in closer. "Never thought I'd get it in the back...not like that," Callahan said.

"I know," said Herschel. "I know." He patted Callahan on the shoulder.

"I gave him morphine," said Pearl. "He'll sleep now." She rinsed her hands in the clean basin of warm water Loomey had the forethought to bring. Herschel hovered nearby.

"I owe you a debt of gratitude," he said, his voice low. "You did some slick work today."

Pearl picked up a clean drying cloth, wiped her hands and dabbed at the dark wet sleeves of her dress. "Don't thank me yet. He's still in real danger with that bullet lodged; more bleeding, possible infection. Do you have any idea how this came about or why someone would do this?"

"Appeared to be a quarreling couple, a domestic flap of some sort," said Herschel. "I'll have John and Zach to the station and we'll file a report. We'll get to the bottom of it."

As the men left, Pearl returned to her patient. Dr. Stevens had offered to stay and was washing up. Loomey was folding a blanket tossed aside in the rush to get the officer stabilized.

"Thank you Loomey," Pearl said. "You were a big help

earlier."

Loomey, silent, continued with her chore.

Pearl turned her attention to Stevens, who was re-entering the exam room. "I'm very grateful for your assistance," she told him. "Do you mind a consult on how best to extract the bullet?"

"Not at all," he said, "happy to help."

"Do you want me to go now, Miss Pearl?" Loomey asked. "I won't bother you no more."

"Yes, you can go," Pearl said, and then added "but Loomey?"

"Yes ma'am?"

"Be here tomorrow at nine a.m."

"What for, Miss Pearl?"

"Why you're hired, of course."

Chapter Fourteen

It took three days for Callahan to regain consciousness after Pearl and Dr. Stevens extracted the bullet and closed the tattered flesh. Pearl worried over his blood loss and the high chance of infection. Had the carbolic acid worked its magic to prevent her from infecting his wounds? There was no way to be sure yet.

She realized with a start that it had been two weeks since she had suffered an outbreak of her psoriasis. Maybe there was something to the healthful mountain air after all.

She sat at Callahan's bedside in her exam room hour after hour, checking his heart rate, cleaning the wound, changing his dressings, administering morphine for pain and brandy to help him sleep while she watched for signs of deterioration. With help from Dr. Stevens and Herschel, Pearl moved him to a sturdier, more comfortable cot in the corner of the room. Herschel took the bullet to file for evidence, along with the witness reports.

Periodically, Stevens stopped in to relieve her, enough for Pearl to run upstairs or have a bite to eat. As peers, they debated the latest techniques in surgical procedures and discussed the many ways a patient could appear to be improving, only to become a victim of new complications.

He seemed eager to share with Pearl some of his earlier cases: a team of horses that had gotten spooked near the Best Depot rail station, collided with a wagon and threw the driver, breaking his hip; a farmer's horse that, scared of a leaf pile, scrambled up an embankment and fell backwards onto the farmer, nearly killing the man; a woman with "hysterical vomiting" who had still managed to retain her flesh and vital functions.

"I'm still puzzling over that one," he said.

Pearl found Stevens intelligent but somewhat pedantic and a man of little humor. He didn't mention family or friends and she wondered if he, like her, was so devoted to medicine he had never sought the pleasures of a companion. Only once did it cross her mind that he might have an interest in her beyond the professional.

"We should dine out after this is over," Stevens said as they sat side-by-side near Callahan's bed on their second consecutive night. Pearl looked up, startled.

"I meant only so that we can continue our medical discussions," Stevens said quickly. But she saw that his face was flushed. Withdrawing a kerchief from his vest pocket, he wiped at several round drops of perspiration that had appeared, dot-like, on his forehead. "Unduly warm tonight," he ventured. He peered over at Callahan. "Do you suppose he can hear us?"

"Unlikely," Pearl said, "though we may someday be proven wrong on such things."

"Remember Garfield's case?" Stevens asked. Pearl nodded. Who hadn't heard of the assassination attempt on President Garfield by a madman two years earlier?

"If you recall," said Stevens, "he was shot in the mid-back and upper arm like our Mr. Callahan here. Had his ten doctors not buried their unwashed hands in his open wounds, I believe he would still be alive today. I heard one of them called the Lister technique a needless rinsing of the wounds. And to say that visible pus is a favorable sign or that it's all too time-consuming... I still find that hard to believe!"

"It's balderdash," Pearl agreed, "and a tragic twist of fate when you survive your injury only to be done in by your healers." It crossed her mind that had she been talking to Herschel, he would have seen the irony and laughed at the remark. Had she been talking to Caine...she was struck by the fact that she had no idea how Caine would have responded.

Like an old tinted photograph, Caine was gradually beginning to fade, at least from her conscious thought. Why hadn't he written to her, sent word through Victoria that he was at least thinking about her? It was as though once he left town and headed west, she no longer existed. Well, that could work both ways.

"By the bye," Stevens was saying, "you would be a great asset to the North Carolina Medical Society. We meet once a year in Raleigh. We're trying to get our licensing laws strengthened so not just anybody can practice medicine in the state. We're also taking on penal and charitable county institutions and their deplorable sanitary conditions. Most facilities are downright filthy. That includes our own county jail. We could use a voice of reason from a level-headed person like you to help spread the word and educate the public."

"I'll think about it," said Pearl. "But I'm just getting settled here. I'll consider it next year." She caught a look of disappointment on Stevens face. Though it was a prideful thought, she wondered if this was his way of drawing her in so they could spend more time together. Hoping she was mistaken, she admonished herself for jumping to such conclusions. Stevens had been a perfect gentleman and she was grateful to him for his time and efforts toward Callahan.

Herschel's visits, on the other hand, were something she found herself looking forward to even as she believed his foremost reason was to check on his officer. Yet he seemed concerned about her too.

"You've got to get some rest, Pearl," he said, "or we'll have two patients on our hands. I'll come by and stay in the evenings. I can call for you upstairs if Callahan takes an unpleasant turn." It had now been a full three weeks since the shooting.

"I'm fine. I've got Loomey coming in each day, and I must tell you, Herschel, she is proving more valuable than I ever imagined." Never late, Loomey arrived each morning with an eagerness to do even the most mundane chores. Pearl was hard pressed to top her stamina. Whenever Loomey was particularly entrenched in her work, she broke into song. Stopping often to listen, Pearl was enthralled by the purity of her voice, and she often thought that if Loomey were not Negro, she could easily find work as a songstress.

As Callahan began to come around and show signs of improvement, Pearl learned that he had a wife and young daughter. Herschel sent for them. Mrs. Callahan had been informed of the shooting just after it happened, but had also been cautioned to wait until her husband was stable before coming to see him.

Nonetheless, Pearl was surprised when a curly-haired little girl peeked inside the exam room looking for her Papa. "Is he all better?" she asked Pearl. "I want my Papa to come home."

Sitting near Callahan, Pearl looked up and smiled. "I'll do everything I can to make that happen. What's your name and how old are you?"

"Pansy and I'm four." But she held up only two stubby fingers. "Can I see my Papa?"

Callahan's wife, a small woman with light brown hair and a look of perpetual fear, hovered behind the child.

Pearl smiled encouragingly. "Come in, Mrs. Callahan. Bring little Pansy too. Your husband is sleeping now, but when he wakes up you'll both be a welcome sight." After the long hours hovering over her patient, Pearl felt a rush of relief that he was finally beginning to heal.

She stepped out to allow them some privacy. Someone had brought a copy of the Asheville paper and left it on the stand in the hallway and she read the blaring headlines: *Dastardly Deed on the Square! Hunt for the Cowardly Shooter Continues!*

On Herschel's last visit, he had told Pearl he feared the quarreling couple had fled the county and their whereabouts were hard to determine. "I've telegraphed every law office I know. They'll surface sooner or later."

"What if they're found?" Pearl asked him.

"The shooter will be hung once convicted. That'll be a first for Buncombe County."

"You mean the hanging?" Pearl asked.

"No," he said, "I mean a woman at the end of a rope here on the Square. That'll be a first."

As she waited for Callahan's family to complete their visit, Pearl went to her office. Sitting at her desk, she pondered writing a much-needed letter to Victoria. She pulled a blank

154

sheet of parchment paper from the desk drawer, dipped her pen in ink and began:

Dearest Friend,   *August 18,1883*

Please forgive my lack of regular correspondence but there was great excitement here my first month and little opportunity to pen a letter to you. Asheville appears full of the eccentric. I have met a few, including the town's Chief of Police who, as it turns out, has befriended me in ways I could not imagine. I have my first (and dare say, only) patient who was shot on the street in front of my office! Can you believe it? I've been attending his wounds these past few days. I also hired a colored assistant who is proving honest and hard-working.

So that is my current news.

Pray tell, dear Victoria, how are you and Walter doing? He loves you a great deal, that is obvious. So I'm certain that all will turn out as you hope. You must let me know, however, of your circumstances. Have you remained in Richmond? I will have my answer if this letter is returned.

A final word if you travel to Tombstone. Give my regards to Caine Lee and tell him I would not be opposed to a letter in his hand.

Your loving friend, Pearl

She re-read the letter and crossed out the last paragraph with reference to Caine. Why should she be the one to initiate a contact with the inscrutable Mr. Lee? Then, realizing she had made a mess of the entire thing, she tore up the pages and started over. This time, she simply asked Victoria to please write to her soon so Pearl would know that all was well. After sealing the envelope with wax, she set it aside to post later.

When murmurs in the exam room next to her office

caught her attention, she hurried to see if Callahan needed her attention.

When she entered, she saw he was attempting to prop himself up so that his young daughter, leaning over him, could plant a kiss on his forehead. "Mr. Callahan!" Pearl admonished, "You mustn't disturb your wounds. Please lie back."

He grunted, winced in pain and repositioned himself on the pillow. "Just tryin' to see my little Pansy. She's a sight for sore eyes."

"As are you," Pearl said, checking his wounds for new signs of bleeding. "You had us all quite distressed for a while."

Mrs. Callahan spoke up behind her. "Are you a real doctor?" she asked. Her voice was so low Pearl could barely hear her question.

"Excuse me?" Pearl said, turning to face her.

"A doctor," Mrs. Callahan said. "I ain't never seen no lady doctor."

"Yes, I'm a real physician." The question no longer bothered her, for it seemed a waste of time to be offended. At some point, she predicted, the issue wouldn't even arise.

Callahan reached for Pearl's hand to indicate he wanted to speak. "Wouldn't allow for some unfamiliar woman to touch me on a normal day," he said, winded. "But I'm glad you was around, or I might not be." He stopped to get his breath.

"You're welcome," Pearl said, knowing that was Callahan's way of saying thank you.

"I want to go home," he said. "My wife here can tend to me. She's as good a mountain healer as any. I even seen her birth babies."

"But..." Pearl began.

156

Callahan grabbed her hand again. "I'm going home. That's that."

"I advise against it," Pearl said. "You still have a long recovery and I can watch you more closely from here."

"Don't matter," Callahan said. "It's done."

"Then I'll need to make the arrangements," she said. "And of course, notify Chief Harkins of your wish. I'll come by to check on you at least once a day for the next week or so. Agreed?" Pearl turned to his wife. "Agreed?" she repeated. Mrs. Callahan nodded. Callahan visibly relaxed.

"Tell me where you live," Pearl asked, smiling at Callahan. This would be her first house patient.

Chapter Fifteen

At home with his family, Callahan continued to improve as the days wore on. While Loomey manned the office, Pearl hired a wagon and made the trip to check on the officer's condition as she had promised. Inside the modest but clean clapboard house, Mrs. Callahan showed Pearl her medicinal supplies: honey, vinegar and moonshine for arthritis, pine tree heartwood for asthma, spirit of turpentine and brown sugar for bleeding and lady slipper leaves, dried and beaten into powder, as a blood builder.

"This is quite impressive," Pearl said. She was familiar with mountain healers, common in the Ozarks where she grew up, and knew better than to minimize their skills, or their impact. In her opinion, seldom shared by her peers, there was room for both natural and scientifically-based medicine. She turned to Mrs. Callahan in order to say something to that effect, but the woman's proud smile was evidence that Pearl had already said the right thing. She reached out and placed her hand on Mrs. Callahan's arm. "You're doing a wonderful job taking care of your husband," she said.

Mrs. Callahan looked down at Pearl's hand and jerked

her arm away. "You got the leprosy?" she said. Pearl, mortified, hadn't even noticed the small scaly patch on her left hand.

"No, it's something called psoriasis, a skin disorder. I have it under control. I'm sorry it frightened you."

"Never hear'd of it," Mrs. Callahan said. "I got no herbs for that. You didn't…my husband…he's not gonna come down with that, is he, since you doctored him?"

"No," said Pearl, her voice firm. "It's not something that appears to spread to another person by touch." But by the woman's look, Pearl wasn't sure she had convinced her. This might be a good time to make her exit. She would bid Callahan goodbye and leave.

Propped in bed, he asked if there was news about the shooter. "The Chief's been by here," he said. "But I was asleep and he didn't leave no word with the missus."

Pearl shook her head. "I haven't seen much of him either. He seems to be out day and night with other officers looking for a couple on the run. I did hear there have been sightings. You might be interested in knowing the newspaper refers to you as "our courageous town policeman.""

In exchange, Callahan gave her a wan smile. The account also referred to the shooter as "the woman who plugged holes in him," but Pearl thought it best to leave that out.

Returning to the office, with no further patients in sight, Pearl began to worry about her rapidly dwindling finances. She hadn't counted on a long spell with no income. So far, Callahan, out of work indefinitely, had not paid a penny. She couldn't fault him. He had a family to support and so had more pressing matters to worry about.

On the ride back to town, she realized she would have

to break the news to Loomey that she could not pay her for a full day's work. She debated what was more important: buy a bit of extra food for her pantry or pay her assistant a meager salary. Rent and utilities were covered but somehow, she explained to Loomey at lunch time, she had to generate more income. They shared a plate of fresh-cut fruit and left-over salted beef Loomey had cooked the day before.

"That's all right with me, Miss Pearl," Loomey said, nibbling at an orange slice. "If you need me, you don't worry none about the money."

"Thank you, Loomey, but I'll pay you through the end of this month. As for today, I don't expect a busy afternoon. You go on and I'll see you tomorrow."

Pearl puttered around the office for the next hour, cleaning glass flutes and wiping down the shelves and counter tops, a job Loomey normally handled. The sound of a tinkling bell at the front door announced a visitor. Hopefully it was a paying patient.

The colored man, accompanied by Loomey, was young, lean and muscular. He was holding his left forearm. Although he was heavily bandaged, blood leaked through the padding.

"Miss Pearl! Miss Pearl" Loomey called. "I just got home and found my cousin here all cut up. I think he's been in a fight. Got him wrapped pretty good but it ain't gonna hold."

Pearl motioned him to a chair. ""Let's take a look. What's your name and how old are you?"

"Abraham. I'm sixteen. And don't call me Abe like most white folks do."

"What happened?" Pearl said, ignoring his impertinence.

"I ain't talkin'.'"

Loomey reached out and smacked the top of his head. The boy yelped. "You better open that trap after I drug you all the way up here!" Loomey said. "Now, you sit up straight and tell Miss Pearl what went on."

The boy grabbed his wounded arm and sat erect. "All right, all right. Got into a scrape down on Eagle. Guy Penland, that no-gooder whose daddy works at the barber shop, why he was tryin' to get my girl. Take her right away from me with his fancy talk. I already warned him once. Came at me with a knife 'bout this long." He held up his good arm and measured the approximate length with his thumb and forefinger.

"Is he hurt too?" Pearl asked, unwrapping the temporary bandage. Loomey had bound the wound with a dry dish cloth to stem the bleeding.

"Don't know and don't care," Abraham said. "I whupped him good after he stuck me. He left walkin' so I ain't worried about him."

Pearl examined the open wound. It appeared superficial. "I'll need to douse this with a solution to keep infection down. And I'll redress it. But you, Abraham, you need to stay out of trouble with this boy and his knife. Next time he might hurt you even worse."

"Amen to that," said Loomey. "I catch you goin' at it on the street again and I'll plumb stick you myself!"

Abraham raised his eyes to Loomey and shook his head. "Never you mind, cousin," he said. "I'm done. Ain't no woman worthy of bleedin' over. Sides, I think she had her eyes on him all this time. Just don't tell Mama, Loomey, that I been fightin' or I'll get whupped again!"

As Loomey left for the second time that day, Abraham in tow, Pearl began to wonder if this was the way her practice might end up: her providing a helping hand with little to no payment in return. Good for the heart, she thought, but a poor way to run a fledgling practice.

The mail arrived at the front door, hand-delivered by a messenger boy about twelve hired by the Asheville postal service to bring letters and packages to downtown businesses. He had a mop of brown hair and an impish grin that always caught Pearl's eye whenever she met him at the front door.

"Here's your mail, Mrs. Stern," he said, handing her a small bundle tied in rope string. Though she had corrected him several times that she was Doctor Stern, with no husband, it must have been too foreign a concept for him to grasp. After a while, she gave up and simply thanked him. Untying the bundle, she felt a letter slip from her grasp. She bent over to retrieve it. The postmark read Richmond, Virginia. Her heart skipped. Victoria! At last she had word, and then realized their letters must have crossed in the mail. There was no way Pearl's last correspondence, posted just the month before, could have reached Victoria so quickly that Pearl was already receiving a response.

Pearl hurried to her office, ripped open the envelope and settled into her chair.

September 21, 1883

My dear Pearl,

It is with great excitement that I inform you of our latest plans. Walter and I are moving to the grand and glorious west – to Tombstone in late October. I should say Walter and I and the child I carry. I am three months gone which means our baby will be born in the Arizona Territory soon after the New Year! Once Walter absorbed the shocking news of my condi-

162

tion, he was beside himself with joy. What a dear husband he is, and what a loving father he will be. I am blessed beyond measure!

I have one more piece of thrilling news. We received a letter from Caine, who has arranged a place for Walter to set up practice on Allen Street in the heart of town! He is immersed in the business end of silver mining and writes to us of places like Toughnut and Lucky Cuss mines. Then he ended his letter by asking about you. He enquired of your welfare and your whereabouts. He wants to write to you. Pearl, can I offer your address to him? Please, dear Pearl, you simply cannot close your heart again, especially not now, with your future so uncertain. If you write posthaste, your reply will reach me before we depart Richmond. You must respond yes!

Your loving friend,

Victoria

Taken back, Pearl let the letter slide from her hand. In a sense, the letter was so Victoria – full of exuberance and lightheartedness. But what about the financial distress that undermined Victoria's and Walter's future? And what did Victoria mean when she said "especially with your future so uncertain?" Did she have no faith in Pearl's ability to rebuild her life? What of the details of their momentous decision to make the move? Victoria didn't even say if the house and practice had been sold. What of the creditors who were after them? Was all of that behind them?

Finally, Caine asking about her was no more relevant than asking about an old acquaintance. Perhaps he just wanted a chance to formally tell her goodbye. Was she ready to grant him such a concession?

A noise at the front door distracted her. Going to the office entrance, she saw Jeremiah Dickson peering in. It had been weeks since Pearl had last seen him. As she opened the door to greet him, she was shocked at his altered appearance.

He was gaunt, his eyes sunken, skin waxy and pale. His hand trembled as he moved forward, steadying himself with his cane. A kerchief, tied in a knot bandit-style, covered the lower part of his face to prevent coughing into the open air. Pearl knew he was well aware of the germ theory that had finally made its way to the Appalachians. They had spoken of it on the train the first time they met. It seemed like decades to her now.

"My dear," he said, "what a delight to be greeted by such a lovely vision."

"And you, my friend," Pearl said, "how good to see you. Please come in." As he passed, she noted that his movements were painfully slow.

When she asked, "What brings you here?" he trailed her into the exam room, his cane tapping its steady rhythm across the oak floor.

"Oh, I'm not here for an examination. You and I both know I am way beyond any substantial treatment."

She turned to face him. "There are viable treatments for consumption. I read in the paper of a sanitarium right here in Asheville opening...well...soon." It could be two years or more from what she read. It would be the first of its kind in the country.

"I won't last that long," he said. "The pleurisy has wasted my lungs. I came here only to tell you that I heard about Callahan and your good work. Both he and the Chief should be very grateful to you." He broke out in a fit of coughing.

Pearl instinctively reached toward him. The racking

noise subsided. She almost told him she was worried about her making it through the next few months. But she thought better of it. No need to burden him with her financial problems. Instead, she went to her medical cabinet.

"I have some ethyl iodine you can inhale that might quiet your lungs," she said. "It requires no apparatus so you can breathe it direct from the bottle until you feel its warmth. For the cough, all I have are liquid drops of Teulene. It's oil-based so it won't taste good. Take two to three times a day. When you run out, substitute a lump of sugar five or six times a day. Here, I'll wrap this for you so you can carry it safely." She unrolled a sheet of parchment and bundled the medication.

"I may not see you again, Pearl," Jeremiah said. "My time is drawing near." It was a simple statement without a hint of pity or remorse.

"Yes, you will," she said. "Who's caring for you now?" Childless and without a wife, Jeremiah had no close relations of which Pearl was aware. She believed that at the end of a person's life, all that really mattered was whether or not there were people around who could provide a sense of care.

"I've hired a nurse," he said. "There's little warmth there, but she's competent enough."

"Then you tell her to send for me day or night," Pearl said. "Is that agreed?"

Jeremiah struggled to his feet, his breathing labored. "Yes," he said.

As Pearl took his arm and helped him to the door, Jeremiah held back as Pearl reached for the heavy round knob.

"I stopped by for another reason," he said, shifting his weight onto his cane. "I wanted to tell you something."

165

"What?"

"The good work on Callahan won't carry you through, Pearl. There's talk in town among the locals about you hiring this new colored woman. It's a highly unusual way to start a practice. Then just today, someone saw a young colored man come here with his arm bandaged. Is that true?"

"Yes," said Pearl. "I've hired an assistant. Her name is Loomey and that was her cousin. He was injured in a fight. Why, is that a source of gossip?"

"I commend you, Pearl, I really do," said Jeremiah. "And I agree with your willingness to treat any and all who come through your door. But a word of caution is due. You're a fine doctor and you have the potential to build a strong practice. Yet you must learn to select your patients more carefully and to be more cognizant of how the locals see you."

"If you mean turning people away who have nowhere else to go, then I'm afraid I can't do that," said Pearl. "As for Loomey, she shows great promise. With some formal education and a few lessons in reading, she might even go on to become a healer herself one day."

He raised his thick white eyebrows. "Not in this town," he said, beginning to cough.

When the fit calmed down, Pearl searched his face. "What do you mean? I thought you were of a more liberal mind."

"I am," said Jeremiah. "Like your new friend, the Chief, I'm a supporter of the Freedmen. It's not the most popular stance in a region with established dens of Klu Klux Klansmen, and others of their ilk. But this isn't about my position. It's about your reputation and your ability to draw new patients. Once you're known as a physician who takes coloreds, you'll have to live with the consequences. It could hurt you."

"I'll take my chances," Pearl said, knowing how stubborn she sounded. "Now, you must go home and rest. I'll come by and check on you on my way to visit Officer Callahan. Remember what you promised. You said you'd have someone send for me day or night."

He tipped his hat. "Your frequent kindness might well be your undoing," he said. "You must learn to say no, Pearl – except to me, of course." His smile was sly as he turned to leave.

Chapter Sixteen

An hour later, Pearl decided to stop by Public Square to let Herschel know his friend, Jeremiah, had come by her office. At the police department entrance, she could hear the clank of metal-hinged wagons as they rolled past and the restless, snorting horses as they headed for the water well. She enjoyed watching the shop merchants, their busy hands filled with colorful rags as they cleaned and rearranged their shop window displays for the next business day.

Across the street, even from this distance she could see the delicate white scroll of her painted sign, Doctor Pearl Stern, Family Medicine. She wished her father were here to witness her arrival in town. He would be proud of what she had accomplished so far.

"Is the Chief in?" she asked at the front desk. She stared at the young man in his dark blue uniform. "I'm sorry. I don't know your name."

"Douglas. I'm Assistant to the Chief. Are you that new lady doctor? The Chief told us about you. Said you was the nicest addition to Asheville he'd seen in a while."

Pearl smiled. "Dr. Stern. I'm pleased to make your acquaintance."

A commotion at Pearl's back caused her to turn. Two women, both appearing flustered, rushed to the desk.

"You have to help us!" said the older of the two. "Something terrible has happened."

"Now calm down ladies. What is it?"

"A kidnapping!" said the younger woman.

Douglas rose and gave Pearl an apologetic look. "Sorry, Dr. Stern, you'll have to wait till I get the Chief and sort this out. You might want to come back later."

"I'll wait," Pearl said. She eyed the two women. Both were dressed in varying shades of rose, their large feathered hats dueling for attention with every shake of the head.

The older of the two was calling to the Douglas as he went down the hall. "Young man," she said, "tell the Chief I am Mrs. Robert Lunsford. He'll recognize the name."

Pearl moved aside, edging her way toward a wooden bench seat that hugged the wall. She could wait. This turn of events might prove fun to watch.

A moment later, Douglas appeared with Herschel at his side.

"Here's the Chief," he said to Mrs. Lunsford. "You can talk to him, ma'am."

The woman gave Douglas an exasperated look. "Chief Harkins," she said, her voice rising. "I know you by name and reputation. We came here because we knew that you would take us seriously."

Pearl scooted down in her seat. From this spot on the bench, there was no way Herschel could see her. Besides, he had now leaned in toward Mrs. Lunsford and was deep in conversation. He motioned toward a small corner table sectioned off with a rickety room divider.

"Bring some chairs, Douglas. We'll take the report here without delay."

Douglas joined them, his bound notebook and Waterman fountain pen in hand. He, too, had forgotten Pearl's presence. Pearl wondered if the department had one of the new typewriters in use in offices across the country. She had read about them. Probably not; budgets were tight, or so Herschel had mentioned.

"First," Herschel was saying, "for the sake of my officer taking your report, may we have your full names and address?"

"I'm Mrs. Robert Lunsford and this is my sister Rebecca. We live together, just the two of us at 131 Woodfin Street since…well ever since my dear husband passed away." Rebecca nodded but remained silent in deference to her older sibling.

"I knew of your husband," Herschel said. "A fine man from what I understand."

"Thank you," she said. "Now may I get to the reason we're here?"

"Of course," said Herschel.

"I want to report a kidnapping. My sister and I received a ransom note early this morning. We came here straight away."

Douglas, head bent, made notations.

"All right," said Herschel. "This sounds like very bad business. And who was kidnapped? You said you and your sister lived alone."

The widow bobbed her head. "That's true. But it's my husband, Mr. Lunsford." Her sister Rebecca nodded once more.

"Your husband," Herschel repeated. "Now correct me if I'm wrong. But hasn't your husband been deceased since early spring?"

"That's right," she said. "Mr. Lunsford is quite dead. You don't understand. He's been...his remains have been kidnapped and there's a *ransom note* demanding five thousand dollars for the return of his body." Her voice caught. Rebecca withdrew a cloth kerchief from her satchel and handed it to her sister. The widow took it and dabbed her eyes.

Behind them, on the darkened bench, Pearl's eyes grew wide. She strained to listen. Fascinating.

Herschel shifted in his chair. Douglas began to scribble furiously. Neither officer looked at the other.

"And why would someone steal your husband's body?" Herschel said.

Rebecca spoke up. "Because they knew of my brother-in-law's prominence and surmised that as his family, we would not want his resting place disturbed. My sister and I plan to be buried in the same family plot so this is very unsettling to us."

"I can imagine," said Herschel. "Do you have any idea who might have done such a terrible thing?"

"No," both women said in chorus. "All we know for certain," continued Mrs. Lunsford, "is that if we don't pay the ransom by four p.m. Wednesday Robert's remains will be tossed into a potter's grave at some undisclosed location. We may never find him again!" She released a loud sob. Rebecca placed a soothing hand on her shoulder.

"Do you have the note?" Herschel asked.

"Yes, it's right here," said Mrs. Lunsford. She handed the

171

folded paper to Herschel who opened and read it aloud:

$5000 upon return of your dead husband

DO NOT GO TO THE POLICE OR YOU WILL BE SORE-LY SORRY.

Leave the money by 4:00 p.m. Wednesday.

Look for detailed instructions in Wednesday classifieds Asheville Weekly.

Pearl's hand shot to her mouth. She must remain quiet or she would be ordered to leave. There must be some rule against eavesdropping on an investigative police matter, especially one as odd as this.

"Have you received further direction on where to leave the funds?" Herschel asked.

"No, but I expect we will today," said Mrs. Lunsford.

"We'll need to take the ransom note into evidence," Herschel told Douglas. "Mrs. Stevens, how was it delivered to you, when and by what person?"

"It was on my front stoop early this morning tucked under the milk can that's delivered three times a week. I have no idea when it was left or by whom."

"Who's your milk deliverer? I'll need his name and the company that employs him," said Herschel.

"I never liked that man," Rebecca offered. "There was always something unpleasant about him."

"Do you mean old Mr. Bowling?" her sister said, aghast. "Why, Rebecca, that's utterly ridiculous!"

The women glared at each other. "That's so like you, Rebecca," said her sister, "always jumping to conclusions, and to think that you would accuse poor ole Mr. Bowling."

"I did no such thing!"

"Mr. Bowling is a start," Herschel said quickly. "He may have seen or heard something as he was delivering the milk. Obviously, it's someone who knows where you live." He turned to Douglas. "Did you get all that?"

Douglas nodded. "I've filled up three pages and underlined Kidnapping – Dead Body." Mrs. Stevens had stopped dabbing her tears.

"You're right, Chief," she said. "They know where we live. It may not be safe to return to our home!"

"Have either one of you been to the gravesite since you received the note?" Herschel said. "That's the first thing any reasonable person would do."

"I did," said Rebecca. "There was a tilt to the headstone and signs of fresh dirt as though the grave had been...I can't go on." She retrieved another kerchief from her purse and blew her nose into it.

"I'll have two officers escort you and stay at your premises until this is over," Herschel said. He glanced toward Douglas who, head down, was shaking his head.

"Not you, Douglas," said Herschel. "I'll assign Clarke and Blevins. Make a note of it."

Pearl stifled a giggle. This was much more exciting than her current lack of patients.

Herschel redirected his attention to the two women. "Have either of you seen unfamiliar carriages, wagons, or anyone on foot near your home?"

"No," said Mrs. Lunsford. Rebecca shook her head.

Herschel rose. "All right ladies. I'll have Douglas round up the officers to accompany you home. We'll also need to

173

go by the newspaper and see if they have the ad that will run Wednesday. I'll visit the grave myself to check for disturbances."

"Yes, Chief," Douglas said. He replaced the pen in its holder, tucked the note pad in his uniform and got up. Moments earlier, Pearl had left the wooden bench and slipped, ever so quietly out the front door. She now had a better understanding of a day in the life of a police chief. It made her realize she should have more patience with Herschel. And it made her realize how very much she liked him.

When she heard the loud knock on the office door downstairs, Pearl was preparing a left-over dinner of cold ham and boiled potatoes that Loomey had cooked for lunch. She set down her plate and hurried to answer. It might be Jeremiah returning, or if he'd taken a turn for worse, someone coming to fetch her. Instead, there stood Herschel in the dimming light. "Oh, hello," Pearl said.

"You sound disappointed," Herschel said. "I'm sorry if I disturbed you." He had removed his police jacket and draped it over his arm. To Pearl, he looked tired and drawn.

She smiled and moved away from the door. "No, not all. Jeremiah came by earlier. I thought he was returning or it was someone asking me to attend him. Please come in."

She wasn't about to tell him that she had been to the police station just a short time ago.

"How is he?" Herschel asked, wiping his boots on her mat. He stepped inside. "I've been too busy to see him. Did he come here for treatment?"

"Not exactly," Pearl said. "I think he came here to …never mind. He came by to visit. He looks terrible, Herschel. So if you want to see him, I suggest you do it soon." Should she tell

174

him that Jeremiah had come by to warn her that her business practices might be jeopardizing her prospects for a successful practice? That could wait for now.

"I'll make sure I do that," Herschel said.

For a moment, they both stood in the foyer that led to Pearl's exam rooms, as though each was uncertain of the other's intentions.

"I'm so sorry," Pearl said suddenly. "I was upstairs trying to find something for dinner. Would you like to join me?" With dusk falling, she wondered if anyone had seen the Chief enter her premises, a single man visiting a single woman. It would be scandalous by societal standards, reason for more gossip. But what was she to do? Refuse to allow him entry?

"Don't mind if I do," Herschel said. "What are you cooking?"

Pearl almost replied 'I don't cook' and then realized such an admission might shock even the likes of Herschel. "Leftovers," she said. "But there's more than enough. Please stay."

She lifted her long skirt and ascended the stairs, Herschel close behind her. Thank goodness Loomey had prepared a noonday meal before she left. There might even be a drop biscuit or two from yesterday, along with a yellow concoction that resembled some type of pudding. At least she hoped it was pudding.

Once inside the kitchen, Herschel reached for a chair, hung his coat over its spine and sat down. "What a day," he said, passing a hand across the top of his head.

Pearl coughed and turned her head so he wouldn't see her knowing look. "Oh, do tell," she said. "I'd love to hear about your day. But first, how's the search coming along?"

Pearl hunted for two clean dinner plates. Now where did

Loomey keep the sharp knives? Was there a graceful art to cutting up a ham? She wasn't sure and didn't want to embarrass herself in front of Herschel. Of course she'd performed autopsies on human beings, but this was hardly the same thing.

"We got word today the Harmons, the couple quarreling on the street when Callahan was shot, were last seen running from an abandoned barn in Madison County," Herschel said. "We've got officers from three counties looking in every cove and holler known in those parts. Mayor Lusk put out notices for a reward, one thousand dollars. That'll bring some new leads."

"Something will break soon, I'm sure," Pearl said. She set the table, picked up the carving knife and handed it to Herschel. "Here, help yourself."

"The search was only half my peculiar day," Herschel said. He seemed in an unusually talkative mood, as though he had been waiting for someone with whom he could share his workday events. "You won't believe the other half. In all my years with the law I have yet to encounter such a wicked breach of trust. By morning, the whole of Asheville will be talking of the case."

She feigned surprise. She poured glasses of cold water, found a pair of linen napkins, and sat across from Herschel to hear him out as they ate.

"What on earth happened?" she asked. It pleased her that Herschel had dropped in unannounced. It was a welcome contrast to the letter from Victoria in which Caine was asking of her whereabouts. What had taken him so long to even mention her name to Victoria? Pearl returned her full attention to Herschel.

176

"I'll give you a little history first," Herschel began. "Since you haven't been here long the name Robert Lunsford won't mean anything to you. He's been dead a while but he was one of the city's better known citizens. Listed his occupation as "gentleman of leisure" if that tells you anything. Family goes way back. They made their wealth in mountain timber. During the war, Stevens fought honorably. He didn't conscript anyone to take his place."

"What do you mean by conscript?" Pearl asked. "I was a child in Missouri during the war."

"Those with money hired others to take their place as soldiers. Those with honor went out and fought just like the rest."

"Maybe there was a reason they couldn't go off to war," Pearl said, "family or business responsibilities they couldn't leave." There it was again, that stubborn practical streak she had inherited from her father.

Herschel placed a thick chunk of ham on his plate along with several large potatoes. "Men fight," he said. "They can hire others to do their bid on the home front."

Pearl knew she wouldn't get far with her viewpoint. "Go on. So what happened to this Mr. Lunsford?"

"I was back at the station today by two o'clock..." He told her of the sisters who arrived at the front desk and their insistence on seeing him to file a report.

Pearl played with her food, her cheeks turning pink. What would he think of her if he knew she'd been there, hiding in the corner like a child, her ears attuned to every word?

When he finished telling her of the alleged kidnapped body of Robert Lunsford, Pearl sat back and gave him a look she hoped was one of pure bewilderment.

"Do you think they're sincere? I've never heard of such a

thing!"

"That makes two of us," Herschel said. "I guess we'll know something by mid-week." They ate together in silence and it occurred to Pearl this must be what it was like to have a husband come home each night, sit across from his wife and share his day. She found it strangely comfortable, as though she and Herschel somehow belonged in the same room.

But a few moments later, he leaned down and flipped open the face on his chained pocket watch. "I'd love to stay longer but it's getting late. I shouldn't have come here uninvited. Forgive my intrusion."

Pearl's instinct was to reach out and touch his hand, tell him she was glad he was here. But something – was it fear? – held her back. Instead, she wiped her mouth with the linen napkin and rose from the table. "You're welcome here anytime," she said. "I'm sorry the meal was nothing more than leftovers." This time Herschel reached out; brushed his hand against hers. She looked down to see him staring at her.

If he stood and she remained where she was, they would be face-to-face. Heart thumping, she chose her next words carefully. "Will you come for dinner tomorrow evening? I must know what happened to the late, poor Mr. Lunsford. This time I promise a proper meal."

Herschel reached for his jacket, averting her gaze. "I'd be delighted. I'll be here at seven p.m. sharp. I'll show myself out. Good night, Pearl."

"Good night," she said. But as he traipsed down the stairs and she heard the front door open then close, she was already looking forward to the next evening. So much so that after he was gone she clapped her hands and in adolescent school-girl fashion – – one she knew would shock most who knew her – – danced about the room.

Chapter Seventeen

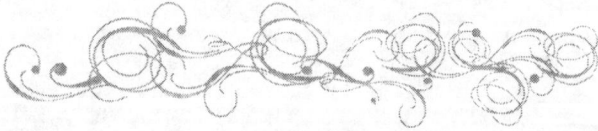

Pearl rose early the next morning as was her usual custom. But with no patient appointments on the books and little else to do until Loomey arrived, she was at a loss as to how best to use her time. After a light breakfast of toast and coffee she wandered downstairs and into her office. From her bookshelves she pulled her notes from her last few months at medical school. She wondered again when she might have her own list of patients.

The cases recorded served to jog her memory on actual cases she handled in medical school. The information was useful as similar patients might come her way. Sitting at her desk, she read through her physician notes, hoping she could soon apply that same knowledge:

February 23, 1882

1st Case – A robust woman, she has lost flesh since the appearance of diabetes. Has a diabetic cataract. One percent of her urine is sugar. Research notes that sometimes depressing moral emotions cause diabetes.

Treatment: Exclude starch and sweets from the diet. Encourage plenty of walking exercise. Brom. Arsenic Solution in one drop doses recommended. One of few remedies we possess.

2nd Case – A man 35 years of age, surveyor by trade. Urine 20 percent albumen. Deposits about the joints and ulcerations. Upon chemical examination, deposits consist largely of urate of soda. Patient states his livelihood threatened due to current limited motion but is also obstinate regarding curatives.

Treatment: Keep joints bound with cloths dipped in a saturated solution of citrate of Lithium slightly acidulated with Citric Acid. Daily intake of large drafts of Liquor Potassi Citratis or the salts of Lithium. Nitrogylcerine a capital remedy in diminishing the quantity of albumin. Follow for compliance purposes.

3rd Case – Colored man with double vision and difficulty of locomotion. States his brain is injured due to overwork. I believe this is a delusion. These symptoms are always due to some disease, a vice or some damage from the outer world. Has headache and vertigo.

Treatment: This patient receives impressions too easily and follows false reasoning. Plenty of walking – from five to ten miles per day. Cold water baths every morning with brisk rub. Chloride Gold & Sodium 1/15 gram. Then 2 gtt arsenic.

Pearl set the paperwork aside and massaged her temples. She should be looking closely at her ledger and her dwindling savings. Maybe Jeremiah was right; she offered her time and services too freely, especially to the less than well-to-do. Yet she knew that would not soon change. It was her nature to help others. She could hear Loomey as she came through the front entry, humming to herself. "Loomey?"

"Yes, Miss Pearl."

"Can you come in here?"

Loomey put down her things and hurried to the office door. "What can I do for you, Miss Pearl?"

"I need your opinion, Loomey. We need more income, more paying patients to help cover those who can't afford anything. You know this town well since you've been here all your life. How do we go about reaching the wealthier clients?"

Loomey's hand went to her chin as though deep in thought. "I may need to study on that. Only big money people I know of is dead. My mama used to work for one and they had so many fine things it took her nigh a year to clean from one end of that house to the other."

"A year? Really?"

Loomey looked down and gave a little smile. "Well, my mama didn't move too fast. That was before she got all her own book learnin'. Now she's a fine lady who can read and write. She's a teacher too. I'm real proud of her."

Pearl wondered how a teacher could have a daughter who had barely mastered the basic skills of reading and writing. Maybe Loomey was an unusually challenged student. Maybe learning from her mother didn't work out. Whatever the reason, remembering her promise to find Loomey a tutor, Pearl felt she should help in whatever way she could. "I'll get a tutor lined up for you as soon as we have some steady income," she told Loomey. "For now, we need paying customers, preferably live and influential − − clients who know others and can refer more patients."

She pushed her chair back, not sure how to make her next request. "Loomey, since we don't have anyone coming in today I wondered if you might help me with something... personal. I have a special dinner guest tonight and I'm not sure,

I mean I really don't know…" her voice trailed off. Then she stood and faced her employee. "I don't know how to cook."

"Why didn't you just say so, Miss Pearl?"

"Actually, I wondered if you might teach me how to make something simple?"

"You want me to teach you?" Loomey said. "I'm not sure I can learn you how to cook."

"Then I'll watch," said Pearl. "Sometimes that's the best way."

As they headed up the stairwell toward the kitchen, Loomey suddenly stopped behind Pearl. "Soup!" she called out.

"Excuse me?" Pearl said.

"People always need hot soup and it's easy to make. I'll show you."

Pearl had been to the markets the day before and had plenty of supplies in the cupboard. In the kitchen, each woman donned a thin cotton apron. Loomey began the search for vegetables and other ingredients needed while Pearl washed up. Soon, she had a cast iron stock pot, a flour sifter, a print of butter and a thick slab of fresh beef covered in ice.

Pearl stood nearby, her hands folded in front of her. "It looks like we're all ready." As she scanned the items on the table, she sighed, for the array of ingredients were confusing. Just for a pot of soup, all this? Suddenly, she remembered the tome *Mrs. Beeton's Book of Household Management* she had unpacked only a few days earlier. Her mother had given it to her, probably in an effort to entice her to try domesticity. Once, she had even tried to read it but its nine hundred recipes brought her to a halt. "I do have a cookbook," she declared.

"Don't need a book, Miss Pearl," Loomey said. "We're gonna put in a dab of this and a dab of that and before you know it, we'll have this place smellin' like Greasy Corner Café at high noon." Pearl watched her carefully arrange a set of silver plated carving knives, a toasting fork, two iron sauce-pans, a large boiling pot, a pepper box, a tin of flour, another decorative print of thick creamy butter and an assortment of unopened spices she found in Pearl's cabinet: bay leaves, tarragon and ginger. A rainbow collection of white potatoes, cherry red tomatoes, orange carrots and purple onions were piled in a neat stack in a corner of the table. Pearl had paid a premium for out-of-season items at the indoor market stall and then nearly let them go to waste.

"Beef makes the best stock, lean and fresh," Loomey said as she pounded the meat to help separate it from the bone. "Veal has less color and taste. Mutton – whew! You get that bad tallow smell. And fowls, they don't add much flavor. I think pigeons add the best, rabbit and partridge too. At least that's what my mama says. My man Jim, he hunts rabbit ever chance he gets."

"Don't you wash it first?" Pearl asked. She watched, amazed at Loomey's speed and agility with the carving knife as she cut the meat into small neat cubes. It reminded Pearl of the local butcher behind his counter, expertly slicing and dicing.

"Oh no," Loomey said, "Never wash it. It takes all the juices away. Now once we get it in the pot and let it boil, all that scum rises to the top. Remember now, the more scum that comes out, the better the stock."

Pearl looked puzzled. "Are you talking about the fat that rises from the meat?"

"Yeah, the scum," said Loomey. "We gotta get rid of it so

we got us a clear broth. Can't make fine soup without a clear broth. If you don't take the scum off, it's like puttin' a filthy ole rag on your patient." She gave a hard whack to the last mound of beef.

Pearl flinched. "You're quite an expert with that big knife."

Loomey smiled. "It's all in the hands, Miss Pearl, just like what you do. Only I don't have nobody hollerin' in pain." She whacked the beef again. "Now, we rub a little butter on it and dust it real light with flour. For every pound of beef you add about this much water."

She picked up a quart-sized iron pot and pointed it at Pearl, "Like about half of this," she said. "Better if you had you some earth pots. When that uglified fat and acid in the gravy gets all mixed up in the metal, why, it can poison you." She set the pot down and moved toward the wood-burning stove, lighting the kindling in one swift motion.

"Make sure your fire is regular so you don't have to add cold water for the scum to rise. When it starts to boil, that's when you put in your salt, your pepper and your vegetables. I like to add turnips, parsley and a bunch of leeks and celery tied together in a big bunch. You can also add a piece of cabbage. If you want to get real fancy stick two or three cloves right smack in the middle." She turned and moved back to the table. Watching her every move, Pearl felt as though she was back in anatomy class on the first day of school, her head swimming with too much information.

Loomey picked at the potatoes, checking for defects. "We'll boil these separate in one of these pots so we can strain 'em good. But listen Miss Pearl. I'm gonna tell you a little secret my mama taught me years ago. Don't ever eat that white mucilage that comes off the spuds when they cook."

185

"Why not, for goodness sakes? I thought all parts of the potato were nutritious."

"Gives you gas," Loomey said.

Soon, the small kitchen was filled with the succulent spicy smells of meat and onions combined with the tang of bay leaves and ginger. The potatoes, carefully selected and washed by Loomey, began a slow simmer on the stove. Next, she made a large batch of floured dough and showed Pearl how to roll and cut its smooth silky surface into fat, round biscuits. Before long, both had their hands and arms coated in white flour up to their elbows.

While the food cooked, the two women worked in tandem cleaning up, Pearl scrubbing pots while Loomey wiped the table with heated water and soap. They talked of the strong autumn storm that had arrived so quickly that afternoon, how to keep skin clean with brown soap and an ounce of lemon juice, how often to wash a head of hair – "Jim's barber recommends once a month to remove troublesome itch," Loomey shared.

She told Pearl how hard it was to keep coal dust and oil fumes from settling on everything in the house. Then Pearl noticed how quiet she grew. Loomey had moved to Pearl's favorite window and was staring out.

"Do you enjoy light as much as I do?" Pearl asked. "Did you know that the more light that comes into a room, the healthier the air?" But Loomey appeared deep in thought.

"Loomey, are you all right?" Pearl asked.

"Today's the day," she said. "One year ago today, I lost my newborn. He dropped too soon; looked like a little kitten when he finally came out, all shriveled up."

"How far along were you?" Pearl could only imagine the

pain and heartache of losing a child.

"I don't really know. Not close enough to time, 'cause he was born dead. That's when my Jim started drinkin' so bad. He wanted that little one ever bit as much as I did."

"I'm so sorry," Pearl said. It pained her to see Loomey's luminous smile replaced with this look of utter sadness.

"Mama says some broken things can't be fixed, 'specially your heart. What time is that special guest of yours comin'?" Loomey asked. She had returned to the stove and was wiping her hands on a linen cloth. "It ain't none of my business, of course, but I can stay and help if you like."

"Oh no! I mean, thank you. But I can handle it from here. The soup smells delicious, by the way. I'll put the biscuits in the oven about an hour from now and by the time he arrives..." She caught herself and stopped.

Loomey didn't look up but Pearl thought she saw a smile form. Loomey bit down on her lip, took off her apron and looked around to see if she was leaving anything behind.

"You left your things downstairs," Pearl said. "I'll go with you." She felt compelled to tell her once more how much she appreciated her help. "I'll repay you in kind."

Loomey lifted an arm and waved it toward Pearl. "Don't worry 'bout none of that," she said, "I just hope the Chief likes it. And I hope...I hope he keeps his promise to help Jim." Then she hurried out the door before Pearl could say another word.

Upstairs, Pearl checked the clock again, stirred the soup and realized she needed to change before Herschel arrived. In her room, she went through her wardrobe, holding up one then another satin dress at the long mirror near her bed. Finally settling on a light blue frock with lace-trimmed sleeves, she dabbed at her neck with the water cologne that sat on her dresser, rearranged her hair and went back to make sure dinner had not somehow mysteriously self-destructed. The pot sat simmering as before, the round, soft biscuits sat waiting on a cast iron pan. She grabbed a heavy cloth and placed them in the oven, closing the door as carefully as she would handle a patient's sore appendage.

The table set, a sprig of fresh mint on the dinner plates, a beeswax candle lit and she was ready for her guest to arrive. She listened for his footsteps up the stairs then remembered, out of habit, she had locked the door behind Loomey. She ran downstairs, found the skeleton key that she kept in a small, rose-patterned pitcher and unlocked the door; but not without peeking out first.

Across the street on the Public Square, she could make out the police station, its arched roof lit with amber lights that glowed inside the lobby. With another look at the clock, she realized Herschel was already late. He said he would be here at seven sharp. Retreating to her office, she pulled a medical book from the shelf and sat down to read while waiting. Upstairs, the biscuits she and Loomey had so carefully prepared continued to bake.

Pearl stared at the clock. Where was he? Her mood darkened as she thought of the labor she and Loomey had performed that day getting ready for this occasion. An odor of something burning caught her attention. She sniffed the air.

The biscuits! Oh lord. If she set this place on fire, she'd never forgive herself, or Herschel. She ran up the stairs two at a time and flung open her apartment door. The room was filled with thick, curling smoke. Frantic, she looked about for a cloth to open the overheated oven. With both hands wrapped in heavy towels, she grabbed at the metal handles and reached inside, pulling the biscuit tray forward.

What began as round pillows of dough were now shards of crisp black circles. She slammed the pan onto the stovetop near the lidded soup caldron and let it sit there to cool. The soup. Oh damn. What did Loomey tell her? Stir the soup every few minutes. She reached for a large metal ladle near the stove and dipped it into the pot. The spoon sank into a mushy concoction, the pot emitting a heavy burnt odor. She let the ladle simmer in the stew, moved to the window and pulled at the sash.

With a rag, she swiped at the smoke, cursing again. The smoke began to fill her lungs. One by one, she opened all of the windows. Two of the sashes stuck. Frustrated, Pearl beat on the pane before giving up. It would be a cold day in hell when she invited that man back to dinner.

Forty minutes later, with still no sign of Herschel, she dumped the burnt bread into the soup pot, grabbed the handles with a cloth and carried the entire mess downstairs and out the back door. "Take that, Herschel Springfield Harkins! You want your dinner? Come and get it," she said, tossing the entire contents onto the back lawn. A stray dog, its tail wagging, ran over, sniffed the concoction and hurried off.

Placing the empty pot at the back door, she extinguished the kerosene wicks room-by-room and stomped upstairs. A lonely candle, still lit on the dining room table, had stubbornly refused to die out on its own. She blew at it once, then twice, till the flame disappeared. Then she marched to her room, slammed the door shut and fell across the bed still dressed in her best finery. Her right elbow and back began their familiar itch.

She sat up. No. No. No. I refuse to lie here like some helpless girl. She pulled at her dress. Where's my mercury ointment? She found a small jar on her dresser, applied the

189

medicinal concoction and changed into a plain frock.

She grabbed her night shawl, extinguished the kerosene lamps and locked the front door, heading straight toward Herschel's office.

Chapter Eighteen

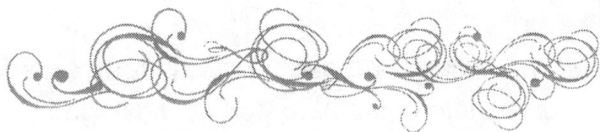

As Pearl entered the arched stone entrance to find and confront Herschel, she heard a loud commotion coming from the front desk. A handful of policemen were gathered about. Unusual, Pearl thought, for such a small department.

Mrs. Lunsford and her sister stood on either side of a uniformed officer, like two boxers waiting for the bell to ring. Herschel had his arms outstretched and was trying to calm them down.

"I cannot understand how you could do this to me and with my own husband!" Mrs. Lunsford yelled.

"You and your 'dear precious' Robert! You have no idea what it was like living in that house with the two of you and you…so oblivious to my feelings."

"Your feelings? What about my feelings?"

Just as Pearl approached, Mrs. Lunsford took aim at her sister's head, flinging a heavy paisley satchel. It landed with a thump, toppling Rebecca's crumpled hat. Pearl stifled a gasp.

"Take that, you deceitful whore! How dare you! How dare you!"

There was a high-pitched squeal. Rebecca ducked then jabbed her closed parasol toward her sister's shocked face.

"Ladies!" Herschel's deep voice boomed. "Stop this!" He stepped between them and grabbed the parasol.

Pearl halted in mid-stride and stared. In all her years of encountering patients and public alike, she had never seen anything like this.

"Go to your corners," he said, "now! George, come here. Take these women into custody." Pearl saw him glance toward the desk where one officer had retreated, realizing Herschel had yet to see her. This time she wouldn't cower in a corner. She would simply wait.

"Sergeant!" Herschel commanded. "Come out from behind that goddamn desk or I'll have you in cuffs too."

Expecting Herschel to spot her at any moment, Pearl caught the eye of one of the officers instead. The young man held up a hand, motioning her to take a seat.

"Custody?" Mrs. Lunsford said. "What do you mean? Chief Harkins, are you arresting us?"

"I'm taking you into custody for a public disturbance in police headquarters," he said. "That's for a start. Now what in God's name is this all about?"

"That woman," she said, pointing to Rebecca, "admitted she slept with my husband Robert. And she was on the verge of admitting to this entire kidnapping hoax when your officers insisted we come to the station."

Herschel turned to his men. "Is that true?"

An officer spoke up.

"The fight started upstairs and got worse as the day wore on. At first, we didn't want to intervene, you know them being sisters and all."

"Just tell me what happened," Herschel snapped.

"When Mrs. Lunsford here found out about her husband and sister..."

"How did she learn that?"

"I told her!" Rebecca said. "I got so tired of hearing 'my dear husband this' and 'poor darling Robert' that, I couldn't bear it another minute. For months, she's been mourning that fiend who didn't even have the good grace to tell the truth. Instead, he just up and died."

Mrs. Lunsford began to sob. She looked up with a tear-stained face. "Such ingratitude! After my dear...that scoundrel...Robert passed I took her in and gave her a decent home, good meals, fine things. And to think this is how she repays me!" The men shuffled uncomfortably. Herschel had his arms clasped across his chest.

"What now, Chief?" said one of the officers.

"We still don't know the truth about this so-called kidnapping," Herschel said. "Anybody want to speak up?" He looked from one sister to the other.

Rebecca took a pleated fan from her purse and began to wave it over her reddened face. "I can tell you," she said, resigned. "But I'm not taking the fall for the entire episode. Robert's remains are quite safe and in their rightful place. I made the whole thing up, though he deserves much worse. His spirit can go to blazes for all I care."

"What about the charges, Chief?" said a young officer. To Pearl, he looked to be no more than twenty.

"If Mrs. Lunsford doesn't want to press criminal charges against her own kin, let them both go," Herschel said. "I'll drop the public disturbance offense if they'll work this thing out between them, peacefully. One more thing. I strongly suggest that you, Rebecca, find yourself a new place to live and a new man to shove around, living or dead. Now good night to all of you."

Pearl stood, watching Herschel's startled face when he finally saw her and approached.

"Pearl! I was just about to leave when this commotion took place. What time is it?"

Pearl gave him a sympathetic nod. "It doesn't matter. Looks like you were indisposed."

He glanced back at his men, some of whom were watching him. "Go on about your business. I'll take care of this young lady."

Pearl tugged at her shawl as she and Herschel crossed the small lobby. Maybe their planned dinner could be salvaged after all. Suddenly, the front door of the station burst open.

"Chief Harkins!" the deputy sheriff said. "We got the shooter! We found her; got her out in the wagon with the High Sheriff. He says come right now!"

All Pearl could do was nod at Herschel, releasing him once again. She did, however, at least hope to catch a glimpse of the infamous female fugitive who had plugged Officer Callahan in the back. But so many officers had scrambled to the wagon, surrounding her in the dark, all Pearl could see was the top of her head, her hair a dark, disheveled mass. As they half-carried, half-dragged her into the station for what Pearl assumed was a preliminary booking, she heard the woman whimper, not once, but over and over.

"Tomorrow," Herschel called to her as he joined his men.

Next morning, when Loomey came upstairs, Pearl's bedroom door was shut tight. She called out. "Miss Pearl? Are you all right in there?"

Pearl gave a low sound and turned over only to see Loomey enter the darkened room.

"Lord have mercy," Loomey said, pushing the drapes open. "You're not sick, are you?"

Pearl moaned and rose from the covers like an apparition. She rested on the edge of the bed, her eyes closed. "No, but I'm very tired. There was a good bit of excitement last night."

Loomey had her hands on her hips. "That must have been some special night you had yourself with your special guest."

"No, it wasn't like that," said Pearl.

"All right then," Loomey said, pulling the covers from around Pearl. "Now you get yourself up and dressed while I fix you some hot breakfast. My, oh my, you're a sight. You go out lookin' like that and you're likely to scare the horses."

An hour later, her morning toilette done, Pearl was dressed in a fresh gingham dress with every hair in place. In the kitchen, Loomey handed her a steaming mug of brewed coffee.

"Thanks," Pearl said. All that was left of the tray of hot biscuits were a few charred remains. The empty pot of soup, its bottom coated with a thick greasy film, sat tipped on its side. Linen cloths and napkins were strewn about. The table, a dead melted candle at its center, was still set with two clean dinner plates, utensils and glassware.

"You sure you didn't have a wild hen party here last

195

night?" Loomey asked, her back to Pearl. "Looks to me like a whole lot of something went on."

"Don't be impertinent, Loomey," Pearl said, sitting down and clearing a space at the table. "I didn't feel like cleaning up, that's all. Come sit and I'll tell you about last night."

Pearl shared the evening's events with Loomey, whose eyes grew wide with the revelation that the shooter had been captured.

"What you think they gonna do to her?" Loomey ask.

Pearl emptied her cup and rose from the table. "I have no idea. But from the rough way she was handled last night as they were hauling her into the police station, I have no doubt this whole thing won't end well. She did shoot an officer in the back. That won't be forgotten."

"And you saved him," Loomey said.

"No. We saved him Loomey. Now I have work to do in my office. Do you mind?" Pearl waved a hand about the kitchen.

"Do I mind cleanin' up this unholy mess?" Loomey said. "Not if that's what you tell me to do, Miss Pearl."

"Thank you. In about an hour would you also bring me a cup of hot tea?"

As Pearl descended the stairwell to her office, she could hear Loomey bustling about, singing to herself, her voice calm and lilting. Having her around was like having the clouds part for the sun. She must tell her so when she came downstairs.

By the time Loomey trooped into her office with a steaming mug and two slices of buttered toast, Pearl was ensconced in too many loose ends to remember the compliment. She was sorting through her files, had started a letter to her parents telling them she was doing well (a fine fib it was), and had

196

a ceramic mortar and pestle on the counter, ready to mix her powders.

She looked up absently as Loomey entered. "A bright spot, that's what you are," Pearl said, almost an afterthought.

Loomey sat down across from Pearl. "Can I ask you something?" she said.

Pearl laid her paperwork aside. "Of course."

"Do you think I'm smart enough to be your assistant? I mean a real one. Not just somebody who cleans and cooks and brings you hot tea."

"Yes I do," said Pearl. "Why do you ask?"

"Because if you already think I'm smart, why am I needin' a tutor?"

Pearl realized she might have, without intention, offended this proud young woman. She took Loomey's hands in hers. "People often judge others by their speech and their ability to read and write, among other things. I want anyone who meets you to know that while you might not be well educated, you're very intelligent. Not to mention kind, funny, quick and a really fine cook."

Loomey grinned. "Got you beat on that one, don't I?"

Pearl laughed. "You certainly do. Now I have a question for you. What are people saying about the practice? You've been here all your life, you know a lot of people in the community."

Loomey studied her hands. "Some like you; some don't. Some are scared of you a little bit."

"What? What do you mean?"

"They think you take just any ole riff-raff that comes through the door. I hear'd that from whites. I also hear'd you have some kind of disease that you don't talk about. That's from whites too."

Pearl was stunned. "Disease? What are you talking about?"

"Mrs. Callahan was talkin' to her neighbors and they was talkin' to people that something strange grows on your skin. She said she sure hopes her husband don't get it, 'specially after all you'd done for him. That you were kind to him, and healed him, but that don't make up for givin' him a whole new worry."

Pearl sat back. "How do you know all this, Loomey?"

"My mama. I told you she was a teacher. So she hears things from all kinds of people and she tells me. So it goes around and around." She made a circular motion.

A small town, Pearl thought. It had its drawbacks.

She rolled up her dress sleeve to expose an elbow. "Let's start with this." She showed Loomey the faint outline of a silvery patch on her arm. "It's a skin condition called psoriasis. Sometimes it appears here, sometimes other places. Sometimes it disappears for a while. But it's not contagious. And it's certainly not something for those I've touched to worry about."

Loomey nodded and reached out to gently run her finger over the patch of skin on Pearl's arm.

Pearl was surprised, and touched by Loomey's unspoken acceptance. If only others could show such compassion. "As for our taking in "riff-raff" there's not much we can do about that. I won't turn anyone away that needs our assistance, not even Callahan's family, despite what they think."

Chapter Nineteen

After she and Loomey talked, Pearl settled into her office chair. A neat stack of papers lay beside her favored fountain pen. With its dark, shiny blue casing smooth as silk in her hand, she felt a special connection to it. It was a graduation gift from her father. He had also given her a cream-colored leather-bound book titled *Volume I* that served as her record-keeping journal.

Most of its pages were blank. She had put off this administrative chore for as long as possible, wishing each time she had the luxury of a secretary who could track her monthly income and expenditures. Not that there was much of the former.

The bell at the front door rang. With Loomey back upstairs cleaning the kitchen and sanitizing cloths used for bandages, Pearl rose to see who was there. A young, well-dressed woman stood in the foyer with a squirming baby in her arms.

"Are you Dr. Stern?" she said.

"Yes, how can I help you?"

"It's my little one here. She's my first child, six months today and just as restless as she can be."

Pearl motioned for the anxious mother to follow her into the exam room. "Were you referred here?" she asked. If so, it would be her first professional referral.

"My uncle is Jeremiah Dickson," the woman said. "He speaks highly of you, though he says you can be a little unorthodox in your practice. I'm Georgia Dickson Shaw. Pleased to make your acquaintance, ma'am."

"Your uncle is a fine person," said Pearl. "Do send him my regards." She didn't want to raise the subject of his poor health to an already-worried young mother. Nor did she want to ask what Jeremiah meant by her unorthodox practice. Instead, she said "Now, tell me more about your baby and why you're here."

"She's had excitable bowels and was peevish all night long," the mother said. "Felt feverish when I put her to bed."

Pearl cleaned her hands and told the woman to sit with the baby in her lap. She gave the infant a cursory look. The child appeared healthy, well-fed and not in great distress. Following several basic questions every medical student is taught, Pearl determined this was not a real emergency. "Does she put her hands in her mouth or attempt to chew on objects?" Pearl asked.

"Oh yes, ma'am, all the time."

The woman spoke as though educated so Pearl launched into a brief description of the signs and symptoms of teething. "Children start with twenty of the thirty-two distinct teeth we have as adults," she said. "The first few are incisors and molars which cut through the gums and can cause pain and irritation. I'm quite certain what we have here is a case of

200

teething."

Pearl then instructed the young woman to sit erect and hold the baby face forward. "Now open her little mouth, but don't ever put your hands inside without washing them," she said. The baby squirmed and shook her head, then settled against her mother's breast.

With a small wooden speculum, Pearl gently moved the child's tongue from one side to the other. "As the incisors break through," she said, "the gums become tense and swollen with a red shiny look. In very severe cases, the gums can be scarified by lancing them. But I can see white lines where her teeth are attempting to come in. This is perfectly normal."

The woman visibly relaxed. "So what can I do for her? The druggist suggested cocaine toothache drops, but I wanted to come here first. I have some laudanum at home. That's the only thing I've found that calms her at night."

"You can continue to use the laudanum but only sparingly," Pearl said. "Keep her cool by putting her in a warm bath. When she cries or seems distressed, allay her discomfort with something she can chew on that has a rough surface. I've seen mothers use ivory rings, even a stale hard crust of bread."

The baby was now gazing at Pearl with a look of intense interest. Pearl reached out and took her miniature fingers as they wrapped around her own. Pearl was struck by the realization she could have had her own child, a baby as precious as this one that would enrich her life and give her meaning above and beyond a career. Was this what her mother had been trying to tell her all along? Had she, Pearl, been so totally blind to her own ambitions that she failed to grasp there was more to life than work and medicine and righting wrongs that occurred in the course of any physician's career?

"I think she'll be just fine," Pearl said. Her voice sounded flat. She smiled at the young mother in an effort to put her at ease.

"Thank you, Dr. Stern. I'll get her home now before her father arrives. He loves to play with her in the evenings. Please tell me what I owe you."

Relieved to finally have a paying customer, Pearl wrote out a receipt for four dollars and handed it to Georgia. "Your next visit is free if you would be kind enough to refer others to my practice."

Georgia nodded. "Of course, and thank you again."

Pearl recorded her first full payment into the ledger, noted monthly expenses coming up for the fall and laid the pen aside. She massaged her cramping hand. One patient every two months would not come close to sustaining her practice. She could hear Loomey traipsing down the steps, still humming to herself.

"Got you another hot tea all ready," she said, placing the floral cup and saucer on Pearl's desk.

"Don't go yet. I have a question for you."

"Yes, Miss Pearl."

"Town council," Pearl said. "That's where to start! We need to offer our medical services to the town council members and their families. I recall a couple of the council who said they were looking for a new physician. They would certainly know other influential people, too." She sipped her tea and got up, pacing the hardwood floor.

"Are you sure that's a good idea, Miss Pearl?" Loomey said. "I remember you talkin' about how they looked down on you and all when you first got here. Didn't give you a job neither."

Pearl stopped in her tracks. "I never told you that. "How did you know?"

Loomey shook her head. "Ever body knows ever bodies' business round here. My mama told me that when I got hired on with you. She heard it from one of her high-flung friends."

Dressed in a white cotton shirt, a checkered skirt and beaded earrings, Loomey faced Pearl with her hands on her hips. Pearl recalled Loomey's shyness the first day they met, when Loomey had arrived for an interview and ended up showing her worth after the Callahan shooting. She marveled at how far Loomey had come since then, not just as an assistant but as a friend.

"What's the worst thing that can happen," she said to Loomey, "that they will all say no?"

"Oh, that ain't the worst. Some of them high-flyin' courthouse folks can be low-down schemers. That Mr. Wilson, why I heard he can call his dog and it won't come till it gets a second opinion."

"I can handle him," Pearl said, recalling Herschel's encounter with city councilman Owen Wilson and the ruckus that ensued. Wilson had displayed sanctimonious contempt for her. She searched the room for her crocheted shawl. "Where is that blasted thing?" she said. "I laid it here yesterday."

"Right in front of your eyes," Loomey said, handing the woolen shawl to Pearl. "Just like a lot of things around here."

En route to the town hall, Pearl had to force herself not to detour to the police station, to find out how the night went after the arrest of the shooter. A quick glance toward the building told her nothing. In fact, there were fewer horses out front and what appeared to be less activity than usual.

At the courthouse, unannounced, she retraced her steps

up the stairs and down the second floor hallway where she and Herschel had gone her first day in town. Herschel again, she thought. Why doesn't he just stay out of my head? She had managed to nearly forget Caine. There was no reason she couldn't do the same with Herschel. She pushed the image of him away.

Owen Wilson was coming from his office, perhaps headed to one of the local cafes. It was almost lunchtime, as evidenced by the near empty offices.

"Mr. Wilson?" Pearl called out as she approached. "May I speak with you?"

He turned, gave her a quizzical look, and then a startled one. "Dr. Stern? What a surprise!"

"Yes," Pearl said. "I'm sure you remember me from my first visit here a couple of months back. I met with your town council."

His face flushed. "Of course. I hope you've been well since then and enjoying our fine town. Actually, I was just leaving. I have a luncheon appointment. Will you excuse me?"

Pearl stood in the hallway, not moving. "This won't take but a moment of your time," she said. "I'd like your permission to leave calling cards for medical referrals with your council members. A few of them said they were looking for a new physician. As you may know, my private practice is now in place on the..."

"I know exactly where your practice is," Owen interrupted. "And I'm well aware of the heroic measures you took to save Officer Callahan. We were most impressed and very grateful for your quick-thinking skills that day. In fact, we second-guessed ourselves on whether or not we erred in not hiring you as our municipal physician."

204

Pearl smiled. "That's wonderful to hear and all the more reason I may be allowed to leave my referral cards. Would that be all right?"

"Now, I didn't say that," Owen replied. "Since then, there have been disturbing reports that you've hired a colored assistant, that you have actually treated patients of that nature and that you are not limiting your practice to women and children, white women and white children, I should add. Why, we even heard a rumor that you took in prostitutes and treated them! That's a most unusual turn from our point of view."

Pearl stood rooted to the floor. "I'm a family physician," she said. "It's my role as a family doctor to treat all members of a family, and all types of families. What if I had refused to treat Officer Callahan because he was a male? What if he had been colored? What then? Do you see my point?"

Owen checked his watch and gave Pearl a contemptuous look mixed with impatience, "I refuse to stand here and argue with you. All that I'll say on the subject of Callahan is that he was an exception. Any physician would have been remiss in not responding to his emergency. But now that is past, Miss Stern, you really should reassess your role as our lone female healer. There are many other physicians in this town who heed our advice and achieve a modicum of success as a result."

Pearl glared at him. "Heeding your advice is not now, nor will it ever be, on my list of priorities. But I thank you for your frankness and I apologize for taking up your precious time." She started to leave then turned around. "One more thing," she said, "do not ever refer to me as Miss Stern in my presence. I am Doctor Stern to you. Good day, Mr. Wilson."

At her office, Pearl returned to her desk in a dark mood. Sitting in front of a half-written letter to her parents she contemplated throwing in the towel and leaving Asheville for good. But go where? She couldn't return to Missouri, not after what had happened there. She wasn't sure where Victoria was at this point, or if Victoria could even fathom what she was going through. Feeling miserable and alone, she slumped in the chair and rested her head against its hard wooden back.

She could hear Loomey come downstairs and enter the front office. There was no mistaking her voice and her familiar reference to "Mama." Pearl rubbed her temples and peered around the corner to see what was going on. "Loomey!" she called out, "What are you doing?"

Loomey's stricken face appeared at the doorway. "My mama's here," she said, quietly.

"What?"

"She's here," Loomey repeated. "She wants to meet you." Loomey turned on her heels.

"Oh I'm so sorry!" Pearl said, jumping up and trailing behind her. "How long has she been here? Why didn't you tell me she was coming?"

Loomey turned to face Pearl. "Because I didn't know it, that's why. She does that sometimes, just appears up like smoke, pops up out of nowheres."

"The word is nowhere," said a shadow at the office entrance. A well-built woman in her mid to late sixties stepped forward. Unlike the sharp angular features on Loomey, her face was soft and round; a creamy dark brown that gleamed in the light, framed by a halo of light gray hair. The style was swept fashionably upward, her clothing classically timeless. She wore a gold and pearl brooch at the spotless neckline of her black taffeta dress.

Pearl's first reaction was that she could have stepped off

the train from any major city in the country. She hoped her stunned look wasn't written all over her face.

"Good day," the woman said, moving forward to extend a gloved hand to Pearl. "You must be Dr. Stern. Loomey speaks of you almost constantly. I feel as though I know you. I am Mrs. Gilbert, Loomey's mother."

"And I feel as though I know you. Loomey also speaks of you often."

Loomey stared at one then the other with a pleased look, as though she had just completed a major achievement.

Pearl re-gathered her wits. "Please, Mrs. Gilbert, come in. Let's go upstairs to my quarters."

Mrs. Gilbert's black taffeta dress swished as she climbed the wooden steps, Loomey traipsing behind her.

"Loomey, would you make us some coffee, please?" Pearl asked. "I'm sure your mother would like something to drink."

Mrs. Gilbert nodded toward her daughter. "She knows how I take it."

Pearl invited the woman to sit across from her near the fireplace. "Please tell me something about you," she said. "I know you have several other children. Loomey is your young-est. Is that right?"

"Yes, I have six children. I'm a teacher by trade."

"A teacher?" Pearl repeated. "My, that's wonderful!" But how could it be that Loomey's mother was a teacher when the poor girl could barely read? Pearl wasn't sure how to raise that burning question.

"I've set up a school, though it's not official. Some of my own children have been students, learning to read and write. I guess you could call me an activist of sorts. Our hopes were high that Loomey would follow suit but instead..." She lowered her voice. "Instead she ran off and married that nev'-do-well Jim. We see how *that* turned out."

Pearl felt a sudden urge to defend her employee. "She's been a godsend to me in getting my practice set up." The mention of Loomey's husband triggered the question: had Herschel looked into Jim's case yet?

Loomey brought the coffee and set it down. Her mother had peeled off her gloves and seemed relaxed, as though she and Pearl were old friends and this was a routine social call.

"I'll get myself downstairs and let you two take a visit," Loomey said. "I got apothecary jars to clean and more pills to grind." As Loomey left the room, Mrs. Gilbert turned to Pearl.

"One reason I'm here is to thank you for your willingness to hire my daughter," she said. "However...and I'll be frank, Dr. Stern. I have another reason for coming to see you. Loomey told me you have also offered to hire a tutor. I'm not sure what your motive is for doing so."

"My motive?" Pearl asked. She leaned back in her chair. It never occurred to her that she might have a hidden agenda for helping Loomey. "Well," Pearl continued. "I suppose it would make her a better assistant."

"For you," Mrs. Gilbert said. "So it would help you in the long run."

"Yes, but it will help Loomey too. Mrs. Gilbert, let me see if I understand what you're saying. It sounds like you think my motive for helping Loomey is strictly for my own benefit. That's simply not true. With training and education, Loomey is quite capable of leaving my employ and returning to the community in whatever role she chooses. For example, she would make an excellent nurse. There could be other opportunities for her."

Mrs. Gilbert set her cup down and looked at Pearl. "Then you must forgive me and my lack of trust in your motives as an intelligent white. I have my reasons. Did Loomey tell you about the baby she lost?"

"Yes, she did. It was a very sad situation." She wondered what that had to do with Mrs. Gilbert's apparent cynicism.

"Did she also tell you she was tended by a doctor who, on principle, at first refused to treat coloreds? By the time he recanted – under much duress and with cash paid in advance – the baby was too far gone. And did she tell you she had worked for this physician in his home as a domestic? And that despite her advanced pregnancy he insisted she continue to perform all of her strenuous duties including heavy lifting that may have contributed to her miscarriage?"

"No, she never told me about that. May I ask the doctor's name?" Ralph Hanson came to mind as it did when anything medically unsavory was mentioned.

"It doesn't matter," Mrs. Gilbert said. "He's no longer in Asheville. He said there was no chance of a lucrative practice here. I think he moved to Charlotte."

"Most physicians don't go into practice to earn a large living," Pearl said. "Medicine is a calling. It doesn't attract wealth. You were frank with me, so I'll be frank with you. My practice is growing but very slowly. I'm barely hanging on financially. In fact, Loomey and I were just talking this morning about ways to increase referrals through influential paying patients who will refer others. So far, I haven't been successful in making that happen." Her face still burned from Owen Wilson's rebuke earlier that day.

"Would you treat coloreds as a regular practice?" Mrs.

209

Gilbert asked.

"Of course I would."

"It's a small town," Mrs. Gilbert said, "so I had to make sure." She went on. "Well, it may surprise you, Dr. Stern. But there are coloreds in this community who are influential in their own right and can pay for medical services."

"I'm not all that surprised," Pearl said. "I've met a few enterprising merchants on Eagle Street. In fact, the settee you are sitting on was purchased from a store in that neighborhood."

"Very well, I'll refer my friends and acquaintances to you," Mrs. Gilbert said, rising from her chair and carefully replacing her gloves, "now that I have met you and seen for myself that you are a sincere woman."

"Well, thank you. Thank you so much."

Loomey's mother gave Pearl a final, appraising look. "I also believe you're a good doctor. I trust my Loomey."

"As do I," said Pearl, extending her hand. "Please don't worry about Loomey."

"That's a mother's lot," said Mrs. Gilbert, "worrying about her children. Do you have any of your own?"

"No. I'm not married. I chose a medical career instead."

Loomey's mother frowned. "There is no greater glory than motherhood," she said. "Some day you may choose another path."

"I think it's too late for me. But I'll remember your counsel."

Pearl felt as though she had been reprimanded and wondered how well her own mother would have gotten along with Mrs. Gilbert, for they thought much alike. Still, hadn't Loomey's mother taken it upon herself to become a teacher, displaying her own ambitions? Here was a woman who named her daughter from a flour sack but went on to become educated and well spoken. How different was that decision from what Pearl had chosen to do with her life?

Loomey pushed at the apartment door. Pearl had not heard her light footsteps as she came into the room. "I think you need to come downstairs, Miss Pearl, right this minute. It's Chief Harkins."

Chapter Twenty

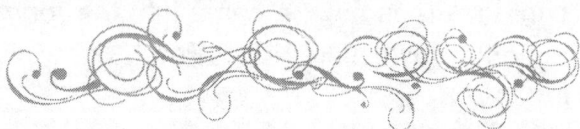

As Mrs. Gilbert took her leave and Loomey made herself scarce, Pearl ran to check her hair and dress in the wardrobe mirror. She felt a surge of emotions including pleasure at the pure sight of Herschel. Damn him, she thought. As she descended the stairs and saw him standing in the foyer, hat in hand, she attempted to give him a cool look.

"Hello Herschel," she said. "What can I do for you?" She was dying to ask him about the arrest of the fugitive and what had happened to her. But her eagerness might appear unseemly.

"Mind if I sit for a few moments?" Herschel asked. Pearl motioned him toward an upholstered chair in the waiting room. She took a seat across from him and arranged her skirt, hoping he would begin with the latest news. He did not disappoint.

"The woman who shot Officer Callahan, Beatrice Goode, she's in our jail and awaiting trial. It'll start this week. There's so much bad blood toward her we can't delay it."

"Where was she caught?" Pearl asked. "What of her accomplice?"

"She was caught in Madison County trying to escape from an abandoned barn. One of the locals recognized her from the newspaper description and thought it odd she and her partner would be staying in an old barn. As for her lover – and that's the word she used to describe him – he ran off and left her. Not much of a man, if you ask me. But then maybe he was scared of her. The woman's mad as a rabid skunk, Pearl. I tried talking to her and she made not a lick of sense. You'll see when you meet her."

Pearl gave him a shocked look. "Meet her? Why would I ever meet her?"

"We need you to pronounce her physically and mentally well enough to stand trial," Herschel said. "Hanson jumped at the chance but no way in hell – sorry – no way will I hire him as an official examiner. I need you."

"There are other physicians in town. You don't need me."

He reached out as though to touch her hand but they were too far apart. "Yes, I do. Not only because I think she will be more amenable to having a woman physician, but I know you will be thorough and fair. Please, will you do this? It doesn't pay much, four dollars as set by the state. But we gotta hire someone. I'd rather it be you."

Pearl had little knowledge of mental aberrations and knew there was a dearth of information on the subject among most physicians. Finally, she spoke up.

"What if my findings are inconclusive, Herschel?" she said. "I may spend hours with her and still not be able to determine her true state of mind."

"I trust you. And so will the court, if you have to get up on the stand. Whatever your findings, it may not make a hill of beans difference to her guilt or innocence. But we owe it to the law, and I guess to her, to find out. It just seems like the decent thing to do. This is a hanging offense so there's a lot at stake. If our circuit rider is a hanging judge, her goose is cooked no matter what. At least we can say we did right by the law."

"That's a generous attitude considering she almost killed one of your officers," Pearl said. "Do you think the prosecutor, the witnesses, his colleagues and Callahan himself will feel the same?"

"I don't know; probably not. A lot of people are still up in arms about this whole event." He stopped talking and stared at her. "Can I count on you?"

Pearl wanted to say no but there was something about the way Herschel was looking at her. She sighed. "I'll talk with her and examine her physically. But I won't commit to anything beyond that. There are some things of which I am not qualified to speak as an expert. I'll do it as long as you understand my position."

"I understand," Herschel said. He rose. "Will you allow me to dine with you in exchange for your kindness?"

She gave him the first hint of a smile. "Depends. What do you have in mind?"

"How about a nice dinner tomorrow evening at the new place on South Main? I'll come by around seven and pick you up. It's a ten-minute walk."

Pearl nodded. "That sounds lovely. But before you go, when can I see Beatrice?"

"Come to the station in the morning around ten. I'll have one of my boys escort you to the jail. And thank you, Pearl. I'm very grateful."

"Good night, Herschel," she said. As he was leaving,

Pearl caught a glimpse of Loomey's shadow from the corner of her eye. She waited until Herschel was safely out the door then turned to find Loomey still standing there.

"Were you spying on us?" Pearl said. If so, she was more amused than angry.

"I was not," Loomey said. "But I will say my piece. My man, Jim, I go see him at least every other day. He's sufferin,' Miss Pearl, sick with fevers and nobody pays him any mind. Can you talk to the Chief about him, see what he can do?"

"I'll do better than that, Loomey." She felt a stab of guilt over not bringing Jim to Herschel's attention as she had promised. It just seemed there were so many other things to get in the way. But that was an excuse. She had simply forgotten Jim, just like everyone else.

"I'll be at the jail in the morning and will see what I can do to check on him."

"Thank you, Miss Pearl."

"No, thank you Loomey, for helping me to keep my word."

Next morning, Pearl, her medical bag in tow, was escorted by an assigned officer to the jail for the purpose of examining Beatrice. Herschel explained they had to place her in a single cell for her own protection, as opposed to locking her up with the male offenders.

The building itself was small, red brick, set behind the police station near Eagle Street. Without signage and the iron bars that dominated its windows, it could have passed for any retail shop, perhaps a shoe repair or a hat shop. Yet once inside, Pearl thought it felt like a mausoleum.

The wardens, all men, were as coarse and poorly dressed as most of the prisoners they guarded. Yet they were polite enough to Pearl, offering to stay close if needed and calling her "ma'am" as they led her down the concrete hall. One threw up his hand to caution a male prisoner who leered through the bars at Pearl.

"Say one word and I'll bust you in the mouth," the guard warned. Pearl felt certain it was no empty threat. As the cell door clicked behind her, she waited for her eyes to focus in the darkened room. God help anyone who entered here.

A metal slop-pail sat in the corner, brimming with ripe, undiluted urine, its metallic odor permeating the small space. Pearl suppressed a gag and then inhaled a deep breath through her mouth. A woman sat huddled in the far corner, her hair unkempt, and her plain cotton dress ratty and torn. The cell itself was filthy, a perfect haven for vermin, Pearl thought. As Beatrice looked up, Pearl noted her pale skin and empty eyes. She guessed her age at no more than mid-twenties.

"Beatrice, my name is Doctor Stern. I'm here to speak with you. May I sit?"

"I don't need no doctor," Beatrice said. "I just need to go home and see my Lord and Savior." She rolled her eyes toward the ceiling. "I'm a-coming, Lord," she said. "Won't be long now. You wait and see."

"Is there anything I can do for you?" Pearl asked, coming closer. She set her medical bag down on the bench next to Beatrice and pulled out her stethoscope.

"Too late for that now," Beatrice said. "But wait just a minute." She cocked her head and stared at the dirt-smeared floor as though trying to remember something important. Then she shook her head as though it was hopeless to recall anything.

There were no chairs in the barren cell so Pearl sat down at the end of the bench. Something sticky clung to her skirt. It looked like some sort of food stain or even spittle, Pearl thought. This is where Beatrice laid her head each night. Pearl unraveled her stethoscope and looked at the prisoner. "May I ask you a question?"

"I know what you want," Beatrice said. "You want what them other folks are after. You want to know why I did it." Beside her lay a thick leather-covered Bible, coated in dust.

Pearl leaned toward her. "No, I want to know how you're feeling."

"What you want to know that for?" Beatrice said. "I don't know you. Who sent you here? And don't be comin' too close in on me." She grabbed the Bible and held it toward Pearl like a weapon. "Here's what I'm believin'. I believe in the power of life but even more in the power of death. Here, let me read you God's word." She opened the dog-eared book and began to mumble something unintelligible.

"It's all right, Beatrice. I just came by to talk with you for a few minutes." It was quickly apparent to Pearl the woman was suffering some type of hysteria, a condition Pearl might never comprehend. She thought it best to start by meeting Beatrice on her own terms. "Has a pastor been by to see you yet?" she asked.

Beatrice smiled, exposing a missing front tooth. The remaining teeth were tobacco-stained and half-rotted. "Oh yes. He administered the sacrament of the Holy Communion this morning." She began humming softly to herself.

An officer appeared at the cell door. "Everything aw' right in here?"

"Yes, officer, we're fine," said Pearl. "I just need a few more minutes." Yet, truthfully, Pearl was uncertain what to do next. Physically, Beatrice appeared normal to Pearl, though under-nourished and with poor color. A fugitive, the woman probably had not eaten or slept well in weeks. But what could one know of the mind and its mysterious workings?

"Beatrice, I need you to put your Bible down and look at me direct. That's good. Now let me see your hands." Beatrice extended both hands to Pearl, palms up. Pearl searched for swelling of the joints and any discoloration. A few odd-shaped bruises were evident on her wrists and forearms, probably from her recent life on the run. Her skin was red and as dry and coarse as a splintered plank.

"Now, if you'll be still I'm going to check your heart and lungs by placing this instrument on your chest," Pearl said. "See? Like this. That's right. Be very still so I can listen."

Beatrice followed Pearl's directions as a child would follow an adult. The rhythmic heartbeat sounded rapid to Pearl and slightly irregular. Her lungs were clear. Next she would palpate her glands about the neck and examine her eyes and ears. Suddenly, Beatrice jerked backwards and reared against the wall.

"You're the Devil's mistress!" Beatrice said. "I can feel it! Don't be touchin' me again." She locked her arms across her chest and began to rock back and forth, humming a tune that Pearl did not recognize. Pearl watched her silently for any physical signs of distress; flushing, perspiration or trouble breathing. Beatrice's exposed calves showed no sign of edema.

"Do you have any pain?" Pearl asked. "Are you hurting anywhere?"

Beatrice nodded. "I was born in sin and will die in sin. That is a pain greater than any mortal can bear." She was mumbling again in words Pearl could not understand. She wondered if Beatrice was suffering from nervous exhaustion,

218

which would manifest itself through her symptoms. She made one more attempt to reach out, tapping her on the arm to gauge her reaction.

"I said don't touch me!" Beatrice yelled. "I will kill you. I'll kill you dead!"

Pearl drew back. Finally, she rose. "I'll be going now," she said. "But I may see you again very soon." Beatrice returned to her humming, her body swaying in rhythm on the concrete bench.

Before leaving Pearl requested that she be taken to Jim Harrison's cell.

"What do you want to bother with him for?" asked the jailer.

"I'm a doctor and heard he was ill. Now please do as I asked."

She was led down two narrow dark passages to a cell in which what appeared was a heap of filthy rags in the corner. The heap moved and Pearl heard a moaning sound. She turned to the jailer.

"Let me in immediately! This man needs attention." She crouched beside Jim and felt his forehead. He was burning with fever. "Mr. Harrison, my name is Dr. Pearl Stern. Your wife, Loomey works with me." The man stirred, attempting to raise his head.

"Jailer, can this man be released? He needs medical attention."

"No can do," the jailer said. "Not without the Chief of Police and the Sheriff's permission. They both run this place. We got prisoners from both of 'em."

"Then I will talk to the Chief myself," she said. "Now

219

please escort me out."

Shaken, Pearl had no idea what to do for Beatrice. The poor woman was beyond her help. As for Jim, she was uncertain what, if anything, she would be allowed to do. She set off for the station. A burning sensation following by an intense itch began at her left elbow and ran like a current down her arm. Why here, why now? She dug her elbow into her side.

Herschel was untying the reins of his horse to the wooden post outside the police headquarters. Pearl wondered if he was coming or going. He looked up, his face showing pleasant surprise when he saw Pearl. "What brings you by here?"

Pearl hurried to meet him. "I've been to the jail to see Beatrice. She's in bad shape, Herschel. Her mind is just gone. I'll write a full report and deliver it to you. You can decide how best to present it to the judge."

He nodded. "I was just leaving. I'm needed down at Rigby's store. Some little mix-up on a few items taken by, shall we say pure accident? At least till we determine otherwise."

Pearl remained by his side. "There is one other thing, Herschel. I also saw Jim Harrison, Loomey's husband. He's quite ill with what appears to be a high fever. I found him slumped over in his cell. If you recall, you said you'd check into his case. I need you to do that…today."

Herschel, still holding the horses' reins, waited till she finished. "Why do you care so much about a common criminal? Jim's been trouble since the day he was born."

"Maybe so," said Pearl, "but he's a human being and he deserves better than what I saw today. Please…can you do something?"

"I'll stop by the jail on my way back from Rigby's place. Check on him myself."

220

"Thank you." She turned to leave.

"Pearl?" he said.

"Yes?"

"Will I see you for dinner tonight? Remember, we were going to the new place on South Main?"

"Of course I remember. But let's see how Jim is faring first."

Chapter Twenty-One

Despite Pearl's carefully written medical report on Beatrice, there was really little to say.

This female subject shows no obvious signs of physical distress or relapsing fever malady but exhibits a form of religious hysteria.

It is also possible she has suffered a brain stunning due to a fall or injury in the course of her recent attempt to evade capture.

Her symptoms include cold skin, weakened pulse and almost total insensibility. However, I did not detect change in pupils, inability to move or an unwillingness to speak.

Hysterics are often preceded by a great depression of spirits, shedding of tears and a palpitation of the heart. Some patients complain of a pain similar to having a nail driven into the head.

While this patient verbalizes no physical discomfort, there is evidence she suffers from various fits similar in design to falling sickness.

No clear history of cretinism or idiocy was established that could be congenital, though medical journals indicate both idiocy and inebriety are on the rise even among civilized people.

She knew her words sounded clinical, cold as she went on to describe Beatrice physically. That the patient was unwilling to allow Pearl full access to her for a physical exam only made Pearl feel sorry for her in her overall condition. In Pearl's concluding statement she wrote:

It is my belief as a practicing family physician that Beatrice Goode, said defendant in any and all upcoming judicial proceedings, is physically capable but mentally incapable of withstanding the harsh proceedings associated with a criminal trial. My recommendation is that Mrs. Goode be housed in the current detention facility until such time that she can be transferred to a state operated asylum for full examination of lunacy before she is subjected to court.

Even as she signed her name and dated the document, Pearl knew that despite her recommendation, it was unlikely Beatrice would be sent elsewhere for a second opinion. Walking alongside the officer who escorted her to the jail, she had gotten an earful of how he felt about anyone, male or female, who would shoot to kill an officer.

"And just about everybody else I know feels the same way," he said. "If she wasn't a woman, she would have never made it back here to Asheville for trial. I can tell you that for a fact."

With so many people calling for blood, it surprised Pearl that Herschel had even allowed her the opportunity to examine his prisoner. At least he was fair-minded.

Pearl sealed the envelope and placed it for pick-up at the door. A young messenger came by daily for pick-up and deliveries, in addition to the regular postal services available. As the day wore on Pearl wondered if Loomey was enjoying her day off and then remembered two more errands she had to complete. She had to find Loomey a tutor and go see Jeremiah.

The brass bell at the office door tinkled. An older woman dressed in business attire stood at the doorway, her hat slightly tilted, a parasol at her side and a folded newspaper in her hand.

Pearl stepped aside so she could enter. "Hello. Can I help you?"

"Are you by chance Dr. Stern, Pearl Stern?" she asked. "I'm Mrs. Harold Ludwick, an acquaintance of Jeremiah Dickson. He sent me to see you."

Pearl's eyes lit up. What a loyal friend Jeremiah was turning out to be. She could hardly wait to see him and thank him in person. "Yes!" she said. "Please have a seat."

The woman handed her the folded paper. "Have you seen our advertisement?" she said. "I'm president of the Asheville Ladies Moral League and we're sponsoring a female lecture at the Normal College for Women. You may find the presentation most interesting and very beneficial to your practice. You're the only physician we are inviting, by the way."

"Oh?" said Pearl, glancing at the letterhead and bordered notice. It claimed this particular lecture drew female crowds from around the country due to its unusual nature, with a guest speaker who had already sold more than ten thousand copies of her book *What Every Young Woman Should Know.*

"That's right," said Mrs. Ludwick. "We simply can't have men in the room. It would be utter madness."

"May I bring my female assistant?"

224

"Of course."

"Then we'll be there," said Pearl. "I look forward to it." She realized too late, after Mrs. Ludwick had left, that she should have informed her that Loomey was a Negro. Would she and Pearl be welcome there? If not, how (that) would that affect Loomey? The fledgling practice? How could she, Pearl, have made such an oversight?

She sat down and wrote a note to Mrs. Ludwick, telling her that she was bringing her Negro assistant along and that if Loomey was not welcome, Pearl would not attend. She would post it on the way to see Jeremiah.

By mid-afternoon, she was sitting with Jeremiah in his book-strewn study, chatting about the week's events, her assessment of Beatrice and the lecture invitation she had received that morning. "You're a wonderful friend. I've had two people come by on your referral alone, including your own niece. Thank you."

He nodded. "Most welcome, my dear. You deserve a good start here despite your tendency to go your own way."

"Speaking of which," said Pearl. "I have a favor. I'm looking for a tutor for Loomey. Do you have any suggestions? I'm not sure where to begin."

Jeremiah leaned back in his chair. He looked peaceful and relaxed today, the coughing at a minimum. "I wouldn't advise it," he said. "Leave it be, Pearl. Retain Loomey as your domestic, nothing more. It will give you a chance to build your practice without further controversy." He glanced over. "You're not listening to me, are you?"

"No," said Pearl. "I made a promise. If you can't or won't help me, I understand. But I will keep looking for someone to teach her the skills I know she can learn."

Jeremiah rose slowly and went to his desk. He opened a leather-bound book on his desk, found a scrap of white paper and wrote something down. Then he returned to his chair and handed the paper to Pearl. "Here. Go by and see him. He's a pastor in the colored church off Eagle. A refined, well-educated man who came south after the war. I've done business with him and found him trustworthy. He might teach your Loomey."

Pearl stayed a while longer, encouraged by Jeremiah's condition. "You seem well compared to our last encounter," she said. "I hope that continues. Take good care, my friend. We'll talk soon." As she was leaving, she bent over and lightly kissed the top of his white head.

"My, my!" Jeremiah said. "You are balm to an old man's mortal wounds."

By six p.m. Pearl had received a message from Herschel asking again if he could call on her within the hour. She smiled at the young boy who delivered the envelope and gave him two copper pennies for his trouble.

"Run over and tell him the lady says yes and that I'll be ready by seven. She hoped he would have news of Jim.

When Hershel arrived, right on time, that was her first question to him.

"I spoke to the Sheriff and we agreed to release him until the next judge gets to town. Loomey came and picked him up. I'm sure she'll tend to him."

Pearl breathed a sigh of relief. "I'm so thankful to you. Yes, Loomey will be an excellent nurse. I expect to see her tomorrow and I'll know how he's doing then."

The sun lowered it rays over the horizon as they walked toward the South Main Café, an intimate diner complete with white linen cloths and colorful fragrant red roses set on each

226

table.

"It's lovely!" Pearl said, impressed by its ambiance. They were one of only two couples in the place. For the first time, no one among the dining staff seemed to know Herschel by name.

"I heard their specialty is fresh mountain trout," Herschel said as he pulled her chair forward. They settled in for drinks, a white wine for Pearl, a shot of distilled Kentucky whiskey for Herschel. They ordered the fish, broiled in butter and garnished with a white sauce tinged with red wine alongside a cluster of fat green beans.

As they began to eat Herschel told her he had received her report. "Sounds like you had an interesting encounter with Beatrice today." He pulled the skin from the trout and separated the meat without breaking its delicate spine. "I can fillet yours too."

Pearl nodded and pushed her plate forward. "Thanks. You know, Herschel, I realize emotions are high over the shooting but this woman has no clear head about her at all. Do you foresee that my report will make any difference?"

"Not likely," he said. "I also got word today that Judge Watson, circuit rider for the Western district, is coming in for the trial. He's a former lawman himself and a judge who likes the noose. It doesn't look good for her. He'll want to send a message that he doesn't tolerate violence on the streets from man, woman or beast. And if she is hung, well, that's a big draw for the town. People will come from all over just to say they were here."

Pearl shuddered. "It'll be a spectacle. I detest public hangings. How long do you anticipate the trial to take?" She pushed back her plate, her appetite waning. Just thinking of a public hanging made her nauseated.

"I've seen it take weeks. I've seen it happen in an afternoon. No way to know. Now, take your fork and scoop up a bite of that brook trout. What do you think?"

Pearl reluctantly picked up the utensil.

"I'm not really hungry now," she said. "The talk about hanging...it's repulsive. Can we change the subject?"

"Of course," said Herschel. "I'm sorry. Tell me your own news." She shared her day with him, including the invitation to the women's lecture, her visit with Jeremiah and her need to find a good tutor for Loomey.

"I think that's a fine idea," he said of her plan to better educate her assistant. "Even the mayor would think so. He's a supporter of the Freedman like me. They called us Lincoln Republicans after the war. Not the most popular stance in a Democratic town."

"It's unfortunate, but not everyone feels the same," said Pearl, sipping her white wine. "Jeremiah has cautioned me on more than one occasion that I could lose good referrals to the practice. Do you think he's right?"

Herschel polished off the whiskey shot and set the glass near his plate. He held onto it, twirling its crystal base while he looked over at Pearl. "I think you'll find there are people in Asheville who believe you're progressive and brave. And some who will think you're an outsider here to stir up trouble so the coloreds can gain an upper hand."

"Into which group do you fall?" Pearl asked, watching his expression.

He met her gaze. "You know the answer to that." He raised his glass. "Here's to progressive brave young women. May they outlive all those who oppose them!"

228

Pearl threw back her head and laughed. Herschel stared.

"What?"

"It's good to see you laugh," he said, "You're somber by nature. You have a beautiful smile, even when you're flustered. You should use it more often."

Pearl blushed. It was the first time in a long while that she found herself embarrassed by a compliment, and the first time in a long while since she had been with someone who took notice.

Chapter Twenty-Two

The trial of Beatrice Goode was already under way on the day that Pearl and Loomey were scheduled to attend the female lecture at the Normal College for Women. To Pearl, it was a nice diversion from the sordid events leading up to the trial, a way for Pearl to be introduced to other women in the community, and perhaps an educational experience for Loomey.

With Jim out of jail and on a full road to recovery, Loomey was even happier than her normal bubbly self. Her face lit up when Pearl told her she had an outing planned.

Once a private home, the three-story Colonial-style house now served the needs of the community for readings and public presentations along with regular classroom sessions.

As she and Loomey entered, Pearl was handed an embossed invitation written in an elegant cursive. Loomey reached out for her cream-colored card. Pearl had heard no reply from her message to Mrs. Ludwick and took her silence to mean that bringing Loomey along would be acceptable.

"I'm sorry, Miss, you can't be here," said a tall woman with sharp features and wire frame glasses. Loomey's hand dropped to her side.

"Why not?" Pearl asked. "She's with me."

The woman nodded toward a corner of the entry hall. "May we speak in private?"

"No, we may not," Pearl said, her voice a notch higher than normal. "I'm Dr. Stern and this is my assistant. We were formally invited by Mrs. Ludwick. I'm sure she will confirm that if she's here." Had Mrs. Ludwick not received Pearl's message?

The woman drew back. "She's quite busy at the moment with our guest speaker. But you do understand we don't open our doors to coloreds."

Pearl took Loomey's arm and moved forward. "If you'll take note, you don't have to open the door. We're already through it. Now if you'll excuse us, we don't want to be late for the lecture."

There were gasps and murmurs as Pearl and Loomey entered the main room. "Ignore them," she said to Loomey. They took a seat together in the far corner. "We'll soon be old news." One woman got up and pointedly moved further from them. Another raised a finger in their direction and whispered something to her companion.

This must be what it feels like to have a highly contagious disease, Pearl thought. She turned to look at Loomey who was staring at the ornate ceiling with its inlaid copper, intricate crown molding, arched-shaped windows and thick russet-colored curtains.

"I've never seen such a fine place," Loomey said softly.

"It is beautiful," Pearl agreed. "I understand it was the home of a man who made his living designing other homes, an architect."

231

"But how would I clean the windows?" Loomey said. "I'd have to shoot right up to the sky."

A woman who chose to sit in front of them turned, gave Loomey a harsh look and Pearl a disapproving one before her attention was captured by a voice at the podium.

"Welcome ladies!" said Mrs. Harold Ludwick. "We're honored to have with us one of the foremost authorities on women and their health. She has come to Asheville to speak to us on subjects most consider too delicate to discuss through public discourse, even among ourselves. But today, our speaker has promised to open wide the confines of our minds. A word of caution. You'll hear things that are shocking by societal standards. If anyone needs to leave the room, please do so quietly. There are fans available in the foyer and a water stand. Now let's graciously welcome Mrs. Mary Allen Woodstein."

"What an elegant figure she has," a woman commented as Woodstein crossed the stage to loud applause. Pearl had heard of the speaker and was intrigued by her willingness to educate girls and woman on topics ranging from the importance of exercise to what was commonly referred to as 'special physiology'. Pearl took that to mean, among other things, sex education.

Pearl leaned toward Loomey. "This should be interesting," she whispered.

"Thank you, Miss Pearl," Loomey said.

"For what?"

"For lettin' me come here."

A guest in the next row twisted in her seat and raised a white-kid gloved hand to her lips. "Shhh!" she said, her pink-flowered bonnet flapping.

The lecture began with the speaker explaining she was a

disciple of Dr. J.H. Kellogg, of Battle Creek, Michigan. Though she had yet to meet him, she added, she agreed with many of his controversial conclusions.

"One of the most frequent afflictions we see among young women today are fits," she said, "those nervous spells that cause headaches, fainting and other female diseases. Well, I contend they come from poor diet, lack of sleep and incorrect breathing. If the body's blood is not thoroughly purified, actual poisons are created and can accumulate in the brain and tissues until one feels overpoweringly weary and stupid."

"I have that ailment all the time," Loomey said, smiling.

"Respiratory gymnastics are the only effective remedy for nervous asthma or pulmonary affliction. If you can't fully breathe, you can't think. So our first order of business is to sit up straight, ladies and breathe in, breathe out."

Woodstein extended her arms, inhaling and exhaling to demonstrate. A rustle of silk skirts; the scraping of leathered boots were heard as the group rearranged themselves to follow her lead. Pearl remained still, Loomey following suit.

"Now we'll speak of bathing," said Woodstein. "A truly delicate woman knows that powder doesn't cover defects in cleanliness. I don't advise daily baths but different parts of the body can be bathed over the space of a week. When to bathe depends upon the amount of blood in the brain. A woman with an anemic brain will not benefit from bedtime baths, while one that is over-charged with blood will find an evening bath quieting."

Pearl winced. There was no scientific evidence to support that.

The speaker took a sip of water from a tall crystal glass thoughtfully supplied at the podium and turned the page on her notes. "But we are here as special creatures," she continued. "And so we shall discuss special physiology – what it is that makes us women. Do we really know?"

Pearl patted Loomey's fingertips. It might be hard to explain the meaning of a rhetorical question to Loomey whose forthright nature was one of her strong suits. But she could tell Loomey was listening.

"Our sex manifests itself throughout our entire organization," Woodstein said. "I'm of course speaking of a young girls' development when she reaches the age that brings on her courses, or in medical terms, menstruation. There are many cautionary tales on this subject. You can read my book in its entirety to gain more knowledge of how you, as mothers, can explain this natural process. And these young daughters must be told."

"I've known girls," she continued, "unaware of what was happening to them, remove and wash their entire clothing in cold water. When they redressed themselves wet, they not only took cold but shocked their menstrual flow. As a consequence they were injured for life, or may have died years later as a result of this conduct."

Pearl took wry note. She was sure they died of something years later, but doubted it was from wearing wet clothes. Woodstein was now telling the audience how to guard against painful menstruation for themselves and their daughters.

"There should be no severe pain involved," she said. Pearl inwardly agreed.

"Guard from taking cold, over-exertion, social dissipation, habitual neglect of the bowels and morbid mental excitement," she said. "There is great evil for young girls in reading romance novels. It excites bodily organs and creates premature devel-

234

opment. There was a girl of eleven who was an omnivorous reader of romances. This hastened her approaching womanhood. At my advice, she gave up romance reading and devoted herself to outdoor sports and nature studies. Her health improved, her nervousness disappeared and three years later her menstruation was painlessly established."

The crowd of women broke into applause and murmurs.

Pearl cast a sideways glance at Loomey, whose bewilderment was obvious in her furrowed brow. Pearl leaned in toward her. "We'll talk about this later."

Woodstein went on to explain that due to restrictive clothing, corsets and overly tight waistbands, displacement of the uterus and other organs could result. Finally, she gave instruction on efficient, economical ways to produce sanitary bandages, the bane of the modern woman.

Here was something she might actually be able to use, Pearl thought, retrieving a note pad from her satchel.

"Cheesecloth is cheap and absorbent," Woodstein said. "Fasten two strips that go over the shoulders and joined together in front and back to an end piece on which a button is sewn. Place buttonholes on each diagonal corner which makes the bandage easy to attach and remove. You can also add an outer strip of muslin. It's practically waterproof." All of this was in her book, she added.

"I'd like to conclude this section by saying that it is a scientific fact that continuous thinking of an organ tends to disturb that organ. So ladies, don't over indulge in fretting about your monthly course." Woodstein then motioned toward Mrs. Ludwick sitting behind her on the stage, who nodded. She turned back to the crowd.

"I've now been given allowance to move into our next

topic which, my dear ladies, may create a great stir within the room," Woodstein said. "What I'm about to speak of is considered the most disastrous vice that any one individual can employ. It destroys mental power and memory, blotches the complexion, dulls the eyes, takes your strength away, causes clammy hands, backaches, irritability and may even cause insanity."

The crowd gasped. Total silence ensued.

"It's a habit most difficult to overcome, engaged in by some women and girls who are unaware of its dangers. And it may not only last for years, its tendency may actually be transmitted to your children! The debasing habit I am speaking of, ladies, is…self-abuse of the sexual organs."

Shrill voices rose throughout the crowd. A woman stood up and raised her arm toward Woodstein. "I'm a god-fearing Christian," she said in a loud voice. "And it is evil to speak of these things before others. I never…"

Mrs. Ludwick rushed to the podium. "Now ladies, please calm down. If you recall, we cautioned you of the subject matter beforehand. Fortunately, this is an excellent time for a break in our presentation. There are tea cakes and punch in the foyer. We'll reconvene in fifteen minutes."

Several women grabbed their purses and shawls, still muttering angrily as they fled the room. Pearl, watching the scene in quiet amusement, took a moment to look over at Loomey who remained quiet. To Pearl she appeared almost bored. "Are you all right Loomey?" Pearl said. "There'll be more talk like this."

"Like what?"

"About sex and other delicate matters."

"It's not natural," Loomey said.

"What's not natural?" Pearl said, wondering if bringing Loomey here might have been poor judgment on her part all around.

"All this fuss and muss," Loomey said, pointing around the room, "this hollerin' and carryin' on over something as simple as people just bein' people."

"I couldn't agree more," Pearl said. "Would you like a drink or something to eat? I think I'll get some punch."

"No thank you, Miss Pearl. I just want to sit here and look at this fine room."

Pearl stood sipping her drink in the nearly empty foyer when Mrs. Ludwick approached her. It was almost time for the lecture to begin again. "Doctor Stern, may I speak with you for a moment?"

Pearl set her cup down. "Of course. And may I say what an enlightened program you've put together here today."

Ludwick cleared her throat. "Well…um…thank you. But there's another matter that's been brought to my attention."

"Yes?"

"Your assistant, she's colored, which frankly is highly unusual. But it's common policy that we don't allow her kind in our building. I'll forgive your transgression this once since you are new to the region. We must, however, ask her to leave."

Pearl stared at the woman. "Mrs. Ludwick, be aware you're speaking of my medical assistant, a person with more skills, and I dare say, more common sense than most people of my acquaintance. I sent you a note explaining that Loomey was a Negro and would be attending this event. Did you not receive it?"

Ludwick's eyes widened. She placed a hand over her

heart. "Why, no I didn't! My goodness; such misplaced loyalty. It's just that our policy is well stated."

"Yes, you've made your policy very clear," Pearl said. "But if you'll look around, you may realize you have more important things to fret about at the moment."

"Whatever do you mean?"

As Pearl motioned toward the open lecture room, Mrs. Ludwick suddenly realized there were more than two dozen empty chairs.

"It appears you've lost a good bit of your audience. If my assistant must leave then I will have to do the same." She turned to go get Loomey.

"All right," Mrs. Ludwick said. "She may stay. But I'll probably never hear the end of this!"

Pearl returned to her seat where she wondered if she had made a critical error in judgment by bringing Loomey here.

The remainder of the lecture series covered topics from whether a true friendship could exist between the sexes – "They are rare due to indulgence in personal familiarities," Woodstein contended – or if love at first sight was real.

"No," Woodstein insisted, "it doesn't exist. There must be a structure built upon a firm foundation of acquaintance with each other's true qualities. Silly girls and impulsive boys imagine only the sweet pain that accompanies the touch of hands or glance of eyes as love. They think it's a sufficient guarantee in forming a life partnership. Thus, they have no way to see personal peculiarities of temper, habits and manners that if seen in time – would prevent many bad marriages."

She spoke of other vices that could easily ruin a marriage and a person's health: the scourge of syphilis "the penalty inflicted for the violation of moral law," and other diseases that followed "an impure life and can lead to nervous bankruptcy."

A round of applause followed, including Pearl who found that she was in full agreement on at least one particular topic. Her thoughts turned to Herschel. Was she seeing him in a true light or was she no different than the silly girls and impulsive boys Woodstein railed about?

She was hoping there would be more medical material covered in the lecture; perhaps new treatments, like a little known cure for stubborn conditions like whopping cough, smallpox, even her psoriasis. Why had she dragged Loomey along on what was proving an intriguing but not necessarily helpful series of talks?

"Loomey," Pearl asked. "Do you think coming here was a good idea?"

Loomey turned her face toward Pearl, her eyes luminous. "I think it's the best present you could ever have given me, Miss Pearl. You brought me with you like I was just as good as you, just as good as any of these fine ladies. I won't never, ever, forget that."

Pearl squeezed Loomey's hand.

At the lecture's end, Woodstein stepped from the podium and positioned herself at a table to sign copies of her book. Pearl and Loomey left their seats and approached as the other women in the audience were still gathering their hats, parasols and other belongings.

"Mrs. Woodstein, I'm Dr. Pearl Stern and this is my assistant," Pearl said. "I wanted to say that while I don't agree with everything you said today, I do admire your willingness to broach such delicate topics. It's important to allow women of all ages to make educated decisions, particularly on matters of their own sex."

Woodstein extended her hand to Pearl but failed to acknowledge Loomey. "That's kind of you, Dr. Stern. And may I say I admire your willingness to, shall we say, reverse tradition by making your own unpopular decisions." She nodded toward Loomey. "You and your assistant are also among the rather interesting topics today," she smiled. "At least that's what I've heard."

Give the woman credit for honesty, Pearl thought, despite her lack of diplomacy. "We'll be on our way. I hope you sell a large number of books to your audience."

However, she nearly added, neither she nor Loomey would be among the buyers.

Chapter Twenty-Three

The criminal trial of Beatrice Goode took three days. At its conclusion, all of Herschel's predictions had come to pass. Judge Watson, a portly former sheriff in Jackson County and prosecutor, arbitrarily dismissed Pearl's findings as "poppycock," and ruled the woman fit to stand trial.

"It's my courtroom and I'll do as I damn well please," he was quoted as saying. A jury of twelve found her guilty on all charges including the attempted murder 'of the brave, upstanding lawman, Officer Donnie Callahan'.

Pearl, never called to testify, attended the sentencing, but sat quietly in the back row. When the judge announced "hung until she is dead," Pearl twisted the lace kerchief in her lap, her heart dropping. There was so little her profession knew about "imbeciles" and "mental defects" in society. But this seemed wrong in so many ways. She left without speaking to anyone, even Herschel, who came and went as his duties allowed.

The public hanging was set for half past noon on the Square. The morning it was scheduled, Pearl read of the event in the *Asheville News* over coffee in her office with Loomey sweeping the floor. There would certainly be no drop-in patients today. They would all be gathered at the Public Square.

"It says here a large crowd is expected," she read to Loomey, "including women and children. Mayor Lusk is scheduled to attend and farmers are expected to bring their families and friends, along with their picnic baskets, by wagon up to twenty-five miles away, Workers will take the day off to see the trap fall. I can't believe it!" Pearl put the paper down and shook her head.

Loomey stopped the broom in mid-stride. "My mama says the Lord giveth and the Lord taketh away, so I reckon that's what people come to see – the taketh away."

"Well, I guess that's one way to look at it. But to have children watching such a horrid spectacle. Have you ever seen anyone hanged, Loomey?"

"No," said Loomey, "and hope I never do."

"Believe me, it's a gruesome sight," said Pearl. She shuddered inwardly.

"You seen it up close?" Loomey asked.

"When I was about fourteen, I witnessed the public hanging of three men in Missouri. The noose slipped as one of them dropped and it took a while before he expired. I'll never forget that."

"I got a cousin down on Eagle that works with a noose man makin' sure all those ropes are done right," Loomey said. "First they have to find out how much the person weighs in his sock feet so they know where to put the noose. If it ain't done proper, it won't take hold good. Makes for a bad day all around."

Someone tapped at the office door. Loomey answered with broom in hand. A young freckle-faced boy thrust a note toward her. "A message for Doc Stern," he said. Loomey took

242

the envelope and pushed the door closed.

"Wait!" Pearl called. She crossed the room, opened her purse and handed the boy his tip.

"Thank you Miss Doc," he said, running down the steps. "Gotta go so I don't be late for the hangin'!"

The note was written on letterhead from the Asheville City Police Station House. Pearl scanned the page and noted Herschel's heavy angular signature with an oversized "H" in which he had simply signed "Hersch." Her heart thumped. She had not seen him for more than a few moments since the trial began a few days earlier.

"Loomey, when you're finished cleaning, you can leave. I'm going up to the station to see the Chief." She fiddled with the small glass buttons on her jacket. "Don't forget to lock the door behind you. I'll see you tomorrow."

Loomey nodded. "You look nice, Miss Pearl. Too bad it's a rope party you're off to." She clucked her tongue.

At the Station House, Pearl found Herschel in the lobby addressing a group of twenty or more blue-clad officers. "All right, you boys know what a crowd we're likely to have today. And some will be more agitated than usual, considering the crime. Your job is to keep the unruly ones away from the gallows. They'll want to get a close-up look."

"Sir, by what means can we keep them at bay?" one officer asked.

"You have batons," said Herschel. "But use them only as a last measure. Your best weapon is your common sense. Many of you will know some of these people. They might even be your friends or relatives."

"Common sense don't work on my relatives," another officer said, causing the others, including Herschel, to laugh, easing the tension.

"You're dismissed," the Chief said. "I'll be with the Sheriff at the gallows shortly. Any questions beforehand, you know where to find me." The officers left through the station door still murmuring among themselves.

Pearl stood waiting.

"I got your message," she said. The badge on his uniform caught a streak of sudden yellow from the sun-lit window, reminding her of gold dust. To Pearl, Herschel in a uniform seemed a natural fit. Caine, on the other hand…when was the last time she had thought of him? It seemed a long time ago. She could never imagine him in this type of setting.

Herschel offered her a hard wooden chair that looked rickety at worst, uncomfortable at best. As she sat, the chair squeaked in protest and tilted slightly forward. Bracing for an awkward fall, she shifted to its edge, pulled the note from her purse and resumed her composure. "I came as soon as this arrived. It must be important as you sent it by messenger."

Herschel raised his brows. "So you were hoping I'd come in person?" he said, smiling.

The corners of her mouth turned up. "Everyone's a little frantic today, it seems, what with the event and all," she said, "as I'm certain you are. What's this about, Herschel?"

"As I mentioned at dinner the other night, Dr. Stokes will officially declare the prisoner dead once the deed is done," he said. "He asked me to send for you. I think he knows we have a sort of… friendship."

It was the first time she had heard Herschel reference their relationship. Of course it was just friendship. What else could it be? She felt a strange sort of let-down. "I don't know why he needs me, except to provide a second opinion."

244

"Precisely," Herschel said. "But no need to argue with him about it. You'll be paid for your time and that's something you can count on. This being a woman and all, he probably wants to cover himself too, in case there's any question of propriety later. She's the first female hanging ever seen in this part of the state. So I can guarantee it'll be a circus. You have a level head. I've witnessed that."

Pearl hesitated. "I don't know, Herschel. I believe in justice but I don't understand why this can't be done behind closed doors." She knew she sounded sanctimonious. Public hangings occurred all over the country and were considered an event open to all as a matter of lessons learned. Yet she felt queasy every time she read or heard about one in which wide-eyed children watched and grinning adults pretended it was just another social outing.

Herschel sat back and rested his elbow on the chair. "You might be surprised to know I agree with you. I don't like the spectacle of it either. But it's here and it'll happen today with or without us. Will you be there for the coroner…and for me?"

Pearl's pulse quickened. It almost sounded as though he would feel better about his own attendance if she was there, nearby.

"All right," she said, finally. But there was no peace at what she had just agreed to do. "But may I speak with her first? That seems the only decent thing to do."

~

At the jail yard, hundreds of people had shown up by mid-morning, some standing on flat, table-sized rocks, others perched on the weed-strewn knoll overlooking the wooden shed that housed the gallows. A few of the women were offering up prayers while the men expressed their disgust over the heinous crime. That a woman could bring a police officer down in such an inglorious way added salt to the nearly mortal wounds the officer had suffered. The pungent smell of tobacco hung in the air coupled with the light sweet tang of the ladies' colognes. A blue sky streaked above.

An elderly man hobbled about on crutches looking for a level place to stand. Two small boys dressed in tattered pants, one colored and one white, zigzagged through the crowd, tossing a ball back and forth. They almost toppled a shawl-draped woman, causing her spectacles to hit the ground. "Watch it you little ruffians or I'll have your hides!" she scolded. They laughed and ran off.

Beatrice appeared at the window of the jail just before eleven a.m. She waved her Bible toward the waiting crowd; her voice rang clear.

"You want to hear from me?" she yelled through the jail bars. "Now you shall. Everyone that wants to hear me speak, pay attention. I know I face my last congregation on earth. Today at noon I face another one. I'm thankful I've done somethin' to die for!"

Loud mutterings rose from the crowd of men. The women gasped.

"God made death for a reason," she continued. "I say to you now, you will make a mistake if you don't prepare for your own day 'cause it comes when you know not. I know my day of death so I'm blessed! I hope this will be a great lesson to each of you. Meet me on Jordan's other shore."

There was a chorus of boos. "If we do, we'll hang you there again!" someone said.

"And now," Beatrice said, "my one last request. I want ever-body to help me sing 'Pass Me Not, O Gentle Savior.'"

"Ain't nobody here that can sing," countered a man below the window.

She put her face between the bars and began the hymn off-key.

Pearl entered the cell just as Beatrice was closing her song. The woman turned and gave her a vacant stare. "Hello, Beatrice," Pearl said. "I was here about a week ago. Do you remember talking to me?"

"No," said Beatrice. "I only been talkin' to the Lord. And he has heard my prayers. Today, I'm goin' home."

Pearl stepped toward her. "I just came to say goodbye and to see if there's anything you want or need."

Beatrice met Pearl's eyes and to Pearl, for one brief moment, she appeared almost lucid. "That Sheriff," she said. "Watch over him. He came by this mornin' and was all a-skitter when he read me the final say-so. I'm worried over him."

"I'll do that," Pearl promised.

"I have one more thing to ask of you," Beatrice said. She was staring hard at Pearl.

"Yes?"

"Would you accompany me up the gallows steps? Would you go with me right up to the door that takes me yonder?" She pointed upwards.

Pearl's stomach knotted. She wasn't sure what to say, so she said nothing.

"You are my only friend in all the world," Beatrice added.

An officer appeared at the cell door. "It's time," he said.

Beatrice was led from the cell, escorted by two officers to waiting officials across the jail yard. Pearl followed a discreet distance behind them, her heart racing. Beatrice shuffled rather than walked, her hands tied in front of her plain brown dress, no bonnet, her eyes cast downward. She mumbled to herself as the small group moved along.

Pearl noted the beaming sun and crisp blue sky. For any other reason than what was about to happen, this would have been a lovely day for an outdoor event. Nor was the irony lost on her that Beatrice was about to be hung for shooting but not killing an officer, while she, Pearl, was free in spite of her culpability in the death of a mother and child. What would her Calvinist mother say of God's will in this? Would He welcome Beatrice, his troubled child, home?

Was Beatrice really her patient or just some poor soul that Pearl had been forced to meet? Where did her obligation begin and end?

As they passed a contingent of young men and women, an argument broke out. "It's not right to hang a woman!" … "It's not right to try and kill a good man! She's worse than the Devil himself!"

The yard, surrounded on the north and west by a grassy embankment, was encircled with a fifteen-strand barbed wire fence a foot taller than Pearl as she passed. Ahead, Herschel was already at the gallows with the Mayor. Both stood erect, their hands clasped before them as though at a church prayer meeting. To Pearl, each appeared as though they would rather be anywhere else than here. She felt exactly the same.

The officers had formed a line to keep the overly zealous at bay. Many had their batons in hand. Only one side of the gallows shed was open to viewing. The crowd pushed forward and a man yelled out "I can't see anything! Move! Get out of the way!"

248

All around her people were jostling for a better view. She spotted Bailey Stokes in a small group near the gallows platform and went to stand beside him while Beatrice was told to wait until the stroke of noon. Pearl had yet to make up her mind about the woman's last, pitiful request.

Stokes nodded as she approached. "Are you as reluctant to be here as I am?" she said.

The coroner shrugged. "My clientele tend to be of the quiet persuasion," he said. "So I am unaccustomed to unruly crowds. But my place is here today. Don't have to like it. Thank you for coming to assist, by the way."

"Just what is it I am expected to do?" Pearl asked.

"Witness my pronouncement and then make your own," said Stokes. "It's an unusual circumstance, her being a female prisoner. First one of its kind, not just here but in the state. Thought it best to have a second doctor pronounce in this particular case. Besides, you've talked to her, right? I thought you might have a personal interest."

"Yes, I've spoken with her," said Pearl. For all the good it did, she thought. "How did you know?"

"Herschel told me," he said. "Said you wrote up a thorough report, and he tried his best to get the court to accept your findings. Got nowhere with the judge. With Callahan on the witness stand, still not able to return to his duties, that was the death knell."

Pearl scanned the crowd. "Where's Callahan?" She had made three home visits as a follow-up to his progress and found him healing properly each time, but had had no contact since then. Nor any payment for any of her services. Across the jail yard, she spotted a tall, thin man with a woman beside him and a small child, dressed in a bonnet matching her mother's. It was little Pansy Callahan. The couple was holding hands, the child pressed up against them.

Then it was time. Pearl could no longer waver. At exactly the stroke of noon, Beatrice Goode was led up the gallows steps, an officer on each side of her. Her hands were tied behind her back. She was placed in position. Pearl rushed forward.

"Wait!" she called. The crowd gasped. Pearl ran toward the gallows and bounded up the steps.

"What the...?" the Sheriff began.

Pearl, out of breath and well aware a good portion of the townspeople were watching her, spoke loud and clear. The crowd grew still.

"I'm with you, Beatrice. I'm here."

Beatrice smiled as the black crepe hood was placed over her head. All catcalls and jeering ceased with the final moment near. Pearl looked away. She could not bear to watch it.

This is wrong, she thought. It's just plain wrong.

When the rope snapped, Pearl felt a surge of nausea. The body, still twitching, swayed back and forth just below the opening in the gallows. As Pearl turned to leave, descending the wooden steps, a small group of officers, led by Herschel, broke into applause. At first Pearl thought they were clapping for the done deed. But as Pearl passed, Herschel spoke up loud enough for his men to hear, "Damn fine display of gumption. Now that's a woman to respect." He was looking straight at Pearl.

Half an hour later, standing beside Stokes in a room set aside at the jail for Beatrice's body, Pearl helped pronounce the woman dead. While Stokes' official pronouncement was swift and cursory, Pearl took an extra few moments to straighten the woman's dress, place her hands across her chest and reach up to gently close her eyes.

"Godspeed, Beatrice," she whispered. "I hope you're home now and finally, finally at peace."

She passed Herschel in the hall as she and Stokes were leaving. Immersed in conversation with a group of men from the gallows, he looked up and nodded toward her as she went by. She was wondering if she would see him again soon when the same young messenger who had been at her door that morning ran up to Herschel and handed him a note.

He read it and called out. "Pearl wait up!" He came toward her. "This is meant for both of us," he said, extending the note. "It's Jeremiah. He's taken a turn for the worse and is asking for the two of us. It may be his time."

Chapter Twenty-Four

Fall had arrived late in the mountains. From her up-stairs window, Pearl could see in the distance what the local paper poetically described as "painted ladies in repose." It was true. The far-flung mountains in November resembled the gentle curves of women resting on their backs. Dressed in earth-tones of russet reds and green-tinged orange, they lay head to head, stark and proud in their finery while above them, wispy clouds appeared as though penciled in.

No wonder people loved these hills. These past two weeks had been a time of deep reflection on many counts. First the hanging, still a source of deep conflict for Pearl, fol-lowed by a summons to Jeremiah's death bed. She and Her-schel had left the group and hurried to his residence where the domestic he hired to clean and cook answered their knock on the door.

"He's in poor shape," she had said. "So when he asked me to send for you, I thought it best to get you right away. I figured everybody was at the hanging."

Jeremiah lay under the covers on his bed in what ap-peared to be a deep sleep. But as Herschel and Pearl approached, he opened his eyes and spoke. "Come close, my friends. What a comfort to see you."

They spent the remainder of the day at his side, Pearl watching his vitals and offering to bring him water whenever his cough turned violent; Herschel talked to him of their early friendship, how they had met, his first impression of the older man and the impact Jeremiah had on Herschel through the years.

"It was because of you, you old cuss, that I decided to go into law enforcement."

Jeremiah smiled faintly. "You thought people like me should be behind bars?" He began to cough.

"Now settle back," Herschel soothed. "No I thought people like you deserved a safe and happy life."

Jeremiah moved his hand and patted Herschel's resting paw. "And I have done so," he said. "Now it's your turn." He turned his head toward the corner of the room where Pearl was measuring his next dose of laudanum. "Don't let that little lady get away from you."

Pearl nearly dropped the bottle. What was Jeremiah saying? She avoided Herschel's expression out of fear of what she might see.

As daylight crept away and darkness settled on the horizon, Jeremiah reached out for Pearl. He took a deep breath. "I have something to tell you," he said. "I want you to know that I was wrong."

Pearl shook her head, not sure what he meant. "Don't talk. You have no reason to apologize to me."

"Listen," he said. "Just listen. I was wrong to tell you that you should be careful with your patients and that not doing so might hurt you. You do what you think is right. That

253

tends to work best, even for an old goat like me." He stopped and closed his eyes. Pearl thought he was gone. But he took another breath and said, "You know, it's funny how things look so different when you're on your way out as opposed to on your way in...wish I'd known..."

Now, a fortnight later, Pearl was still feeling the effects of the loss. Jeremiah had been her first true friend in Asheville. She felt honored that of all the people who knew the elder gentleman, it was she and Herschel who were asked to come to his bedside. In some respects, it was as though he also knew his death could bring the two of them together. And it had. They had seen each other nearly every day since then, planning Jeremiah's funeral, exchanging stories of their mutual friend as they sat by the hearth in Pearl's apartment, often talking late into the night.

"I'll miss him for a very long time," Pearl said. "He was a wonderful, intelligent man."

Herschel nodded. "He was capital, and few will measure up against him." He had stretched his long legs toward the fireplace and leaned back to light his pipe, a one-time gift from Jeremiah.

Pearl watched him in the firelight and noted "You're smoking fewer cigars and more on your pipe."

Herschel smiled. "Is that against your medical policies? You do know smoking cures many ailments, don't you, including nervous prostration?"

"Not proven," said Pearl. "Perhaps someday it will be."

They sat in companionable silence until the clock struck again, talking of Loomey's new tutor, another, long-lasting gift from Jeremiah. It was his referral that had led Pearl to the colored pastor who agreed to see Loomey twice a week. Twilight

254

came and went.

"How's Loomey coming along?" Herschel said.

"She's learning to tell time. Of course, I get reminded of the clock about every half hour. But she works hard and her tutor is a man of great patience."

Herschel chuckled. "I imagine he would need to be." He lifted his boots from the hearth and stood up. "Will you be all right? If not, I can stay a bit longer."

"I'll be fine," Pearl said. She reached down to retrieve a splinter of wood that had escaped from the kindling box. As she straightened, she could almost feel his breath on her neck. He was that close behind her.

"Have you ever been kissed in the firelight?" he whispered into her neck.

Pearl, her mind racing, turned to face him. "Not in a long, long time," she said. The blood rushed to her head, mortified that she had admitted such a thing.

"We can change that right here, right now," he said, taking her in his arms. He kissed her slow and tender. "I didn't plan that," he said, releasing her. "I swear to it. Do you want me to go?"

"No," said Pearl. Her head was still swimming. It wasn't that she had never imagined kissing Herschel. Her attraction toward him was real and strong. She just wasn't sure of its outcome, on what uncharted path it would take her. "But I can't let you stay, either," she said. "Do you understand?"

"Yes," he said. "No. Not really. But I'll do as you ask." He gave her another quick kiss on the lips, retrieved his coat and left.

Next morning, Pearl was just getting up when she heard

Loomey in the stairwell. Once she entered the apartment, Pearl knew exactly what was coming next.

"It's SEVEN a.m. in the daytime morning Miss Pearl," Loomey said. "It's past time for you to rise up and shine." She could hear her cross the room and whip open the curtains, allowing a painful brightness to enter.

"We have a patient coming in I think right at the stroke of EIGHT a.m. at least that's what I told her. Be here EIGHT o'clock, I told her."

Pearl came into the parlor. "I don't recall making any such appointments. What are you talking about? And please shut that curtain. The light is giving me a massive headache."

"She's been to Doc Hanson and told my mama she don't think he's helpin'," Loomey said. "Mama told her about you when we were at the market and I told her to be here at EIGHT O'CLOCK a.m. in the mornin' time." Loomey jerked at the offending drapes.

Pearl put hands to her hips. She had yet to have her first cup of coffee and was not in the best of moods. "Loomey, are you telling me you made a patient appointment on my behalf without my permission?"

"I'm your assistant, aren't I?" she said. She went to the stove and poured two cups of coffee, handing Pearl one. "I was just tryin' to help, Miss Pearl. It's not like we got a whole slew of patients comin' through the doorway."

Pearl softened her tone. "I know. But assistants follow direction. You must follow my direction. Understood?" She knew she was being unreasonable in light of the fact that so few patients were under her care. In fact, finances were so dire that she was living off the remnants of her savings in order to pay her rent.

Loomey nodded. "But you aren't gonna send her away, are you, Miss Pearl? She's real worried about her little one."

Pearl set her cup down. "A child? Why didn't you say so? Of course we won't turn her away." Not that she had any intention of doing so anyway. If someone came to her door she had an ethical responsibility to treat them. She glanced at the clock. The woman would be here in twenty minutes. She should dress and get downstairs.

A little after eight, a woman rang the bell at the entry to Pearl's office. She was medium height and thin, her young face drawn and pale. Wrapped in a thick soiled quilt was a child of about two. Pearl hurried the mother in so she could lay the bundle down.

"Are you the new lady doctor?" the woman asked.

Pearl nodded. "Yes, I'm Dr. Stern. Here, let's get your little one in the exam room. Just follow me. Boy or girl?"

"It's my little Sarah. She's burnin' up and has these fearsome marks. God help us, I think she has the small pox."

Pearl's heart skipped. Still referred to as formidable disease, small pox was not as prevalent as it was twenty years prior, but Pearl knew it could still kill quickly. "Well, let's take a look. I'll wash up while you unwrap her. But don't allow her to get chilled."

"Loomey," Pearl called, "would you stay in the front office? No need to expose you unnecessarily until we know what this is." She turned to the young mother. "What's your name?" she asked, drying her hands.

"Watson…Elsie Watson."

The name rang a bell with Pearl and then she remembered. "Are you by chance related to Judge Watson? He was just in town for the Beatrice Goode trial."

"Oh, I know all about that," the woman said. "He's my uncle. But he don't claim me, at least not anymore."

"What do you mean?" Pearl asked. Beaded sweat had snaked along the child's forehead as Pearl examined her small frame. The toddler moaned but didn't open her eyes. She appeared sick, but not deathly so.

"I'm not what'd you call respectable, at least in his eyes," Elsie said. "My little girl here. She was born out of wedlock. I still got no husband." Her tone was matter-of-fact, as though she had given up defending her position and no longer cared. "I can't prove nothing, of course, but I think that's why Doc Hanson won't give me the time of day. Afraid I'll hurt his reputation, I reckon."

Pearl had to restrain herself from blurting out her low opinion of Hanson. She checked for telltale signs of a coated tongue and eased the little girl onto her back to look for the distinctive flat depressed circles which could indicate an outbreak of smallpox.

"Didn't know where else to go till I ran into Loomey's mama," Elsie continued. "She told me to come here. I'm most grateful."

"Has your daughter had any problem breathing, any nausea or vomiting?"

"No, just mighty restless and riled up," Elsie answered, "said her head hurt. Then today, she got these little red spots."

"Yes, I see them," Pearl said. "Has she ever been vaccinated?"

"Been what?" Elsie asked.

"Given a shot to keep her from getting sick with a bad disease like smallpox."

258

"A shot of what?" Elsie said. "You don't mean shot at, do you?"

Pearl glanced up. The woman's sincerity shone through her exhausted expression. "It's medicine," Pearl said kindly. "Some people are given medicine through a needle that goes in their arm and keeps them from getting really sick."

"No ma'am, she's never had nothing like that."

"Well, I don't think she has smallpox. I think she has measles which is a much milder form, and not nearly as dangerous." Pearl said. "See these little spots? They look like tiny blisters, don't they? In a few days they'll turn straw-colored and dry up. She'll start feeling better and should be fine within about two weeks."

"Oh, my," Elsie said. She took a deep breath. "That's good, ain't it, doc?"

"Yes," said Pearl. "Do you have other children?"

"No," Elsie said. "But someday…maybe someday someone will marry me and I'll have a whole slew of kids."

"In the meantime, you should know that measles are catching. If you can, keep Sarah away from other children and adults until the spots begin to dry. You can wash her with warm water and mild soap. Have her stay in bed and give her gruel, beef broth and plenty of water. Don't force any food until she asks for it. This will run its course in due time."

The child stirred and Pearl reached down to run her hand across her forehead. "She doesn't appear to have a high temperature, though she's a little warm to the touch. I'd keep her in bed for a couple more days."

Before gathering up her little girl Elsie reached in her purse and handed Pearl a silver coin. "It's a fifty cent piece," she said. "I was saving up for bad times. It's all I can give you

259

right now."

Pearl wanted to refuse the scant payment but knew that based upon her ledger receipts, her practice was perilously close to the red. She could not keep operating on good will alone. Nor could she accept only bartered items in return for her services.

"Thank you," Pearl said. "Let's do this. Stop at the desk and have Loomey give you a receipt for your payment. I'll charge you only what you have today. In exchange, please let your friends know of my practice. Is that fair enough?"

Elsie nodded. "That's real kind of you, doctor...Miss Pearl."

As they were settling the bill, the small brass bell at the door rang again. A second young woman with a small child hurried in. She seemed to recognize Elsie but swept past her as though she was contagious. One look at the woman's face told Pearl something was wrong, very wrong.

"It's my little boy, he can't breathe!" she cried. "Help me, please!"

Pearl rushed forward and grabbed the blanketed toddler. He appeared about fourteen months old and was gasping for air.

"Tell me his other symptoms," Pearl said to the child's mother as she laid him upon her examining table. Loomey had followed her in and was helping Pearl unwrap the child. His perfectly formed face, framed with dark wet hair, lay plastered to his forehead.

"He's real pale, Miss Pearl," Loomey said, shaking her head.

The boy was also listless and wheezing with a short dry cough. Every few moments he reached up and plucked at his throat, releasing a pitiful sound that resembled a kitten mewing. A thick rope of mucus hung from the side of his bow-shaped mouth.

"He's been like this since four days past," his mother said. "Gets a fit of coughing and then I believe he's gonna stop breathing altogether."

From medical school, Pearl had learned that among the most formidable diseases of childhood was croup, which attacked the mucous membrane lining of the windpipe and bronchial tubes. "All dull fat children are predisposed," her professor had insisted, "and those with short necks."

Pearl made a mental note to keep an open mind on his, as yet, unproven theory. What she knew for sure was that croup was sudden in its attack; its progression rapid. It could be fatal in as little as three days. She turned to the child's mother. "Have you noticed the veins in his neck swelling up? Restlessness followed by languor? What about vomiting or loose bowels?"

She answered yes to all three questions. "And he had a bad chest cold about two months back. He was just getting over that when this came on."

"Has he been exposed to anyone with consumption or flu?" Before the mother could respond, Pearl stopped and peered at the child closer. "Loomey, look at this."

Loomey bent over to get a better view. "I can see it, Miss Pearl, but I don't know what it is," she said. Streaks of bright red marks were visible on the mid section of his throat, his left foot, his thigh and along the bony ridgeline of his spine.

Pearl looked at the boy's mother, to whom she had yet to address by name. The woman's demeanor had changed from visceral fear to one of apprehension. "Your name, ma'am?"

Pearl asked.

"Flo Sawyer, call me Flo. I had to take him somewheres yesterday cause I feared he would stop breathing so I went to our regular man down South Street,' she said. "He leeched and blistered him on different parts. Told me to take him home, put him in a hot bath up to his neck and give him senna tea and lumps of sugar to make his bowels move. Didn't help none though. I heard about you from Chief Harkins. He knows my husband."

"Is your physician Doc Hanson?" Pearl asked. Flo nodded. The leeches and mustard poultices Hanson had applied to the child's body had left angry red marks and Pearl surmised the emetic had drained the boy of vitality.

She sighed. "I'll be honest," she said. "I'm not sure what I can do for him. We have no real treatment for inflammatory croup. All I can suggest you do is keep him as quiet as possible, make sure the room is warm, even humid and don't force any foods on him. Give him liquids only and watch him closely."

Flo's eyes filled with tears as she stared first at Pearl and then at Loomey. "But you gotta do something," she pleaded. "I already lost one to the flu three winters ago. I can't go through that again."

These were the moments Pearl dreaded most, first in her training and now in her practice with a very sick patient and a terrified mother standing before her. "What's the boy's name, Flo?"

"Samuel Gaston Taylor. He's named after his father and grandfather. We call him Little Sammy. He's the light of our lives." She began to sob quietly.

Pearl reached down and gently lifted a wisp of hair from

262

the child's closed eyes. Exhausted by his efforts to gain air into his small lungs, he had drifted off to sleep, his breaths coming in quick shallow movements. A terrible sadness crept over her. She had little doubt the child was near death and it pained her to watch his mother suffer through it.

She glanced up to see Loomey's round eyes brimming over. "Let me see what I have on hand," Pearl said. At this point, offering hope was all she could do.

Chapter Twenty-Five

Before Flo left with her sick child, Pearl went to the tall oak cabinet that held her apothecary jars, some of which she had mixed with her own hands to ensure quality. Removing chloride of mercury and a jar of ammonia-muriate, she poured small amounts into two glass containers. Loomey had hand-pressed cork tops so enthusiastically, the cabinet was nearly over-flowing. Pearl grabbed two and inserted them into the containers.

"Take this," she instructed, "and give Little Sammy half a grain – about a teaspoon full – of the mercury and one full grain of the ammonia every two hours. If you have any thick flannel, fold it into a square, dip it in warm water and place it over his upper chest and throat."

"What about bleeding him?" Flo asked. "Can we try that? Doc Hanson says that's a last resort but it might work."

Ralph Hanson. I'd love to walk up to him and slap him hard in the face, Pearl thought. "We've learned that bleeding is not very effective, especially in these cases," she said, forcing an even tone. Loomey was not nearly as diplomatic.

"That Doc Hanson has struck again," she said, causing

Flo to give her a startled look. Pearl shot a warning look at Loomey.

"I understand if you need to try another physician," Pearl said. "You might call on Dr. Stevens. He worked with me on a shooting case and is a very good physician. Or, if you can afford the trip perhaps take Little Sammy to a hospital in Charlotte or Raleigh." Gauging by Flo's shocked expression, Pearl immediately regretted the advice.

"Hospitals are where people go to die," Flo said with a vengeance. "We'll take our chances right here in Asheville." Then her tone softened. "I'm sorry," she said. "I'm just so worn out. And we have little money. But we can pay you something next month or bring you one of my husband's hand-carved chairs. They're fine pieces."

Pearl motioned for Loomey to help her as they wrapped the small boy in his woolen blanket, tucking the sides papoose-style so he wouldn't chill. Pearl handed him back to his mother. "There's no fee," she said. "All I offered was an opinion."

Pearl accompanied them to the front door while Loomey straightened the exam room. "I'll need your address," Pearl said. "I'll come in the morning to check on him. Please send word if there's any change tonight. In the meantime I wish you and your family well."

"Thank you for your kindness, Dr. Stern." Her voice quivered.

As they left, a sudden weariness overcame Pearl. There was something about this case that reminded her of the incident in Missouri, leaving her drained of all but gloom and anxiety. She sat down on a chair in the waiting room and was still there when Loomey came in.

"You all right, Miss Pearl?"

"That baby is going to die," Pearl said. "And there isn't a thing in the world I can do about it."

Loomey grabbed her apron and flapped its folds as though to fan Pearl. "I'll pray hard all night long," she said.

As the day progressed, Pearl and Loomey stayed busy with two additional patients, a fifty-six year old colored woman referred by Loomey's mother who presented with a history of eating starch, fourteen pounds in the past two weeks, she reported. Pearl noted her right carotid gland was swollen but with no soreness present. She treated her with an iodine solution to reduce swelling and told the woman to return in two days, giving Pearl time to research the case and consult with Dr. Stevens.

The next patient was a woman in her twenties Pearl suspected had syphilis. "I saw your sign on the street," she told Pearl. "I got nowhere else to go and don't want no man 'touchin' me that don't pay for the privilege." A woman of negotiable affections, as Pearl's father would say – a street-walker – not her first such patient and probably not her last.

She examined the fistulas present on her lower extremities and treated her with mercury and iodine ointments. "Do you have children or do you suspect that you might be with child?" The disease was often passed along to infants by the mother, exhibited by cracked, sore lips on the baby that resulted in an inability to nurse and subsequent malnourishment.

The woman shook her head. "God help me, no. Can't afford to feed myself, much less a young'un. Just been lucky, I guess, that I never been in an awkward way. But I can pay you, Dr. Stern, don't you worry 'bout that."

That evening, exhausted from her long day, Pearl sat

down at her desk to write her clinical notes. Feeling slightly dizzy, she folded her arms and laid her forehead down just for a moment. Five minutes was all she needed. She found herself back in Missouri in an exam room with another young woman and infant, Pearl trying frantically to save them as the room filled with blood, first up to her high-top boots, then her waist until it enveloped and swallowed her whole as she gasped for air.

A tap on her shoulder awoke her. A voice boomed in her ear. "Pearl, wake up! You sound like you're having trouble catching your breath. Are you all right?"

Pearl shook her head to clear it and looked up. "Herschel! My lord, what are you doing here? And what time is it?" She sat up. Her mouth was parched.

"It's past dinner. I saw your office light from across the street and walked over to see if everything was all right. The door was unlocked. Not a good idea, Pearl, to leave the place wide open after dark. And not like you to be sleeping in your office chair. What happened?"

Pearl smoothed her disheveled hair, stood up and ran her hands along the wrinkled crevices of her dress. Her shoulders and neck ached from the awkward position in which she had fallen asleep...how many hours ago? She glanced at the clock standing guard near the doorway. Seven p.m. "I'm fine, Herschel," she said. "I was just having a bad dream." She glanced toward the front office. "Was there a note at the door or have you heard anything from little Samuel Taylor's family? He's very ill. I sent him home with his mother earlier today."

"Not a word," Herschel said. He studied her face. "I haven't eaten yet and I bet you haven't either. Come on, I'll take you to the Eagle for some of their better fare before they stop serving."

"No, I need to check on Samuel," Pearl said. "I don't have a good feeling about him."

"Now?" Herschel asked. "Well, let's get some food in you first. Then I'll go with you. No need to be out alone, especially tonight. The skies are rumbling like they'll crack wide open any minute."

Pearl considered his offer. "You'd go with me?" she asked. "Why would you do that?"

He took her arm. "Because I'd accompany you anywhere. Now come along. There's a very ample steak, well-done, calling our names at the Eagle."

By the time they had eaten and Pearl had two cups of coffee to clear her head, the storm was in full force. Wind battered the hotel windows and flipped large umbrellas inside out as hotel guests pushed hard against the wind in an effort to come inside.

At the table they shared, Pearl explained to Herschel her concern about little Samuel and how sick he was in his mother's arms as they left that afternoon. But she said nothing of the dream that carried her back to Missouri, dredging up the incident that drove her here.

"It's a terrible sight to see a mother suffer such a loss," she said. And it's even more terrible to be a part of it, she thought.

"Maybe we should wait till morning to visit the family," Herschel suggested.

"No," She could tell the sudden edge to her voice startled him. "I mean I don't think that's a good idea," she said more kindly. "I'm really worried about him, Herschel. He might not live through the night."

He made a last swipe of the linen napkin across his whis-

268

kers. "As you wish." He motioned for the tab. "We'll need a carriage too," he told the waiter. "Can you have it brought out front?"

"Of course, sir. As you may know we have our own stable. For you – as a police officer and your lady – it's complimentary, part of our public service." Herschel smiled as he rose and moved to assist Pearl with her chair. "I like the ring of that... my lady."

"Don't be so familiar," Pearl scolded. "You too are in public service."

She regretted her sharp rebuke. Normally entertained by Herschel's playful nature, her mind was elsewhere tonight. Somewhere a child lay dying. Yet she knew that in his own awkward way, he was just trying to divert her attention. She gathered up her purse and the medical bag she had remembered to bring as they left her office.

As they stood at the doorway waiting for the carriage and watching the beating rain, Herschel mentioned their lack of an umbrella. "Here take this," he said. He removed his jacket and draped it across her shoulders. It swallowed her small frame.

She gazed up at him. "Thank you, and Herschel, thank you for coming with me, especially on a night like this."

They rode in silence in the dark covered carriage, the streets of Asheville casting a silvery glow against the backdrop of drooping oaks and beaten-down maples huddled against the storm. Lightning sizzled then sliced the sky followed by a thunderous clap. Pearl's thoughts were on what they would find at the Taylor home. The carriage stopped at the edge of the city limits before a small frame house, its only sign of life the flicker of a kerosene lamp from the front room.

"How long should I tell the driver?" Herschel asked. "He

won't be able to sit here and wait for more than a few minutes."

"Whatever you think," Pearl said. "I am here as long as I'm needed." As she climbed out of the carriage, she could hear him talking to the driver, telling him to return in an hour if the weather hadn't cleared. If the night grew calm, they would walk the mile or so back to the Square. The plan made perfect sense to Pearl.

They must have appeared an odd pair at the door, the towering coat-less man, his thick hair a wet mat flattened in the rain, and the small woman beside him with the heavy blue jacket pulled tight around her. The door opened and Flo, Samuel's mother, appeared.

"Dr. Stern?" she asked, "is that you?" Her face, pinched from worry and sleeplessness, looked even more haggard than Pearl recalled.

"Yes, and this is Herschel Harkins, the Chief of Police. May we come in?"

"Oh my!" she said. "Has something else terrible happened?" She drew back, hand across her mouth, as though about to be struck.

"No, no," Pearl said quickly. "And I'm so sorry we came unannounced. We...I'm here to check on Little Sammy and the Chief was kind enough to escort me."

"Of course," Flo said. "My manners, forgive me...please come in." The place was small but tidy with minimal furnishings and plain linen curtains at each window; four rooms from what Pearl could see. A closed door led to what must have been Samuel's bedroom. The only concessions to excess were a few children's toys scattered about: wooden building blocks, a set of blue and white rope-tension drums and a red mahogany hand-carved rocking horse that gleamed in the

270

dim light. Topped off with golden brass hardware and a dark leather saddle and bridles, it must have cost several months wages.

This child was cherished, Pearl thought. "Is your husband here too?"

"Yes, he's in there with Little Sammy and Doc Hanson. We've hardly left our boy's bedside."

"Did you say Doc Hanson was here?" Pearl asked, removing Herschel's jacket and placing it over a spindle-back chair. She looked at Herschel. He shook his head as if to caution don't say anything, not here, not now.

"I'll wait in here," Herschel said. "You two go on."

In the boy's darkened room Samuel's father and Hanson sat on either side of the bed. Little Sammy lay on his back, still and ghostly, as light from the parlor crawled across the floor. At the doorway Pearl searched for signs that he might have already stopped breathing.

Hanson looked up and nodded. Pearl gave him a curt acknowledgment. At least he appears sober, she thought. "How is he?" she whispered, moving toward the bed.

Hanson shook his head and motioned for her to step outside the room. As he entered the light, Pearl was shocked to see evidence of tears on his fleshy face.

"I've known this family for over twenty-five years," he said quietly. "Birthed the young mother and watched her grow up to have a little girl she lost to the flu, recover and then have Little Sammy." His voice caught.

"I'm so sorry," said Pearl. "What's his condition?" Despite their prickly past and Pearl's complete lack of respect for him, he at least seemed genuinely affected.

"He's been sleeping for the past hour but has frequent pulse, flushing and laborious breathing. I almost had him cured from an earlier episode of bronchitis but I fear with his prostration from the fever and croup, he will not be able to withstand this latest pertussis."

"Is the coughing still spasmodic?"

"Oh yes. I had his mother steam a tin of water and vinegar so he could inhale into it. I've read of cases where asafoetida may be found to have some good effect."

He hesitated, as though seeking a reaction.

"Are you asking for my professional opinion?" Pearl said, taken aback.

A woman's shriek was heard from the boy's room. "Help us, please!" yelled Samuel's father. "He's not breathing!"

Pearl and Hanson rushed in. Sammy was splayed across the bed, covers tossed onto the floor. "What happened?" Hanson said, bending over the boy.

"He had some kind of fit and threw off the blanket. Then he just seized up and stopped...help him...do something," Samuel's father begged. Flo was behind him, hands covering her face. Sammy's face turned a dusky blue. Hanson forced open the child's mouth and stuck his hand inside.

"What are you doing?" Pearl cried.

"Trying to excite vomiting," Hanson said. "If I can tickle the fauces at the back of his throat it might help him breathe better."

Pearl reached for Hanson's open case sitting next to the bed. She spotted a small blade and a thin silver metal catheter. Pearl estimated more than a full minute had passed since Little Sammy had taken a breath. His tiny face was growing

272

darker, his bow-lips turning a purplish-blue. His parents had now turned to each other and were weeping in each other's arms. Herschel, alerted by the noise, came and stood at the door, watching the unfolding scene.

Pearl grabbed Hanson's arm. This was still his patient, though he was fast losing him. "I want to open the trachea," she said. "Will you allow it?" For a moment, their eyes locked.

"Do it," he said. He removed his hand and took a step back. "I'll help you."

With no time to waste, Pearl prayed the scalpel was relatively clean and set the blade just below the boy's thyroid. She sliced the skin in a swift, determined motion. "Now reach for that catheter," she told Hanson. "Let's see if we can thread it in. Use gentle pressure. It may relax the chest wall."

Hanson, hands surprisingly steady, inserted the silver hollow catheter. Almost immediately, the boy's chest began to rise and fall followed by a hint of color around the lips and face.

"Oh, thank god, thank god," Flo whispered behind them. She pushed her way forward and knelt by the bed, grabbing her son's small hand. She held it to her face.

Don't thank Him yet, Pearl thought. *This child is still critically ill.* For the next hour, no one moved. All five adults remained in the crowded room, including Herschel, seemingly transfixed by the two physicians' heroic measures. Finally Pearl, needing to use the outhouse facility to relieve her aching bladder, slipped out quietly. Herschel followed her into the kitchen.

"Were you able to save him?" he asked.

"I don't know. I don't even know if he will wake up," said Pearl.

"Where did you learn to do that?" Herschel persisted. "I've never seen that done, even when I trained with my uncle."

"Case studies I've read about," Pearl said. She had forgotten Herschel once wanted to be a doctor. "Now, if you'll excuse me, I must go outside to the privy." Normally, she would blush at even saying the word aloud, especially in front of a male who was not her husband. But not this night. The close proximity among the adults over a very sick child made such social niceties seem frivolous.

"It's dark and there may be snakes even this close to town," Herschel warned. "I'll escort you."

"No!" Pearl said, horrified at the thought he would follow her to the outhouse.

"Then I'll wait for you here," he said. "I can see you from the window."

"Oh, for god's sake," Pearl said, gathering her skirt and stepping onto the back stoop. Unable to discourage him from waiting on her, Pearl completed her business in the outdoor privy and carefully worked her way back to the house. If there were snakes, as Herschel kindly pointed out, she wouldn't see them until she stepped on one. She wondered if he was actually peering at her from the window. That man, she thought, smiling to herself. It was the first time in days she had had even the semblance of a light moment.

As she and Herschel re-entered Little Sammy's room, Pearl immediately noted a change in the boy's breathing pattern. It was no longer shallow and erratic. But Hanson turned toward her and shook his head. Her heart sank, knowing that what they had achieved could be temporary at best. The child was just too sick.

"At least he's sleeping peacefully," Hanson said, as

though to add we gave him that much. Pearl leaned toward Hanson and whispered something into his ear. "You should talk to his parents," she said. "Herschel and I will sit here with him."

He nodded, rose and led the boy's parents from the room. As Pearl and Herschel sat silent in the still room on either side of Sammy's bed, Herschel reached across the covers and took Pearl's hand, squeezing it once before releasing it. Not knowing what to say Pearl simply nodded in the dark, hoping Herschel would see that she was grateful for his presence.

The child stirred, his breathing so shallow Pearl had to lean in to ensure his tiny chest was moving. She could hear his parents sobbing in the parlor. A pervading sadness rippled through the house.

And then she heard something else, a soft wheezing noise as the little boy attempted to speak. He could make no further sound with the tube inserted in his throat.

"Herschel, hurry," said Pearl. "Go get his mother!" Flo was in the room within moments, kneeling close to the bed. Sammy's father came and stood beside her. Their collective grief was palpable and Pearl, who suddenly felt as though the room was closing in, had to struggle to catch a good breath.

"What is it, my precious?" Flo said. "Come back to us, please come back."

But the child had stopped talking; stopped moving; stopped breathing.

"I'm so sorry," Pearl whispered.

"No! No, no, no, no, no!" Flo wailed. She grabbed the child and held him to her, refusing to let go.

Hanson, in tears himself, placed a hand on the father's shoulders. The man was weeping, his entire body heaving.

Behind them, Pearl pulled at the smothering lace collar on her dress and attempted to loosen it.

"I can't breathe," she told Herschel. "I need to go outside." She knew at this rate she might even faint. Herschel instinctively put an arm around her waist and guided her toward the door. Then in one fell swoop he grabbed her and lifted her into his arms.

"What are you doing?" she said, gasping for air. Her head felt light; her stomach queasy.

"I'm getting you outside." He sat her down on the wooden stoop at the back door and settled in next to her. "Now don't move. And don't say a word. Just sit."

"I have to go in," she said, pulling at her collar. "They might need me."

Herschel reached out and held her arm. "Hanson is with them. And there's nothing you can do now. Leave them be." He loosened his grip but refused to let go.

Nothing you can do. Nothing you can do. A memory floated to the surface of another young mother, another child. Pearl felt sick. She doubled over. Her body began to shake and she clasped her hands over her ears as though to drown out the memories. "I tried to help," she said. "I tried so hard! Everything, I tried everything…but it was too late…too late."

"What?" said Herschel. "What are you talking about, Pearl?" But it was as though she was lost to him. In the dark, he held her close and waited. The rain had stopped and the night had taken on a glittery calm. Starlight twinkled through the haze. A silver moon peeked through a feathery gray cloud.

"Are you up to walking back to town?" Herschel finally asked. "I told our carriage driver not to return if the weather cleared." Beside him, Pearl was quiet and still.

"Yes," she finally said. Physically and emotionally depleted, she didn't even realize what she was saying. "I mean, no... I don't know," she said. "Let's go back inside. I must see how the family is doing."

They returned to Little Sammy's room. Hanson was quietly gathering his supplies. The boy's dazed parents were sitting on either side of their son's bed. No one spoke. Pearl placed a hand on Flo's back. "I'm so sorry," she whispered. The woman, weeping into a kerchief, nodded.

"Do either of you need anything?" Herschel asked.

"I need my boy," the father said. "I just need my boy." His shoulders heaved. Herschel gave him a comforting pat.

Pearl turned to Hanson. "Is there anything I can do to help you?" It crossed her mind that only yesterday such a question to Hanson, of all people, would have seemed absurd. Even now, she was uncertain how she felt about the man and his professional skills, or lack thereof. What treatment had he provided besides the outmoded blistering and leeching? Was there a lack of hygiene that perpetuated Samuel's infection? How long had Little Sammy been sick before Hanson noted his deterioration? Was he even sober when ministering to the child? She would never know.

"No. I'll stay here with the family until daybreak," Hanson was saying. "You and Herschel go on. And Pearl," he added. "Thank you."

"For what?" she said. "We lost this precious child."

"For your help, of course, and for being here."

Frustrated, she knew nothing else to do but make an exit. "We'll show ourselves out," she said. She began to feel better when she and Herschel reached the night air. She was almost grateful for the brisk walk back to town.

"It's chilly," she said as she increased her stride in an attempt to keep up with Herschel's long legs. He slowed his pace and offered her his arm. But she pushed on, pointedly ignoring his courtesy, her sober mood as dark as the surrounding night.

"Sorry," he said, "didn't mean to get ahead of you. I can find a carriage if you like."

"No, I'm fine."

He stopped in mid-stride and stared down at her. "Pearl, you're not fine. You just lost a patient, a young child. You're upset and rightly so. You have a claim to grieve, just like anyone else."

"You don't understand, Herschel." There was much more, so much more.

"Understand what? For god's sake, woman, you can be as convoluted as a Chinese puzzle. What don't I understand? And why are you so hard on yourself? You're a doctor. Losing a patient is an unfortunate but not uncommon occurrence. Am I right?"

She tightened her arms against the autumn cold, looked up at him and nodded. "Yes, of course. We lose patients. It's part of the nature of medicine. It's just that this case…this one…it reminded me of something that happened in Missouri."

"You lost a child there too?" he asked.

"A mother and a child," she said, her voice flat.

They resumed walking.

"What happened in Missouri?" Herschel said.

She shook her head. "I really don't want to talk about it," she said, "not right now." It occurred to her that she sounded like Victoria who, more than anyone she knew, wanted unpleasantness to disappear like smoke.

Herschel was silent. "Is that why you nearly collapsed in Samuel's room?" he said.

"I didn't collapse," she said sharply. "It was a very long and arduous night."

"I said nearly." Approaching the Square, Herschel escorted her to her office door and stood behind her while she turned the key in the door. It was now well past two a.m. Her back was to him as she fiddled with the metal device.

"I'm sorry that I was discourteous to you, Herschel," she said. "You were a true gentleman, taking me to dinner, accompanying me to Samuel's home, all of it, everything."

She turned to look at him. "I appreciate all that you've done, all that you do for me. Now, if you'll excuse me, I'm exhausted. You must be too. Good night."

"Good night," he said. But the look he gave her was one of bewilderment, as though women and she in particular, were mysterious creatures he would never understand.

"Herschel?" she called after him.

He turned. "What?"

"Can we talk tomorrow?"

"Yes, of course."

Then he disappeared into the night.

Chapter Twenty-Six

Pearl was bent at the young man's side examining what appeared to be a leg wound. She glanced up to see that Herschel had entered, called out a hello and went back to her work. "You say you're a surveyor, Ian?" she asked. "Here in the city?" It had shocked her that a nice young man chose to come to her office when there were several male physicians close by.

"Yeah, though I may need to carefully reconsider my profession after today."

"Oh?" Pearl said. "I thought the life of a surveyor was an exciting one. You do know our president Thomas Jefferson was a surveyor, don't you?"

"Oh yeah, and it has its good days. We're authorized to cut down trees and do other damage. Also has its drawbacks. I've been pelted with cabbages by angry property owners, arrested for trespassing – though Mayor Lusk bailed me out of that one. And now this dog bite. Damn thing attacked when the owner sicced him on me. Said he didn't want no hell-fire city street being plowed through his property. I apologize for my language, ma'am." He flinched as Pearl probed the wound.

"I gotta say, you're the best-looking doc in town. That's why I came to you instead of subjecting myself to those other medical mugs. But you got a wicked pair of hands."

"It's a nasty bite," she said. "I'll need to clean it first and then dress it." She looked up to see Herschel still patiently waiting in the foyer.

"Will you excuse me just a moment?" she said to Ian. "I'll be right back."

"What are you doing here in the middle of the day?" she said, greeting Herschel with a smile.

His look was as solemn as she had ever witnessed. Her smile faded. "What is it?" she said. "Has something happened?" She thought of her parents in Missouri, then Loomey, who was out sick with a cold that day. Said she caught it from Jim. Word must have come through about something tragic.

"I need to speak with you in private, Pearl. I can see you're busy but I'll wait. This is important."

"Has something happened to anyone I know?" she said. Her heart was thumping hard against her chest.

"No one's died or been injured. This is more a...legal matter. I'll explain shortly. You get back to your patient."

"Of course," said Pearl, turning away from him. What now? Had someone complained about treatment here? The bane of too many doctors, worry over unhappy patients threatening them in some way. Physicians had been shot, stabbed and sued at various times by disgruntled patients. She struggled to regain her focus. One thing at a time; the person before her needed her attention.

"Ian," she said, re-entering the exam room, "the dog that bit you didn't appear unusually aggressive or have foam coming from its mouth, did it?"

281

"No ma'am. But I can't say the same about its owner."

Only half-listening, her head was still spinning from a sense of impending doom. "All right then," she said. "I'll wash the wound with a dilution of carbolic acid, apply nitrate of silver and wrap your leg with cotton bands. Leave them on for three days, clean the area with some salve which I'll give you and rewrap. I'll see you back here in a week and we'll check for infection. Do you need something for pain?"

"Nope," he said, setting his injured leg onto the floor. He tugged at his pants leg. "That's what my buddy corn liquor does for me, among other things."

Pearl searched her medical cabinet for the salve.

"What about my work, Doc?" he said. "I've got a plot of land to lay out and a map to draw, all due by end of the week."

"Use your own judgment," Pearl said. "But I'd stay off it as much as you can the rest of the day. It should heal completely in about a month." He thanked her, paid her four dollars in cash and hobbled toward the door, acknowledging the Chief of Police on his way out.

"Just a minute Herschel," Pearl called from the exam room. "I'm washing up and I'll be right there." She soaked her hands in a basin, reached for a towel and waited for his usual banter. Silence greeted her. "Are you still there?" she said loudly. All she could hear was the ominous tick of her grandfather clock. Briskly wiping her hands, she went to the foyer. Herschel stood at the window, his back to her, his police cap still planted in place.

"Herschel?" Pearl said. "You look so official. Whatever brings you here?"

He turned and she caught a look on his face that she never wanted to see again. It was one of anguish, disappoint-

282

ment and if she didn't know better, something akin to fear.

"What's going on?" she said.

He reached in his coat pocket and pulled out a folded sheaf of thick parchment paper.

"I might ask you the same," he said. "I received this today. It's from the state of Missouri." He read the words out loud:

On or about September 1, 1882 in the state of Missouri, county of Taney, Pearl A. Stern, M.D, Defendant, did willfully and intentionally commit Manslaughter against said Winifred R. Singleton and her unborn child.

Color drained from her face. Pearl steadied herself against the heavy oak counter. "And that is?" she managed to say. It was the day she had been dreading since she first met Herschel.

"It's a warrant signed by the Governor stating that you're charged with manslaughter in the case of Winifred R. Singleton, represented by the State of Missouri. You, Pearl A. Stern, M.D. listed as the Defendant."

Pearl gripped the countertop. The large grandfather clock chimed in the other room, as though mocking her. She had expected something bad from the incident in Missouri, but a criminal warrant? Yet what did she think would happen? That it would all disappear like the morning fog that enveloped the mountains?

"I can see by your reaction there's some merit to the case," he said. "I prayed otherwise."

"Are you here to arrest me?" she said. She felt like a trapped child, instinctively clasping and unclasping her hands.

"I'm here to find out what the hell happened and why

283

you never told me. I trusted you with everything in me." He grabbed a chair and in one swift motion crossed the room.

"Sit down." Then he went to the front door and locked it, snatching another chair on his way back to Pearl. He was angrier than Pearl had ever seen him.

"No one comes in, no one goes out until I hear this from your own lips," he said. He sat directly across from her, looming over her small frame. He shifted in his chair, unbuttoned his jacket and removed his hat, setting it aside. "Pearl," he said, in an almost pleading tone. "Talk to me."

Pearl took a deep breath. It was all she could do to keep from passing out. Had she collapsed right there in front of him, he would no doubt still be standing over her when she awoke. This was the moment of truth she had dreaded most.

"All right," she said. "It was last year. I'd just received my medical degree from the Women's College in Pennsylvania and was home in Missouri with plans to set up my own practice. But I felt that I needed to intern first with an experienced physician as I had little practical work behind me. So I arranged a six-month internship with the oldest and most respected physician in town. His name was Dr. Walter Stone."

"Go on," said Herschel. He had folded his arms and leaned back in the chair as though the day had no end. The warrant lay straddled on his knees.

"Mrs. Singleton was his patient," Pearl continued, "a para-prima."

"A what?" Herschel said.

"Someone with multiple pregnancies," Pearl said. "Anyway, this was her fifth child and there were complications right from the start. She was plagued with hemorrhages and weakness through much of her pregnancy."

"Why?" Herschel said. "Was she not being treated by this experienced doctor?"

"She didn't come to him until this pregnancy. Her husband forbade her, said he wasn't persuaded that the natural function of childbirth could be dangerous. He didn't want her seeing a doctor during this pregnancy either. But I think she willfully disobeyed him; came to see us behind her husband's back. Of course, we had no way of knowing that at the time."

"Then what happened?"

"As she got closer to her confinement date, she stopped coming in. Right before her due date, Dr. Stone had a heart attack and just…died. I was left unattended with his practice and his patients. People needed help. Some patients had been coming to him for decades. I felt morally compelled to treat them as best I could."

"What about the confined woman? Did she return?" Herschel asked.

"Yes, but her case was dire by then. She was carried in by family members who were quite distressed at her condition. That day…" Pearl stopped. "If you're going to interrogate me, I need a drink of water."

He rose quickly and brought her a cup. "This is not an interrogation. I'm just trying to get to the bottom of it."

Pearl sipped from the cup, ran her tongue over her lips and continued. "What the woman really needed was hospital attention, but once again her husband refused. When her mother and sister demanded that she get medical help, they gathered other family members and brought her to us. It was my first unattended delivery."

"What did you do?" Herschel asked, his tone level, non-accusatory.

285

Pearl bowed her head and sighed. "I had to use instruments to deliver the baby. It was alive but very weak." Her voice caught at the memory.

"I'm sorry Pearl, but I need to hear the rest," Herschel said.

Pearl's hands gripped the half-empty cup. "The mother was feverish and had already lost a good amount of blood. But I made mistakes, some bad ones. I tried to staunch the bleeding, make a repair and thought I had done so. But she grew weaker and I almost lost her on the exam table. At one point she revived enough to ask about her baby, and all I could tell her was that the infant had been delivered, that now she needed to rest and get well."

"Was she dying?" Herschel asked.

"Yes, and possibly the baby too."

"Where was the husband in all of this?" Herschel asked.

"He came storming in just as I was working over his wife, demanded to take her home. He started yelling that I had done this and there would be retribution and that he hoped to send me to hell. I found out later that she had died at home, along with the baby. I suspect it was blood poisoning and that it was my fault."

"I don't understand," said Herschel. "What are you saying?"

Pearl cleared her throat, took another sip of water. "I missed the most fundamental step of all. I failed to wash my hands, having just come from attending another patient. I don't even know if the instruments I used were clean. There was no time…" her voice trailed off.

"To minimize germs, a level of cleanliness is required," she said. "It's called the Lister Technique. I knew about it. I just

286

didn't follow it. Nor did I fully persuade Stone of its value. That day, I should have…"

Her voice broke and she leaned over, put her face in her hands. "I may well have killed her and the infant. At the least, I contributed to her death with my incompetent care," she sobbed.

Herschel leaned back in his chair and closed his eyes. He snatched up the warrant and re-read the wordage out loud.

"It says here 'willful neglect of said Plaintiff that led to her untimely death and the death of her newborn infant.' Willful means intentional, Pearl. What you've told me, it sounds like it was neither willful nor a direct result of your care that day. From what you've said…"

Pearl looked up, caught Herschel's steely gaze. "Stop saying from what I said. You do believe me, don't you? Herschel, tell me you believe me."

For a moment he didn't speak. Pearl felt her chest heave and her stomach constrict. She gagged once then twice, on the verge of vomiting. It was like she was suddenly transported to the dark night at Singleton's front steps when he held a gun to her chest and told her to never return. To think she could leave all that behind just by moving to a new town.

"Yes," Herschel finally said. "I believe you. But it's not what I believe that matters. It's serious business to have a governor sign off on a warrant. It means someone wants you back in Missouri pretty bad and is willing to go to the expense and trouble to extradite you. It also means someone there has influence with officials, enough to get the warrant drawn and signed. This Dr. Stone, was he married?"

"Oh yes," said Pearl. "The widow Stone is very well

known. Her father was a lumber magnate, owned nearly half the trade throughout central Missouri. She had a great distaste for me; refused to sell me her husband's practice even though I was the logical person to take over the business. Do you think...do you think she's behind this?"

"Why did she dislike you?"

Pearl glanced about for something to dab at her eyes. A cloth apron hung on a hat rack nearby, no doubt left by Loomey. She was glad Loomey was out today. This all would have been a huge upset to her. She grabbed the apron, dipped it into the water cup and ran its cool cotton surface across her face. "I was never sure why. But she was determined that I would never be her husband's replacement in his practice."

"Let me think about this," Herschel said. "We have a woman with child; history of complications; inconsistent medical attention due to husband's unwillingness to allow doctor visits. She arrives at Dr. Stone's practice. You attempt to save them both. Granted, you made procedural mistakes and didn't sterilize."

He stopped. "On average, how many doctors around the country believe in and practice sterilizing? Do you happen to know?"

"Well, three years ago, when I was still in medical school, I would say about fifty percent," Pearl said. "That number is rising now. I keep up with it through lectures and journals."

"All right," Herschel said. "So in 1880 about half the doctors anywhere in the country actually believed in and were practicing these...what you call...Lister techniques. Dr. Stone wasn't one of them. You were young, just out of medical school, new to his practice. Not likely you could have persuaded him, regardless of how hard you tried."

"You sound like an attorney in a courtroom," Pearl said.

"This is what it would sound like," Herschel said, "only in a worse light for you. I'm actually defending your position."

Pearl blinked. She was beginning to understand for the first time how her case might sound from an outsider's point of view. Herschel went on, one hand on his knee, the other still grasping the warrant.

"Mother returns home and dies within days."

"You forgot about the husband barging in and threatening me," Pearl said quietly.

"Yes, irate husband already at odds with the family. They return home where God knows what kind of condition the place is in and what kind of follow-up treatment she might have received."

"I was told by the patient's husband to never darken their door. He'd care for his wife on his own. I'm sure he squabbled with the entire family over how and where to care for her. Whatever happened next, I have no knowledge of it. Though Singleton did point a gun and threaten to shoot me."

"What?"

"The night I went to his house, the same night he took his wife home. I had to go see about her."

"You could have been killed," Herschel said, shaking his head.

"I had to go. She was my patient, or at least I thought she was."

"So the woman dies," Herschel said, "and the husband, now left with a household of motherless kids, seeks revenge. That he threatened you – drew a weapon – will bolster your case. Did you speak to the widow after the incident?"

Pearl struggled to recall. "Actually, no. I got a visit from the county sheriff instead." She told him about the eviction papers.

"How long did you stay around after the incident?"

Pearl looked down at her hands. "I took a few months off from Dr. Stone's practice. I went home to my parents to consider my next move. On a visit to town I saw that the practice had been boarded up, which surprised me. I tried calling on Mrs. Stone but there were always excuses that she was ill, or that she was unable to take visitors at the moment. I'm sure now she was just unwilling to see me."

"What happened that made you decide to move to Asheville, so far from home?" Herschel asked. His tone had grown more conciliatory from when he arrived in her office.

She had the first stirring of hope that he believed her. "I needed a fresh start. After a few weeks went by, people in Taney County began to talk. Apparently the husband had been telling everyone that I killed his wife and baby. True or not, the talk was there and the damage done. I was tainted goods. It would have been nearly impossible to start a successful practice in the region. I chose Asheville at random."

"I understand why you couldn't stay there," Herschel said, "but that still doesn't account for the warrant. Someone went to the trouble to build a case against you and have this thing issued, signed and sent. I doubt the dead woman's husband had that kind of influence. But the doctor's widow did, maybe to protect her husband's image by laying all the blame at your door. Maybe she was even threatened by this lunatic man who lost his wife and baby so she decided to turn the tables onto you."

290

Pearl sat motionless, taking it all in. "I was still at fault," she said. "There were so many things I should have done differently. Any first-year medical student would have done a better job."

"Yes, it sounds like there's ample fault to go around," Herschel said. "But keep in mind what I said. A criminal matter must involve willful intent. And I see no evidence of that. The parties involved could sue you for civil damages and perhaps win their case, but I don't think this criminal warrant will stand."

"So what should we do?" Pearl said, well aware she had used the pejorative we.

"I don't know yet. But I do have one final question."

"What?" Pearl asked. A pounding headache was starting at the base of her neck.

"How did they know where you went next? It had to be through your parents, Pearl."

Pearl stood up. "My God! They know about everything that happened. But someone had to contact them about the warrant!" She paced the floor, shaking her head. "My poor parents. I must go to them. I have to go to Missouri. Mother will never forgive me for this." This time, in this case, her patient, understanding father might not either.

"And I have to go with you," Herschel said. "You're now officially in my custody."

Chapter Twenty-Seven

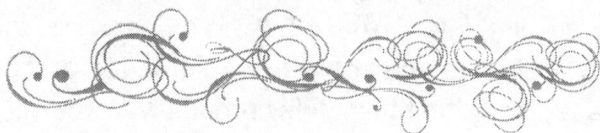

It had been months since Pearl had traveled anywhere and she fretted over the mode of travel Herschel insisted upon, a stagecoach. It was the final topic they had discussed before he left her office the previous afternoon. He wanted to minimize their departure; she just wanted it over with the quickest way possible.

"Take me to the depot in Best where I arrived," she had pleaded. "The cars will get us there much faster. If we're seen by someone we know, then so be it. All I request is that you don't cuff me or treat me like some dangerous criminal in public."

Herschel was adamant. "If that's what you want, you're both foolish and naïve. I know how this town operates. Once word gets around that you're in legal trouble and that I'm escorting you to Missouri for extradition, it's all over for you. Your reputation will lie in tatters, and you'll never be able to rebuild your fledgling practice."

"It sounds like you don't think I'll be exonerated." This was turning into a miserable conversation. She felt despondent; as trapped as a caged animal.

Herschel shook his head at her. "I'm confident your name will be cleared. At least I intend to do everything in my power to make that happen. But I can't control all matters here or there. All I can do is try to protect you while we're here. Trust me, Pearl."

She considered his position. "I know you're an honorable man and that you believe what you're saying. But I already feel bad enough about this whole thing. I don't want to slip out of town like a thief in the night." Placing a hand to her chest, she sat down again, the enormous impact of the words she had just spoken hitting her full force. It was true – a heart could physically hurt from emotional distress. "What a mess," she said.

"I think the mess has just begun, so I get to make the decisions about our mode of travel. That's the end of it," he said, as he left her sitting there.

Pearl slept little that night, her unmade bed a knot of sheets and tousled blankets a vivid testimony to her restless state. Having no idea what awaited her in Taney County, she found no comfort in the new light of morning. She spent the entire morning preparing for the trip, including a plan to tell Loomey that she would be away for an estimated three weeks. Reasons and details must be left unsaid. It made her feel disloyal toward Loomey but it was for her own good, and that of the practice, at least for now.

After pulling her faux alligator luggage from the wardrobe, she filled it with plain muslin dresses, an extra bonnet, thick cotton stockings, combs and various toiletries. She was half-way through when she heard Loomey enter the office down-stairs. She could always tell it was Loomey because she was usually singing or talking to herself as she made her way up to the apartment. At least she had her own key. That was one less thing to worry over.

Loomey entered Pearl's room and spotted the open bag across the quilted spread. "Oh my, Miss Pearl! Where are you goin'?"

"I'm returning to Missouri for a short time," Pearl said. "I need to check on my parents and I have some business to attend to."

"All by yourself?"

"No, in fact…uh…Chief Harkins is going with me."

"Well, if that don't beat all. You and Chief Harkins."

"It's not what you think," Pearl said quickly. "It's business, strictly business."

"Most women I know would be pleased to ride any distance next to that big handsome man," Loomey said. "I know Missouri is somewhere on this side of the world, and when a man friend travels that distance with a woman friend, that's some serious business all right."

Pearl folded a cotton undergarment. "I have to insist you keep the details between us like where I'm going and with whom. I'll post a notice for our patients letting them know I'll be out of town for a while. There's a list of chores for you to complete, and if an emergency arises, one or two physicians will surely take care of my referrals. I'll arrange that later today."

"How will I know where you are?" Loomey asked.

"I'll leave my parents' address. You know how to send a telegram, don't you? There's a Western Union office on South Street."

"I'll get my tutor to help me," said Loomey. "He won't mind."

Sunlight streamed through the upstairs window and caught a glint of gold in Loomey's large hoop earrings. On a normal day the pair would have sipped their first cup of coffee and exchanged light banter, now that they had established a friendship. But not today. Today was far from normal.

"I have to finish packing," Pearl said, turning away. "Please go downstairs and check the patient list in my record book. Put a mark by the names of those scheduled to come in between now and the end of the month."

"Don't forget your warm wrap."

The last item Pearl thought of placing in her bag was a medical journal, the one she used to record all patient visits, entries, medications and follow-up after graduation from college. She opened the bound leather book to September 1, 1882 and noted that she had failed to make an entry that day.

She knew she had been in shock from Stone's sudden death, and then it was bedlam every day while trying to keep up with his patients. Still, she should have made entries with full details, especially for those patients with complications. She meant to. Would that now, too, haunt her forever? She tossed the journal aside.

Since then, she had obsessively recorded each patient's medical details, reflected in page after page of her flowing, delicate cursive. Though she had seen only a handful of patients since July, her journal was more than half-filled, containing each patient's name, age, gender, occupation, whether they were colored or white, date of first and all follow-up visits, diagnosis, planned treatment, prescriptions and follow-up. If a patient died – so far no one had except little Sammy – she noted the date, time and circumstance for future reference.

At the stroke of four Douglas tapped on the window

pane of her office.

"Dr. Stern?" he greeted her when she came to the door. "Your ride's here. Herschel is walking over from the station to meet us. He had some paperwork to locate and bring along."

Paperwork, she thought, my extradition documents. She wondered if Douglas knew anything about her predicament. If so, he gave no hint. To her, he was as bland and pleasant as ever. Of course, good police officers were naturally coy, a reason to never play poker with them, her father advised.

As Herschel arrived, Pearl gathered her things. Loomey followed her every move, as though it had just dawned on her that Pearl was actually leaving. It occurred to Pearl that things could go horribly wrong in Missouri. There was a real chance she might not return.

"You go have yourself a fine ole time," Loomey was saying. "But we want you back here soon. Me and Jim will miss you while you're gone. He asks about you ever since you helped him out."

Pearl set her bag down. A rush of regret followed by anxiety caused her to approach Loomey for a farewell embrace. Then she thought better of it. Loomey might suspect something if she was unusually effusive. Instead, she reached out and clasped Loomey's hand, squeezing it tight.

Pearl released her grip and Loomey rocked back on her heels. "Just be careful, Miss Pearl. You be careful and come home safe."

"I'll do that," Pearl said, realizing Loomey was one person she would never forget. She had come to not only rely on her, but cherish her warmth and good humor. "Why, I'm already anxious to come home and I haven't even left yet," Pearl said, her smile wan.

Herschel helped her into the hack and tossed her bags into the black luggage bin at the rear of the carriage, slamming the lid tight. An eerie silence had settled between them, and Pearl had no idea what he was thinking. Perhaps she was merely his prisoner now. The entire episode seemed surreal. It was as though they had taken a sudden detour and were about to embark on a voyage to some strange and distant land with nothing to guide them except the damning paperwork tucked next to Herschel's heart.

Chapter Twenty-Eight

Leaving Asheville, Pearl found herself strangely nostalgic for a place she had only begun to know. Unlike Missouri, where she had felt the need to leave her past behind, here she was leaving behind a future, incomplete and not yet fully tested. There were already signs within her of roots slowly taking hold: affection for the grand Swannanoa where she encountered Jeremiah and met Herschel for the first time; the Public Square where Asheville's lifeblood ebbed and flowed; the courthouse; South Main; and Eagle Street, where she and Loomey had spent the day shopping in the rain.

They passed the shops where Pearl made her frequent purchases for medical and personal supplies, the post office where letters, though infrequent, were sent to her parents and Victoria, and the gravesite near the Central Methodist Church where Jeremiah Dickson was buried. She fought back tears. This was where she belonged. She turned to look at Herschel, but he was talking to the driver. With or without him, she thought, this was now her home.

On the west side of town, where they were scheduled to catch the stage, three passengers stood waiting on the wooden platform. Bordering Hominy Creek, it served as a departure point for those going west to Tennessee.

Herschel fiddled with their bags while Pearl looked about. This was a side of town she hadn't seen. The rolling hills were much the same, though their elevations slightly higher in the west and there was more farmland. The summer crops now gone, tall fields of tobacco spread outward, white clapboard homes and small log-hewn cabins perched in the valleys and on the ridgelines. Pearl could hear an occasional cowbell in the distance and the squawking of crows overhead. A chill wind began to blow and she drew her cloak around her. At least they'd be in Missouri before real winter weather hit.

"I hear the coach coming," Herschel said.

Pearl saw the swirl of dust before the stage came into view, smelled the over-heated horses and heard the driver call their names. As he approached, she could see him perched atop the empty rumbling carriage, thick leather reins in each hand.

He pulled up, climbed down from his seat and faced the small band of customers before him. His thin face was covered by a gray-speckled beard spiked with faint bits of brown tobacco juice. He wore a working man's Fedora, its wide sweat-soaked band discolored from his daily toil.

"Howdy there, folks," he greeted them. "You might want to know this is my first stop of the day and you might not. I don't really care much either way. Now before we get started, there are certain rules for stage passengers. So let's go ahead and get that all said and done."

Propping his weight against the side of the stage with one arm, he reached down to adjust a gold-buckled belt with the other. "First off," he said, clearing his throat, and proceeded to rattle off the exact list of rules Pearl had seen in the pamphlet in Richmond. When he got to the part about rules for chewing tobacco, he released a large wad of black juice from his corner of his mouth, as though to emphasize the point.

Pearl glanced toward Herschel. He did not return her gaze. Arms crossed, his eyes flitted about the group, paying scant attention to the driver. It must be the lawman in him, always leery of strangers.

Pearl suspected the stage driver had given this well-rehearsed speech before, but the small group tittered appreciatively, encouraging him to continue. He ended with "Now everybody on board, ladies first since we have no young'uns in this bunch."

One of the passengers was a moderately attractive man who looked in his mid to late twenties, slicked back hair and saucer eyes so deep-set Pearl thought when he settled his riveting gaze on either sex, they couldn't turn away. As though reading her mind, he flashed a dazzling smile. She quickly turned her attention toward Herschel.

"I guess we're ready," Herschel said. "Let me help you into the carriage." She took his hand as he helped hoist her up.

The New Concord Coach, advertised for "elegant travel," was suspended on strong leather straps that served as springs, making it sway like a ship in rough seas. Up to nine passengers could be seated inside, led by the driver of a six-horse team. But even with five adults tucked inside, the carriage, pungent with the scent of leather and old cigars, felt a bit crammed to Pearl.

"Are you in law enforcement?" the man with the slicked hair asked, as though appraising Herschel. "You look like a

300

man who means business."

"And you are?" Herschel asked, turning the tables.

"A bailiff. But they call me the Inspector. I go after those who fail to appear in court."

Herschel frowned. "I know what a bailiff is. Now we still have a long ride ahead. Any one of you ever been out west?"

"Me," said the inspector. He was fully animated as the attention turned to him. He soon launched into a series of stories about his multiple adventures in the great Rockies, and his first-hand knowledge of notorious renegades, rascals and red men he encountered in his unusual line of work.

"Why, I once saw a skilled bowman shoot six arrows per minute," he said. "And do any of you know that most doctors out west carry a gun? There was even a case I investigated in which the doctor was attacked, shot his attacker, and then promptly treated the wound! The scoundrel was so grateful he went to work for the doctor, became his stableman."

"How about you, sir?" the inspector asked.

"Went to Denver in '73," Herschel said. "Found the antelope on the menus much to my liking. The meat's supposed to cure you of the tobacco habit." He flicked an ash from his cigar. "As you can see, it didn't take."

Nearing the hamlet of Pigeon River, they passed a saw mill, its large wooden wheel spinning near the river, two small boys fishing on the bank and a barefoot man in a wagon waiting for their catch. A group of what appeared to be Masons had gathered on the grounds of the Freewill Baptist Church and someone, his hand raised, was trying to get their attention.

The stagecoach came to a sudden halt, nearly lifting the passengers from their seats. As the tallest and bulkiest, Herschel's head collided against the carriage roof.

Instinctively, Pearl's protective arm shot outward. "Are you all right?"

"This head's been in a lot worse places," he said, rubbing his crown. "Driver must have hit a rock in the road, or one of the horses reared."

The driver appeared and the carriage door opened. "We're near Waynesville," he said. "You'll find refreshments at the Haywood White Sulphur Springs Hotel just up the road. Would you folks like to get out a spell and stretch your legs? It may be December but it's not too cold out here."

They walked the short distance to the two-story white hostelry, its double veranda housing several guests sipping drinks and conversing among themselves. A man mounted on a stallion watched them approach from a grassy knoll. An enticing aroma of beef, vinegar greens and cornbread wafted toward them.

Herschel turned to Pearl. "Do you want to stay over here or continue on?"

"No. I don't want us to be delayed. Let's keep going so we can get this over with."

The inspector moved in close beside her while Herschel entered the hotel to purchase two coffees.

"So you want to get this over with, eh?" the inspector said, his hands clasped behind his back.

"What do you mean?" Pearl said sharply. There was something odd and slightly sinister about the man. She wished Herschel would hurry back.

The inspector leaned over and whispered in her ear. "Just making conversation."

302

Pearl took a quick breath. "How dare you be so familiar with a complete stranger!"

She could see Herschel coming. He walked up and handed her a steaming cup of coffee. "What was that about?" he said. "Did that weasel say something to you?"

"Nothing," said Pearl. "It's just that everything I see and hear right now is subject to suspicion."

Herschel took a sip from his coffee as he watched the inspector's slender frame slink toward the hotel entrance. "That means you would make an incompetent criminal," he said, "much to my relief."

Well, at least he was talking to her. That was progress.

"Let's head back to the stage," he said. "We've lost two passengers here, Hazel and Mr. Gilmore. So I guess it's just the three of us all the way to Knoxville."

Pearl released an exasperated sigh. "I don't like that man."

"Who?"

"That...that inspector whatever his name is...there's something not right about him."

"I've found that to be true of most people in his profession," Herschel said. "Don't worry about him. He's of no consequence to us."

Chapter Twenty-Nine

With the inspector sitting across from them in the stage leaving Waynesville, neither Pearl nor Herschel sought to engage him in conversation. Instead, while Herschel nodded off beside her, she tried to see out the dust-encrusted windows for views of the rolling Appalachian Mountains. But it was little use. Only faint outlines of the distant ridges appeared and then dusk fell.

By evening, they had reached Knoxville, taken a light dinner at the station and had boarded the train. Inside each compartment, stewards had placed decorative Christmas decorations. Pearl thought they brightened the dull compartments.

Across from their designated seats was a stiff-looking gentleman with a walking cane propped against his knees. His round spectacles gave him a professorial look.

"Ex-military," Herschel whispered to Pearl as they approached the bench seat.

"Maybe not."

"Sir," Herschel said, formally greeting the man.

The man looked up, the soft light from the train's interior throwing a glare onto his glasses. "Good evening," he responded. The three of them positioned themselves as the train inched forward.

Pearl's trained eye instinctively went to the bone-tipped cane and what appeared to be a missing limb under his trousers. She wondered if he had ever suffered from "the soldier's heart," a mental state that many of the Civil War veterans had reported. By all accounts, he appeared of sound mind.

He spoke up first. "Traveling far on this fine night?"

"Just a ways into Missouri," Herschel said.

"Business or pleasure?"

"Business," Herschel said. Pearl thought he must have decided to become reticent on this last part of their journey. Or else he was tired from the long stage ride and in no mood for theatrics. At least the inspector was nowhere to be found. She was beginning to worry that he was following them.

Pearl was about to ask the man's name when he offered it up.

"A privilege to meet you both," he said. "My name is Colonel Daniel York, en route to the great state of Kentucky. I'm retired now from the Union army."

"Ex-military," Herschel said. "I thought so. You have the bearing."

"You're a Kentucky native then?" Pearl asked. She wondered if Herschel would remind her later that he was right.

"No, born and bred in North Carolina. Joined the Union Army in '62."

"A Union soldier?" Pearl said. "That surprises me."

"It surprised a lot of people at the time, though there were thousands of us," the Colonel said, "but I happened to agree with the President about owning slaves. Didn't believe in it then or now."

"I happen to agree with you, sir," Herschel said. "But there are many brave Confederates who believed they were fighting for states' rights."

"True enough," he said. "It's one of numerous tragedies of the war."

While he and Herschel engaged in a civilized debate, Pearl realized this was another facet of Herschel of which she knew little. She had no idea that though a Southerner he was opposed to slavery. The topic had never come up. At least the man wasn't asking personal questions; perhaps the war conversation was part of Herschel's strategy to deflect attention from their real reason for traveling to Missouri.

The Colonel went on to tell them that his family had moved to Cades Cove, Tennessee – neutral territory during the war and a safe confine away from the strife.

Pearl's interest piqued. She studied him as she would a new patient. He appeared around forty, but looked fit for his age. Nearly as tall as Herschel, he had a leaner frame, and was less muscular. His hair was a rich chestnut brown, and his eyes were cobalt blue. "May I ask how you injured your leg?" Pearl said.

"It's a war wound," he said, patting his right thigh. "Found myself on the receiving end of a Whitworth breach load cannon at Gettysburg. It kindly removed part of my lower limb. The thing now pains me nearly all the time. And I'm tired of it. I'm going north to find a progressive doctor to see what they can do."

Pearl had to bite her tongue to keep from making suggestions. "Well, this has all been lively," she said to Herschel and the Colonel, "but I think we should get some sleep before we arrive, don't you gentlemen?"

Herschel gave her a sideways glance. "You go ahead," he said, as the train rolled through the night's deep shadows. The coal-powered lights were soon dimmed in the car as each passenger, alone with their thoughts, sought sleep or solitude in the dark. Pearl placed her purse against the window and nestled her head against it. She doubted she could sleep in this position, especially with Herschel beside her sitting upright, seemingly awake. But within minutes, helped by the soothing rhythm of the train, she had nodded off.

The train depot in Springfield, Missouri, just north of Taney County where Pearl's parents lived, was an imposing red brick building with arched windows and a decorative white cornice. Its clock tower was encircled by four small spires, each capped in matching white masonry. A stylishly-dressed woman brushed past Pearl in a blue satin bustle gown with cheerful pink rosettes at the neckline. White gloves set off her matching wide-brimmed floral hat. Pearl felt downright dowdy by contrast, especially after the long night on the train with nowhere to freshen up.

Herschel seemed surprised by the hustle and bustle. "You were expecting a one-horse town on the railroad tracks?" Pearl asked him, smiling. Then it struck her again why they were here, and she dropped her attempt at idle chatter. She glanced about the depot for signs of her parents. "They're here somewhere," she said. "Mother doesn't like the sun on her face."

Pearl spotted them coming toward her across the marble lobby. Her mother, wrapped in an ivory-colored crocheted shawl, hands clasped near her waist, looked more aged than when Pearl had seen her last. A handsome woman in her prime, she was now in her sixties and somewhat stooped from chronic arthritis. Her face bore signs that she had been crying. She gave Pearl a perfunctory hug.

"Mother, I know...I'm so sorry," Pearl said. "And Papa," Pearl said, catching her father's eye. He had removed his bowler hat exposing a thick shock of white hair. He grasped the rim of his hat with hands calloused from years of farming and watched her as she embraced her mother. Neither parent had yet to acknowledge Herschel.

"Hello Pearl," her father said stiffly. But within seconds he reached out and drew her to him. Pearl hugged him tight. He smelled of old leather, tobacco and the scent of her mother's handmade lemon soap.

"My girl," he whispered.

Pearl reluctantly pulled away and turned to Herschel. "My manners," she said. "Mother...Papa, I'd like you to meet Herschel Springfield Harkins, Asheville's Chief of Police." The formality made her wince.

"Madam," Herschel said, extending his hand to Pearl's mother, "pleased to make your acquaintance."

"Not under these circumstances," her mother said. Pearl sensed her defensive tone and wondered whom she blamed more, Pearl for getting herself into this fix or the towering stranger here on official business.

"Sir," Herschel said to her father, each nodding toward the other.

"Well," said Pearl's father. "Let's get your bags and we'll be on our way. The carriage is outside."

"You must both be weary from your long trip, Pearl," her mother said. "I have a pot of soup simmering at home. And we have your guest room prepared, Mr...Chief Harkins."

308

"Please, call me Herschel," he said. "And I'll most likely take a room in town."

A brief look of panic crossed her mother's face. "But Pearl...she's allowed to stay with us, isn't that right?"

"This is an unusual circumstance," said Herschel. "I have discretion to make allowances."

There was little talk en route to the farm. Instead, Pearl kept her eye on her surroundings. It had been well over six months since she left. On the street that formed the main thoroughfare into Taney County, men in bowler hats sauntered by, one with a cane tucked under his sleeve, its tip projecting like a well-worn weapon. Street signs set atop wind-blown canopies provided a burst of red and blue colors. A series of large wooden barrels filled with merchandise were set on display along the storefronts. A horse attached to an open carriage kicked a stream of dust that circled upward to its driver who coughed and slapped the reins. They passed the boarded-up office front once belonging to Dr. Stone. Pearl looked away, stung by the unpleasant memories it evoked.

"At least the streets are dry today," her father said as he called to Mildred, the family's sturdy work horse. Six miles ahead lay the family farm, the place where Pearl had been born and raised.

The house was just as Pearl remembered. L-shaped, with a low covered porch balanced by three white columns offset with gingerbread trim, it sported two chimneys rising like beacons on either end of the house. A few scrubby bushes along the clapboard side were struggling to bloom one last time before winter set in. Large rectangular windows at both ends offered up sunlight for the parlor and Pearl's bedroom. In the kitchen, Pearl noticed her father had installed new electrical lights that were all the rage. Her mother's large black kettle sat on the coal-burning stove, its decorative soot catcher above. A pot of soup bubbled on the stovetop.

Still draped in her shawl, her mother cleared the table so the four adults could sit while she set about to make coffee. Her father took his usual seat and laid his hands palm down on the table.

"All right," he said. "Let's hear what this is all about. Chief Harkins, I understand your official role here, so if you'll abide by it, I'd like to hear Pearl's side."

"Of course," Herschel said.

This was probably the last place in the world Herschel and her father wanted to be right now, Pearl thought. Normally a cheerful room where she would be laughing alongside her mother, the kitchen was full of tension and a palpable sense of awkwardness.

Pearl began. "Papa, I'd like to know first how you and Mother learned of this current situation and then by all means, Herschel and I will tell you what happened."

"We got word from our neighbor Tom Wilson that someone was looking for you and needed your address in Asheville. When I asked for what purpose, he told me it was a legal matter involving the Taney County authorities. You can imagine my surprise."

Pearl hung her head. She had never felt such humiliation. "Go on."

"I immediately took the carriage into town and went to the High Sheriff. He explained that a governor's warrant had been issued…a warrant! Course I didn't even know what the governor had to do with anything but there it is. All we knew then and all we know now is that you're in legal trouble. I'll be honest, my girl, I can still barely believe it."

Her mother served the coffee along with a plate of still-warm ginger cookies and sat down. She looked at Pearl with such sadness that Pearl reached out and grabbed her hand.

"I'm so sorry you both had to endure this," Pearl said. Launching into the circumstances surrounding the young mother's death, she omitted a few of the details she had recounted to Herschel.

Her mother spoke up. "But I don't understand why you were charged with…what's it called?"

"Manslaughter," Herschel said. "In legal terms it means that a person willfully caused another person's death, either by accident or some other means. In Pearl's case, as I explained to her, there was no willful intent. So I don't believe this charge will stand. I'll be speaking to the Sheriff myself."

For the first time, Pearl's mother gave Herschel a look that resembled gratitude.

"Do you really think this case has no merit?" her father said.

"I do," Herschel said. "And I intend to see that Pearl is fully exonerated, not only here but in Asheville where we have come to trust her judgment and depend on her. She has already proven her worth to the community medically and from a more…personal standpoint."

Her mother shot a glance at Pearl and then at Herschel. "Yes, of course," she said. "We certainly know our daughter well enough to understand she's a young woman of great character. That's why this was so utterly devastating to us."

"We need to get to the bottom of several things," Herschel said. "Who placed the original complaint? Was it the young husband now left with several children or a family member? Or Mrs. Stone, the doctor's widow? It had to start from someone followed by an investigation. Once all the facts were in and Pearl's whereabouts determined, a decision was made to issue an out-of-state warrant signed by the governor. That normally requires a very serious charge and enough influence to back it up. Do you think the dead woman's family has that kind of pull?"

Both parents sat silently, considering each question. Pearl found her hand quivering as she reached for her coffee. Now that she was here, before her distraught parents, she felt an almost nausea-inducing sense of remorse that she had placed them in such a horrendous situation. Would they ever forgive her? Would Herschel?

Her father looked at Herschel. "I don't know the poor woman's family, the woman that died, but I do know Dr. Stone's wife has a great deal of wealth. I also heard she put her husband through medical school so that she could rightly claim she was hitched to a doctor. Don't know much else about her except she's not well-liked."

"With great wealth comes great influence," Herschel said. "That bears a closer look."

"She's too snooty for the townsfolk," said Pearl's mother. "At least that's what I hear in my weekly quilting bee."

"What do you mean?" Herschel asked. Aware that this entire conversation would soon circle back to her, Pearl felt like a child with an ear to the wall.

"I mean she seems much taken with how other people see her," her mother said. "I've only met her once, in town, and she doesn't speak to any of us regular folks so I can't fully judge, but I know people who are familiar with her background. True or not, that's what they say, that she's high flung and unfriendly."

Herschel turned to Pearl. "You worked with her husband. You must have known something about her."

"She stopped by the office maybe once or twice, that's all," Pearl said. "And her sole purpose was to speak to her husband, always behind closed doors. Other than that, Dr. Stone and I didn't exchange details of our private lives. She was quite upset at his funeral; I recall that. It seemed genuine. As for me, it was obvious through the eviction she wanted me gone."

Herschel stood up. "I'm grateful for your willingness to let me into your home and the gracious hospitality," he said. "But if you'll excuse me, I'll head into town, find a room for the night and begin asking my own questions in the morning."

"Would you like me to drive you in or borrow a horse?" Mr. Stern said. "I have a young mare that might serve your purposes while here."

"I'll gladly pay you," Herschel said. He reached into his pocket for cash.

"No," he said. "You get our Pearl out of this fix with her good name intact and that will be more than adequate payment."

"I'll do my best."

"Will I be arrested and put into jail?' Pearl asked. Though the thought had crossed her mind, the reality of it was making her physically ill.

"Not if I can help it," Herschel said. "Let me find out what I can first and I'll return to the farm as soon as possible tomorrow."

"I'm going with you," said Pearl.

"No, this is business better left to me," said Herschel.

He looked at Pearl's father for support.

But the elder man shook his head. "Once she makes up her mind..." He promised to take her into town the next morning to meet Herschel.

That night, tossing in her bed, Pearl could hear her parents' low tones in the next room as they discussed, no doubt, the day's events. She thought of all the years of hard work, sacrifice and commitment both they and she had endured to get her through medical school. And now she had her own practice, albeit a small one, in a peaceful part of the country. A new home, new friends, the start of something more between her and Herschel. The possibility of losing all of that was almost more than she could bear. She smothered her face in her feather pillow to absorb the noise and let the bitter tears come freely.

Chapter Thirty

The next morning, in town, after an early breakfast of country ham and biscuits, Herschel and Pearl walked toward the Sheriff's office. Pearl wondered if he would remember her.

A group of locals had gathered across the street: women in their long checkered dresses as they wove baskets; men in muslin shirts and suspenders stirring cast iron pots filled with ashes and lye. A covered, green-painted wagon featuring "Pickles for Sale" sat on a street corner.

They entered the Sheriff's office and found him hunched over his desk, a short wiry man with a Manchu mustache that rested on his chin like two exclamation points. He got up when he saw Herschel, a look of shock on his face when he spotted Pearl.

"Dr. Stern!" he said. "So you've returned after all."

Herschel extended his hand. "Chief Harkins of Asheville, North Carolina. I'm pleased to meet you, Sheriff. And of course you know Pearl."

"I do." He gave her a curt nod and turned his attention back to Herschel.

"I've heard of you," Fred Billings said. "Used to be a Federal Marshal, right? Ran all them revenuers right off their moonshine stills." He grinned, exposing a set of teeth yellowed from tobacco.

"Something like that," Herschel said.

"You were in that famous Blue House fight in…what's that little place…Polk County? The story made the papers all the way up here, how you fought them scalawags till the last man dropped. Read you were stabbed and shot but still standing. Guess that's obvious since you're here in my office. What can I do for you?"

"That was a long time ago," Herschel said. "And that's not why we're here, Sheriff."

"Call me Fred," Billings said. "I know why you're here. We contacted you about the governor's warrant. We don't get many of those, you know." He stopped and glanced behind Herschel. Are you here to turn over your prisoner?"

"I can speak for myself," said Pearl. "I'm here, voluntarily, with Chief Harkins, to get to the bottom of this travesty."

"She's in my custody," Herschel added.

"It don't look that way. Looks mighty amicable to me."

Herschel started to pull up a chair. "Mind if we sit?" he said. He pulled out a chair for Pearl.

"By all means," Billings said. "Just so she don't run off." He gave Pearl what she considered a leering grin, a far cry from the respectful officer who had delivered her eviction papers just a few months earlier. Had someone gotten to him too?

"She's in no danger of leaving until we straighten this out," Herschel said.

316

Billings toyed with his mustache. He eyed Herschel, one suspicious lawman to another. "Well, this is nothing like what we're used to goin' after. But according to the complaint..."

He shuffled in his desk for the paperwork. "Here it is." He pulled a dog-eared sheaf from his desk and flipped through the pages. "This here states..."

"Can I ask who filed that?" Herschel interrupted. His voice had taken on an edge.

Pearl spoke up beside him. "This has to be the work of Singleton, or the Widow Stone. Perhaps both."

"Singleton did come in to see me about two months after you left town, Dr. Stern. Said you had killed his wife and baby and he wanted to press charges."

"I did no such thing," Pearl said.

Billings tapped the document. "Manslaughter. Says so right here." He tossed the document toward Herschel. "Read it for yourself. And sir, if I may be so bold, I need to know why you did not report here immediately with your prisoner. Need I remind you that despite your reputation you are now in my territory?"

"I know where I am," Herschel retorted. "Need I remind you this is a complaint not a verdict?"

"Just read it," Billings said.

Herschel crossed his legs, propped a hand on his folded knee and scanned the document, having seen only the official warrant. The complaint was where the real details were spelled out. "The date on this is more than three months past the incident," Herschel remarked. "Why did he wait so long?" He handed it to Pearl so she could study its contents.

"Said he was grieving for his wife and trying to care for his little 'uns," Billings said. "The man got left high and dry with all those kids at home."

Pearl handed the complaint to Billings while Herschel leaned back in his chair.

"I still see no evidence of willful intent," he said. "Sounds like Dr. Stern did all she could do in a bad situation."

"No offense, Chief Harkins," he began. "But do you by chance have some personal interest in this case?"

"Well, I take offense!" Pearl shot back. "How dare you!"

"Dr. Stern is a friend," Herschel said evenly. "She's also one of our best physicians in Asheville. What are you getting at, Billings?"

"Call me Fred," he said, his tone belying the friendly reminder. "I'm just curious to know why you're so intent on this woman's innocence when you hadn't even made her acquaintance at the time of the alleged crime. Don't make sense to me."

"Let's get down to the basics, Fred," Herschel said. "You and I both know there's a good chance this whole thing is bogus. At the very most, the plaintiff may have a civil case. If the facts support it, he can sue Dr. Stern for his losses. But to charge her like a common criminal and have her brought in here in shackles and thrown in your filthy jail, that's what doesn't make any sense."

Billings drew back. "My jail is not filthy," he said. "You may think you're some hotshot lawman with a big reputation to uphold but I assure you, sir, that don't fly here in Missouri. We don't care who you are and where you've been."

He turned to Pearl. "You have twenty-four hours to turn yourself in or we will come and arrest you at your family home. You don't want that now, do you?"

318

Pearl rose while Herschel stood beside her, towering over her small frame. "We'll take that twenty-four hours," she said.

Herschel stood. His gray eyes flashed. "I'll have her here at nine o'clock tomorrow morning. In the meantime, we have some business to conduct in your community, a few questions of our own to ask. Just letting you know, Sheriff, as a courtesy. But hell, maybe that don't fly here either."

Billings watched them go. "Be here nine sharp!" the Sheriff called out.

Their next stop was at the physician's office where Pearl had worked with the older physician until he had suddenly died. The place was still boarded and a sign tacked to the door that read: *Doctor Stone, may he rest in peace, will not be returning anytime soon.*

Just below the hand painted notice someone had written and then attempted to cross out: *Those who enter here don't always come out alive.*

Pearl felt as though she had been transported back to a living nightmare. "This place," she whispered to Herschel, "it's cursed. I'm so glad to be in Asheville."

They continued down the plank sidewalk until they came to the corner pharmacy, its large roof-top sign announcing ownership to *Henry A. Casebeer, Apothecary.* A series of colorful green, red and amber show globes nestled like oversized gems inside the street front window. Pearl had once told Herschel that according to pharmacists, medicinal globes were deliberately set in sunlight to help in the mixing of their medicinal properties. The more complex the mixtures, the greater the tendency to show off the colorful displays.

The brass chime tinkled as the couple entered. The gentleman behind the counter looked up, his back to a wall of cedar cabinetry filled with assorted apothecary glass bottles and jars. The place was large but relatively empty of customers. Only two roamed about the well-stocked aisles.

"Henry A. Casebeer at your disposal," the clerk said. "I have a special today on Warburg's Tincture, one hundred gelatin capsules, up to sixty-four grains of opium in each little coated pill." He looked from Herschel to Pearl.

"Are you here for marriage advice? I give that freely." He smiled.

Herschel shook his head. "Well, Mr. Casebeer, you're quite the salesman. No wonder your establishment has such a predominant place on Main Street. Actually, we're from out of town and looking for information on Dr. Stone's practice. We noticed it's been boarded a while. Can you tell us anything about it?"

Casebeer threw him a sideways look. "And who are you? What's your business here?"

"I'm a friend and advisor of someone who worked with the good doctor." He motioned toward Pearl.

"The man's dead," Casebeer said. "Dropped like a stone...no pun intended. He'd come in here with his face all flushed and out of wind. I told him he needed tonics, and I had 'em all here, but he wouldn't heed my advice. Wasn't too proud to give 'em to his patients though. I actually miss the old bastard. He was a steady, good paying customer."

"No doubt," said Herschel. "What happened after his practice closed?"

The garrulous clerk seemed eager to converse with someone.

"There was talk," Casebeer said. "Lots of talk about what happened to that poor mother and her little one. It was sad,

320

tragic if fact be known. Truth is, it wasn't the first time something like that took place."

"What do you mean?" Herschel said. Pearl remained silent. If she kept her identity unknown, she was likely to hear a great deal more.

"Well, I don't aim to speak ill of the dead, but it's like this. Doc Stone was not the most progressive man of medicine and he had a habit of conducting business by means of certain – shall we say – shortcuts. I seen it myself on more than one occasion. That's why he was such a good customer. He was always in here trying to find some quick cure for this ailment or that. While I was more than happy to sell to him, I heard complaints from some of his patients."

"What kind of complaints?" Herschel asked.

"Oh, things like he didn't take time to listen, he was old-fashioned. He just wanted to get 'em in and get 'em out. And he sure didn't like it when that pretty little woman came in, that lady doctor. Can't think of her name."

"Pearl?" Herschel asked. "Dr. Pearl Stern." Pearl stood by, biting her tongue.

"Yeah, that's her. I had a few folks come by here and tell me they were going to see the doctor 'cause they never seen one, at least one made from the gentler sex." He laughed at the recall.

Herschel stared at him.

Casebeer dropped his smile. "I thought it was amusing," he explained. "You know, see the doctor cause they never seen one?" He paused. "Okay now. So what is all this to you?"

"It's a legal matter," Herschel said. "Just tell me what you know if you don't mind."

"I believe rightly that ole Doc Stone saw her as a threat to his practice," Casebeer said.

"How do you figure that?"

"For one," Casebeer said, "she was well-liked by the patients. Not that Stone wasn't, you see, but this new doc, she was a breath of fresh air. Come to think of it, it was Stone's wife who had the greater trouble over Dr. Stern."

"Meaning?" Herschel asked. Pearl knew he was accustomed to enticing people to talk and instinctively knew Casebeer was an easy mark. Give him a cracked door and he'd walk right through it.

"You'd have to know this woman," he said. "About as high and mighty as you can get and still be earthbound. Grew up with everything she wanted. Her daddy owned half the town. I reckon she loved being hitched to a doctor so she could flounce about in high society, though if you look around Taney County, you might say our social circles are a big dead end." He chuckled at his own remark.

"Where does Mrs. Stone live?" Herschel asked.

"Why? You don't aim to go see her, do you? She won't take kindly to strangers in her business, not when it comes to her late husband."

Herschel's well-groomed mustache twitched. He made a futile attempt to control his annoyance. "Can you just answer my question?" he said.

"Who did you say you were?" Casebeer insisted.

"I'm Dr. Pearl Stern," Pearl volunteered. Casebeer's jaw dropped.

"I didn't mean...I mean I just...I'm sorry, Madam, Doctor."

"It's all right," said Pearl. "You've been a great help."

To close the conversation, Herschel opened the flap of his jacket, removed his police badge and slapped it down on the counter. It twirled on the glass-top counter like a child's golden spinner. "Officer Harkins," he said, purposely omitting his full name. "I told you this is legal business. That's all you need to know."

Casebeer took a step back. "Holy Jehovah's Witness!" he said. "Are you here to arrest somebody?" All movement in the store ceased as the two would-be shoppers halted at the front door. One woman audibly gasped.

Herschel glanced their way. "No need for alarm, ladies," he said in his best take-charge voice. "Now go on about your business." They hurried out the door.

His attention reverted to Casebeer. "Where is she?" he said.

"She lives in that big white house on the ridge just as you're coming into town," he said. "It's got an arched entrance and everything, real fancy-like. Even got a name, Heavens Estate, if that don't beat all."

Herschel retrieved his badge. "Thank you for your help, sir," he said. "I'll be on my way."

"She still does business here," Casebeer called out. "I can't afford to lose no more customers. So don't tell her I said anything! Please officer? Please Dr. Stern?"

Outside, Herschel and Pearl passed a harried woman attempting to raise her parasol against the rising sun with two rowdy children in tow, an older man whose business suit reeked of unwashed tweed and old cigars, a slightly built man in his thirties with a long mustache who bumped against them, dipped his head and then hurried on.

Pearl grabbed Herschel's arm. "Is that the inspector?

What on earth is he doing here?"

Herschel stopped and turned to call out to the man. "Inspector, is that you?" Herschel said. "What the blazes are you doing here in Taney County?" Herschel remembered the stage ride to Knoxville they shared and how the man's superior attitude had irritated him no end.

"Business," he answered. "And you?" He tipped his hat to Pearl.

"Same here," Herschel said. The two men eyed each other before the inspector walked away.

"Good day," the inspector said before disappearing into the crowd.

Chapter Thirty-One

At her family's home, Pearl was finding little comfort in their presence or her familiar surroundings. Herschel had gone to see the Widow Stone and then Singleton, father of the mother and infant Pearl had lost months earlier.

"I must go alone," he told Pearl, "so that we don't inflame this situation."

She paced the carpeted floor, stopping only long enough to periodically lift the lace curtains her mother had carefully sewn and hung this past summer. Both parents sat nearby, her mother crocheting an almond-colored table scarf, her father reading a new novel by General Lew Wallace, author of *Ben Hur.*

"Why this is nothing more than an ole love story!" he said. But Pearl noticed he kept on turning the pages.

"Pearl, will you please sit down?" her mother implored. "You're giving me a nervous tic with that constant peering out the window."

"Your mother's right," said her father, placing the book facedown across his lap.

Ignoring the faint scolding, Pearl called out, "I see him!"

"Hard to miss a big man like that," her father remarked. "Does he come bearing shackles?"

"That is not amusing, Papa," Pearl said, rooted at the window. She could barely restrain herself from running to the door and flinging it open. She felt her parents looking at her and wondered if they were curious about her rare emotional display. Was it related to the situation at hand or the man who had brought her here? Even she didn't know. Herschel's large-sized shoes stomped at the outdoor mat.

Pearl reached for the smooth ceramic knob and pulled at the door, catching Herschel off-guard. He gave her a startled look. "Thank God you're back!" she said. "I've been beside myself."

Herschel crossed the room without a word and turned to face all three adults. In his hand was a holster that contained a Colt .45. Pearl's parents eyed the weapon while she stood behind them, clasping her hands in an effort to keep them still.

He wasted no time. "There are some vengeful people in this town, especially that Mrs. Stone. She's got it in her head that Pearl was after her husband."

Pearl's hand went to her throat. She could feel her heart pounding against her rib cage. The nightmare was finally coming to a head. "That's absurd!"

Her mother set her crochet aside. "My lord, I've always heard when that woman takes a mind she can cause all kinds of grief," she said. "She practically owns this town."

"She knows more than she lets on," Herschel agreed. "That's a fact. If we dig a little deeper we may even find she's at the root of these unfortunate events."

He now had their full attention. Her father leaned forward

in his chair. The book slid from his lap. "How do you figure that?" he said.

"I suspect she had something to do with the charges brought and the warrant issued," Herschel said. He raised three fingers, one at a time. "She has the money, she has the power and she has the influence to make things happen her way. And she sure has the will, especially if her image is threatened. Everyone has a motive for what they do. Hers is maintaining her sense of importance in the community, and extracting a little revenge when she feels threatened."

"She's a jealous, bitter woman," Herschel added. "She thinks her husband had an eye for Pearl and that Pearl may have encouraged him."

"Pearl looked as though she'd been slapped. Standing behind her father, she grabbed the back of his chair for support. "That's completely, utterly ridiculous."

"Of course it is!" said Mrs. Stern. "How dare she say such things!"

Pearl saw her father peer down at the carpet. He slowly nodded, rubbing his white beard. "Kinda makes sense. It was way before your time, Pearl, but ole Doc Stone, well, let's just say he had an eye for the ladies."

Pearl came around and sat on the settee near her father. She put her hands in her lap.

"I don't understand. How could she think so little of me? She doesn't even know me."

"It's not about you, Pearl," Herschel said. "I know it's hard for you to see that right now but trust me, this goes way beyond you. This is about revenge."

"He's right, Pearl," her mother said. "Until she met you at her husband's office, she wouldn't have recognized you on the street. She and Dr. Stone mostly kept to themselves and socialized only with people of wealth and standing."

"But I'm a physician, too," Pearl pointed out. "Doesn't that put me in a better social light in her eyes?"

Her mother shook her head. "She made many disparaging remarks around town about the audacity of women physicians in general, and probably you in particular, though never in my presence," she said. "I'm sure she saw you different than we do." She reached out and patted her daughter's hand. It was the first real sign of support Pearl's mother had displayed.

"What she saw," said Herschel "was a means to an end. Once you left town, it was easy to lay the full measure of blame on you, especially since your parents are not part of her social circle."

She should try to think logically, just as she would over a complex medical issue, not be swept up by emotion. She glanced at Herschel, still commanding attention at the room's center. It struck her that she had included him in her small family circle. But it felt right, just as his standing in the parlor of her childhood home felt comfortable and right.

"Whatever we think, it's nothing more than an opinion without evidence," Pearl said. "Isn't that right, Herschel?"

He nodded.

"So what do we do next?" she asked. "How do we prove it? Or I should say how do you prove it? I may well be sitting in a jail cell this time tomorrow." The thought made her stomach roil. Through her friendship with Herschel, she knew the judicial system had its own ways, both just and unjust, of resolving legal problems. He once said justice could, at times, be nothing more than an afterthought.

"We have until tomorrow," Herschel said. "In the meantime, I intend to find the widower, this Keith Singleton, and learn what he has to say. He wasn't home earlier."

"Is that legal?" Mr. Stern said. "I mean, can you do that when Pearl hasn't even turned herself over to the Sheriff yet?"

Herschel repeated his now familiar line. "I'm here on official business," he said. "Pearl is in my custody until tomorrow morning. That means I can talk to anyone I please. But we won't advertise the fact." Their silence was a tacit agreement.

Pearl rose and reached for a wool shawl her mother had crocheted and folded over the chair. "Then I'm coming too," she said. "I should meet my accuser face-to-face. It may be my only chance to speak with him."

"No you're not," Herschel said. "You're likely to set him off and ruin everything. Let me handle this as official police work."

"Listen to him, Pearl," her father said. "I know you, daughter. You have a strong will and a tendency to take things into your own hands. That serves you well at times. This is not one of them." Her mother's imploring eyes seemed to agree. When united, her parents were a formidable pair.

"All right," she said. "I'll stay put, for now. But Herschel, I want every word spoken between you and Mr. Singleton relayed to me. Don't hold anything back. He needs to know I take some, though not all, responsibility for what happened to his wife and baby. Agreed?"

Herschel nodded. "Well, I'll be on my way," he said, fingering the revolver and holster which he proceeded to strap about his waist. Pearl knew he had carried a weapon in his bag from Asheville. He had told her he was determined never to travel without a gun.

"Is that necessary?" Pearl asked, watching him.

329

"Don't know," said Herschel. "But from here on out, I'm taking no chances."

"He's a lawman, Pearl," her father said. "It's part of his job. To be honest, Mr. Harkins, I've been surprised to see you without one."

"Won't you stay and have something to eat first?" her mother asked, eyeing the weapon nervously. "I have chicken pot pie in the oven. But please leave that gun at the door."

"Sorry, Mrs. Stern. I'm afraid I can't do either one." But before he could close the door behind him, Pearl had stepped into the foyer.

"Herschel, remember. That Mr. Singleton – – he has a bad habit of greeting unannounced visitors with a weapon. Please be careful."

Chapter Thirty-Two

While Herschel was gone to see Singleton, Pearl heard someone at the door and thought he had returned. But when she opened it, there stood deputy marshals. One carried an official-looking paper in his hand.

What happened next was a blur. All Pearl remembered was that the paper was read to her, one of the men grabbed her arms, cuffed her and pushed her toward their wagon. She could hear her father yelling, "What's going on? Where are you taking my daughter?"

She rode into town in shocked silence.

Escorted into the jail, Pearl sat on a plain wooden bench in a dim light filtered through the jail cell window. Not only was it bleak and dark, it was cold, dirty and smelled like rotting food. With only five cells inside the jail, she was surprised to see she was the lone prisoner. Apparently, crime was not rampant in Taney County.

She clasped one arm over the other in an attempt to get warm. Her teeth chattered and for the first time in her life, she felt the beginning of something akin to hopelessness. This was her deepest, darkest fear come to life. It must have been how Beatrice had felt, her mental aberration her one and only escape. Given time and without a great deal of effort, she could go crazy too. All it took was a flash of fate, a certain set of circumstances.

How long had she been here? She was already having trouble distinguishing the passing of time. The realization sent her into a state of near frenzy. She closed her eyes and took deep breaths in an effort to stem the fear. Calm down.

She thought about the past year and what it had wrought. Maybe her mother was right. Maybe this was God's way of punishing her for not following His will. She had clung to science, not religion, and wasn't sure she believed in much of anything except the randomness of life. It was a random act that had brought her to Dr. Stone's practice. Had she been offered a position anywhere else, she would not be here; a random twist of fate that Dr. Stone had died and Lori Singleton was brought to her, Pearl, in her weakest moment. It was certainly random that Asheville, North Carolina was chosen as the place where Pearl would start over.

But it wasn't randomness that had led to Lori's death and the death of her baby. Pearl played a role; a role that could have turned out very different. She bowed her head. *I need forgiveness, forgiveness for all of my mistakes and bad judgments, forgiveness from you, God, from Lori Singleton, from my parents and from myself.*

What seemed like hours later, she heard a noise coming from the front office. Men's voices, someone yelling. She stood up, grabbed the iron bars. "Herschel! Is that you?" she called. "Please, can you come in here?" There was no answer. A few moments later more yelling; the scraping of chairs.

A shadow loomed at the hallway entrance to the cells. She looked up. "Herschel, thank god. I thought you'd never come." She clasped the bars and he reached out, entwined his fingers with hers. His look was somber.

"What?" she said.

"I can't get Billings to release you," he said. "Son-of-bitch says the warrant was issued in his district and you're no different than anyone else. Says you have to stay here until tomorrow. I tried every way I could to talk him out of it."

"I heard arguing," Pearl said. "I guessed that was you. She leaned her head against the bars. "Then that's that," she said. "What about my parents? How are they? I couldn't even tell them goodbye at the house. Is that how you found out I was here?"

Herschel nodded. "They're upset, naturally. Have every right to be. But we'll work all this out in the morning. I can promise you that. I think this was more about Billings showing me who's in charge than it was about you. Slimy son-of-a-yellow-dog-bitch." He was still cursing when Pearl spotted his injured hand.

"You're bleeding!" she said. "What kind of wound is that? Did something happen at Singleton's? Tell me."

"It's a scratch," he said. "Got myself shot at by a kid with a rifle bigger than he was. But it's fine. You've got a few more important things to worry about right now."

"Here, slip your fingers through the bars," she said. "Let me take a look while you tell me exactly what happened."

Singleton had responded much the same way to Herschel coming to his home that he did when Pearl had shown after Lori Singleton gave birth. Only this time, he had put a gun in his oldest son's hand and it had gone off, grazing Herschel's finger.

Pearl turned his hand as best she could and examined

it in the dim light. "It needs to be cleaned and bandaged," she said. "When you get to my parents' home, have Mother take care of it for you."

"I'm not going anywhere," Herschel said.

"What do you mean? You can't stay here!"

"The hell I can't," he said. "If Billings wants to throw me out, that's one thing. But I don't think he gives a damn now that he's got you locked up and made his point. So I'm here until the morning. Besides, I want to see if Singleton shows up. I gave him good incentive to come in." He took off his jacket and pushed it through the narrow bars at Pearl.

"Take this," he said, "You look cold. After Billings leaves for the night, I'll find a blanket or whatever's lying around." He settled himself onto the concrete floor in a corner near the cell door. "I'll be fine right here."

"Herschel!" Pearl said, as though admonishing a small child. "Don't be insane! It's bad enough that I'm in here without having you spend a horribly uncomfortable night too. Please go check on my parents, stay with them, have a hot meal and come back in the morning. I can assure you, I'll still be here."

"As will I," said Herschel. Back against the wall, he had folded his hands in his lap, stretched out his long legs and propped his hat over his eyes. "Now quiet down. I'm trying to get a five-minute nap. We'll talk more in a bit."

"Not until you tell me what incentive you gave Mr. Singleton."

"That he might be facing some serious charges of his own, including assault on a public official, that type of thing. I told him to come in at nine a.m. here and we'd make it square."

Pearl knew he had been in motion since early that morning. She released a loud sigh that seemed to echo down the narrow corridor. "You're impossible," she whispered.

"Heard that," he said.

The deputy who had brought Pearl in opened the door and spotted Herschel sprawled on the concrete floor.

"What the hell you doin'? he said. "If you need to talk to Billings again, he's already gone for the day."

Herschel opened his eyes. "Then he won't mind if I partake of his hospitality for the night," he said.

Pearl, gazing through the bars at both men, shook her head.

"Suit yourself," said the officer. "I came in to see if the little lady wants something to eat. We got beans and cornbread. I could even round up a little buttermilk."

"I'm not hungry," said Pearl. "But please bring it anyway." Herschel might want something if he insisted on staying. That's the least she could do for him after all he had done for her.

The officer closed the heavy metal door and Pearl remained standing. Herschel adjusted his position and patted a spot near the cell bars.

"Come sit," he said. "I'll tell you what happened at Singleton's."

As he talked, Pearl felt a wave of sympathy for the struggling father and his motherless boys, then anger at the extreme reaction which could have killed Herschel, followed by the hope that Singleton might come around and tell the Sheriff his story. "Do you think he'll actually appear?" Pearl asked. "From what you're telling me, he's more mad than afraid."

"True," Herschel said. "But for all his bluster, he knows

that if I press charges – and I will, by god – he'll be in worse straits than he is now. He's got those kids to think about."

Together, they sat in the darkened jail on opposite sides of the cell, Pearl with Herschel's jacket around her, him propped against the wall.

"Reach into the inside pocket of my jacket," he said. "You'll find something useful."

She tucked her hand in the jacket and felt a small hard object. She pulled out a metal flask, held it up. "You mean this?" she said. "Why you scoundrel."

"Comes in handy sometimes," he said. "Take a swig then pass it over."

Pearl, unaccustomed to drinking hard liquor, decided this might be the time to make an exception. She opened the flask and let the sharp liquid burn her lips, tongue and throat. "That's wicked stuff!" she said, coughing. She handed it to him through the cell bars. "You know you could have been killed tonight."

"And by a ten-year-old!" Herschel said. He took a large sip of whiskey. Then he burst into a hearty laugh. "Come on now, Pearl, that's funny" he said. "Can you see that on my tombstone? Here lies Herschel Harkins, dead at the hands of a killer child." He handed her the half-empty flask through the bars.

She took another sip. At least the brew was making her warmer. "I guess so," she said, attempting a smile. Her eyes darted toward the door. "Shhh! Let's be quiet. We'll have that deputy back in here and this time he might throw you out."

Herschel, the whiskey taking hold, attempted to put his injured finger to his lips to mimic her and missed the mark. "Hmm, guess I need this thing after all," he said, examining his wounded digit. He laughed even harder, Pearl giggling along with him. It was the first time in days she had felt something other than dread.

They sat, silent for the next few minutes.

"I'd play you a little tune about now if I had my fiddle with me," Herschel said in the darkness.

"You play the fiddle?" It was something else she never knew about him.

"Used to play for Mary Jane, my late wife."

"Tell me about her," Pearl said. It was the first time he had ever mentioned her name. In the shadows, she saw him lean his head against the wall.

"Loved to dance. Couldn't cook worth a damn."

We have that in common, Pearl thought.

"A sweet-natured woman, knew her all my life. Our families expected us to marry and so we did."

"Do you still miss her?" Pearl said.

"Yes," he said, "but not as much as I once did." He turned to look at her in the dark.

"What about you? Did you have someone special in your life?"

"There was someone...his name was Caine. But we didn't get to know each other that well. Now he's clear across the country, somewhere out in Indian Territory."

A silence ensued. "What took her?" Pearl said. "What took your wife?"

"Diphtheria. We had a scourge of it running through Asheville."

"I'm sorry," said Pearl. She wasn't sure what else to say.

"She didn't have your iron," Herschel said quietly.

"What do you mean?"

"Your strength. I don't think she could have handled all this. Or what you do every day as a doctor. She wasn't strong like that, depended on me for everything. Not that I minded."

Pearl had no response. But she felt that a door had opened and they had crossed a threshold. She wanted to tell Herschel how much it meant to her that he was sitting here with her on the floor, in the dark, in this god-forsaken place. But he had gone quiet again, his head bent forward onto his chest. He was sound asleep.

She remembered little after that. When she awoke next morning, the side of her head was sore from sleeping against the bars, her shoulders ached from her hunched position and her legs felt like they were weighted down. Herschel was nowhere in sight. Had he really been here all night? Or had she dreamed it? She couldn't recall. Yet as she struggled to get to her feet, his heavy dark blue jacket slid forward. He must have been here. Where was he now? Her temples began to throb.

The hall door opened. Sheriff Billings stood in the entrance, Herschel on his heels.

"Heard you had a little company last night," Billings said to Pearl. "Irregular, if you ask me, but then this whole case is not what you call your usual circumstance."

Pearl swayed on her feet. She felt a mess and knew she probably looked even worse. "Are you releasing me?" she said.

"It's almost nine," he said. "I'm letting you out so you can sit on the bench in my office. What happens after that depends on a lot of things. There's one condition, though."

"What's that?" Pearl asked.

338

"That you don't say a word. You just sit there and listen."

"But I..." Pearl glanced over Billings' shoulder toward Herschel. He was nodding.

"All right," she said. "I'll be quiet as a jailhouse mouse, but not for long."

At the stroke of nine, the front door opened to the Sheriff's office. Pearl, Herschel and Billings all looked up at the same time. Please let it be Singleton, Pearl prayed. Beside her, Herschel didn't move.

A slender man wearing a dark derby entered. When he reached up and removed the hat, the color drained from Pearl's face.

"What are you doing here?" Herschel asked.

"And good day to you too," the inspector said, bowing slightly toward Pearl. "Why, I'm here to represent my client, Mrs. Stone. I see you have the prisoner."

Pearl could feel her pulse quicken. This was not what she had expected and neither did Herschel from the look on his face. "No Mr. Singleton," she whispered to Herschel. "I bet he isn't coming."

The Sheriff had leaned back in his chair, hands clasped behind his head as though he had all day and nothing better to do than engage in idle chatter.

Pearl attempted to keep her hands from visibly shaking. She clutched Herschel's jacket and held it tight against her bosom. Each man in the room held her fate in his hands. The thought terrified her. A glance at the plain wall clock over Billings' head announced it was ten minutes past nine. She was now certain Singleton wouldn't show.

"We're expecting someone," Herschel said. "He should

339

have already been here."

Billings allowed his chair to tip forward. Its hardwood legs thumped against the dusty plank floor. "Expecting who?" he said. "You aren't trying to pull a sneak on me, are you Harkins?"

Herschel nodded toward the inspector and asked the Sheriff, "Why didn't you tell us he would be here?"

The inspector pulled a print kerchief from his vest and dabbed at his face in a decidedly feminine gesture. Then he meticulously folded the cloth and tucked it back inside his coat. "I'm in the room," he said. "You may address me directly."

"All right," Herschel said. "What the hell are you doing here?"

"No need for coarse language," the inspector said. "There is a lady present, even if she is a rather – shall we say – uncommon criminal."

Herschel started up from his seat. Pearl reached out with her free hand, grabbed his sleeve and pulled him toward her. "Stop," she said. "He's goading us."

"I was hired by Mrs. Stone to investigate the circumstances surrounding Dr. Stern's deceased patient and infant," the inspector said. "Through my investigation, we determined that criminal charges were warranted against the good doctor."

"I'm in the room," Pearl pointed out. "Please address your remarks to me."

"And did you investigate the good doctor Stone as well?" Herschel asked. "Talk to his prior patients? Visit the family that lost its wife and mother after Stone's death?"

The inspector, fingers bent, was examining his neatly trimmed nails. "In due time," he said, "all will be revealed through proper court proceedings,"

Billings had pulled the governor's warrant from his desk and allowed it to rest in plain view, its gold seal sparkling in the natural light. The governor's signature was clearly visible.

The gesture was not lost on Pearl whose eyes kept returning to the layers of parched paper. She could feel her heart thumping through her chest. She struggled to keep her breathing as normal as possible.

"Enough," said the inspector. "Let's get on with details for the court proceedings. When can we expect the judge, Sheriff?"

The front door creaked. "Singleton!" Billings said.

The inspector turned in his chair. His face went white. "What the devil is he doing here?"

Herschel went to the open door as though to usher in a welcome guest.

"I'm not here for you, Chief Harkins," Singleton said. "I'm here to make sure you don't show up at my door to arrest me for assault."

"What'd you say?" Billings asked. "Assault? What he's talking about, Herschel?"

"This here police chief from parts unknown showed up at my house and threatened my family," Singleton said.

Billings turned to Herschel. "You did what?"

Pearl bowed her head. Could things get any worse?

"That's not what happened," Herschel said. "I did show up to talk to Mr. Singleton and he and his boy pulled their guns on me."

"Is that true?" the Sheriff asked Singleton.

"He was on my property without my say-so," Singleton replied. "Wouldn't leave and then barged right in. He's as bad as that lady doctor!"

Pearl jumped up. "I'm Dr. Stern to you, Mr. Singleton, and I won't be addressed as though I'm not here."

Billings looked from Singleton to Herschel. The inspector spoke up.

"Well, looks like we have ourselves a little tit-for-tat."

"You! Shut up!" Herschel said to the inspector.

Pearl was biting her tongue to keep from interfering further. But Billings had warned her about speaking up and making matters worse.

"Sheriff," Herschel said, pointing at Singleton, "this man and his son fired three shots at a law enforcement officer even though I clearly identified myself. That's assault with a deadly weapon, a felony in most states. If you want a signed affidavit, you got it. He held up his still bloodied hand. "And I have an injury to prove it."

"You want to press charges against him?" Billings asked.

"Damn straight and the boy too," Herschel said, turning to Singleton. "I warned you this would happen."

"That's a serious charge," Billings said to Singleton. "I know you got a reputation as a hot head but I can't have you firing shots at the law. How do you expect us to do our jobs? And did you know Mr. Harkins here was a Deputy U.S. Marshal before he was a Chief of Police? You'd have a lot to answer for if this got into a court of law."

Singleton appeared to reconsider his options. Then he

shrugged and took a step back. "I didn't mean no harm," he said, "just trying to protect my own."

"Sheriff, before we go any further," Herschel said, "you might want to hear what else Singleton has to say."

Billings retained a grip on the paperwork. "You beat all I ever saw, Harkins, with your blasted interference!"

"Just listen," Herschel said, "listen to the man."

Pearl could stand it no longer. She rose and placed herself between Herschel and the Sheriff, her small frame casting a slight shadow on the jailhouse walls.

"Stop it!" she said. "This is my life we're talking about, my professional and my personal life. Stop acting as though I'm not here! Now let's sort this out once and for all."

The two men looked momentarily taken aback.

The inspector got up. "This is outrageous!" he said. "Singleton has no business coming here before this case even gets into court. Sheriff, put this woman in a cell where she belongs and find out when the court convenes."

"Now you giving me instructions," Billings said. "Why don't I leave the three of you alone and let you work it out? I'll go down the street and have a nice sarsaparilla."

"The four of us," Pearl said. "There are four of us here."

Herschel motioned toward Singleton. "Tell him," he said.

"I want your word that neither one of you lawmen will take any charges against me or my son," Singleton said. He glanced toward the inspector. "You neither," he added.

"On behalf of Mrs. Stone, I promise you nothing, Singleton," the inspector said. "And you, Sheriff, will regret this transgression. Now if all of you will excuse me, my presence here is no longer needed."

Billings let him go.

"Never mind about him," Herschel said after the office door slammed. "Just tell us the truth, Mr. Singleton, and start at the beginning."

Singleton purposely avoided Pearl as he walked past her to take a seat near the Sheriff's desk. "I'm not here 'cause of her," he said. "I'm here 'cause I don't want no more trouble for my family. I'm sick of it."

Herschel pulled up a chair for Pearl and the two of them sat nearby as Singleton faced the Sheriff. Pearl made a gesture toward Singleton. "I'm so sorry about your family," she said. He gave her an icy stare.

"Don't want nothing from you," he said. He began by telling the Sheriff that even before Dr. Stone died he had heard gossip from unhappy patients around town. Some felt the doctor was getting too old to practice, others that he was incompetent, even dangerous.

"It's a small community," the Sheriff said. "I already knew of that talk. But you have to admit Stone did some good. And after he died, you did go work for his widow."

"I didn't believe none of it," Singleton explained. "Ole Doc Stone was all right by me when you wanted doctoring. I just didn't think we needed help with the birthings. Most young'uns are born just fine on their own."

The Sheriff motioned for Singleton to continue.

"Well, after he dropped dead, his widow lady hired me to do some carpentry work around her house so, yeah, I was there a lot. All she could talk about was her husband's...what did she call it – legacy – and how that new lady doctor had come in with her fancy ideas trying to take over Stone's busi-

344

ness. And how she liked to flaunt herself all over the doctor's office."

"I never!" Pearl interjected. "And fancy ideas like washing his hands? Dr. Stone was still using methods from twenty-five years ago. I did not try to take over his practice. He invited me to work with him."

"Please Dr. Stern," the Sheriff said. "Don't interrupt. You're not on trial here, at least not yet. Go on Mr. Singleton."

"She wouldn't let it be. Finally, one day I got tired of hearing it and said 'now Widow Stone, what do you expect me to do about it?' And she went to a desk in her parlor, opened a wooden box and handed me a big wad of cash. Said 'here take this.' In return, you let everyone in town know it was that woman doctor who killed off your wife and infant. Leave my husband out of it.'"

Billings pulled out a sheaf of paper from his desk and began taking notes. "How much money was it?" he asked.

Singleton hung his head. "Enough to keep my boys and me afloat for near up to two years," he said.

"How dare she!" Pearl whispered. Herschel shook his head as though cautioning her to remain quiet.

"And I assume you took the money?" Billings asked.

"My kids had to eat," Singleton said. "Didn't know when I'd get more work."

"So," Billings said, still scribbling, "you're telling me Widow Stone bribed you into keeping quiet about her husband while you slandered the name of Dr. Stern here. Is that about right?"

Singleton shifted in his seat. "Wouldn't exactly call it bribery," he said, "more like an agreement between the two of us not to blame poor ole dead Stone for what happened."

"Bribery," Herschel said, "plain and simple."

"I couldn't agree more!" said Pearl.

Billings placed his pen on the desk and made a prayer-like gesture with his hands. "Got a little dust-up here. Singleton, did you know you can be charged with accessory to blackmail, sued for slander and – unless you agree to go against Widow Stone – we can also make the assault charges stick."

"What do you mean go against Widow Stone?" Singleton asked. "What...what do I have to do? I can't be put in jail, Sheriff, I just can't. I got a family to feed."

"You'll have to sign a sworn statement that you accepted money from Mrs. Stone to spread false rumors and that Dr. Stern did not, in fact, intentionally kill your wife and unborn child as stated in this governor's warrant."

Singleton's face flushed. Tiny rivulets of sweat dotted his forehead. "Am I going to jail?" he said. Pearl was shocked by his sudden meekness.

"Depends on me and this other lawman here, I guess," said the Sheriff, "and on any retribution from Dr. Stern. She's the one that might want to sue you for slander."

All eyes turned to Pearl. She rose and took the few steps to Singleton near the Sheriff's desk. Standing over him, she waited for him to meet her gaze. "Do my bidding and look at me, Mr. Singleton," she said. He remained head down. She continued, "You have wronged me with your false accusations and I have suffered on account of it. But you and your children have suffered a great deal more. I'm truly sorry I couldn't save your wife and infant. Circumstances and perhaps...well perhaps even my medical inexperience at the time didn't allow it. So if you will forgive me, I'll forgive you." She reached out to him with her bare hand, hoping he would take it.

Singleton didn't respond to her request. "Lady doctors," he mumbled. "It ain't right."

Pearl sighed. There was no changing his attitude. But she also knew that in order to be freed from her part in this terrible situation, she must extend herself even further.

"Sheriff," she said, turning to Billings. "As far as I'm concerned there are no grounds for slander against Mr. Singleton. Any pending criminal charges against him, of course, are out of my hands. My only request is that you assure me the governor's warrant can be rescinded."

"I can do that," Billings said. "Chief Harkins and I will discuss the other legalities on their own merits."

"What about Mrs. Stone?" Herschel asked. He had remained seated near Pearl's empty chair. "She's the one that set this buggy in motion. What are you going to do about her?"

The Sheriff shook his head. "I don't know. She's a powerful woman throughout Taney County. And my position is an elected one, Chief, you know that. It kinda ties me up."

Herschel stood, his anger resurfacing. "Why, you coward."

"Stop!" Pearl said. "This blaming will get us nowhere. Let's just get the sworn statement from Mr. Singleton and be done with it."

Singleton raised his head and looked at the Sheriff. "If I sign something, you sign something," he said. "I want a guarantee that I won't be in no more legal scrap. I'll have enough trouble with Widow Stone as it is, once she finds out about this."

The Sheriff gave Singleton a stern look. "You, my friend, are not exactly in a bargaining position. So I advise you to sit there, keep your ears open and your mouth shut. Chief Harkins," the Sheriff said, "a moment of your time."

The two men moved to a corner of the room and began to converse in low tones while Pearl stood at the window, her back to Singleton. Outside, sunlight skipped along the busy main street. Country farmers in their muslin shirts and women in their bow-tied hats and gingham skirts bustled past. A black leather-strapped buggy was stuck in mud and the driver appeared to be cursing his labored horses to move along. The world was going on about them in its normal fashion. Maybe soon, very soon, Pearl thought, this would all be nothing more than a bad memory.

She turned to find Singleton watching her, a hateful look on his face. He quickly glanced away. It occurred to her he could have a pistol hidden in his clothing, just missing another prime opportunity to shoot her in the back, this time with both officers a few feet away.

She had never known cold hatred directed toward her and it gave her the shivers. Then she recalled his children, the driving force that brought him here and probably saved her from his direct vengeance. Knowing her casual chatter was not welcome she didn't speak to him but instead, returned to her seat, contrite.

Herschel and the Sheriff must have come to some agreement. They both appeared calmer. The men came back and sat down.

"All right, Singleton," the Sheriff said. "Here's what we're going to do."

Pearl leaned forward toward Singleton. "I want that affidavit signed first in which you release me from any criminal intent. You can say you were displaced from your normal mind through your grief. Say you will not be a witness in any court proceedings and you will not pursue any further allegations against me."

Singleton glared at Pearl. "And what do I get in exchange?" he spat.

"You get to go back to your family in one piece," Billings said. "Chief Harkins has agreed not to press assault charges with the firearms. But if you ever aim or fire a weapon at him again he says he'll shoot you down – – your boy too if necessary."

Arms crossed, Herschel neither flinched nor altered his expression.

Singleton slowly nodded. "All right," he said. "What about the money I got from Mrs. Stone? Can I keep it?"

"That's between you and the good widow," the Sheriff replied. "But if I was you, son, I'd be thinking about taking my family elsewhere and starting over. She's liable to bring a wagon load of misery into your life after all this."

Singleton's hand trembled as he wrote a few simple statements directed by the Sheriff and signed his name. The Sheriff made notations, signed and dated the new paperwork and attached it to the warrant.

"I'll get a message off by telegraph this afternoon," he said, "and then send the original documents by rider."

"Something signed," Pearl said.

"Excuse me?" Billings said.

"I want something for my own records," Pearl said. She watched Singleton get up and wondered what he was thinking.

"Can I go now?" he said. The Sheriff motioned him toward the door. Singleton said nothing as he left.

"Well, ma'am," the Sheriff said, looking at Pearl. "Is my word not good enough for you?" He seemed put out.

"You can't blame her, Sheriff," Herschel said. "This whole episode has been one long set of troubles. What if your telegraph doesn't go through, or your rider gets lost with the documents?

"Herschel, I think it's time I speak fully for myself," Pearl said. "Sheriff, a statement similar to what Mr. Singleton signed will suffice. And please know I'm very grateful for your help."

"Humph," Sheriff grunted. But he picked up the pen and began writing. "You owe this big officer here most of your gratitude," he said, scribbling a note. "If he hadn't gone to see Singleton – which would have been against my better judgment had he asked me – then we wouldn't have seen hide nor hair of him until time for court. He was the star witness against you."

"I know," Pearl said. She looked at Herschel. "I owe him a great debt."

Herschel grinned. "A debt of which I'll frequently remind her."

Billings handed Pearl the requested statement. Herschel reached out to shake the Sheriff's hand, who reluctantly took it.

"We'll be on our way," Herschel said. "Appreciate your cooperation, Sheriff. It's always good to meet a fellow officer. If you ever get down to the Blue Ridge Mountains, look us up."

Billings crossed his arms. "Not likely," he said, watching them leave.

Outside, Pearl turned to Herschel. "Was he angry about my asking for proof that he would follow through?"

"You pierced his pride. His word would have been good enough for most men."

"Well I'm not most men," she said.

"Yes," Herschel said, "I note that every time I see you."

Pearl jabbed him playfully with her elbow. For the first time in months she felt an exhilarating sense of freedom and pure...no other word came to mind but joy. Without Herschel as a witness, who would have thought her a fool, she might well have skipped down the street.

"I can't wait to tell my parents the news!" she said as they hurried toward the wagon. She knew her father would be pleased, but what about her mother? Was this another black mark she would hold against Pearl for the rest of her life?

"Then you won't have long," a familiar voice said. Her father came up behind her. "We couldn't sit at the house while your future was at stake. From the look on your face, I would say things have worked out."

Pearl rushed into his arms. "It's over," she said. "It's all over, no small thanks to Herschel. He convinced Mr. Singleton to drop the charges and the Sheriff is rescinding the warrant. Isn't that wonderful news?"

"You had much to do with it, Pearl," Herschel said. "Had you not been so willing to stand up to the charges, this might have been a lifelong grief for you."

Mr. Stern released Pearl and shook Herschel's hand. "We're most grateful, Mr. Harkins," he said.

Pearl's mother reached out to Herschel. "May an old woman give you a hug?" she asked. Herschel laughed and reached down for her embrace. "It was good luck and better timing," he said. "I'm as thankful as Pearl that it's done."

Pearl's mother had a sly look on her face. "My, you two look happy together."

"Well," said Pearl's father, "I say this calls for a celebration. Let's all go have a fancy lunch at the Candlelight, one of our best eateries. Ever seen a ten-pound skillet of fresh corn succotash, Mr. Harkins?"

"No, can't say that I have."

"Then you're in for a treat," he said. "You and my two favorite ladies in all of Missouri."

Chapter Thirty-Three

The return trip to Asheville was smooth, marked by a distinct change in Pearl. She felt lighter and more relaxed than she could remember. Herschel sat close, taking her hand as he spoke.

"Think about all the things that have happened since the day we met," he said. "I wasn't even sure I knew you till now. Something always held you back. Now that you're free of it, maybe we can put it all behind us and get to know each other even better."

She linked her arm through his. Turning, she caught a scene from the rumbling train. "Herschel, look!" Pearl said. "I just saw a glimpse of Old Fort. We're getting close to home." She caught herself: *Asheville. Home.* Somehow the words fit together.

To expedite their return trip, they had taken the train from Springfield, Missouri, to Old Fort, following the route to the depot south of town where Pearl had first arrived in midsummer. Now it was nearly Christmas. Signs of the coming holiday were everywhere.

"I should have told you this earlier but I like your parents,"

Herschel said. "They seem like solid people to me."

"Yes," Pearl said, "and there's a good chance they like you too, especially my mother." She squeezed his arm.

"Didn't appear that way at first," Herschel said. He crossed his legs and folded his hands in his lap.

"That's because my father, in particular, believes a person must first show his worth through his actions. And my mother, well, she probably doesn't understand why the two of us are not, you know."

"What?" Herschel said.

Pearl pulled on his arm. "You know. Why we're not officially...together."

Herschel grinned. "Looks to me like we're pretty together, right here, right now."

"You know what I mean." She looked away. Time to change the subject, she thought. Allowing Herschel fully into her heart was like lighting a cannon fuse and standing in front of the barrel. There would be no turning back from its repercussions.

"Seems as though we've been gone for months instead of just weeks," she said. "I hope Loomey has done well without me and the practice is still intact. I hope Jim is still all right. What about your office? Have they notified you of any new developments?"

"I told them not to telegraph me unless somebody died or something caught on fire," he said. "No word is good word."

As the train rolled along, Pearl diverted her attention from Herschel, no easy task, she thought. Her mind turned to the more practical: tick marks of chores undone while she was gone, Loomey's untested ability to maintain the office, which patients had been referred and why. Staring out the window, she realized two things: her psoriasis had not flared up despite the recent stressful events and her thoughts of Caine now seemed far away, a distant memory.

At the depot in Best, Herschel grabbed both their bags and followed Pearl off the train. The air on this clear December day was crisp. Across from the station, the trees had shed their leaves, some still carpeting the walkways below. Pearl took a deep breath, thankful once more to be living in this peaceful place cradled by the surrounding hills.

A hack driver sat waiting for arriving passengers. He recognized Herschel. "Hey Chief! Over here," he said. "I'll take you folks wherever you need to go."

"Let's get Pearl home first," he said, helping her into the open carriage. "She's a mite anxious to see how her practice fared while we were away."

"Did you say Pearl…do you mean that Dr. Stern?" the driver said to Herschel as they lifted the travel bags onto the hack.

"Yeah, why?"

"No reason," the driver said, hurriedly returning to his seat atop the carriage.

He gave Pearl a glance in passing but failed to acknowledge her in any way. How rude, she thought. Any gentleman would at least tip his hat, especially one for hire.

"What's wrong with that man?" she asked Herschel as he climbed in beside her. "He was friendly enough to you but whipped past me as though I wasn't even here."

Herschel's brow furrowed. "No idea," he said, "did seem a bit off. But I know him from his frequent visits to the courthouse. He can be an odd fellow at times."

Two miles further north they arrived at the Public Square just as dusk was beginning to settle. Pearl's office was dark; its windows shaded by the curtains Loomey had helped her select and hang before Pearl left. The driver sat still as Herschel lifted her from the cab.

"Need a hand here, Coggins," Herschel called out. The driver dutifully climbed from his perch to unload the baggage. Pearl untangled her cloth purse from her arm and smoothed her skirt.

"Thank you, Herschel, and Mr. Coggins," she said. Once again, the driver ignored her. No way was she tipping him. Let Herschel do it.

She reached inside her purse to locate her door key when something caught her eye. A small hand-written sign was posted on the front door of her office. It hung sideways from a crooked flimsy nail. In the dimming natural light, she could barely see the words.

What is that, Pearl thought. She moved in close and cocked her head to see a string of crude words: *Nigger and whore lover. Now baby killer.* She reared back as though stung. "Oh my God," she said. "Herschel, look at this!"

The hack driver had sped off as soon as Herschel paid him. Herschel set the bags down and took the few steps to reach her. She pointed to the sign and placed a gloved hand over her mouth.

"What the thunder?" Herschel said. He read the words then quickly scanned the street, searching in both directions.

"How could this happen?" Pearl asked. "It's as though they knew why we were in Missouri."

The flush began on Herschel's neck, snaked its way upward and settled into his jowls. "Douglas."

356

"Your assistant chief? That's absurd!" Pearl felt light-headed and sick to her stomach. "Douglas wouldn't betray a confidence, or you." Or me, she fervently hoped.

"No, but he's got a very big mouth. Get behind me. We're going inside to make sure the place hasn't been disturbed."

Hands shaking, she fumbled with the skeleton key, managed to turn its end and open the door. Herschel stepped around her and entered first. "Where's the damn light?" he mumbled, bumping against a protruding chair. In protest, it scraped across the hardwood floor.

"What was that?" she whispered. Despite her rising fear, she crossed the room in near darkness, located the kerosene lamp and turned the knob. She always carried extra matches in her purse. She reached inside to grab one and quickly lit the fuse. The lamp immediately cast soft shadows.

Herschel's frame filled the center of the room. "Be still," he said. "Let me listen."

Pearl froze in place but all she could hear was the loud ticking of the grandfather clock in her office. Eyes now focused, she took in the waiting room looking for overturned furniture, open drawers and rifled cabinets. "Nothing appears disturbed, at least in here," she said.

"Do you have a lantern behind the desk?" Herschel asked. "Thought I saw one here a while back."

"Yes!" Pearl said. Shifting her purse, she snatched the metal handle of the portable light and handed it to Herschel. Then she fumbled in her bag for another match.

"Now," Herschel said, once the lantern was lit. "Stay behind me but not too close." He reached for his pistol, held it forward in one hand while he carried the swinging light in the other. Together, they went room by room, searching for anyone hiding or anything damaged.

Upstairs, Pearl found the door to her living quarters locked. Thank goodness for Loomey, she thought. Doors secured just as she instructed. Key in hand, she was still trembling as she unlocked the entrance to her apartment. "I don't see anything amiss," she told Herschel after they had entered and examined both rooms. "I don't think anyone has been here."

"Well, somebody sure as hell was outside," he said. He had removed the offensive message and tucked it into his pocket. "You shouldn't stay here tonight," he told Pearl. "We can find you a hotel room down the street and get some answers tomorrow."

"I'm home and I'm not leaving," she said. "I'll be fine."

He shook his head at her stubbornness. "I can't make you go, but I don't like it, Pearl, not a bit. Why don't I come back here when I'm done?"

"Where are you going?"

"To the station. I need to check in and let them know I'm back. I'll also enter this note into evidence."

"You're not fooling me for one instant," she said. "You're looking for Douglas, aren't you? Herschel, we have no idea where this note came from. Don't go off half-cocked and accuse him of anything."

Once he was gone, Pearl went room by room turning on each kerosene wall lamp. Her bag, heavier than she recalled, had to be dragged up the stairs, step by step. Home again, she thought, and yet am I really? It would be another sleepless night.

Chapter Thirty-Four

Pearl had slept little. Every creak and groan in the aged building made her sit up and wonder if someone was in her office downstairs or here in her living quarters. She couldn't wait for daylight. At eight she heard Loomey. Pearl rushed down the steps to meet her.

She opened the door and grabbed her startled employee, hugging her tight.

"Good gracious, Miss Pearl!" Loomey cried. "If you don't turn me loose so I can breathe, I might drop right here in front of your eyes."

Pearl pulled her forward into the office, away from the street. "I'm just so glad to see you, Loomey," she said. "It seems like I've been gone forever. And I have so much to tell you."

"That makes two of us," said Loomey. "Three, countin' my tutor. My learnin's goin' real good, Miss Pearl."

They spent the next two hours catching up, Pearl filling Loomey in on the events in Missouri and what led up to the stress-filled trip.

"No!" said Loomey, looking surprised. "Not you, Miss Pearl. I can't believe it!"

"Believe it," said Pearl. "But that's all behind us now. Your turn. Tell me everything that happened while I was gone."

"Well, let's see," said Loomey. She told Pearl of two new patients who said they would return when Pearl was back in town.

Pearl described the note on the door upon her arrival last night.

"If they come while I was here, I didn't see nobody," Loomey said. "Course I hadn't been here all day every day. No need to be."

"Well, someone was here," said Pearl. "And they want me to know it."

When Herschel sent for Pearl and Loomey later that morning to show them the daily paper, Pearl scanned the headlines and looked up at the Chief with a hurt expression. "And we thought it was over."

"And I thought you were goin' on a trip for your health," Loomey said. "Lordy, Miss Pearl, I had no idea you were in such trouble. I'm mighty glad the Chief was there. You could have been locked up for good right now."

A familiar sense of helplessness was creeping back. How could such wicked intent follow her all the way back to Asheville? She had to fight her way back, but how?

"I have an idea," Herschel said. "But let's not stand out here all day. Come down the hall and we can talk in my office."

Loomey held back. "I need to go check on Jim. He's still feelin' kind of poorly."

"Then go back to the office and wait for me," said Pearl.

"I'll be along soon." She watched Loomey cross the Public Square and then followed Herschel inside.

"What's your idea?" she said once they were seated in his office. "At this point, I'm open to anything." For all of yesterday's buoyancy after the ordeal in Missouri was over, today she felt exhausted, as though she had gotten up only to be beaten down again.

Herschel leaned back in his chair. "We go straight to the source of this story," he said. "Hold a...don't know what you call it...but a gathering on the Public Square and invite the publisher, his reporters, every member of the town council and anyone else who wants to attend. People will come out if they think there is news to share. Then we make an announcement that runs counter to this story. We tell them what led up to the arrest and the end result, the gist of what happened in Missouri."

"I'll get up and speak," Pearl interjected. "I'll be forthright. It will clear my name and give the paper something new to write about. We'll tell everybody. The more people that show up, the better."

After this hopeful declaration, she suddenly crinkled her forehead and spoke more softly. "Do you really think it will work? You know how the town council already feels about me. And most people will believe a lie before they believe a fact."

"What do you have to lose, Pearl?" Herschel asked. "If we do nothing, you might be right where you started, in a situation similar to Missouri."

"I won't go through that again," she said. "And you're right. What more do I have to lose?"

"Then I'll go see Clay Higgins, the publisher. You start thinking about what you want to say and when you want to say it. We can pull this together in a matter of days."

Pearl reached up and rubbed the back of her neck. "I'm so sorry," she said.

"For what?"

"For dragging you back into this."

Herschel came around the desk and reached for Pearl's hand. She stood and he held her gaze. "Don't you know by now," he said, "that wherever you are, that's where I want to be?"

"Herschel," Pearl said softly. Douglas burst through the door.

"Chief!" he said. "There's a fire! The whole place is going up!"

"Where?" Herschel said.

Douglas looked from one to the other. "It's your office, Dr. Stern."

Chapter Thirty-Five

By the time Herschel, Pearl and Douglas reached the outside steps, the tower bell was already ringing at the volunteer fire department next door. Lifting the hem of her dark skirt, Pearl began to run toward her building. Watching the flames lick against the walls of her office and her home, she tried frantically to recall if she or Loomey had left something on the cooking stove, failed to extinguish a kerosene lamp last night, or inadvertently knocked something over. But nothing came to mind other than...Loomey! Was she in the burning building?

Behind her, she could hear Herschel and another man yelling. "Have you got the horses ready for the fire wagon, Joe?" It was Herschel.

"No time!" said Joe. "It'd take thirty minutes to get them here and hitched."

"Then we'll just have to pull the thing by hand," said Herschel, motioning to Douglas and six more officers who had rushed forward at the sound of the bell. Pearl could see the fire wagon sitting in its berth, weighted down with large leather hoses and a round metal cylinder bolted to the top board.

She saw men in street clothes who must have heard the

fire bell and come running. One gentleman, suspenders and pantaloons exposed, hobbled out from the public privy. He quickly redressed himself and ran toward the fire wagon to help move it. Someone grabbed a wooden bucket and rushed to fill them with pumped water from the nearby well.

"Pearl," Herschel called to her as she passed. "Where are you going? Stay here until we can get some water on the flames!"

"No!" Pearl called. "It's Loomey! I think she's in there. I have to go find her!" She neither heard nor felt the motion as Herschel grabbed her from behind. As he clutched at her, they both nearly fell to the ground.

"Are you crazy, woman?" he said. "You're not going into a burning building that has already near collapsed. If I have to, I'll have your feet bound together."

Pearl's eyes filled with tears. "But Loomey," she said, "what if she's in there? We have to get to her, Herschel. We can't just leave her!"

He grabbed her shoulders and forced her to turn in his direction. "We'll find her," he said, "I promise. But look Pearl. Turn around and look at the building." She had seen it as soon as she came out of the station, but refused to acknowledge that it might already be past saving.

Images were searing themselves in her memory: Twelve foot flames lapping at the sky, black smoke curling and spreading outward, one-half the building crumbled into mounds of ash, while the other half was obscured with smoke and fire. Anyone inside could not have survived.

"As hard and fast as that went up, it looks like an explosion to me," Herschel said. "I'm sorry, Pearl. All we can do now is try to contain it so that it doesn't spread down the street. Now I've got to get back and help the others. Please, please, step back and let us do what we can."

Despite his warning, Pearl found herself moving forward in slow motion. If she was dreaming, now was the time to wake up. Now, before she found Loomey.

Near the site, a group of townspeople had gathered, some to watch the fire in morbid fascination, others to pitch in and do what they could to help. Donnie Callahan was there, his shoulder and chest wounds still obvious in his slower movements. Despite his infirmity, he joined the other men in helping hoist the heavy leather hoses from the fire wagon, now parked on the street. Behind him, Joe Tallent, the fire chief, pushed at the levers on the hand pump to build enough pressure to make the water flow. Sweat dripped from his bright red face. Overweight, he was struggling to get his breath. Pearl wondered briefly if he was on his way to a heart attack.

She turned to see merchants from the businesses she had frequented running to help: the druggist, the realtor, even the retailers who had forced her and Loomey onto Eagle Street. She recognized a few town-council members, Owen Wilson among them. Little Sammy's father was here, the strong young surveyor Ian, Dr. Stevens and Ralph Hanson. There were colored men as well; Loomey's nephew whose injured arm she had treated and two of the department store clerks where she had purchased used furniture; the pastor who tutored Loomey, his white collar covered with black soot and smoke.

She knew some came from self-preservation, worried about their own stores catching fire. She was grateful for the heartfelt condolences they shared: "So sorry, Dr. Stern," "No one deserves this," and "How could this happen right here on the Square?" But it ran counter to the "baby killer" headlines in the morning paper. She felt conflicted, unsure of what was real and whom to trust. Did they believe what they saw in the paper or had enough townspeople come to know her as a good person and dismissed the latest gossip? And who had written the horrid note? Surely time would tell.

As the leather hoses failed to deliver, the men threw off their coats and rolled up their sleeves to form a water brigade. Meanwhile, the building continued to flame.

Pearl ran to Abraham, Loomey's young nephew. "Have you seen Loomey?" she said. The teen gave her a startled look and shook his head.

"Don't stop the line, boy!" someone yelled. Abraham redirected his attention. Pearl stepped away from the men struggling to relay the heavy wooden buckets.

She looked back to see Herschel and the fire chief organizing the volunteer brigade at its head. They moved up and down the line, giving direction for steady movement. She joined in, one of the few women hauling buckets of water hand over hand.

It might already be too late, she thought, too late to save anything, or anyone. Everything she owned, everything she was, now lost inside the burning building. The leather hoses had proved nearly useless. She forced herself to push harder, the heavy buckets making her nearly breathless as they made their way across the brigade.

It took another half hour but the line, with bucket after bucket of water, managed to douse the adjoining structures. At Pearl's office, now an empty charred site, the fire was wearing itself out. The angry flames had grown smaller but smoke continued to billow. The gray heated air grew thick, snaked upward and wrapped itself around workers and spectators alike. Pearl felt her skin heat and her eyes burn. She held one hand against her throat, coughed, and put the sleeve of her dress against her mouth, breathing into it for relief. All around the Square, people were doing the same – some hurrying to-' ward the courthouse in an effort to escape.

"Thank God there's no wind today," Herschel said, coming to her side. "It looks like rain, so that'll help too." He stood beside her, coughing loud, his face and hands smudged with smoke. "As soon as we can get onto the premises, we'll look for...we'll look for anyone who might have been inside," he said. He coughed again, pounded his chest with his fist as though he could force the acrid air up and out. The smell of charred wood and chemical-like odors filled the space around them.

"I can't believe it, Herschel," Pearl said. "How on earth could this happen? And Loomey, my poor Loomey." Herschel patted her shoulder then reached out and drew her to him. They stood there for what seemed like a long time to Pearl.

"I can see Bailey Stokes," Herschel finally said. "He's across the street with the fire chief. Someone must have notified him to come to the site in case there are victims."

Leaning against Herschel, Pearl rubbed at her eyes.

Heat from the blaze had been so intense it had cracked the brick walls and melted the tin roof. As Stokes and the fire chief walked toward the premises in their thick-soled boots, each step produced a flurry of black ashes.

"We'll have to wait until this mess cools down a bit," Stokes said. "It's tragic. Such a terrible way for us to meet again, Pearl." All she could do was nod.

Stokes stepped over a broken roof beam and was about to speak when the fire chief, having forged ahead despite the heated ashes, called out to them. "Better come this way," the chief said. "There's something here at the edge."

Pearl clutched at her chest as they approached the chief. The body lay on its back near what was once Pearl's entry to her upstairs apartment.

"Hard to tell but appears like a small person, someone slender," the fire chief said.

"Is it her? Is it Loomey?" Pearl asked. She could hardly bear to look down. Yet her eyes were continually drawn to the charred remains on the same ground upon which she and Loomey had forged both a practice and a friendship.

All three men squatted and began to study the blackened corpse.

"This is odd," Stokes said. He had found a shard of broken, blackened glass, sniffed at it and held it up. "Hard to tell at this point," he said, "but if I had to venture a guess I'd say this was ether. Could account for the explosion, along with whatever other tinctures and formulas Pearl had in her supplies."

"Let me see," said Pearl. Anything to keep her mind and her eyes off what was probably all that was left of Loomey. She raised the shard to her nose. "I can't tell either," she said. "Too much smoke, too much of…everything." She let the glass remnant fall from her hand and fell to her knees, head in her hands. Her weeping grew into a deep wail as she cried over the loss of her friend.

Herschel stood up. "I don't think there's anything more we can do here until the ruins cool down." He went to Pearl and bent down, putting his arms around her to comfort her. They remained there for several minutes.

Then Herschel looked across the street toward the station. The crowd of spectators and volunteer bucket brigade were moving toward the Square.

"Where's everyone going?" he said.

"My wife got a bunch of the townswomen together to set up tables and food," said the fire chief. "They'll all be inside at the courthouse, away from the smoke. Let's go. We're done here for now. Herschel, you and Pearl come along."

Everyone left except Stokes. "Think I'll poke around a bit," he said.

Pearl knew she couldn't eat if her life depended on it, but Herschel was steering her in the direction toward the others.

"We can't stay here among the ruins," he said. "Besides, where else would you go?"

"I don't know. Right now, I don't know anything."

Chapter Thirty-Six

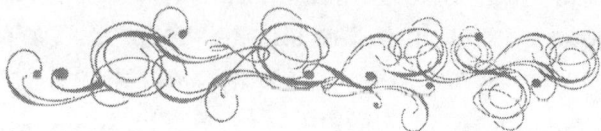

At the courthouse, Pearl was surrounded by people expressing horror over the fire along with their sympathy. Bathed in Christmas wreaths, mistletoe and holly, the decorations seemed at odds over what had just taken place on the Square. It would be a very dismal Christmas.

"You can always start over," said Ralph Hanson, handing her a cup of a pink-like substance that Pearl tasted and found sickly-sweet. She set the cup down. "We'll help you," Hanson said. "All of us here and others. Many others."

Dr. Stevens was nearby. "He's right, Pearl," said Stevens. "This community knows how to come together, despite its differences." He glanced at Hanson. "Within a fortnight, we'll have a new building going up on that same site if you choose to stay there. And I'll round up other physicians to get your supplies restocked. The state and local Medical Society will help too. Of course, they'll want you to join the group."

"I can sew and get household goods," said Donnie Callahan's wife. "The women-folk here know what it's like to be hard up. We tend to each other. You're one of us now." She reached out and patted Pearl's arm. Pearl wondered if Callahan's wife had forgotten the rumors she had spread about

Pearl's skin condition, implying it was some horrible, contagious disease. Maybe she had finally come around.

"Thank you," said Pearl. "Your kindness means a great deal." She looked around the lobby for Herschel and saw him standing among a group of officers near the entrance, no doubt talking about the fire.

Owen Wilson, the councilman Pearl disliked most, expressed sympathy and support at her plight. He had come to her when she and Herschel had entered the courthouse. Aside from the holiday trimmings, the place now looked and smelled like a diner. Against the marble walls, hastily constructed plank tables groaned under heavy bowls of mashed potatoes, fried chicken, corn on the cob, cornbread, green beans, fried tomatoes, double and triple-level cakes, fruit pies and canned jars of pickles and beets. Pearl was stunned at how quickly the women had pulled this together. Wilson, thumbs tucked inside his jacket leaned back on his heels as he spoke.

"I'll convene a special meeting of the Board next week and we'll re-consider your position," he said. "Maybe we can find it in the budget to hire a municipal physician after all, at least on a partial basis."

"I'm obliged," said Pearl, wondering if he was sincere.

Herschel had come over to stand by her side. "Don't promise things you can't deliver," he said to Owen, then led Pearl away.

Now desperate to disconnect from the stifling crowd, Pearl told Herschel she needed to step outside, get some air. "There's little smoke this far from the fire," she said.

"I'll go with you," he said. They strolled to the same bench where they had sat months earlier after the disastrous board meeting in which Herschel had threatened Owen Wilson and

Pearl had wondered what she might do next. Now she was back in a similar situation.

Both sat, saying nothing. Pearl stared into the distance. Someone approached them from behind. She turned to see Stokes, the coroner.

"Found something you both might want to take a look at," he said. From his pocket he retrieved a tattered burnt scrap of fabric. "It was near the body. Either one of you recognize it?"

Herschel took the scrap and turned it over in his hand. "No, not something Loomey would normally wear."

Pearl sat up straight. She snatched the fabric. "I remember this! From the stage on our way to Knoxville. The inspector, he was wearing this tweed design. But why him, Herschel? Why would he come here and destroy everything I own?"

"Oldest reasons in the world, I reckon," said Herschel. "Revenge, spite. Maybe just wanted to earn his big salary from the Widow Stone. Who knows? We'll never have all the answers. I suspect he's also the one that went to the newspaper and spilled your story. I can find that out easy enough."

"Bet he didn't count on blowing himself to kingdom come," said Stokes. "The place went up like a box of railroad dynamite. Took most of our evidence along with it."

Pearl jumped to her feet. "This means Loomey could be all right. But where is she? The last time I saw her she was heading toward the office."

"Maybe she changed her mind," Herschel said. "Remember she said something about her husband, Jim?

"Then I have to find her," said Pearl. She rushed the two blocks to Eagle Street from the courthouse, asking everyone she met along with way if they had seen Loomey.

"I reckon she's at home with Jim," a young woman said. "She must be somebody important for a white woman to be on Eagle Street."

"She's someone important to me," said Pearl, hurrying away.

When Loomey came out of her front door to learn what the commotion was about, Pearl rushed to greet her. The two women embraced. "I'm so glad you're all right," Pearl said. "I was worried to death about you."

"Me too," said Loomey. "I mean, I was worried about you too. When they told me the blaze was on the corner at your office I tried to run back and find you. But it was too late. So Jim and I just prayed together. Prayed that you and the Chief and everybody was safe. Are you okay, Miss Pearl?"

"I am now," said Pearl, releasing her hold on Loomey.

~

A week later, Pearl sat in Herschel's office. She had returned to the Swannanoa Hotel, written of the fire to her parents and made sure that Loomey was paid through the end of the month. Loomey told Pearl she and Jim might even try for another baby.

There was no hard evidence of who had started the fire. Rumors had swirled that it was someone in the community upset by the nature of Pearl's patients, someone biased and full of contempt. Both Pearl and Herschel continued to believe it was the inspector – that he had come to Asheville to find out everything he could about Pearl, and that for the right amount of money, there was nothing he was unwilling to do. A scorned woman has no bounds, Herschel had said. Pearl chose to believe that rather than consider someone in her own, adopted community could be so cruel.

"What now?" Herschel asked.

Pearl pulled a letter from her purse. She tugged at the envelope, opened the parchment and looked up at Hershel. "I never told you about my best friend in college, Victoria. Her husband, Walter is a doctor and they live…or lived in Richmond, Virginia. I actually went to see them for a short visit before I came here."

Herschel leaned back in his chair. "Oh? Are they coming to Asheville?"

"No. In fact, they're living in the Arizona Territory now. This is a letter from Walter telling me that they moved to Tombstone a few months back, that they had a new baby on the way and that Victoria is very ill. Apparently, she contracted consumption. It's running rampant in the silver mines."

Her left elbow began to itch, and she realized the other thing she had failed to share with Herschel was her chronic skin disease. What if he rejected her in a moment of intimacy? He had never seen her naked, of course, but what if…"

Herschel was watching her face. "What are you saying, Pearl? Are you thinking of…you are staying here, aren't you?"

Pearl shook her head. "I don't know if I can start over here or not. It was hard enough before to get the practice going. And it'll take time to rebuild, time for the town council to hire me if they keep their promise. Time for me to decide if I even want to work for them. Time to recover. I think that's what I need most. And my friend, Victoria, we go back a long way. She's asking for me. She wants me to be with her. She needs me, Herschel."

Herschel got up, came to her, reached down and pulled her toward him. "Stop. Stop running Pearl. You have a home here and a life -- a life built by your own valor. I need you, too, need you more than I can put into words. If you stay, you won't have to worry about starting over, at least right away. Together, we can do a lot for this town, be a powerful force. Don't run away again. You tried that in Missouri. It never works."

Pearl's surprised look was matched only by Herschel's next move. He kissed her once, then again, hard. Breathless, she said nothing, settling into his embrace.

"I'll think about it," she whispered. "But right now I have to think of Victoria, too and how best I can help her." Walter had also mentioned Caine in her letter. Along with Victoria he, too, was asking for her. All three were begging her to come to Tombstone.

As Herschel accompanied Pearl to the department exit, Pearl knew their conversation about Tombstone was far from over.

Outside, in the bright December sunlight, a wagon pulled up and a young man dressed in coveralls and hat jumped from the buckboard. Pearl, standing next to Herschel, shaded her eyes and watched him run toward them.

"S'cuse me, folks!" he said. He pointed toward the back of the wagon. "My wife there, she's 'bout to have our first baby and she heard tell there was a lady doc in town. Won't agree to see no man and didn't want no granny midwife. Either one of you know where she might be?"

Without a second thought, Pearl took the steps two at a time. "I'm Dr. Stern," she said, "And I'll be glad to take a look at your wife, though I have no medical bag." She pointed toward the ashes. "That was my office."

The young husband nodded. "Heard there was a big fire

in town," he said. "But I'd be most grateful if you could just take a look, make sure ever'thing is all right."

Herschel followed close behind her. "Pearl," he said, "are you sure? We can find someone for them. This might not be a good time for you."

"I'm sure," she said. "Now, if you don't mind, would you send someone to find Loomey? I may need her help with the birthing. Just tell her we have a new patient."

End

CPSIA information can be obtained at www.ICGtesting.com
Printed in the USA
LVOW12s1317020414

380014LV00001B/7/P

9 781940 224121